Didymus

Didymus

A Novel

LARRY ELIE

credo
house publishers

Published in the United States of America by Credo House Publishers,
a division of Credo Communications LLC, Grand Rapids, Michigan
credohousepublishers.com

ISBN: 978-1-62586-246-4

Cover and interior design and layout by Believe Book Design
Editing by Donna Huisjen
Back cover photo courtesy of the Ford Motor Company. Copyright © 1986.
Reprinted with permission. All rights reserved.

Printed in the United States of America
First edition

Prologue

Thomas of the Bible demonstrated stubborn doubt and fatalistic thoughts, very much as any cynic would. Thomas (Aramaic) is also known as Didymus (Greek); both words are usually interpreted as "twin." This means that Thomas is more a title or nickname than a given name. The assumption is that Thomas was the younger of a birth pair. Identical twins are a special case; they have identical genetics. I know how similar they may be; two of my older brothers were identical twins. Thomas's twin is never mentioned in Scripture. I believe that Thomas, like any convert, wanted to see the people he loved come to Christ. Perhaps Thomas in this story subconsciously represents me.

The most engaging parts of the Bible are ones we can identify with. This story will help people of many ages identify with the Gospels in a way that does not modify their content, yet explains what is told in them in an engaging way. This story is filled with the Bible, which Isaiah 55:11 promises will accomplish a work for God.

We don't find the name of Thomas's twin in the Bible. We will call the twins Jahzeel, meaning "God hastens," and Jezer, which means "island of help." Thomas will be the nickname of Jezer—and the name by which he is called exclusively in this story. The older twin will not have a nickname. Thomas did fish later in the Gospels, but there is nothing in the Bible confirming that this was his occupation. Here, Thomas's father is depicted as a Galilean vineyard owner.

The Gospels are not particularly concerned with timing; they are organized by substance. The order of the calling of the apostles and the timing of their calls is somewhat spread out—surprisingly, over nearly a year. Significant events occur before all the apostles have been called, and some are introduced to Jesus before they are called.

I prayerfully worked out how to introduce Thomas to Jesus. That meeting is not recorded in the Bible. To create a realistic narrative, I have Jesus talking to Thomas.

This is a historical fiction work and as such is not a substitute for the biblical account.

This book is dedicated to the memory of Dr. Ronald Elie and Dr. Donald Elie, my identical twin brothers, who, between them, pastored for over seventy years.

Bind the Enemy. Loosen my mind.

I

Family

AD 27, FIRST WEEK OF THE MONTH OF NISAN (MARCH/APRIL) JEWISH YEAR 3787

The sun was hot again today. Not as hot as yesterday, but hotter than normal. Not even a breeze. The reason for doing terracing in the spring is to get the heavy work done before the heat of summer. The sweat that trickled down the small of my back felt like a stream. My beard itched. Hours ago, I had pulled my robes back to expose my shoulders and also girded my belt, lifting the hem of the robe above my knees. A sweat bee got the back of my neck; I had thought it was too early for them. Too hot for spring before Passover. Had I not argued with Jahzeel this morning about which face of the hill I would train the vines for, this work would have been completed before the sun was so high. I knew he wanted to go to the bakery to see Anna without smelling of sweat, and I could not fault him for that. Her name means grace, or favor, and anyone meeting her recognizes that God has given her special favor. I suppose the real favor for Jahzeel is that Anna is drawn to him. Even when we were look-alike children, she was cordial to me but drawn to him. I was envious.

The arranging of the rock terraces and the training of the vines had to be done, and pruning will have to be done, too; vines without early training become much harder to train or become of little use at all if never trained. The pruning will be later, in the month of Sivan, after Passover. I knew that, as the elder, Jahzeel would not be working the rock terraces on the hillside facing south; that's the steeper side. Moving vines around rocks is hard; moving the rocks to hold the vines is much harder, especially facing the sun. If the terraces are not steep enough, the clusters of grapes will not hang, and creeping insects will more easily get into the fruit. Bees help pollination, and wind pollinates, too; air must get to the vines. The taller bunches are more marketable. Terraces need no earth, but the root of the vine needs deep, rich soil and water, especially in summer when the grapes are filling. Keeping roots low also makes watering the vines easier if the summer rains fail. My calluses, skinned knees, and stubbed toes proved how much time I spent doing this.

It wasn't worth arguing this morning. Besides, I know that I am really better at terracing, training, and pruning than Jahzeel is. I'm no taller or stronger—just more determined and able to concentrate better. I'm more careful with the pruning knife, more willing to spend the time necessary to do it right.

He has always been better at quick and clever haggling, like Father. It's not bad to prune, though. I wouldn't tell Father or Jahzeel, but I enjoy working on vines. Moving the rocks on the terraces . . . like now . . . what's there to like? Still, it's better when there is shade or a breeze. The breeze Jahzeel likes is talk. I smile thinking of that; I'm pretty clever with words, too. I am just as good at reading Torah as he is. I like to see work finished; he is always ready to put it off. I like to hear Father say, "Well done, Thomas," even though he always seems to ask me for even more. When he does, I give it. I take pride in my work.

Don't get me wrong, Jahzeel is a good man, but why did the Almighty have to let him be a few score of heartbeats the elder? Since we were young, Jahzeel has been pruned by father to take his place running the business. It used to bother me being called Thomas, or "twin," instead of my given name, but eventually I just accepted being a shadow. I've enjoyed watching Father pruning Jahzeel at times, but it has never seemed quite fair. I've been pruned enough, too, but I seem to be placed as a terrace, a solid foundation. The foundation is necessary, but it doesn't get much notice, except by Father.

There was a time not long ago when Jahzeel and I did everything together. The vineyard will someday belong to Jahzeel. Father always insists that family is more important than the vineyard, but sometimes the vineyard seems to be part of the family. I've looked at other opportunities. Oh, Jahzeel wouldn't ever kick me out, and Father will make sure I have a place, but sometimes I think working at the seaside would be easier than on the hillside.

I know a number of fishermen, and it's nice to be in a boat, where there's usually a breeze. Jahzeel gets seasick! He thinks I just naturally don't. Actually, I did at first, but I wouldn't want Jahzeel to know that; it's one of the few things he realizes that I do better. If he were to go out in the boat a few times, he probably wouldn't, either. Besides, Mother likes it when I bring home a big biny—the biggest fish in the Sea of Galilee! Even Father comments on it. I like to see the look on Jahzeel's face when I do. If he knew that he could get accustomed to the water, then he might be out there, too.

As it is, fishing is my activity. I can't go out often. Besides, when I'm on Zebedee's boat I really should let him have the catch; that's what he and his workers live on. He's more likely to let me keep a few little musht for my efforts—fish barely big enough for a boy's meal. For now, I work the vineyard.

When I finished the last rock and the last vine, it was time to go home. I expected that Mother would have something ready to eat and Father would be back from market. Jahzeel? Who knew?

Our home is only a few stone throws from the hill I was working on. We are not far from our tiny village: a few houses; small market; a bakery; a tanner; and, the heart of any village, a good well. We have a real synagogue close by in the town of Korizim, but even there we barely have the fifty men required to form one.

Father remembers when they had only a minyan, a meeting of as few as ten Jewish men, a gathering Grandfather had helped start.

As I entered the main room of our small stucco house on the south face of a smaller hill on the edge of the vineyard, I found Father quietly seated on our stool near the window for light and what little breeze there was, sharpening a pruning hook on the top of the family chest. "Shalom, Father," I greeted.

Father replied, "Shalom. Did the training go well? The terraces?"

"The vines do well." I elaborated, "The terraces are solid."

Jahzeel, already back from the bakery and sitting on a mat peering out the lattice, interjected, "He could have finished sooner instead of trying to get me to do the south face of the hill."

Father announced clearly, "Jahzeel, Thomas does well. I have two good sons, Jahzeel and Jezer. I will not have Cain and Abel."

Jahzeel replied properly, but still making sure I understood his displeasure: "Yes, Father, Thomas is good. And I am Thomas's keeper."

I gave my brother a stare before replying. I had caught his reference to Cain but recognized that, not only was Jahzeel no Cain, but he was hardly my keeper. "Yes, Father, the delay was my fault," I dutifully acknowledged.

Mother walked in from the small open courtyard where she had been cooking and addressed us all: "Shalom. Sit. Cool yourselves. I wish there were a breeze; we could go to the roof to sit. As it is, the shade is better. Thomas, you look tired. There is still water in the pot if you need to freshen a little." I'm sure she could smell my sweat, but she kept that to herself. I am glad that Father has always given Mother, as well as us twins, the freedom to speak at home. Not many Jewish men, and even fewer Gentile men, allow such freedom of speech in the home. Father would still control if the conversation were to become more serious, but his allowing the blessing of banter within the family is something I give him praise for.

Father, smiling, replied, "Yes, dear. Sometimes I wish my grandfather had started the vineyard closer to the sea and its breeze. But what you inherit, you inherit."

Didymus

Jahzeel commented curtly, "I think we are in a good location. Rome doesn't bother us much here where it's hot. And it's only a Sabbath day's journey south to the bigger markets in Bethsaida, or even Capernaum."

I agreed, half-heartedly: "It's not bad for Galilee."

Father, realizing that there was no real praise in my statement, replied sternly, "No! We are of the tribe of Naphtali. This is where our tribe first settled, long before the Assyrians came. This is why my father returned and settled here with the few who still know themselves to be of Naphtali. This is where we belong. We will not wander looking for a better situation; this is what the Lord has given us. He is our Yehovah Jireh: "the Lord will provide." We have all we need, and we have the favor of God. We grow grapes as good as in the Valley of Eshkol."

Mother refocused the conversation: "Good enough that my sons should be finding wives soon . . ."

Jahzeel reacted: "Mother!"

Father, in agreement, put in, "Your mother is right. Jahzeel, I see you looking at Anna. She is lovely. We should have arranged the engagement years ago. Would you like me to speak to her father?"

I interrupted, laughing, "Yes, Father, do!"

Mother said calmly, "Thomas! You must be serious, too! We could have chosen a wife for each of you two years ago, but we thought it best to let you be involved in the decisions."

Jahzeel and I were both well aware that few families allowed men, even of our age, to choose their own brides. Perhaps we took such a blessing too much for granted. Father spoke again: "Yes, but we can add only one room this year. As the elder, Jahzeel must come first."

Jahzeel responded, "No need for haste; I'm still young."

Father spoke clearly: "It's not hasty; you know your mother and I could not have any more children. We should have decided for you two long years ago."

Mother wistfully admitted, "We were blessed with two sons, but I want grandchildren on my lap."

Father agreed, "More hands to pick . . ."

I interjected, jestingly, "Jahzeel just wants Anna."

Jahzeel defensively shot back, "She is a good girl."

Mother, again placating us, replied, "Yes. A baker's daughter. Her mother is a fine woman. She has her mother's grace. Not that any woman is good enough for either of my sons . . ."

Father, his decision made, stated more than asked, "It's settled, then?"

Jahzeel, trying to retain some semblance of control over his life, countered, "Let's wait until the grapes are in."

Father, realizing that Jahzeel was stalling, proclaimed, "Like Job I should be patient? We will wait. Hard work will help with patience; it takes our mind off other things."

Jahzeel realized that he had traded time for Father's expectation of hard work— not the bargain he had intended. Still, I realized that Father had relented a bit, so I spoke, changing the subject: "Father, the training and terracing of the south hill is done. I don't know about the north face of the hill (looking at Jahzeel). May I go to Bethsaida this afternoon?"

Mother, speaking with a grin, "Is there anyone you are seeing?"

I blushed slightly as I replied, "No, no. Philip told me more about a new young rabbi, Jesus, who has been speaking about shalom. Real peace—not just the greeting, or a lack of malice, but an attitude of serenity between people. I want to know more about him."

Mother, requiring detail as she always did, "Philip, the fisherman? We have a rabbi to *fishermen*?"

I answered clearly, knowing that Mother was simply curious, "No, Andrew bar Jonah is a fisherman, like his father was. Philip helps out Andrew and Simon only when they need him."

Father, always questioning, asked, "Didn't Andrew think the Baptist was the Christ?"

I answered somewhat defensively of my friends, "No. Well, he was John's disciple, but John never claimed to be the Christ.

Didymus

Andrew just liked to hear his words."

Jahzeel, tried to posture himself as though he were above the conversation, declared, "Words! I prefer actions."

I spat my reply, "You of all people love words. Did you finish your 'actions' on the north face of the hill?"

Jahzeel, realizing he had angered me, goaded me on: "You never listen to my words."

Jewish people, like most people born in our region, often argue violently with words, especially in haggling. In our house Father never allowed it—or the spitting, shaking of fists, or raising of hands that often go with it. Father, realizing that our teasing was quickly going deeper, spoke clearly: "Sons! I trust Thomas to think on his own. His wisdom is not so great as Solomon's, but good enough for our vineyard."

Jahzeel, trying to appear wise, spoke, seemingly in my support: "Yes, Father. He is not easily swayed."

Mother, also recognizing our growing animosity, again changed the subject: "This rabbi talks shalom? I should see peace between my sons. Take Jahzeel with you."

Jahzeel, realizing he could be forced to go, relented, insisting, "I have work to do."

Although I was relieved, I wanted a final word about Jahzeel and muttered, "Only because you didn't finish the north face of the hill yet."

Jahzeel, unwilling to relinquish his favored position, countered, "I have responsibilities."

I wasn't done with him yet. "Because you didn't finish the north face of the hill yet! You went to the bakery to see Anna! Not that I blame you; she is charming. Mother, we are at peace. I just want to think for myself."

Mother replied, "Peace? You and Jahzeel have a truce, not peace. Perhaps if you two should marry . . ."

Father agreed but ended the discussion. "Peace is a good thing. A wife and children bring perspective. Family is everything. In time. For now, you may go, Thomas."

I realized that Father had shut down our discussion and knew that our meal would now be very quiet. We would recline at our low table but talk very little. Still, I smiled, realizing I had been granted some freedom. "Thank you, Father. Shalom."

II

A Dream of Freedom

ndrew and John had been impressed by the Baptist. They went to the wilderness of Perea to see him. They said the Baptist had been born after a vision from angels. He taught them to pray. I would love to pray as they do. Better than the rabbis, even; they seem to talk directly to God. And they do so often, as well. Others went to the wilderness, too, but Andrew and John were real disciples of the Baptist. The Baptist is the son of a priest, and I don't know why he would leave the temple for the wilderness. I thought about going to the wilderness, but Jahzeel would not forget my absence if I were to leave for long. Now, my friends had returned to Bethsaida.

It was nearly dusk. They sat near Simon's nets, waiting for them to dry and be put away. As I approached them, I called out, "Andrew! Philip! Shalom!"

Andrew replied first, "Shalom."

Philip's customary greeting was also "Shalom."

I sat and entered their conversation. "I wasn't sure I would be able to make it here."

Andrew replied honestly, "I'm glad you did."

Philip let me in on the current subject: "We were talking about the wedding."

I was still unaware of the implication of the discussion. "You are getting married? I didn't know you were even espoused!"

Philip, in shock, "No!"

I looked at Andrew. "You, Andrew?"

Philip chuckled, "Ha! He has no prospects!"

Andrew went on, "No, no, I want freedom for now; this wedding is not about us."

Still ignorant, I asked, "Who, then?"

Philip gave a more thorough explanation: "It's David ben Beriah; he is finally marrying Elizabeth. The espousal has taken a year. All is ready. The room has been added. His father will give the blessing any day. They will be good for one another."

Andrew continued, "It will be at Beriah's home in Cana. I'm sure Jesus will be there for the wedding. His mother, Mary, will be hosting; she is from Nazareth, and since David's mother is dead, she volunteered. It is not far but will require a half-days' notice. The call will go out hours before the feast begins."

I asked, "Jesus, the young rabbi?"

Andrew answered, "Rabbi, yes, and more . . . a prophet! He has been away for nearly two months. He left after being baptized by John, in the area of Bethany across the Jordan, near Perea, where we were for a time."

I wanted detail. "Was it on business? I heard he used to be a carpenter. Now a prophet?"

Andrew replied, "No, it was some sort of pilgrimage in the wilderness. He's the son of a carpenter, but prophets are called from all walks of life—farmers, shepherds . . ."

I was still in the dark about this man they were so delighted with. "What about the Baptist, John? He at least is the son of a priest. An only son—why he didn't become a priest only God can know. This Jesus cannot be called as a prophet; no prophet was ever a carpenter."

Philip replied seriously, "No Thomas, it wasn't business; I heard Jesus was alone for forty days."

Andrew agreed, "That's what I heard."

I wanted to hear more. "For what purpose did Jesus go—to study?"

Philip replied, "To be tempted."

Didymus

I was puzzled, "What?"

Now Andrew replied, "He said he had to be tempted after the baptism by John."

I could not understand. "You two didn't go into the wilderness after baptism. Besides, I see plenty of temptation here, and even more in a town! Why go to the wilderness? What is the temptation there?"

Philip simply replied, "He was tempted of Satan."

I replied, "Aren't we all?"

Andrew resisted, "Not like this; he fasted the whole time."

In shock, I answered, "No one can do that."

Philip quietly answered, "The prophets of old did."

I realized where they were going. "Forty days like Moses? That was supernatural. He was actually with God. Why so long for Jesus?"

Philip answered again, "Yes, Moses accomplished two of these fasts, back-to-back, and Elijah did a long one."

I still was unconvinced. "Forty days seems impossible. A few raisins would do well after so long."

Andrew stated, "He still doesn't look weak. After forty days and nights he should be."

Philip reasoned, "He was a carpenter, and likely thirty years old; he has muscles. He seems even stronger now."

I was not giving in. "That's hard to believe. He should not be able to walk . . . if it was the full forty days."

Andrew tried to explain: "The strength is in what he says, not what he looks like."

Philip spoke softly: "He looks into your soul."

I wanted to meet him for myself. "Father gave me permission to hear Jesus. Where can I see him?"

Andrew explained, "The Baptist told us to follow Jesus. Then Jesus disappeared for forty days! Even now, we spend time with him only at his choosing. He spends so much time alone in prayer!"

Philip again gave me hope: "He will be at the wedding."

Andrew agreed, "He will be there, but it won't be like when we can talk to him."

I didn't care. "For now, I can just see him. My mother wants me to listen to him talk about shalom."

Philip smiled. "He talks shalom. He has more peace than anyone else I've ever met."

Andrew agreed. "His peace rubs off on you."

I interjected, "He needs to rub some off on Jahzeel."

Andrew clarified, "Your brother?"

"Yes."

Philip stated, "I've not seen him; he is never around."

I explained, "He looks like me, but he doesn't act like me."

Philip retorted with a laugh, "Lucky for him . . . or for you?"

I grumbled, "He had all the luck. What fortune. What favor. A few hundred heartbeats older than me!"

Andrew, laughing too, "You said you have his looks."

"He would charge me money for them if he could!" I had replied before I realized how angry I sounded, adding now, "No, that's unkind; he isn't all bad. I know he really cares."

Philip pointed out, "Everyone calls you Thomas, or Didymus—nicknames. You call your brother Jahzeel, his given name. No one calls you by your given name, Jezer. Why not?"

I replied, "Jahzeel has Father's name, and Grandfather's. I was always known as Thomas or 'the twin.' I really don't mind any longer, but see how little I'm respected?"

Andrew replied understandingly, "I know what it's like to have to work with an older brother. Follow, follow. That's partly why I went to the Baptist: for independence. Besides, there is no luck, only God's favor. That's why God has some born first—that, too, is part of his favor."

Philip, also trying to calm me down, stated, "Thomas, you don't know what it's like to fish before dawn, day after day!"

I still pitied myself. "In the cool of the day! If a fisherman is hot, he can dip in the water; I have to wait and sponge off. I pick and prune in the daylight, I train vines, and I move rocks! I prefer the cool of the morning, but it's not always my choice. Independence would be grand."

Didymus

Philip jested, "Yes, people say they can smell a fisherman. I can smell a farmer."

I ignored his joke, but Andrew again answered understandingly, "You pick and give to the Romans. There is no real independence. No real favor."

I was glad to have his sympathy. "Yes. They take what they want. We are lucky to keep just the spoils. As long as they don't knock down the terraces . . . They took many years to put up. They look too much like walls, which the Romans realize could be used for a defense. That's all the favor we get in this day; we're fortunate they don't knock us down." I went on, changing the subject, "Is there enough wine this time of year for the wedding? Nothing very fresh is still available. We use yeast for everything not going to the Passover. You know about requiring the removal of yeast for Passover. The best without yeast was saved for Passover; the skins are already in caves. Any yeasted wine available for the wedding will be old. Anything not in caves will not have aged well."

Philip pointed out, "That isn't our worry. Would your vineyard give David a deal?"

I replied, "Jahzeel? He is a businessman. He wouldn't give me a deal! Old wine. Raisins."

Andrew asked, "What about your father?"

I answered, "He's letting Jahzeel do most of the sales these days. Father wants to become a quiet man—less involved with day-to-day business. He is at least trying to put the cares of the business behind him. He's not nearly as negative as he used to be. He used to complain about everything. He couldn't believe anything until he saw it with his own eyes."

Andrew spoke with a smile. "So, that's where you get it. My brother Simon is never quiet! I don't know how he can quiet himself enough to fish."

Philip bantered back, "All fisherman are loud when they don't have a net in the water. Look at Zebedee's sons, James and John. There's a pair!"

Andrew again seemed understanding. "Loud, but James will be inheriting the business someday, just as Jahzeel will inherit Thomas's vineyard; it's God's will. God's favor."

Philip agreed, "Yes, but their mother will not let James take anything from John. He will be fine."

Andrew, still contemplative, went on, "We do still have the favor of being the Chosen people. John will be fine, but what Simon tells me is true: the oldest has the responsibility of the business. In some ways we with older brothers have more freedom than our brothers do. Besides, a good mother can keep peace."

I spoke: "You are too philosophical. I have a good mother, too. I think she rubbed off some of her attitude on Father. Perhaps because she is with him so much more, now that Jahzeel and I do most of the work. I must be going back home; she will worry. It's close enough to home that I will hear the wedding cry. I'll be at the wedding; I can't train vines in the dark! Shalom."

Philip agreed, "Shalom. I want to talk to someone before dark. I must make haste."

Andrew quietly replied, "Shalom, friends."

They are good men. I'm not the only one who doesn't really fit into the life that was planned for me. But it can't be as simple as leaving home to follow the Baptist. Even Andrew and John were cast away by the Baptist! You just don't get to choose your life. What will be will be. I cannot plan my future. It often seems as though God's plans don't include me. That's not the sort of favor I want. Still, Andrew and Philip have a sparkle in their eye that wasn't there before. It's as though they expect something good— expect it to the extent that they are sure of it. Like expecting a great harvest before you pick it, all the while knowing that nothing will spoil the harvest. I know it's better to not expect good than to be disappointed. Andrew and Philip will be back to reality soon enough.

III

At the Wedding

When the call for the wedding came, I left our home for Cana. The call occurred near dusk, after people had finished their day's work. By the time I arrived the ceremony was over, but the celebration would last for many hours. As usual, most of the guests were in the courtyard, celebrating or milling about. I quickly found Andrew, and he greeted me first: "Shalom!"

"Shalom." I replied, "You beat me here. I'm glad I heard the call. Where is Philip?"

Andrew replied, "He is with a friend, Nathanael."

"I don't know him."

"Philip knows him well. A thoughtful man. He found Nathanael after we met last time. He brought him to Jesus. Now he also follows."

"So soon? What did Jesus say to him?"

"Here they are; let him tell you himself."

Philip smilingly greeted me with "Shalom, Thomas! This is my friend Nathaniel. He is from Bethsaida, like Andrew and Peter."

I gave a warm greeting, "Shalom," and Nathaniel greeted me in kind.

Philip got to the point. "We are here hoping to see Jesus. Have you had anything to eat or drink yet?"

I acted disappointed, as usual. "No. Judging from the looks of their barrels, you may not want to. The flies tell me that the wine has not been kept well. The barrels weren't properly sealed."

Andrew gave weight to my assessment, which I enjoyed, conceding, "You do know your wine, Thomas. I hope no one is unhappy with the host."

Philip, more concerned, commented, "Unhappiness lasts only a while. The marriage lasts forever. The host looks unhappy now."

I asked, "Who is the woman talking to the host?"

Andrew replied, "That is Jesus's mother. Her name is Mary, the widow of a carpenter, Joseph ben Jacob, of the tribe of Judah."

I went on, "The host is talking to her. He looks worried."

Philip remarked, "I had some of the wine. They should be worried. It's nearly gone. And not at all fresh."

I replied condescendingly, "You are a judge of wine, Philip?"

Philip simply replied, "I would rather drink vinegar. Here, try some."

I looked at it, sniffed it, and then touched it to my lips without swallowing any: "Phew! Worse than vinegar; we make vinegar because it does not spoil. Only a drunk would enjoy this. Not only has it turned; the fining was not done right. The lees were not separated regularly. Fining, as I'm sure you know, is moving the liquid wine from one bottle to another. They didn't do it. They did not rack it, either. That's separating the lees at the bottom from what you finish. The lees are mostly the dead yeast left in the bottom when you are done. Instead of being separated, it has gotten mixed in. If you do everything right, the wine will age well. The best of our wine, processed well and stored in caves would not be fresh, but it would still be pleasant; this wine has not aged well."

Philip, realizing that I knew what I was talking about, replied, "I'm impressed. You are an expert. All I know is that it's bad."

Andrew, paying attention to the master, stated, "Look, there is Jesus. His mother is talking to him."

Philip, watching, reported, "He seemed brief; then she left."

I was watching now, too. I said, "She speaks to the servants of the host. The servants look to Jesus."

Philip went on, "Jesus is speaking to them. They look confused."

Didymus

Andrew was confused, too. "They left with water pots. I wonder where they were going. What do they need to wash for?"

Philip commented again, "Who knows? Nathaniel, you have been quiet."

Nathaniel replied quietly, "Jesus has asked something of them. He knows things."

Philip blurted out, "You told me that he is the Son of God."

I interjected, with what I thought to be an appropriate degree of anger in my voice, "What? He's Galilean. He can't be Messiah."

Andrew appeared to be nonplused. "What's wrong with Galilee for a prophet? Jonah was from near there, and he was a mighty prophet."

I tried to cover my anger by a rational response: "Jonah was a prophet mostly to Gentiles. We are not talking prophet but Messiah. Your friend said *Son of God*."

Philip also seemed defensive. "Nahum was from Capernaum, in Galilee; you grew up near there; you should know Capernaum means city of Nahum."

I replied again, "Fine. But Nathaniel said *Son of God*."

Nathaniel simply stated, "I believe he is."

Andrew, not questioning but inquisitive, pointed out, "You just met him."

To which Nathaniel answered, "He has known all things I ever did."

Philip offered his opinion without taking sides: "I believe he is a mighty prophet."

Nathaniel went on, "He did not deny it."

Andrew asked, "Did not deny being the Messiah? Perhaps you didn't ask clearly."

Nathaniel continued, "Philip brought me to him. He knew me without ever before having laid eyes on me—and what I had done before I got there. He told me I would see heaven open and the angels ascending and descending on him!"

Andrew, asking for clarification: "Jesus *is* Jacob's ladder? He is the way from God to man?"

I interrupted before Nathaniel could answer. "Look, the water pots have been filled. I saw them pour much water into them at the city well just down the street; you can see it from here."

Nathaniel continued, "Jesus asked them, and they dipped into the jars. They are taking the water to the master of the feast."

Andrew, taking everything in, invited, "Listen to the master of the feast! You can hear him from here! He said, 'This is the best wine; why have you saved it for now?'"

Now I was indeed disturbed. "Absurd. It was water. I saw them draw it from the well."

Nathaniel, for his part, appeared very pleased. "Let's try some."

I was not moved. "No. I know wine."

Andrew challenged me, "Are you afraid?"

I would not be goaded into this. "No. I just know better. You should know better, too. You men know fish. They grow. It takes time. You catch them. You don't catch them in water pots. The same with wine. You grow the grapes. You tend them. You water them. You pick the fruit when it is ripe. You crush them. You jar it. It takes many weeks or even months."

Philip, no longer sitting on the fence, declared, "I'm with Nathaniel; what can it hurt?

And Andrew went along: "Coming, Thomas?"

I replied sternly, "No!"

Nathaniel spoke again, with sweetness in his voice: "We will save you some; looks like plenty . . ."

I replied even more sternly, "*No!*"

Nathaniel, Philip, and Andrew went to try the wine; it was not half a stone's throw away. They grinned broadly, to which I shook my head. Philip came back with a dish of wine. Smiling, he offered, "Here, Thomas."

I angrily retorted, "NO!"

Philip goaded, "Come now. I've never had better."

I was now angry with my friends. "You can't trick me. It won't work. I don't mind a joke, but this is silly."

Didymus

Philip went on, "Look at all the people, Thomas. Some others must know nearly as much about wine as you do."

I looked around and replied, "If it ends the joke."

I sniffed the dish, puzzled, after which I looked into the dish, swirled the liquid slowly, and sniffed again. Then I conceded softly, "It smells fresh. Perfect. No sparkle. Clear and sifted. Impossible before Passover."

I sipped, coming away even more puzzled. I took more and swirled it in my mouth. I stopped, then drank again. I closed my eyes. Then I waited for what must have been a long time.

Finally, I responded quietly, "I need to take some to my father. We grow the best grapes in all Galilee. Mature vines. Some years we have the finest wines anywhere in the region; everyone says so. This wine is better than I've ever tasted. It is fresh and cool, not overwhelming. Perfectly sifted. No yeast. It has not even fermented. It comes from mature vines; I can taste it. That's impossible for this time of year; the grapes would have to be only a few weeks old, but it's not the right season. How could they have brought it in and kept it fresh nearly until Passover? When we keep wine, we get the best fresh skins we can; the tanner is required for anything good. They are sewn closed to seal. The skins shrink a little as they dry on the outside. We add yeast for most wine; it helps it expand. If the skins split or leak, there isn't enough pressure. We store them in a cave to keep them cool. The sweetness turns and ferments, preserving the wine so it doesn't spoil, at least too quickly. If it ferments too much, it splits the skins. This isn't like that. Not at all. I need to sit and think. It *must* be a trick."

Nathaniel, walking up at last, asked, "Well, wine expert?"

I could not talk now. This was serious. "Leave me alone for a moment. Please."

Nathaniel stood quietly as Andrew walked up. Andrew reported, "I just talked to the servants. Mary told them to do whatever Jesus asked. He told them to fill the pots with water. They thought that was to give the guests fresh water to drink, as the wine was gone. They took plain water from the city well. It took time, as they had to draw so much. They brought it back, and Jesus simply said to take it to the master. He didn't *do* anything."

Philip simply stated, "It couldn't be a miracle, a direct intervention of God. Jesus didn't even touch it or pray over it."

Nathaniel disagreed. "Jesus did the miracle quietly. Peacefully. With shalom. Only the servants and ourselves know what happened."

I finally looked up, saying quietly, "This was a miracle, Philip. I've always heard about them. This is what they look like. Not so grand, but so very real. I never knew. Most people at the feast think this is wine from grapes, as usual. God always fills our grapes; we just tend and water the vines. It takes time. We squeeze the grapes. But God does the whole thing, from start to finish. I suppose I didn't really believe in miracles, or at least expect that I would ever see one. Not everyone who is here saw the miracle, yet they still partook of it. They took it for granted. They lived it and didn't even realize what it was. One moment water—the next pure and fresh wine as from perfect grapes. But there were no grapes . . . not even pulp. No squeezing. I can't imagine this. I don't know what this means. Why now? Why here?"

Philip asked, not in jest, "You didn't believe in miracles, Thomas?"

I answered honestly, "Not really. Just stories. Oh, I believe in God. I go to synagogue. I believe in the Passover, but it's never been *real*. I believe in my hoe, my pruning knife, the rocks, the vines, the grapes. I can touch them. Miracles? No. You can't touch them."

Nathaniel pointed out softly, "You just did."

I nodded slowly.

Nathaniel asked, "Would you see Jesus?"

I answered, "No. I'm not worthy . . . not ready."

Philip stated, "Too late; he must have stepped out. He didn't even try the wine."

Andrew spoke, "He doesn't seem at home, even in his mother's house. He's the eldest, yet he let his brother take over the business. He yielded his favor to James. He has other brothers, too. They seem to resent him."

I spoke, surprised at first. "The eldest leave? He would have been heir." Then I added, "But then he would not be free . . ."

Philip agreed, "His freedom is not given by men. It's fruit."

I asked, now really interested, "What does *that* mean?"

Philip went on, "The Baptist talked of fruit. You know fruit, Thomas. How does one get fruit?

"I already said. You prepare the earth. You plant good seed or cuttings from another vine. You dress the vine and tend it. You water it. You care for it. Finally, it produces fruit of the vine."

Philip continued, "Yes, grapes. What is in the grapes?"

"Fresh wine, pulp, and seeds. They change in maturity with time, but they are there from the beginning."

Philip asked, "What are they good for?"

I wasn't sure where he was going, but I explained in more detail, "We squeeze the grapes and get the wine, and we remove the seeds for planting, or they can be ground into oil to be used for cooking, for hair, and for medicine. Actually, we rarely plant seeds; we plant cuttings. The pulp and skins may also be eaten, or dried into raisins, unless you have made a Nazarite vow."

Philip went on, "The fruit has seeds that could be used for another crop of fruit?"

"Certainly. Sometimes we crush the seeds to use for a poultice. There is no waste. We even burn the old vines; they burn quickly but are excellent for kindling."

Philip explained his line of thinking, "Then the fruit is free. It has clear purpose, but it's no longer tied to the vine. It needed the vine to grow, but now it has purpose of its own. Jesus's family was sort of like that. He has more purpose than to be tied to that vine."

I complained, "You are too philosophical."

But Philip went on, "And you just touched a miracle."

I changed the subject, not wanting to think so deeply about this. "I need a jar. My father must try this wine."

Andrew and Philip walked off, looking for a receptacle.

Then Jesus walked up behind me and spoke softly: "Shalom, Thomas."

In shocked amazement, I replied, "Yes?" And then, remembering my manners, "Shalom."

Nathanial also greeted Jesus: "Shalom, Lord."

Jesus asked me pointedly, "Was the wine satisfactory, Thomas?"

I replied, "It was perfect. A complete wine. I've never had as good."

Jesus replied, "I'm pleased. Why do you think I made it?"

I replied, "For the guests. They were out of wine."

Jesus agreed but continued his line of questioning. "They were. I made the wine to be used by many. Did it matter to those who drank it where it came from?"

"I suppose not."

Jesus complimented me. "You have answered well. All things given are for the use of them to whom they are given. The Father has given you all things to enjoy. You have been given much wine over the years. You also have given much wine."

I agreed but was puzzled. "We worked for that wine . . ."

Jesus agreed, "You did. But did you cause the seed to grow or the vines to produce? Who filled the grapes?"

"I suppose God did . . ."

Jesus looked pleased. "Wonderful. You have answered well. If I choose to take weeks to fill grapes or moments to fill jars, what difference does that make?"

I answered humbly, "None, Lord."

Jesus asked, "Was it any less wine because there were no vines, no aging, no skins, no seeds, no pulp, no squeezing?"

Once again I conceded, "No. It was perfect. As though grown from the best aged vines."

Jesus again complimented me: "Well said. You did not come for the wine."

I answered with trepidation. How could he know? "No . . ."

Jesus went on, "You came for shalom. True shalom. Not just

as a greeting. Not what the world can give. You want an end to what you see as an adversarial relationship, don't you?"

I admitted, "Yes . . . You know what I think."

Jesus explained, "I know *you*, Thomas. I've always known you. I've always seen your desire for shalom. Nor do you want it just for yourself."

I admitted that, too: "I suppose I want it for my whole family."

Jesus probed bluntly, "For Jahzeel, too?

I could not believe he knew. "Yes. Especially for Jahzeel."

Jesus went on, "I know you do. My child, I want that shalom for both of you. You can't have real shalom until you know Jahzeel has shalom as well. Do you understand?"

I had not thought of that. I replied, "I've never seen it that way. Yes, shalom for Jahzeel. I would not have shalom if he did not have it."

Jesus smiled. "You understand your need. You will have shalom. Just as it takes time to make the wine in the grape skin, it will take time to develop shalom in Jahzeel's heart. It will even take time in your heart. Do not lose heart. Just as the grapes appear, shalom, too, will appear in due season. Do not give up."

I suddenly realized that I could never give up, and I answered as such. After a brief pause, I asked, "Lord, did you do this miracle *for me?*"

Jesus, with a smile, replied, "I would have, had you been the only one here, but no—many were blessed by the wine. There is abundance. Many more will be blessed by this miracle over a great number of days to come."

I replied genuinely, "Thank you, Lord."

Andrew and Philip returned with the small jar, now filled. They looked calmly and quietly at Jesus, who continued to speak: "Thank you for bringing Thomas the jar. It will make for lively and enlightening discussion at his home. Thomas, don't try to save any of it as fresh wine for more than a few days; it's real wine, but wine, like manna, spoils quickly. Manna spoils in a day, and fresh wine spoils in only a few days. Why waste perfect wine? Use it for the purpose for which it was intended; let it not go to waste. Now friends, I must speak with my own family. It will take time, but they, too, will some-day have shalom. The wine is just a small step. Like you, they cannot have shalom unless I bring it to them. Shalom, friends."

I quietly took the jar, nodding my thanks to Andrew and Philip, and then locked eyes with Nathaniel and slowly walked home. I didn't even say "Shalom" in departing; it didn't seem appropriate right then.

I was in deep thought all the way home. So much to think about. Shalom. Peace. I had been promised shalom. I already felt more shalom than I had ever experienced since I had sat on my mother's lap long ago. There would be even *more* shalom. How did Jesus *get* such shalom? How did Jesus come by such love? Such favor. Jesus must indeed be Messiah. Yet, he did not say so. If Jesus were Messiah, why would he not say so? Yeshua. The name Jesus means "God is salvation"; it seemed to fit. Yet perhaps it was rash to think so.

One thing was clear: I had witnessed a miracle. I had touched one. Or had I? I must have: I had the wine jar in my hand. Prophets did miracles. But would my family believe me? I hardly believed it myself. It's too much too quickly . . . Wait, what did Jesus say? It would take time. Tonight had come about so quickly, and yet the process would take time. How could both be true? It was like the wine: the grapes we grow take time, but when Jesus stepped in the normal process was circumvented.

Why would he not always simply step in? Oh, of course, then Father would be out of a job. That must be it: miracles are special, . . . but participating in growing grapes and producing wine is also special—a different kind of special. How could I know when mira-cles should happen? I couldn't trust my own mind any longer. Only Jesus knew when. He could be trusted—of that I felt unaccount-ably certain. There was only one way to find the answers for sure: I must follow Jesus. Only he could explain what was happening. Only he could explain why. Only he knew when. Passover was coming soon. Jesus would be at Jerusalem. I must find him there.

Didymus

I returned late, and only my mother was awake. "Shalom, Mother," I greeted her. "What a wedding. What wine!"

Mother replied, "Shalom, Thomas. You had your mother worried. I knew you went to the wedding; we heard the cry. But the paths are dark, and a mother always worries. We can talk about it in the morning. Now I can rest."

I replied softly, "Yes, Mother. We will all talk in the morning." Then, silently, to myself: Jesus promised we would!

IV

First Family Witness

I woke early, in excitement. The sky was barely pink. I had not slept much. So much to think about. I slipped out from behind the curtain without waking Jahzeel. Only Father was in the main room; Mother was cooking in the courtyard.

I called out, quietly, in order not to wake Jahzeel, "Father, Shalom!"

Father, replied, "Shalom. You are up early after getting home late. What excitement is in your eyes! Did you meet a girl?"

With a grin, I said, "No, Father, it's the wine."

Father looked disappointed. "I was afraid they would have old wine at the wedding. Are you sick?"

I went on, "No, it's the best wine ever."

Father, looking puzzled, "As good as ours three years ago? Impossible; it's not even the season . . ."

I interrupted, "I know, Father—that's the point."

Jahzeel, coming in, interjected, "What is all this noise so early?"

Father courteously greeted his son: "Shalom, Jahzeel. Thomas had some wine."

I spoke clearly. "No, it's not just the wine, it's so fresh . . ."

Jahzeel, laughing, "Fresh? At this time of year? Ridiculous. Thomas, you know better."

Defending my position, I responded, "I do . . . I did. Here, try some. Save some for Father."

Didymus

I got out the jar and gave it to Jahzeel, who smiled, sniffed, and then swirled and frowned, looking puzzled.

I commented, "See . . .

Jahzeel took a sip, looking startled. Incredulous, he asked, "How . . . ?"

Father held the jar to the light, looking carefully at it and sniffing before taking a sip. He, too, appeared startled.

Father spoke clearly but softly: "It's impossible."

I replied enthusiastically, "I know! Isn't it *wonderful*?"

Jahzeel, still nonplused, countered, "No, it's not wonderful—it's a trick!"

I went on, "How is it a trick if he admits to doing it?"

Jahzeel, confused, asked, "He . . . ?"

Mother, coming in, invited, "It's time for breakfast. What are you up to? Which of you ever admits to doing anything?"

Father handed the jar to mother, who took a sip.

Mother spoke thoughtfully: "Excellent. Where did you get this at this time of year? Fully strained. Very dark blood red, yet fresh—no sparkle. How?"

I replied, "From Jesus!"

Father asked, "The young rabbi? I heard he was a carpenter, not a vinedresser. Where did he get it?"

I replied clearly, "It came from water. A miracle!"

Jahzeel, still unconvinced, queried, "What's the trick. Where did this come from?"

I replied, "I just told you. Jesus performed a miracle. He turned water into wine."

Father spoke contemplatively. "Moses turned water into blood. No rabbi, or even a prophet, has ever done so since."

Jahzeel, plainly rejecting the explanation, still insisted, "It's a lie."

Mother looked hurt. "Jahzeel, Thomas does not lie! Thomas, how did he do this?"

"He asked men to fill the water pots, then to draw the water."

Father asked for detail. "Did he pray? Wave his arms? Put a stick in the water, as Moses did at Marah?"

"He wasn't even close to the jars. There were six pots, ceremonially clean vessels for washing, four or five bath of water each!"

Jahzeel, seeming interested, though still incredulous, probed, "That much! Impossible. Then someone else did it. Someone else put wine into the jars."

"No, he did it. I'm sure he did. He admitted it!'"

"You're smarter than that. You know it's impossible."

"It's a miracle."

"Miracles like that don't happen."

Father interjected, "Jahzeel, you don't believe in miracles?"

Jahzeel, realizing he had gone too far for Father, elaborated, but taking care to use the informal title for God "The great miracles were long ago. Not at weddings. Why would Hashem make wine?"

I spoke again, not at all careful, formally calling God my master: "Can't Adonai do as he chooses? I believe it was a miracle."

Mother defensively replied, "Thomas, I'm sure that's what you believe."

Startled at how much my family doubted, I reminded them, "You have tasted it yourselves! Where did it come from to taste fresh this time of year? It had to have been a miracle. So much at one time; even if it were not fresh, it would take many dozens of skins to hold that much wine properly."

Father agreed, "It is incredible."

Jahzeel conceded reluctantly, "It's odd, but I want to know how to make this new wine before Passover. What a market there would be. No fermentation, no leaven! There must be a new way."

Father seemed to agree with Jahzeel. "Yes, but what is one jar of wine?"

I pointed out, "He made six large water pots of wine."

Jahzeel asked, "*Who* made it? You said Jesus didn't touch them."

Father added, "That is a lot, but we sell that in a few days sometimes. We would need more."

I was beginning to get upset, but I declared, "You miss the point: Jesus does miracles."

Didymus

Jahzeel condescendingly replied, "We make wine, and no one calls it a miracle. When it doesn't rain, and we don't water the vines, the grapes never fill. If there is enough water, it fills the grapes, and we still make the wine from the grapes. I *suppose* God makes the wine over the long run, but it's no miracle."

Father, hearing Jahzeel's tone, corrected him: "Don't make fun of your brother. We say we are winemakers, but we know God really makes the wine. We say doctors heal, but we know God does the true healing. This is amazing. It's as though God did in seconds what usually takes months and much work. Think of the time we could save."

Mother, wanting to end the discussion before a fight began, spoke plainly. "Wine-spine, come and eat breakfast."

I was not to be shut down. "But he gave me shalom!"

Father asked, "Who did?"

"Jesus did."

Mother, still trying to keep peace, put me off with "That's nice, son. I'm glad for you—now let's eat breakfast."

Jahzeel could see that I was on the defensive. "Shalom? Peace? You look more excited than ever. That peace didn't last as long as this wine of yours will. I'm not angry, Thomas. It's good wine, but we'll have baths of fine wine in a few months, at your own hand. No miracle—just hard work, . . . and God's favor."

I continued, excitedly, "Jahzeel, he can give you shalom, too."

Jahzeel sneeringly retorted, "I hope whatever you have isn't contagious."

Mother would not have it. "Stop this and eat."

No longer able to contain myself, I blurted, "I want to be his disciple!"

Silence. I realized that I had spoken too much.

After a score of heartbeats, Father spoke: "I always thought you would follow me. Do you know what you have just said?"

"Yes, I do, Father, I do follow you. I have followed you. I must now follow Jesus."

Mother, genuinely concerned, asked, "Are you sure?"

Jahzeel, now showing some concern, though not for Thomas, asked his own question: "What makes you think any rabbi would accept you? You were not prepared for that. Even if you were ready, can't it wait until the grapes are all dressed? Then picked? And pressed?"

I replied, "I feel in my heart that Jesus will accept me just as I am. I don't think I can wait. I must find Jesus at Passover."

Mother asked, "You would break with the family?"

Father ended the conversation with "We will talk. Later. Now we will eat. No more of this now."

Breakfast was very quiet. The next days were quiet. The wine was all finished by the second day, long before it sparkled. Thomas went about the dressing of the vines, and Jahzeel and Father even helped a bit, which was very unusual for the time before Passover. As Mother was preparing for the Passover, she asked Thomas for help.

Mother spoke lovingly: "It's so good to have you boys at home. A daughter God did not bless me with, but you are good boys."

I replied, "I like to help."

Mother spoke again. "I know you do. I will miss you. I know you must go. You are of age. I believe you; the wine was a miracle. You have found not only a rabbi but also a prophet. Who knows, perhaps I am mother to a future rabbi!"

Relieved, I replied, "Thank you, Mother. I'm glad you believe me."

Mother replied, "Your father wants to believe, but he is afraid . . ."

"Afraid of what?"

Mother replied thoughtfully, "Perhaps the vineyard is not as important as he thought. Perhaps *he* isn't as important as he thought. He tried to raise you both well. Family means everything to him."

Realizing her concern, I replied comfortingly, "He did, Mother. And he is important. You are important. Jahzeel is important. Family is important. The vineyard is important. They are all gifts from God. But doesn't that mean that God is even more important?"

Didymus

Mother acknowledged in a knowing voice, "Your father knows that in his heart. Even Jahzeel does. You are honest; we know you believe. It's harder for us to know, as we have never seen."

"You saw the wine. You touched it. You sipped it. It was good. Very good."

Mother replied politely, "It was only wine. We can believe in wine. This Jesus—we have never touched *him*."

"I haven't touched him, either, Mother, but I know he is a great prophet. You will see."

"Yes, I suppose I will see. Someday. But we haven't seen yet. We trust you, Thomas."

"Thank you, Mother."

"Show your father you care. He cares for you, Thomas, more than you can know . . . until you yourself are a parent."

"I know he does. I will show him."

"Do it now. Before Passover. Shalom. We will all travel for the pilgrimage, but you will stay in Jerusalem. This is our first Passover when we know you will not return with us. You can't expect me not to have tears." Tears, as though bidden, did appear in her eyes . . . I held her close . . .

Finding Father repairing the grape press in the tool shed, I greeted him with "Shalom, Father."

Father cordially replied, "Shalom, my son. This press tells me I am not a very good carpenter."

"You have always made it work. You will again. Father, you know I have nothing but respect for you."

"But not for our vineyard?"

"You are more than a vineyard."

"Perhaps. But most of my life is the vineyard. That and you two boys. And your mother."

"Your time was not wasted. It was precious."

Father replied wistfully, "I taught you not to trust a deal that's too good. But thank you—that was kind."

"It's true, Father, I would be nothing without you."

Father, chuckling, "That is a fact."

"No, I mean the way you brought us up. We studied Torah. We went to synagogue. We celebrated the holy days. You taught me to be careful, honest, and truthful. To believe God."

"Yes. I think your mother and I did well. Thomas, I'm not angry, only sad. I feel I've let you down."

I could feel the pain in Father's voice. "Never, Father! You did not let us down. I'm a branch of your vine. I need to be grafted into a new vine. I cannot bear fruit unless I do. I'll always be your son."

Father acknowledged gratefully, "Thank you."

I elaborated, "I told you Jesus gave me peace. Do you know what it reminded me of? When I was little and we had to work at the vines until after dark. I was afraid."

"I remember."

"I had peace when you held my hand."

"I had peace, too. If this Jesus gives you such peace, follow him . . . but don't forget us."

"Never. I will always be a part of you. I will be back. Many times. I will always be a part of the family."

I departed quietly then to find Jahzeel. I located him near the grape vat, inspecting it to see whether it needed repair. I spoke without a greeting: "Jahzeel, we must speak."

Jahzeel replied mockingly, and without a greeting, "You, a prophet in training talk to a vinedresser?"

"You know better. You are the closest person to me on earth."

Jahzeel replied tersely, "Don't you mean second? Now you will follow Jesus."

"I will follow. But you are still my brother. You are always with me."

"I'm just surprised that in one night you could change."

"Do you not like the change? Have I argued with you once?"

"You have not. Yet you are different. And this is happening so fast. It is scary."

"It should not be. It was peaceful to me."

"Not from where I stand. I believe in what I touch."

Didymus

"Come then, touch Jesus; you don't have to be his disciple. Just come and hear him. You tasted the wine. You can always return home. Jesus knew why I was there before I spoke to him."

Jahzeel replied with a sting in his words, "Then he knows I don't need him. I have a vineyard to run. Jesus does not need me, either."

I entreated him, "Don't say that."

Jahzeel continued, hoping to drive home his point, "Does that hurt you? Now you feel hurt for your new master? What makes you think you are good enough for your miracle worker?"

"I'm *not* good enough. But he will still let me follow—I'm sure of it. I need him. He doesn't need me. He never told me I have to follow him. I want to."

"Fine. Go. Then grow up. And come home. We still have a family. There will be work for you to do here after you have wasted who knows how many days?"

No longer angry but trying to sound compassionate, I assured him, "I will miss you. I will tell you what Jesus says."

Jahzeel spat out his reply: "Just tell me when you are back to normal. No, that's too easy; tell me what he says, so I can point out to you his tricks. Shalom." He turned away.

Downcast, I replied, "Shalom, . . . my brother."

V

First Passover

Our family was quiet as we made the annual three-day pilgrimage to Jerusalem for the Passover. Most of the conversation was talk with other travelers about the heat. The pilgrimage was mandatory for males, but many people couldn't afford the trip every year. My own family as a whole didn't show up every year. This year was different. The household knew of my plans and were expecting me to stay. Mother made sure I had extra clothes And Father made sure he had a few extra coins sewn into the clothes in case I had to hurry home. The whole affair was somewhat humbling. Jahzeel suddenly didn't sound as dominant as he had just a few days earlier. I knew he wasn't bitter; he just wanted me to get over the phase he thought I was going through and get back to my normal life.

Jerusalem was bursting with people and animals. Even after prior preparations, one had to make it through the crowd of the temple for sacrifice. The smells of all the sacrifices filled the air. Things were not at all quiet. Barkers offering animals for sacrifice to those who had brought only money. This spoiled the romantic aura of the temple, but it was a part of life. Then suddenly, the tempo of the barkers changed, and shouting was heard.

Jesus spoke loudly and authoritatively: "It is written, 'My house will be a house of prayer,' and you have made it a den of thieves."

Didymus

There was a clatter of noises as tables were overturned and animals and people were chased out of the temple. The worshipers were at first shocked, then grateful; everyone knew the moneychangers cheated the people, but they were astounded that something the priests and temple guards had never been able to accomplish had been done by the ordinarily unassuming young rabbi Jesus.

The temple officials, their clout usurped, spoke loudly to Jesus: "Who gave you authority to do these things?"

Jesus's response, though hardly direct, was calm and peaceful: "Destroy this temple and in three days I will raise it up."

The officials, miffed, "It has taken forty-six years to build this temple, and you will raise it up in three days?"

After that, there was so great an uproar that no one could hear anything. Father looked amazed. "What we heard—that was your Jesus speaking?"

I replied, strangely exhilarated, "Yes!"

Jahzeel insisted, "He had no right to stop legitimate business."

To which Mother countered, "Those thieves are not legitimate."

Father agreed, shaking his head. "That's true. The best of the flock from outside the priests reject, but the runt they sold to you at the Temple they claim is without flaw."

I asked, "Did you hear the words?" to which Jahzeel retorted, "Nonsense. *Three days* to rebuild the Naos, the inner sanctuary?"

I interjected, "I don't think he was talking about the hieron—the building—at all."

Father reflected, "Perhaps not. It was strange."

I went on, "Let me look for my friends; they may know more."

Jahzeel spoke again. "Always off when there is work to do!"

Father stopped him, stating firmly, "Jahzeel, it is fine. This is a pilgrimage, not a workday. We will find lodging where we normally do with others of Naphtali. You may find us there, Thomas. Shalom."

Eventually I found Philip. "Shalom, Philip."

"Shalom. Did you see it? Jesus cleansed the temple!"

"Is that what that was? We heard it but could not see much."

"He came up with his mother and brothers from Capernaum last night. They were there since the wedding. Andrew and I followed. Nathaniel is here somewhere, too. Jesus is doing miracles here!"

"I want Jahzeel to see one!"

"Many have seen them. Even the leaders. Everyone knows he is a great prophet."

I spoke excitedly again, my twin still on my mind: "If Jahzeel sees, he will believe."

Philip reflected more calmly, "The leaders saw. They know he is a prophet, but he frightens them. They refuse to believe."

"Why?"

"The Levites have worked their way to power, even within the priesthood, and the Pharisees all came to power through training from a Pharisee rabbi or master. Jesus is no Levite. And who was the Pharisee master of Jesus? If he had a master, then his master would have to have been greater than he. At least the Baptizer was son of a temple priest. This man is the son of a carpenter."

Undeterred, I remarked, "Many prophets of old were not priests, or even Levites. There were no Pharisees until after Ezra's temple."

"That was hundreds of years ago. The rabbis have added much to our Law. Jesus shows no great respect for the rabbis, or for their rules."

"He performs miracles."

"Yes, he does. But if Jesus were to turn all the water to wine, what would your father do for a living? This is why the rabbis fear him. If the people follow Jesus, will they still follow the rabbis?"

Now I was more thoughtful, conceding, "I don't know."

"Neither do they."

"Have they seen the miracles?"

"Yes. He was healing here on the feast day. Jesus has power—power that can only have been given by God: Yehovah Rophi, the

Didymus

Lord our healer. They believe he is a prophet, but he does not seem to seek them. He is talking to the crowds but not preaching, as the Baptist did. Not here, at least not at this time. I don't really understand what his purpose is. Perhaps he is showing the Pharisees that he is not trying to take the people from them."

"He is keeping people away from himself?"

"No, he keeps no one away. Some seek him out. Some seem drawn to him. I can't explain it. Jesus came to Bethsaida, in Galilee, where I live. Thomas, Jesus came there and *asked me* to follow him! Andrew brought his brother Simon to see him, since they live so close. Simon was frightened by what he saw, and by what Jesus said about him. He watched from far off. He didn't even speak . . . and you know Simon; that in itself seems to be a miracle! Jesus said Simon would be called Cephas from then on. It's humbling to see him perform a miracle."

"Then I could bring Jahzeel?"

"I'm sure you could, if he would come. Andrew and John asked if they could follow, and Jesus permitted it."

I stated with enthusiasm, "I can *compel* Jahzeel!"

To which Philip replied tentatively, "I'm not sure that works. Andrew worked hard to get Simon to come, but Simon simply left quietly, without speaking with Jesus. Think of it: Jesus called him Cephas—a little stone, Peter!"

"I know what the word means, Philip. Does Jesus not want disciples? That is why I came: to become a disciple, not a little stone."

"Andrew and I had followed the Baptist, and he did not forbid us. We learned so much; he taught us to pray, not like the synagogue rulers, but in a more personal way. I can't explain it. People came, but on their own. Perhaps Jesus will do it the same way. The Baptist told us to follow Jesus."

"Then I must do so."

"I feel compelled, too. So do Andrew and Nathaniel. I see it in the faces of others, as well. With the Baptist, we went to the wilderness to learn discipline and more about God. Jesus went there all alone. He appears to want to be among the people—to go to them, not to expect them to come to him on their own, as they did to John. I can't explain it. Jesus draws us, like the Baptist, but to *himself*, not just to the place where he is located. He is hospitable; he allowed those of us who follow him to come along with his family to their home in Capernaum after the wedding."

I interjected, "It is getting late; I must find my own family. Where is Jesus staying?"

"He is from the tribe of Judah. He has much family in Jerusalem. You can find him. See if you can convince your brother to talk to him."

"I will try. Shalom. It sounds strange, but I feel as close to you as I am to my brother. I now feel I should call you brother, as well."

Philip, smiling, replied, "I feel that connection, too. Shalom, brother."

I worked my way through the city to find my family. As I went, I thought of the events that had transpired. Jesus truly is a prophet. Yet the Messiah, I felt certain, would have entered the temple and announced himself. Jesus did not. That meant he was not claiming to be the Chosen One. Andrew said the Baptist never claimed to be the Messiah, either, but Andrew still became his disciple. The Baptist had said, "His shoes I am not worthy to unlace," and Andrew explained that he had been talking about Jesus. Perhaps there is yet another; I do not know. One thing I do know: I must follow Jesus.

I found my family. The bustle of Jerusalem had quieted because of the memorial meal about to take place: it was time for the Passover Seder—a reflective time. Addressing us, Father began, as the patriarch of each family had for thirty generations: "How is this night unlike any other night?" With every fiber I wanted to blurt an uncustomary reply: *Because of Jesus!* But I knew the festival is a commemoration. So it must remain. For now. Patience. So hard to learn. Miracles are so much quicker. But there had been 1,200 Passovers, and there would be Passovers to come.

Didymus

The next day there was much talk about Passover, Jerusalem, and Jesus. Father seemed impressed with Jesus's actions in the temple. Mother, hearing of many miracles, was also moved. Jahzeel was not. My brother saw Jesus as someone who fooled himself or, worse, as a fraud. Jahzeel kept asking about money. Was Jesus asking for money or service? He was trying to determine what reason Jesus had for having left the carpentry business. It hurt me to hear such lightly covered accusations.

I asked, "Jahzeel, do you really think I am more naïve than you are?"

"Brother, you seem to prove it."

"Jahzeel, that hurts."

"If you continue to hold your hand in the flame you will be burned. Pull it out, and the pain will end."

"It isn't like that. Do you remember when Father first talked to us about marriage? Marriage should be of our own volition, not the arranged kind. He told us that, although some young people think that infatuation or physical attraction is enough, that's unlikely to last. He explained that more mature people say it's all about love—which is far better. Those wiser still realize that mutual commitment or trust is even more important and is absolutely required for a marriage to work. Although those qualities are good, he told us that the only real reason to marry someone is that you know union with that person is the only path for your life. You will see *only* that path, and you must take it."

Jahzeel answered briskly, "Father was speaking wisely, but this isn't about marriage; this is about becoming a disciple of someone you have talked to only once."

"You've talked to Anna a hundred times. No one ever asked you to stop seeing her after the first time."

"No one talked marriage after our first chat."

"Jahzeel, can't you trust me? If you marry Anna, it will be forever. You can't stop just because you learn she might snore. I can leave Jesus any time."

"But I have learned all about Anna over time."

"Do you know whether she snores?"

"How could I know that?"

"You can't. It just shows that you don't know all about her. You would have to be married to her to completely know her."

"It's true, to marry means to know. But I know what is important about her. We are committed to each other. I know she is the only path for my life. I'm sure she sees me as the only path for hers, as well. You know I would not divorce for a frivolous reason like snoring."

"I know you would not, brother; you are an honorable man. But how do I learn all about Jesus without following him?"

"Your point is well taken. Follow him. Learn of him. When you learn enough, come home." My twin smiled ruefully before continuing, "If you want good advice about his teaching, come, talk to me."

With a smile of my own, I concurred, "That's all I ask. I guarantee I will come and tell you what I learn."

VI

A Disciple with Much to Learn

Eventually my family made their way out of Jerusalem, back toward the vineyard. I was surprised at how unemotional they were. Even my mother was not in tears. My farewell had gone well. My final word to my brother had been, "Jahzeel, let me know in time for the wedding with Anna. I will be home from time to time, but I would not miss your wedding."

Jahzeel sheepishly responded, "The betrothal will be after the grapes are in, if the lord wills. Shalom."

Now on my own, I sought out Jesus. I first found my new friend Nathaniel. I greeted him, "Shalom, Nathaniel, my brother. It is good to find you."

"Brother? Yes, brother Thomas. Shalom."

"I seek to follow Jesus."

"I know you do. Come with me. Did you hear who else sought out Jesus? Nicodemus, the teacher of Israel, no less!"

"You are joking! He is a Pharisee, a great teacher of Israel, and in the Sanhedrin. He has so much to lose!"

"No, he did it at night, thinking no one would know."

"Then how do you know?"

"John was there. Nicodemus is an honorable man; I would not tell any who would spread it."

"You told me!"

"You want to be a follower."

"Will Nicodemus follow, too?"

"I don't know. Jesus said that Nicodemus must be born again."

"What does that mean?"

"I don't know. He told Nicodemus he must be born of the Spirit."

"How does one do that?"

"I'm not sure. I don't yet understand everything Jesus says."

"Doesn't he want us to understand?"

"Of course! Did your father teach you to be a vinedresser with words?"

"No, he showed us."

"Yes, because you remember what you actually do better than what you are only told."

"Of course. We must *do* in order to understand."

"Yes. I think we are going through Judea. We are going there to learn, as John's disciples did."

"Who is going?"

"A number of us are following. I'm not sure exactly how many. You already know some. James and John are here. They came into town for Passover. Their father is watching the nets, but James is only traveling with us; he will be visiting his home when we are nearer. Simon is minding nets back in Capernaum, too, but Andrew is here. I'm sure no one like Nicodemus will be going. Most of us are from the area of Galilee; we were just in Jerusalem for Passover."

"Do we start soon?"

"I would guess so. I'm glad you didn't miss us. Look, there is Philip. Shalom!"

Philip greeted his friends, "Shalom. I see I am not too late."

Jesus approached then and invited in his understated way, "Come. We must walk in the day."

Jesus walked north, toward the Damascus Gate of Jerusalem. The small group followed. The procession quietly filed out of Jerusalem.

Didymus

We first went about Judea and east to Perea—to baptize, as John had. We were all happy. I've never felt so clean. The Pharisees heard that Jesus was gaining and baptizing more disciples than John, but it was we who baptized and not Jesus. Eventually, we left the area near Judea and went back on our way, more slowly north toward Galilee. For weeks, and then months, we were constantly following and listening.

VII

Updating the Family

After synagogue one day in Capernaum, I had time to find Jahzeel. Being less than a Sabbath day's journey from home, I found the walk easy. So much had happened over these months that I could only update the family with highlights. As I expected, they were in the warmth of the house, resting as they should.

I greeted my family warmly, "Shalom!"

Mother replied, "Shalom! Let me look at you!"

Embarrassed, I replied, "Mother, it's been only a few months."

Father spoke. "Yes, and you haven't changed a bit."

Jahzeel, without a smile, "No, he changed *before* he left."

Father scolded Jahzeel. "What sort of a greeting is that?"

Jahzeel, embracing Thomas, replied with more sincerity, "I'm sorry, Father, I'm delighted to see him back where he belongs."

I spoke civilly. "I'm here for a visit. Jesus is in Capernaum."

Mother, trying to hide her disappointment, "You are going back?"

"Yes. I'm here to tell you all that is going on."

Mother, facing away from us to prevent her expression from giving away her emotion, invited, "Sit. Let me get some food. I made fresh bread before Sabbath."

Going and getting a skin, Father called, "Here, come over by the brazier and warm yourself. Have some wine. It's nearly as fresh as what Jesus made for you. Tell us all about everything."

Didymus

Jahzeel, pushing away from Thomas: "You still haven't realized the facts . . ."

Ignoring the implicit insult, I responded kindly to all three in turn, "Thank you. Mother, I would like food. Father, you make the best wine. Jahzeel, I am learning truth."

Scowling, my twin replied, "Facts, truth—What is the difference?"

I started to explain, "Sometimes there is no difference. Sometimes there is."

Father, genuinely interested as he poured wine into a bowl, asked, "How is that?"

"Remember the wine I brought from Jesus? The truth was that it was wine. Good wine. Most people who drank it thought it came from bottles, and before that from grapes, and the grapes from vines. The truth was that Jesus turned water from jars into wine."

Father concurred, "Yes, the wine was good. I believe you when you say Jesus made it."

Jahzeel commented, "I don't. It was a trick."

I sipped from the bowl and continued, "Perhaps that wasn't a good enough example. Jahzeel, do you remember years ago when you came in with what you thought was a cut on your back from tripping and falling against a terrace? The fact was that your back hurt; it felt like a scrape or a cut. Father looked at it and pulled a tick from your back. That was the truth. You could not tell. If you had waited for it to heal, you could have gotten sick. The fact was only the pain. The truth was a tick."

Jahzeel replied, "Of course I remember: it hurt to have it cut out."

Father recalled soberly, "I remember, too. I used a pruning knife, as clean and sharp as I could make it. The tick had burrowed deeply, and the spot was infected badly. I know it was painful. I think *I* hurt more in extracting it than you did, Jahzeel. But it had to be removed. There was no doctor. I did what had to be done. Mother put a poultice on it afterward to draw out the poison. We did what had to be done. Is that the point? God does what has to be done, even when it is painful or messy?"

"Excellent wine, Father. No, that isn't the lesson I intended, but that is a good message, too. My point is that Jahzeel believed he had a scrape based on the pain. The fact was that it felt like a scrape, but the truth was that he had a tick. He may believe the wine was a trick, but it was truly wine. What you believe about the truth does not change it from being the truth."

Mother interjected, "Wine-Spine. Fine. But let's not talk about ticks while we have food. What *truth* have you learned?"

"A lot. Let me just tell what has happened since Passover."

Father replied, "Start telling already.

"For a time we went to an area east of Jerusalem, Perea, to baptize, for the remittance from sin, as John had. The Pharisees heard that Jesus was gaining and baptizing more disciples than John, but it was we who were baptizing, not Jesus. John and Andrew baptized me; then I baptized others. Because of the Pharisees, we left Judea and went back once again toward Galilee.

Mother, seeking clarification, "Who is 'we'?"

I added, "Philip, John the son of Zebedee; Andrew; and some you don't know: Nathanael; Joseph ben Barsabbas, whom some call Justus; Matthias; and a few others."

Jahzeel reflected sarcastically, "The prophet to the fishermen . . ."

"Only John and Andrew!"

Jahzeel, still trying to disrupt the story, pointed out, "That's almost half the group."

Father, seeing the problem, chided him with "Jahzeel, let Thomas tell his story already."

Jahzeel relented, at least overtly, "I'm sorry. I'm not trying to disrespect you."

"It's fine. Eventually, we went through Samaria."

Jahzeel, still getting in jabs, "A true prophet traveling through Samaria?"

Father countered with "We travel though Samaria, Jahzeel."

Appreciative of Father's comments, I went on, "It's fine, Father. I was surprised, too. But what happened there was more surprising. We came to Aenon."

Didymus

Father interjected, "Yes, I've been there. Near Salim. Jacob's well is there. I've drunk from it."

"Yes, now I have, too. We got there at midday. No one was about, and we were thirsty. We all went to find food and a pot to draw water."

Jahzeel commented, "Being in Samaria, they couldn't leave a vessel there; it would be stolen."

Ignoring Jahzeel, I went on, "Jesus stayed at the well. A woman came with a vessel."

Mother, looking surprised, asked, "At midday?"

"Yes. She was an outcast."

Jahzeel spoke again: "I didn't know Samaritans could have outcasts; they are all outcasts."

Father, realizing that the thinly veiled ridicule was not ending, spoke again, *very clearly*: "Let Thomas tell the story."

Jahzeel mouthed, "Sorry."

"Jesus asked her for a drink."

Now Mother was surprised. "A Jewish prophet asking a Samaritan woman for a drink?"

"Yes, even the woman was shocked. That's not all. He offered her 'living water.'"

Jahzeel, thinking he understood, asked, "Is that the water he made the wine from? I knew there was a trick."

"No. That's not what Jesus meant. Water satisfies thirst. He was offering her satisfaction in life. She was an outcast because she had been married five times and was living with someone not her husband."

Mother, now understanding, reflected, "No wonder even Samaritans would not want her about."

"Yes, exactly. Why do you think she had been married that many times?"

Jahzeel threw out an answer without thinking: "She was a bad cook?"

Father answered, thoughtfully, "No, she has never been satisfied. She lusts for what she does not have."

"Exactly. Some people always want more. When Jesus told her about living water, she misunderstood him, too. She said, 'Sir, give me this water, that I won't thirst or have to come here to draw.'"

Mother, beginning to show compassion, realized, "She didn't want to come to the well. The women must have treated her horribly. That's why she came at midday."

"Yes, Mother, you have pity on her. Jesus did, too. He said, 'Go, call your husband and return.'"

Jahzeel, on the alert for inconsistency, countered, "You said she wasn't married. A prophet would have known."

"Jesus knew. Her reply was 'I have no husband.' Jesus got her to admit it. Then Jesus said, 'You are right when you say you have no husband. The fact is, you have had five husbands, and the man you now have is not your husband.'"

Father spoke understandingly. "I see now—what she said was a *fact*, but it was not the whole *truth*."

"Yes, Father, exactly. The woman had been caught, so she tried to change the subject. She said, 'Sir, I recognize that you are a prophet. Our fathers worshipped at this mountain; you Jews say that Jerusalem is the place where people should worship.'"

Jahzeel spat out, again missing the point, "Samaritans. They don't understand the Law."

"They don't understand it completely. Jesus told her, 'Woman, believe me, a time is coming when you will worship the Father neither on this mountain nor in Jerusalem, You Samaritans worship what you do not know; we worship what we do know, for salvation is from the Jews.'"

Jahzeel, again speaking superficially, remarked with evident satisfaction, "That's telling her."

"Wait, Jahzeel. Jesus went on, 'Yet a time is coming and has now come when the true worshipers will worship the Father in the Spirit and in truth, for they are the kind of worshipers the Father seeks. God is spirit, and his worshipers must worship him in the Spirit and in truth.'"

Didymus

Jahzeel, realizing that he was not tracking, echoed, "Worship *in spirit*?"

Father replied, "Truth again. The fact is that we worship, but my spirit is not always in it. That is the truth. This Jesus is a wise man."

Jahzeel, incredulous, asked, "Not you, too, Father?"

Father replied simply, "I am still a Jew."

I went on quickly, saying, "Let me finish. The woman again tried to move away from the truth. She said, 'I know that the Messiah, the Christ is coming. When he comes, he will explain everything to us.' Jesus replied without hesitation, 'I, the one speaking to you, am he.'"

Jahzeel declared angrily, "Blasphemy!"

Father spoke slowly but clearly. "That is only if it is not the truth."

Jahzeel seemed even more shocked. "Father!"

Father looked squarely at my twin and admitted, "Jahzeel, I'm not yet convinced, but I will not accuse someone without knowledge of the truth."

Jahzeel, looking again for an error, asked, "Wait. How do you know all that was said? You told us his followers had gone to find a vessel to draw with?"

I picked up a few nuts from the dish before replying. "We had just returned at this point. We heard the whole story from the woman later."

Jahzeel scoffed, "You believed a story told by a *Samaritan woman*?"

"There was plenty of evidence. Let me go on."

Father, genuinely interested, urged, "Finish already."

"When we returned, Jesus was still talking to her. No one, not even John, asked her what she wanted or asked Jesus why he had talked to her. She left her water jar and went back into town."

Mother, catching the detail, asked, "So upset she left her jar?"

"No, she was excited. She went into town and told people about Jesus. She said, 'Come, see a man who told be everything I ever did. Could this be the Messiah?'"

Jahzeel, grasping for any hint of error, echoed, "Everything she ever did. Exaggerates like a Samaritan."

Mother stated, "I'm surprised she sought out anyone in light of her background."

Father spoke, "Many of the men knew her, but to believe her . . ."

I went on, "She was persuasive *because* she believed. She could not keep silent."

Jahzeel, trying another approach, asked, "Is that true of you?"

"I suppose it is."

Father prompted, "Either it is, or it is not."

"Then it is. I am his disciple, or I am trying to be. Let me finish the story. We urged Jesus to eat what we had brought back. Jesus said, 'I have food to eat you know nothing about.'"

Jahzeel spouted again, "More mysteries."

I ignored him. "We discussed it, thinking that someone, the woman perhaps, had fed him. Jesus said, 'My food is to do the will of him who sent me and to finish his work. Don't you have a saying, "It's still four months until harvest"? I tell you, open your eyes and look at the fields! They are ripe for harvest. Even now the one who reaps draws a wage and harvests a crop for eternal life, so that the sower and the reaper may be glad together. Thus the saying "One sows and another reaps" is true. I sent you to reap what you have not worked for. Others have done the hard work, and you have reaped the benefits of their labor.'"

Jahzeel interjected, "What nonsense."

Now Mother stopped him. "No, I understand. He was satisfied not with food but with knowing he was honoring God."

Father agreed, "Yes, Mother, and the fields are ripe; that must mean that people are ready to repent. The prophets and teachers have planted, and now is the time to gather."

I was surprised at how much insight my parents were showing and enthused, "Wonderful. I'm sure that's what it means. You got the message more quickly than any of us."

Jahzeel, not giving up his attack, asked, "Am I the only sane one here?"

Didymus

Father, smiling broadly, asked me, "Is there more?"

"Much more. I still can't believe it; he spoke there for two days! Father, you gave us a good education, and we had good synagogue. The Samaritans don't know the Law all that well, but, as I listened, I learned more about the Law and the kingdom and God than I had learned in all my days at synagogue! Many Samaritans believed in Jesus because of the witness of the woman. They came to see, then urged him to stay. We did, for two days, and we heard the story from her repeatedly. Jesus verified it as true. Because of his preaching, many more repented. They said to the woman, 'We no longer believe just because of what you said; we have heard him ourselves, and we know that this man really is the Savior of the world!'"

Jahzeel, sneering, "*Samaritans repenting?*"

Father, ignoring the insult, spoke: "Yes, light does let one see truth. I remember the prophet Isaiah saying, 'The people living in darkness have seen a great light.' I always thought he was talking about the people living here near the coast and Galilee among the Jews; there are many who live in darkness all around us. He could also have been referring to the people in Samaria. Light changes everything."

Jahzeel, speaking under his breath; "A prophet staying in Samaria . . ."

I replied, "Even Samaritans know hospitality. They wanted us to stay longer. Jesus told them he had others to attend to."

Father prodded, with genuine interest, "There is more?"

"Yes. After leaving Sychar, my friend Nathaniel sought me out, wondering why I was not much troubled about staying in Samaria. I explained that we had learned that many Samaritans are honest and honorable and that when you show them respect they do the same to you. We have had Pharisees cheat us on occasion. Not even all Romans are evil; some have dealt fairly with us. Nathaniel felt that Samaritans could not be trusted. I reminded him of what God did through the prophet Jonah for the Ninevites."

Jahzeel countered, "Yes, but they did not stay with God. In just a generation he destroyed them."

"That's true. But he forgave a whole generation and let them learn the truth. They were given shalom. God did that. It was a gift they did not deserve. Jonah did not want it for them, but God did. We have no right to decide what God can or should do. How many generations of Jews were in the dispersions, or under the judges?"

Jahzeel simply shook his head.

I went on, "We went to Aenon, near Salim, right on the water."

Father asked, "Where the Baptist is now?"

"Where he *was*."

"Was?"

"That's another long story."

"So, tell it already."

"You know that Andrew, the brother of Simon, as well as John, the son of Zebedee, were the Baptist's disciples."

"So, that's why you went to Aenon?"

"It was something like an appointment . . ."

Jahzeel asked another superficial question: "Jesus made an *appointment* to see the Baptist?"

"Not the way we do; it was divine."

Father asked, "God makes appointments?"

"Appointed or chosen, I can't tell. You remember that Rebekah was appointed for Isaac?"

Father answered, "Yes, but who would have told Jesus or John of the appointment?"

I replied, "I don't know. Let me tell the story; perhaps you can tell."

Jahzeel interjected, "So, you don't have all the answers?"

As Father gave Jahzeel a scowl, I replied, "We began to baptize, too. As you would expect, Andrew and John went to visit the Baptist and his disciples. Those of John's disciples not following Jesus complained to the Baptist that 'everyone' was going to Jesus."

Father stated, "John is a good man. Everyone says so. Brave. Had they all gone to Jesus?"

"Not at all. It was exaggeration, a figure of speech. You just mentioned that everyone says John is a good man; Herod does not."

Didymus

"Yes, but you know what I meant."

"Yes, and John knew what his disciples meant. He answered them with much grace. He said, 'A person can receive only what is given them from heaven. You yourselves can testify that I said, "I am not the Messiah but am sent ahead of him." The bride belongs to the bridegroom. The friend who attends the bridegroom waits and listens for him and is full of joy when he hears the bridegroom's voice. That joy is mine, and it is now complete. He must become greater; I must become less.

The one who comes from above is above all; the one who is from the earth belongs to the earth and speaks as one from the earth. The one who comes from heaven is above all. He testifies to what he has seen and heard, but no one accepts his testimony. Whoever has accepted it has certified that God is truthful. For the one whom God has sent speaks the words of God, for God gives the Spirit without limit. The Father loves the Son and has placed everything in his hands. Whoever believes in the Son has eternal life, but whoever rejects the Son will not see life, for God's wrath remains on them.'"

Father, seeking clarification, asked, "John bows before Jesus?"

"He does. John's disciplines realized that he was sending them away, much as he had dispatched Andrew and John only months earlier. It was as though he thought he had nothing more to teach, or perhaps that he would be going away soon. They seemed startled. I suppose Andrew and John had believed themselves to be better prepared than the others and therefore sent to follow Jesus. Now it seemed as though their requested departure had just been expedient. In a short time, most of John's disciples dispersed. Suddenly, Herod's troops appeared. They arrested John! It happened suddenly, when only a few disciples were still there. I'm not sure they would have arrested the Baptist if the crowds had remained; there would have been trouble. As it was, John went quietly."

Father, in shocked disbelief, "No! John arrested?"

Understandingly, Mother pointed out, "It's because of what he says of Herodias. There is nothing good an honorable person can say about that woman."

I agreed, "Yes, Mother, that was it. Herod was angry because John had not kept still about his living with Herodias, his brother Philip's wife. Everyone knows, but only John is brave enough to say it publicly. Even Philip, Herod's brother, said nothing. No one but John. John fears only God."

Jahzeel interjected, "Herod and Herodias might as well be Ahab and Jezebel. No, Herodias is slyer."

Father quietly predicted, "John will be dead soon . . ."

I agreed, "Probably. When Jesus heard about John, he left for Galilee. When Andrew and John, the son of Zebedee, saw what had happened and knew that a few of John's disciples were following the troops to ensure that John would be cared for, they came with us. Jesus began preaching the good news of the kingdom of God: 'The time is fulfilled, and the kingdom of God is at hand: repent and believe the good news!' It was as though Jesus had known John would be arrested, as though this were somehow a necessary step."

Jahzeel spoke, and I think he was serious: "If Jesus were truly a prophet, he could have stopped it."

Father disagreed. "Jahzeel, you know that John is a prophet, and he did not stop it. Did Jeremiah stop the wicked? You know better."

I continued, "We went on to Nazareth with Jesus preaching; that's where Jesus had grown up. On Sabbath Jesus went to the synagogue there."

Father expressed, "It's nice to be back where everyone knows you."

"At first it was. Jesus stood up to read. The ruler gave Jesus the scroll of Isaiah. He unrolled it to where it is written,

'The Spirit of the Lord is on me,
   because he has anointed me
   to proclaim good news to the poor.
He has sent me to proclaim freedom for the prisoners
and recovery of sight for the blind,
   to set the oppressed free,
   to proclaim the year of the Lord's favor.'

Didymus

"Then he rolled up the scroll, gave it back to the attendant, and sat down. The eyes of everyone in the synagogue were fastened on him. He began by saying to them, 'Today this scripture is fulfilled in your hearing.'"

Jahzeel interjected again, "Blasphemy!"

"Everyone was shocked, Jahzeel. We all knew this was a scripture about the Messiah. Jesus was claiming that he is the Messiah to anyone who knew the scriptures. He didn't talk of vengeance, which is what we all would have expected from the Messiah. The people gathered started talking about the facts of who they knew Jesus to be; they could not understand the truth of the grace that came from his lips. They asked, 'Isn't this Joseph's son?'"

Mother quietly expressed a more compassionate perspective: "His family must have heard these things . . ."

"Yes, and Jesus knew what they were saying. They had come expecting miracles and signs, as he had done elsewhere. He said to them, 'Surely you will quote this proverb to me: "Physician, heal yourself!" And you will tell me, "Do here in your hometown what we have heard that you did in Capernaum."'

'Truly I tell you,' he continued, 'No prophet is accepted in his hometown. I assure you that there were many widows in Israel in Elijah's time, when the sky was shut for three and a half years and there was a severe famine throughout the land. Yet Elijah was not sent to any of them, but to a widow in Zarephath in the region of Sidon. And there were many in Israel with leprosy in the time of Elisha the prophet, yet not one of them was cleansed—only Naaman the Syrian.'"

The people of the synagogue were angry when they heard this. Jahzeel, this wasn't just about the thought of blasphemy; they had expected miracles, not preaching directed against them. Besides, Jesus had grown up there, and now he was calling himself the Messiah. They were enraged. They pushed him out of the city and led him to the cliff of the hill Nazareth is built on, to throw him off. Jesus simply passed through the crowd and went his way. The people had no idea how he had escaped. We watched, startled, as he returned to us."

Mother commiserated, "His poor family! The people must hate them."

"I know."

Now Father showed concern. "They are carpenters. No one will hire them in their own town. They will have to look in other places for business."

I replied, "Perhaps. Or Jesus's followers may give them business. Jesus has brothers; they looked upset, if not worried."

Mother asked, "Will you be alright?"

"I have shalom. We went our way toward Bethsaida. Knowing where we were going, and knowing the area well, John left for Bethsaida to see his father. Not to stay, just to let him know what was happening. It was very close by. Andrew had gone to visit his brother Simon, too, on that Sabbath; his house is near the synagogue in Capernaum. The next morning, we followed the lakeshore of Gennesaret toward Capernaum. People who saw what had happened pressed in on us. They wanted miracles, but also to hear Jesus's words as we passed along the shore. We came upon ships at the water's edge, with fishermen washing nets on shore. Jesus entered Simon's ship and asked to put out a short distance into the water, because the people pressed so hard upon him. He sat in the ship and taught the people as we watched. Once Jesus was offshore, they stopped mobbing us and begging for miracles. Everyone could hear plainly."

Father explained, "Sound travels well on water."

"Yes. After Jesus had spoken for quite a while, the crowd went off. Jesus told Simon and Andrew to move out deeper and drop the nets. Simon told Jesus, 'We worked the nets all night, taking nothing. Now it's midday, too late for fishing. But I will put out and drop the net.' When they dropped the net, the fish swarmed into it. It was so full it began to tear. The fishermen called for their partners in Zebedee's boat to come out and take hold of the other side of the net to prevent it from tearing worse. The fish filled both boats so full that the men were afraid of sinking. Huge biny! We were all shocked, but even more so the fishermen."

Jahzeel threw out a comment: "Fishermen and their stories . . ."

"No, if you fished you would know this was a miracle. Simon fell to his knees, right on the ship. He told Jesus to depart, for he was a sinful man. Jesus called to both Simon and Andrew: 'Come after me, and I will make you into fishers of men.' They dropped their nets and followed!"

Father, showing concern, asked, "What? Their livelihood? Simon has a family."

Mother stated her opinion: "Simon is no sinner. A bit loud, but he is honest."

I replied, "We are all sinners, Mother."

Jahzeel seemed defensive. "How is that?"

I answered carefully, "How many people does a man have to kill to become a murderer?"

"One!"

"How many lies does one have to tell to be a liar?"

Jahzeel was catching on. "One, . . . but you would not call him that yet."

"One sin and you are a sinner, just like all of us. I, too, was shocked that Simon left all. Andrew I understood, but Simon had to provide for his family. They simply followed. Without delay, Jesus called James and John, as well. They left the nets and followed, too. Zebedee saluted them; he has servants to do the work. I asked Andrew what would become of Simon's family. He said that they are partners; Zebedee has men enough to fish from Simon's boat, too, and he will make sure none will be in want."

Mother asked, "But what about Simon being apart from his wife and children?"

I agreed, "It will be hard. But it appears to be the only path Simon can see at this time."

Father put in, "Zebedee is a good man. He will not allow Simon's family to starve. Still, to give up so much . . ."

Jahzeel pointed out, "We gave up Thomas."

Mother disagreed: "We still have him!"

Father clarified, "We gave up his hands. We have his heart."

Smiling at Jahzeel, I replied, "Yes, you still have my heart. All of you. We came back to Capernaum this Sabbath to visit the synagogue. I was glad to be near home. Here I am. If Andrew and Peter and the sons of Zebedee can go home on a Sabbath, as they did last week, so can I."

Mother asked, "What now?"

"I will return before the end of Sabbath."

Jahzeel interjected, "Before you can be given work."

Father spoke sharply: "Jahzeel!"

My twin replied, "I know. I'm sorry, Thomas. I do wish the best for you."

"I know you do. And I want the best for you, too. Speaking of best, tell me, Jahzeel, what about Anna?"

Jahzeel replied shyly, "It's been only a few months . . ."

To which I replied, holding out a dish to him with a smile, "I know, brother. Here, the nuts and dates are good, the raisins moist. The wine fresh. The bread wonderful!"

VIII

Martus (Testimony)

A number of weeks later, on another Sabbath when we were
close to home, I returned for an afternoon. The atmosphere
at home was refreshing; all were resting on mats.

I greeted warmly, "Shalom, Father! Mother! Jahzeel!"

Father, rising quickly, "Thomas! Shalom!"

Mother, smiling, "Shalom. You look well, though perhaps
lean; let me get some food . . ."

Jahzeel's tongue-in-cheek greeting: "Shalom, brother. It's nice
to see you, even if it's not on a day you can help . . ."

Father interrupted with "Jahzeel!"

I brushed this off with "It's fine, Father. I do miss the vineyard
some days. So much walking. So many people. So much to learn."

Father spoke up. "Jahzeel has news . . ."

Looking toward Jahzeel, I asked, "Anna?"

Jahzeel, looking sheepish, answered, "Yes. Father has met
with her father. We are espoused."

"Wonderful news! I am truly happy for both of you!"

Mother concurred, glowing, "Yes, we all are."

Father went on, "We will be adding to the house."

"Do you have a time in mind? A year? When the grapes are
in . . . ?"

Father explained, "Anna's parents want this to happen slowly.
They will prepare, too. After a year, when the addition to our house

is completed, and her father is satisfied. Perhaps sometime after the next season when the grapes are in. When the time draws near, I will get word to you."

"Betrothal takes time."

Jahzeel admitted, "I knew it would, but it gives me something to work for. You aren't here to help . . ." He stopped. I realized that he was disappointed, not angry. He was not trying to cause pain this time.

I responded, "I'm truly sorry that I am not with you, my brother. It cannot be helped."

Father interjected, "Enough of our news . . . So, what truth have you learned?"

"Much. I've learned that the Pharisees are not to be trusted."

Jahzeel laughed. "That sounds more like my brother . . . I could have told you that."

Father cautioned, "Be careful what you say. But you are right, trust must be earned, and we regularly see some leaders who want to spend trust, even when it has not been earned. Honesty must precede trust."

I answered, "I'm not really afraid, at least not of what they will do to me. I'm afraid of losing favor."

Father asked, "Favor? With whom?"

"With God. I'm really feeling I have his favor now."

Jahzeel asked, trying to sound genuine, "Are you sure you are doing God's will?"

Father stopped Jahzeel. I don't think he knew whether or not Jahzeel was going to attack but preferred to cut him off before his elder son could elaborate on this thought. "Jahzeel, what a thing to say! Thomas, you always have our favor, and I think we have God's favor."

I explained, "Father, growing up I heard from you a lot of times that God hadn't given our family the best growing conditions. . ."

Father explained, "That was just an old man spouting. You know we are grateful to God."

Didymus

"Yes, I know you are. It's just a fear I can't seem to shake off. Jahzeel, we are certainly doing God's will. The lame walk, and people are healed. People repent. We take from no one."

Father asked, "Do you need money?"

"No, God has provided."

Jahzeel, again sounding more genuine, stated, "I wasn't really questioning you, Thomas; I know you are honorable. I know you are honest. The Pharisees know God's Law in all its detail so much better than we do; if they think you are wrong, then perhaps the facts are on their side."

Father questioned, "Facts, or truth? The truth is that the Pharisees like to be able to raise themselves up by putting others down."

Jahzeel conceded, "I know, Father. I'm sorry I even asked the question."

I smiled. "I wish you could see a miracle of God . . ."

Mother, returning with a bowl of raisins and some bread, announced, "Here, this bread was fresh from last night."

Father acknowledged her offering. "Thank you. See, Thomas, we have favor!"

I smiled, "Yes, I know I have your favor now. Don't be upset, but I used to think Jahzeel was the one with favor. Now he has the favor of Anna, too!"

Father countered, "That's not true. Well, it's true of Anna. Growing up, you might have thought it, but it wasn't true. Don't forget that Jahzeel had the responsibility."

"How many times did Jahzeel say he was going into the field to work but did not? He was not challenged. Yet, when I said I would not go out to work, and yet repented and did go out, you remembered what I had said, not what I had done."

Father explained defensively, "I could not have let your refusal go unchallenged, nor could I have disowned Jahzeel."

Mother, sounding thoughtful, put in, "Yes, but perhaps we showed too much favor . . ."

Father asked her honestly, "Do you think so?"

Jahzeel, interrupting, "No, I received nothing special that wasn't required by the Law."

"Please. Shalom. I'm fine. I love you all. I have no regrets. These are the things that made me who I am. I was young, and repenting of my attitude was exactly what I needed. Had I not, I would have grown up to think I was the center of everything. I know now that I am not the center—God is. He used those things, even mistakes you may have made, to mold me. The last thing I want is to hurt any of you. Let's change the subject; let me tell you what has been happening."

Father, obviously hurt, invited, "Tell on."

I had not intended to cause Father pain. I set aside the bowl, thinking it best to proceed with my report: "So much to tell . . . I've seen so many miracles . . . Jesus healed a Capernaum official's son while he was still in Galilee. The official asked, and Jesus just told him that his son was healed."

Father asked, surprised, "No prayer?"

"None we heard."

Jahzeel stated, "Then Jesus didn't really do it."

"No, Jesus did it. It happened just when he said it had. I suppose God always does the miracle in the end, but Jesus caused it to be done."

Father asked, "The official believes?"

"Everyone who sees what happens believes, at least on some level, even among the Pharisees. Some *choose* unbelief, but I think they have no real doubts. They are afraid of losing their influence."

Jahzeel asked, "Yes, but if they believe he is a prophet . . ."

Father spoke with deeper understanding. "Then they will be sure to keep him away. They worked hard to gain influence; they were not born into influence like the Levites. They would do anything to keep it."

I agreed, "Yes. Jesus himself told us he came to preach. Yet in Capernaum Jesus healed a man with an unclean spirit right in the synagogue."

Didymus

Jahzeel pointed out, "That should convince them."

"It was on a Sabbath."

My brother continued, "Still, if it was a healing . . ."

Father stated, "No, they would have said it was work. A doctor is not permitted to set a bone on the Sabbath."

"Exactly. It angered them. They had actually planted the man there, expecting Jesus to heal him. But what angered them more were the words the spirit shrieked out: 'Let us alone—what have we to do with you, Jesus of Nazareth? Have you come to destroy us? I know you are the Holy One of God.' Jesus at once commanded, 'Hold your peace and come out of him.' The spirit tore the man, but with another shriek it came out of him. Everyone was amazed. The others talked about Jesus's authority, and whether this were some new doctrine, as the spirit had obeyed him. When all those who had seen what happened left the synagogue, they told others, and his fame spread all around. That simply angered the Pharisees more. They are envious of his power and envious of people following him and not them. Even the spirits know Jesus."

Mother asked in dismay, "Yet could they not praise God that the man was healed?"

"Some may have. You have compassion, Mother, but most of these Pharisees don't. They don't have room for compassion because of their hate, or their fear of losing place. We returned to Simon bar Jonah's house because it is large. You know Simon has a big heart. Andrew lives there, too, and Simon's wife's mother stays with them. We told Jesus she was sick with a fever; he touched her hand and spoke, and the fever left her; she got up immediately and started to feed us all. At sunset people began to bring the sick and possessed to him, and he healed the diseased and demanded the demons to come out of those possessed. Some of the demons cried out 'Christ' or 'Son of God,' but Jesus would not let them testify as to who he was. It seemed as though the whole of Bethsaida had gathered there."

Mother interjected, "I knew about Simon's mother-in-law. She praised God."

"She did. When morning came, before full light, Jesus went to a quiet place and prayed. Peter (now all except Andrew call him Peter because there is another Simon among us) told Jesus that everyone in Bethsaida was seeking him."

Father mused, "Still, . . . calling a man 'a little stone.' What does that mean?"

"I'm not sure. It does not sound flattering. Jesus said to us, 'Let us go to other towns to preach; that is why I have come.' We went on through Galilee, Jesus teaching in synagogues; preaching of the coming of the kingdom; and healing the sick, possessed, lunatic, and palsied. Why, all *Syria* knew of his fame. His following grew, as people from Galilee, Decapolis, Jerusalem, Judea, and even beyond the Jordan followed. Some came to learn, others to watch."

Jahzeel noted, "Decapolis—that's Gentile. Do any of the Decapolis population give him money?"

"Decapolis is mostly Gentile. Jesus never asks for money, and yet we never lack. Jesus gets up before full light to pray. His quiet place has often been high on a hilltop, where there is less distraction. When he comes down, multitudes are often waiting, ready to follow him."

Father commented, "You know how to get up early, and the fishermen do, but city people typically do not."

"True, but Jesus is up before anyone else. The crowds come after dawn. Once, before the crowd arrived in a city, a leper came; standing apart, he kneeled and entreated, 'Lord, if you desire, you can cleanse me.' Jesus, with pity, put out his hand and *touched* the man! We were shocked! A rabbi, or even a prophet who touched a leper would become unclean until he washed. They usually yell at a leper unless he stays at least a stone's throw away. Instead, Jesus's touch cleansed and healed the leper. Jesus told him, 'Tell no man, but show yourself to the priest, and offer the gift Moses commanded as a testimony to the priests.' Instead, the man told everyone what had happened, and people came in droves. Jesus healed them all. So many came that afterward Jesus could not even enter the city."

Didymus

Jahzeel asked, "Why did Jesus have to *touch* him? You said he had healed others at a distance?"

"He showed that he had no fear of touching him. It was an act of compassion."

Mother commented, "Imagine how long since the man had been touched."

"Yes, Mother, that must be it. Some follow only to see what Jesus does. Many are Pharisees. One Sabbath, as we passed through the grain, we were hungry, picked grain, and rubbed it between our hands to remove it from the husk. Blowing off the chaff, we ate the grain."

Father offered, "You have a right to glean if you are hungry."

Mother, showing concern, asked, "I thought you had enough to eat."

"We have plenty. We were just hungry at the moment."

Jahzeel observed, "Mother, he has not lost weight."

I replied with a grin, "No, I haven't. When the Pharisees saw us gleaning, they reprimanded Jesus: 'Don't you see that your disciples are breaking Sabbath by harvesting?' Jesus asked them, 'Haven't you read what David did when he and his men were hungry? They went into the house of God, and Abiathar the priest gave them shewbread to eat, which is not lawful. Don't you know that the priests in the temple profane every Sabbath and are blameless?'"

Father, chuckling, remarked, "He knows the Law and the history better than they do."

"Yes, but then he shocked them. He said, 'In this place is one greater than the temple. You should know that God says, "I will have mercy, and not sacrifice," and then you would not condemn those who are without guilt. The Son of Man is Lord even of the Sabbath.'"

Jahzeel spoke clearly, but without malice: "That's blasphemy. No one is greater than the temple."

I replied, "God is. The temple would be nothing without him. Jesus finished by saying, 'The Sabbath was made for man, and not man for the Sabbath.'"

Father pointed out, in case I had missed the ramification, "Thomas, Jesus is right that the Sabbath was made for our rest, but in saying he is greater than the temple, Jesus really is claiming to be the Son of God."

"I believe he is. This time some had called him 'Son of David, the king.'"

Jahzeel commented, "That would have had their blood boiling."

Father predicted, "They will try to destroy him."

Jahzeel made a surprisingly positive comment: "I'm impressed."

Mother asked, "Are you safe?

"I'm fine. There seems to be no safer place to be than with Jesus. It all continues, day by day: Jesus preaching repentance, being pressed by people wanting a miracle, and the Pharisees watching to see if he might make a mistake. Some people healed on the Sabbath had been planted by the Pharisees just to catch Jesus breaking Sabbath so they could accuse him. I told the other disciples what I thought. They still say I am too cynical, and they are partly right: these people needed healing. They think it just happened to be at the feet of the Pharisees, that Jesus simply had compassion for those in need. But I'm sure Jesus knew exactly what was going on."

Father confirmed, "As wise as he is, he knew."

Jahzeel concurred, too. "I agree. I may not believe, but you can tell these people are dishonest."

Mother continued to voice her concern: "Just stay safe."

"I feel safe. On our last visit to Capernaum, the people heard ahead of time that we were coming. They gathered so thickly there was no room even to stand as he preached in a house. Four men came with a paralytic, hoping for his healing. When they found that they could not come close, they climbed on the roof, pulled it open, and let the man down through the thatched roof on his mat. Jesus, seeing what was happening, commended their faith. The people all expected to see him heal the man, but he shocked them all by saying, 'Son, your sins are forgiven.' Some teachers and scribes who were there were, of course, thinking that no man could forgive sin and that the statement was blasphemy. They hadn't yet spoken when Jesus intercepted them with 'Why are you thinking this? Which is easier to say, "Your sins are forgiven," or "Take up your bed and walk"? I want you to know that the Son of Man has authority on earth to forgive sins.' He said to the man, 'Take up your mat and go home.' Everyone saw him do so—and were amazed. Many said they had never seen anything like this."

Father acknowledged, "That is a dilemma; if I can do neither of those two things, I cannot tell which is harder. This is indeed a wise man."

Jahzeel commented candidly, "Yes, but he had already healed many times over; that must have been simpler for him. Besides, prophets have healed."

I replied with a smile, "Yes, but God really did those healings, not the prophets. I understand miracles and faith better now. First, God *saw* the faith of the prophets, and responded, 'God healed only after he saw their faith.' We humans can accomplish neither healing nor forgiveness. So, how can we know which is harder? Is *anything* hard for God?"

Jahzeel replied, "I just assumed that the prophets did the healing. Of course, God did the work."

Mother reflected, "This is too deep for me . . ."

And Father agreed, "It is too deep for anyone."

I went on, "I agree. Jesus keeps proving who he is: the Son of God."

Father, not countering my words, merely asked, "Is there more?"

"Not yet." Then, feeling pleased with myself, and as though nothing unusual had just been discussed, I asked casually, "How are things in the vineyard?" (and turning toward Jahzeel) "How is Anna?"

Jahzeel, blushing, replied, "All is well. Please share that bowl . . ."

After the enjoyable Sabbath visit, during which even Jahzeel had seemed willing to listen, I returned to Jesus and the disciples. I tried to ignore my awareness that I had hurt Father briefly, rationalizing that, since I was doing something important, it didn't matter. My fatalistic bent and doubts had seemed to disappear. We were learning so much. For some reason most of us (except Simon Peter or occasionally John) were afraid to ask Jesus when we had questions; we would instead ask each other. Jesus answered every question we did ask, but he did so in a teaching manner—sometimes making us uncomfortable. We were grown men asking things he had a way of making seem so simple—his explanations at times seeming childlike. We seemed to be answering our own questions as we tried to explain ourselves. Often, he responded with questions of his own when we didn't really understand what we were asking.

IX

Testimony with Little Progress

Eventually, it was time again for Passover. It didn't seem possible that I had been with Jesus for nearly a year, as had most of us. I finally had a chance to see my family again, as they were in Jerusalem for Passover. We had stayed in the usual inn for as long as I could remember, so I found them easily, even with the crowds. I had so much to tell, and only Sabbath afternoon to tell it on. Staying in Jerusalem even at a family inn left almost no privacy. I wasn't about to talk freely about so many things to strangers. I realized that it was hard to be frank in my witness with others around, and harder for my family as well. Happily, there was no one about early, when I entered the inn. There are many inns because of the feasts. This one was a "family" inn because it was owned by a family from our tribe of Naphtali. It is actually more of a large, covered space with curtains for a little privacy. The family owning it lived in one corner of the structure year around, near a common indoor kitchen and eating area with a small courtyard for cooking, and yet another corner and courtyard serving as a stable.

I greeted my family, "Shalom, Father! Mother! Jahzeel!"

Father, rising, "Thomas! Shalom!"

Mother, grinning, "Shalom. You need some food . . ."

Jahzeel spoke, with a twinkle in his eye, "Shalom, Thomas. Coming home to stay?"

Father cautioned sternly, "Jahzeel!"

"It's fine, Father. He isn't being mean; he's just being my brother."

Father asked, "What has happened?"

"So much. I don't know where to start . . ."

Father, rhetorically, replied, "Where you left off the last time we met. Where else would you start?"

I nodded and began, "We were beside the Sea of Galilee, with a large crowd. Jesus taught as he walked. We came upon Levi, the son of Alpheus, a tax collector. Jesus shocked us all by saying simply, 'Follow me.' Levi left all and followed with us."

Jahzeel scoffed, "A tax collector! Ridiculous!"

"It did seem strange at the time. But Jesus preaches repentance, and Levi left all and turned to follow. That's the definition of repentance. Matthew (the other name he is known by) really is not what I would have expected. I don't think any of us realized that Levi's association with Jesus would open doors for Jesus to speak to other wealthy people. I didn't even realize the wealthy could be lonely. Some have shared their misgivings about collecting taxes for the Romans. Matthew is in truth a Levite, but because he works with Romans he is outcast."

Father also seemed surprised. "We sell to Romans, but a tax collector . . ."

"Jesus just walked right up to the tax booth to call him!"

Jahzeel mused, "I don't see why he followed—he has money."

"Money does not satisfy. Matthew uses it for the ministry now. He held a huge banquet and invited many other rich people, including tax collectors, to hear Jesus. They listened well. They were not what I might have expected."

Jahzeel spoke up. "I *knew* money was involved somewhere . . ."

"Jesus takes none. Besides, Matthew takes note of what Jesus says; he writes well and fast."

Father agreed, "As a tax collector, he would, and accurately."

72

Didymus

"He believes a written record is important. It will help us remember all of Jesus's teaching. Some Pharisees and teachers of the Law were there at the banquet, not to learn or eat but again to try to trap Jesus. They know better than to question Jesus directly, but they ask hard questions of us disciples in the hope of sewing discord. They asked us, 'Why do you eat and drink with tax collectors and sinners?' I was afraid for Nathaniel, for he worried about what the Jews thought. But Jesus knew what they were doing, and although the questions were asked of us, he answered them plainly, 'It is not the healthy who need a doctor, but the sick. Don't you know what Hosea meant when he wrote, "I will have mercy, not sacrifice"? I have not come to call the righteous, but sinners.'"

Father commented, "He knows the prophets well."

"He speaks as though he knew not just their writings but *them* personally. The Pharisees accused Jesus directly, saying, 'John's disciples often fast and pray, as do the disciples of the Pharisees, but yours go on eating and drinking.' Jesus answered them, defending us, 'Can you make the friends of the bridegroom fast while he is with them? The time will come when I am taken, and in those days they will fast.'"

Father asked, alarmed, "What is this 'taken?' Who will take him? Will you fast?"

I answered as best I could. "I don't know. He gave a parable: 'No one would tear a piece out of a new garment to patch an old one; it would damage the new, and then it would not match the old. No one pours new wine into old wine skins; the new would burst the old skins, and the wine and the skins would both be ruined. New wine must be put in new skins. No one after drinking old wine wants the new, for, they say, the old is better.' The Pharisees and the teachers realized that he was talking about them, but they didn't look as though they really understood him, and they were too embarrassed to ask exactly what that meant."

Father reflected, "I think I understand. The Pharisees are the old skins; they cannot contain what is happening. They are too stiff, too rigid. This new doctrine is for the young. For those who are not so set in their ways. Yet he does not insult the old ways. What a marvelous way to answer."

Jahzeel protested, "Our ways are good."

I corrected Jahzeel's understanding. "Jesus said as much, but, just as Father has said, the new way won't fit into the old skin. His response was marvelous. They had no answer."

Father again mused, "A wise man. A true prophet."

Jahzeel asked, "Why would he use a parable, a story? Can't he express himself well enough in Greek or Hebrew to just tell them outright? The teachers of the Law always use big words in Greek or Hebrew to show their wide knowledge. A great teacher would, too."

Father disagreed, "I think not. There are no words in Greek, Hebrew or even common Aramaic for some things; you boys know the smell of a ripe bunch of grapes; you know it is ripe and have learned that by experience. Even I can use a big word for learning by experience: *ginosko*. Instead, I prefer just saying 'learning by experience' because it fits, and everyone understands it. Even now, you can't *describe* that nuance of ripeness, but you learned it well even before you had a term to describe how you learned it."

I nodded. "The teachers think big words prove that they understand. But what does their use really prove? Who does it teach? I don't think any language can completely express certain thoughts and concepts. Jesus paints pictures with simple words that put you in a situation where you understand his meaning far better than you would through the use of lofty words. You discern his meaning— almost like experiencing it yourself. When Father told us how to prune a vine, he told us plainly to be careful, but when we were there and used the knife, we *learned* to be careful in cutting with it, remember?"

Jahzeel agreed, "You *would* bring that up. I remember getting cut. I see the point, much as I felt it then . . ."

I smiled at Jahzeel's joke. "It was a painful lesson for you, and a memorable one for me. That's the first time I learned by watching someone else make a mistake. After following Jesus and listening to how he used scripture, I realized I should also learn by under-standing the mistakes people made in the days of the prophets. I would rather learn without the pain of making the same mistakes myself."

I paused before continuing, "Here we are for Passover. So much has happened in the last few days. There is a pool near the Sheep Gate called Bethesda."

Father spoke, "I know the place. So much sorrow there. Those who have no hope."

"Yes. It has five covered porches surrounding it for shade. Many infirm, blind, maimed, and paralyzed gather there, hoping for a miracle. People believe that, when the still water of the pool is stirred, it is a sign that an angel is about to appear and that a miracle might follow for the first one to the water."

Jahzeel opined, "It sounds like superstition. The only healings I have heard of were done by Jesus. No angel of the water."

"It may indeed be superstition, but it has been accepted as fact by those without hope. Jesus asked an invalid there, 'Do you want to get well?' The man said he had been crippled for 38 years and that someone else always beat him to the water. Jesus simply said, 'Get up. Pick up your mat and walk.' The man did so—he was healed. Jesus didn't even talk to the others around the pool."

Father asked, "Why did he not heal the others there?"

I answered simply, "None asked to be healed."

Jahzeel stated his opinion. "Neither did this one. Jesus should have healed them all."

"I have learned that miracles are always done for a reason. Miracles are direct acts of God. When he does them to show some-one something in particular, they become a sign. When they are truly awesome, they are a wonder. This one had a reason, so it was at least a sign. It had taken place on a Sabbath. The man was caught carrying his mat by Jewish leaders. To them it became a sign. They stopped him, saying, 'It is Sabbath; the Law forbids you to carry your mat.' He simply replied, 'The man who made me well said to me, "Pick up your mat and walk."' They asked him, 'Who is this man who told you to carry your mat?' The man healed did not even know who Jesus was—Jesus was now in the crowd. Later, Jesus found the healed man at the temple and told him, 'You are well; stop sinning, or something worse may happen.' The man went and told the leaders that it was Jesus who had healed him."

Father exclaimed, "They will not accept Jesus going around the Law."

I agreed but pointed out, "*All* miracles go around the Law—either the Mosaic or the natural law! To want a miracle is to want to get around some law!"

Jahzeel agreed. "For once, I see what you are saying. Even I pray for things beyond the Law. Miracles are outside the usual course of things."

Glad that Jahzeel was following and not just looking for my errors, I concurred, "Yes. But Jesus did this to cause a confrontation he knew would happen, to get the chance to preach directly to them. The leaders tried their hardest, probably because in their eyes he was undermining their authority, right in Jerusalem, and right at Passover. Jesus answered them clearly: 'My Father is always at his work to this very day, and I too am working.' I don't think it occurred to them that God the Father is working; it had not occurred to me. I had assumed that God's work was completed on the sixth day."

Father put in, "I never thought about that, either. Yet when we pray, we ask God to work. We pray even more on the Sabbath."

I nodded and went on, "Now they wanted to kill him, for he was calling God his own father, making himself equal with God. But Jesus went on, as though to tell them enough that they could no longer be ignorant about who he is or what he was doing. That they did not interrupt him until he was finished was a miracle in itself!"

Jahzeel agreed, "Not interrupting doesn't sound like the leaders of the Jews. They are trying to catch him."

I went on, "Jesus explained his ministry. He said, 'Truly I tell you that the Son can do nothing by himself; he does what the Father does, because what the Father does the Son will do. The Father loves the Son and shows him all he has to do. He will show him even greater works than these, so that you will be astounded. Even as the Father raised the dead and gives them life, so the Son will give life as it pleases him. In addition, the Father judges no one but entrusts all judgment to the Son, that all may honor the Son, just as they honor the Father. Whoever does not honor the Son does not honor the Father who has sent him.'"

Jahzeel asked, "Why does he have to call himself 'the Son of God'? He has to stop that; it's blasphemy."

I disagreed, "It's not blasphemy if it is true. Jesus said, 'I tell you, whoever hears my words and believes him who sent me has eternal life and will not be judged but has crossed from death into life. The time is coming and has already come when the dead will hear the voice of the Son of God, and those who hear will live. As the Father has life in himself, he has also granted the Son to have life in himself. The Father has given him authority to judge because he is the Son of Man. A time will come when all who are in their graves will hear his voice and come out, the good to be raised to life, and the evil to be condemned.'"

Father looked very interested. "I believe in a resurrection, but I have never heard such detail."

"Nor had I, Father. Jesus said, 'By myself I can do nothing; I judge only as I hear, and my judgment is just; I seek only to please him who sent me. If I testified of myself, my testimony would not be true, but you know there was another who testified in my favor, and I know his testimony is true. You sent for John, and he testified to the truth. I do not need earthly testimony, but I say this so that you might be saved. For a time, you enjoyed the light of John's testimony.'"

Jahzeel concurred, "The Jews did follow John for a time."

"Jesus went on, 'I have a testimony greater than that of John; the works that the Father gave me to finish, these very works you see me do, testify that the Father has sent me. These works are the Father's testimony concerning me. You have never heard the Father's voice, or seen his form, nor does his word truly dwell in you. If it had, you would believe me. You search the Scripture because you think that it will give you eternal life, yet these are the very Scriptures that testify of me. You refuse to come to me to have life.'"

Mother entered with a plate of food. She asked rhetorically, "Who would not want life?"

"Thank you, Mother. Everyone wants life. The problem is that we want the life of our own choosing. Jesus offers so much more, zoe, the eternal life of God. Jesus told us, 'I will not accept glory from men, but I know you. I know that you do not have *agape* love in your hearts. I have come in my Father's name; you will not accept me, but someone who comes in his own name you will accept. You cannot believe because you accept glory from men and will not even seek the glory that comes only from God. Yet do not think that I will accuse you before the Father. Your accuser is Moses, on whom is your hope. If you had believed Moses, you would believe me, for he wrote of me. But since you do not believe what he wrote, how are you going to believe what I say?'"

Jahzeel mused again, "The leaders always want the praise of men."

Mother asked, "Jesus says they do not have agape in their hearts? This is an odd term to choose."

"It's unusual. Agape is a love that is determined, like khesed in Hebrew; it's a choice, not a reaction. He must mean that they have chosen *not* to love. Agape will continue, regardless of circumstances. Their unbelief is a decision, not a response."

Mother reflected, "I determined in my heart to love my child, no matter whether it was a girl or a boy. Then we had two boys! I simply continued to love you both. I suppose that was agape. I could never have loved either of you more than I already did before I met you! What a blessing!"

I smiled, impressed with her practical understanding, and went on, "All of the disciples were amazed. The leaders had kept silent. Jesus had just performed a miracle to keep them quiet—until he had told them all that he thought of them."

Didymus

Father asked, "Is there anything more?"

"I wish I had notes like Matthew, but this was just yesterday. You are up to date."

Mother prompted, "I heard something about fasting when you were talking?"

"Jesus said that there will be a time when we fast. A time of sorrow. It's not yet."

Mother smiled and invited, "Then eat. With all this you need to keep up your strength."

Father continued to think aloud: "The leaders are not finished. Jesus has put them to shame. They will consult together. They will try to destroy Jesus, in order to keep their place."

Jahzeel agreed, "At least you see the leaders for who they are. I just hope this prophet doesn't disappoint you."

"He won't. If you could meet him . . ."

Jahzeel stopped me. "No! I have listened politely. This Jesus may be a good man, perhaps a prophet. Nothing more."

"Jahzeel, you remind me of myself with the miracle of the wine. At first, I refused to believe. You heard the claims he made. A good man could not make such claims unless they were true. A good man does not lie. If Jesus is good, he must either be God in the flesh, as he claims, or he has convinced himself that he is God, which would mean he is not good. Or he would be a deceiver, which would be very bad."

Father agreed, "Thomas's logic is correct. If you understood him, then what you say is true. Perhaps he is not so good, or perhaps he has fooled himself . . . or perhaps he really is the Son of God."

Mother looked at Father, her eyes wide. "Thomas does not lie. He understood Jesus."

Jahzeel admitted, hesitantly, "I . . . I am not ready."

Father unexpectedly agreed. "I, too, feel unready. I suppose I don't know what to expect. Of the Pharisees, I know what to expect. Jesus never does what I expect."

I spoke again: "We can't meet Jesus until he decides we are ready."

Mother murmured, "It is enough that he takes care of my son. Perhaps I will meet him when he chooses. I always like to know the friends of my sons."

I changed the subject. "That is fine. Speaking of friends, . . . you have news, too? What of Anna and the wedding?"

Jahzeel, blushing, "Not yet. We have begun to work on the room. Pass the bowl . . .

X

Emotional Testimony

Over the next months, Jesus preached to multitudes. We finally had a Sabbath near home. I had learned so much that I was bursting to tell my family. I returned as early as I could to tell them all that Jesus had taught and done.

I found them on the roof, in the breeze. "Shalom, Father! Mother! Jahzeel!"

Father, rising from a mat to greet me, replied, "Thomas! Shalom!"

Mother, clapping her hands and rising as well, "Shalom. You need some food. . ."

Jahzeel, with a grin, but not rising, also replied, "Shalom, Thomas. Here to help?"

Father looked at him. "Jahzeel!"

I, too, laughed. "My brother and I love one another enough to banter a bit."

Father seemed satisfied and asked, "What has happened?"

I began, "So much. Ever so much!"

Father asked, "Start where you left off, at Passover."

I spoke quickly: "The Pharisees keep trying to catch Jesus doing something unlawful. They planted someone to accuse him in front of the people. They told a man with a need at which synagogue Jesus would be expected on Sabbath. When Jesus was about to teach, there was there a man with a withered hand. Jesus asked the man to stand. The Pharisees asked Jesus, publicly, 'Is it lawful to heal on the Sabbath?' so that they might make him break their Law. Jesus asked the Pharisees plainly, 'Which of you who has one sheep, if it fell into a pit on the Sabbath would not lift it out? Of how much more value is a man than a sheep! Is it lawful to do good on the Sabbath, or evil? To save life or kill?' The Pharisees refused to answer."

Jahzeel saw through this and confirmed, "It was a setup."

"Yes, it was. This was the first time I saw Jesus look on them with anger, yet even then he was grieved that they were not open to the truth. Without even touching the man, he said, 'Stretch out your hand.' When the man did, it was fully restored. The Pharisees went out angry, knowing that Jesus had not touched the man or even prayed out loud over him. Every one of us stretches out his hand every Sabbath. How could they accuse him?"

Mother remarked, "That's terrible!"

"Yes, Mother, it is terrible. I'm sure they are planning how they might destroy Jesus. Jesus, knowing this, withdrew from the place, yet multitudes followed him. He continued to heal them all, telling them not to make him known. Their plot had been foiled, and the people were now more drawn to Jesus than ever. We also realized that the Pharisees and Herodians now intend to kill Jesus at any cost."

Mother asked anxiously, "Are you safe?"

"I feel total shalom when I am with Jesus. Don't worry. Jesus did heal, because of compassion for those being healed. I'm sure Jesus knew what was going on. That may be part of what made him angry. These Pharisees have no compassion. Later, they brought us a man possessed with a devil that was making him both blind and speechless. Jesus healed him so that he both saw and spoke. The people were as amazed as I was and asked if this was the Son of David, the promised king of Israel. I don't think you ever get used to miracles. The Pharisees don't get used to miracles, either."

Father asked rhetorically, "What could they say? Healing someone is a great work. It is the work of a prophet; they know this."

Jahzeel concurred, "They know. That's why they want to stop him."

"Yes Jahzeel, I'm sure that is it. Later, Jesus brought us to the Sea of Galilee, and a large crowd followed. People from Judea, Jerusalem, Idumea across Jordan, Tyre, and Sidon followed. Jesus asked that a small boat be prepared, as the crowds pushed him almost into the sea. He healed all who even touched him. The impure spirits cried out that he was the Son of God, but Jesus commanded them not to speak; he would not accept the testimony of demons."

Jahzeel reasoned, "I would have expected him to want *any* testimony."

Father answered, "Not of the unclean. Think of the logic; do I want a known liar to tell the judge that I am telling the truth? The testimony of the liar would make it sound as though I were being deceitful. Jesus is right."

"Father, your logic is excellent. There is so much more to tell. On another day Jesus went out to a mountainside to pray and spent the entire night praying to God. The next morning he called his many disciples to him and set apart twelve whom he designated apostles, or called out ones. There was Simon, whom he called Peter; his brother Andrew; the brothers James and John ben-Zebedee; Philip; Bartholomew, whom I call Nathanael; Matthew, also known as Levi; James ben-Alphaeus; Simon the Zealot; Judas ben-James; Judas Iscariot; and me. We all felt pride in having been chosen to be among the close followers."

Mother beamed. "You are his chosen! I'm so proud!"

Father agreed, smiling, "Yes, I too am proud. One of twelve. Apostles, called out ones. I know he has many more followers. This is a great privilege."

Jahzeel, looking pleased, couldn't resist commenting, "A Zealot and an ex-tax-collector in the same group; this Jesus must be persuasive. Imagine, my little brother called out to be assistant to a prophet. I taught you well. Just joking, Father. I'm proud of him, too!"

I replied with a smile, "I expected no less from you, Jahzeel. Now the teaching truly began. Jesus brought the twelve of us and stood on a level place near Capernaum. A large crowd of disciples was there, as well as people from all over Judea, Jerusalem, and along the coast from Tyre to Sidon, most of whom had come to hear him or to be healed. Everyone knew the power coming from him and that he was healing everyone. When Jesus saw the crowds, he went up on a mountainside and sat down. He preached a great sermon."

Father mused, "The side of a mountain above a flat place for the crowd. His voice would have carried well."

Jahzeel agreed, partially, "Yes, but sermons take place in synagogues. Orations may be for theaters or palaces. But a sermon on a mountain?"

I replied, "Yes, that's what it was: a sermon on a mountain. We twelve came closest to him, but he began to teach all of the disciples gathered there. I believe it was to encourage us, but also for the benefit of the disciples who had not been chosen to be among the twelve. Jesus offered powerful promises to us all."

Jahzeel, seeking clarification: "You say this is him *beginning* to teach? What was everything until this point?"

I answered as best I could, "It was to prepare us. I've never before heard anything like this:

'Blessed are the poor in spirit,
　　for theirs is the kingdom of heaven.
Blessed are those who mourn,
　　for they will be comforted,
Blessed are the meek,
　　for they will inherit the earth,
Blessed are those who hunger and thirst for righteousness,
　　for they will be filled.
Blessed are the merciful,
　　for they will be shown mercy.
Blessed are the pure in heart,

for they will see God.
Blessed are the peacemakers,
for they will be called children of God.
Blessed are those who are persecuted because of righteousness,
for theirs is the kingdom of heaven.

Blessed are you when people insult you, persecute you, and falsely say all kinds of evil against you because of me. Rejoice and be glad, because great is your reward in heaven, for in the same way they persecuted the prophets who were before you.'"

Mother responded first, "What beautiful promises. Who would not want comfort, or mercy?"

Father agreed, "Who would not want the kingdom of heaven. And to see God!"

Even Jahzeel enthused, "And such rewards. Imagining such rewards would give you a better attitude to face the troubles of the day."

Father commented, "It sounds as though the second half, the final four, had to do with things we do, while the first four are more about what we feel or fear."

I agreed. "Father, you are so insightful. The last four are the righteous things we need to do, but I don't think we can do them without getting help from our Yehovah Tsidkenu: the Lord our righteousness. They occur only after the recognition of our needs within the first four. It will have to be God working throughout all eight. The first are so we can receive the holiness of God by recognizing our need, which results in the righteous behavior of the final four. You can't get one without the other. I knew you would all be impressed. But Jesus was just getting started. Jesus started to preach more to those who were not followers. Some Pharisees, Sadducees, and Herodians there as spies were feeling plenty of guilt by the time he was finished:

'But woe to you who are rich,
for you have already received your entire reward.

Woe to you who are well fed now,
   for you will go hungry.
Woe to you who laugh now,
   for you will mourn and weep.
Woe to you when everyone speaks well of you,
   for that is how their ancestors treated the false prophets.'"

Jahzeel commented, "I like this preaching. Whether he is a true prophet or not, I'm not sure, but I'm glad he puts the proud in their place."

I agreed, "He does. Then came a series of warnings to us all: 'You are the salt of the earth. But if the salt loses its flavor, how can it be made salty again? It is no longer good for anything, except to be thrown out and trampled.'"

Father concurred, "Yes, what good would it be if you couldn't do what you were made to do? You would be useless."

"Yes. Jesus went on, 'You are the light of the world. A town built on a hill cannot be hidden. Nor do people light a lamp and put it under a basket. Instead, they put it on a stand so that it gives light to all in the house. In the same way, let your light shine before others, that they may see your good deeds and glorify your Father in heaven.'"

Father reflected, "You are to be seen . . . Light is useful; it keeps us from stumbling.

And Mother, still beaming, breathed, "You are a shining light, Thomas . . . I want you to shine before others."

"I want to. Jesus said, 'Don't think I have come to abolish the Law or the Prophets; I have not come to abolish but to fulfill them. I tell you truly, until heaven and earth disappear, not the smallest letter or stroke of a pen will by any means disappear, until everything is accomplished. Because of this, anyone setting aside even the least of these commands and teaching others the same will be called least in the kingdom of heaven. Unless your righteousness exceeds that of the Pharisees and the teachers of the Law, you will not enter the kingdom of heaven.'"

Didymus

Father interjected, "He knows how bogus these Pharisees are . . ."

I nodded, continuing, "He went on. Now he began to make me feel guilty, too."

Mother seemed shocked. "You, Thomas? What have you ever done wrong?"

I admitted, "I'm not without flaw, Mother. Jesus told us, 'You have heard it said long ago, "You shall not murder, and anyone who murders will be subject to judgment." But I tell you that anyone who is angry with a brother or sister will be subject to judgment. Anyone who says to a brother or sister, "Raca," or worthless, is answerable to the court, and anyone who says, "You fool!" is in danger of the fire of hell.'"

Jahzeel interrupted, "Wait, *Raca* is a mild term of contempt, and it's natural to be angry with a brother."

"Yes, it is. You know I'm guilty, too. But that isn't God's plan for us. Everyone there eventually felt guilty and realized why we need a covering for our negative attitudes."

Father added, "That's what the sacrifices are for: a kophar; a covering for our sins."

"Yes, they are. But listen again to Jesus's words: 'If you are offering your gift at the altar and there remember that your brother or sister has something against you, leave your gift there in front of the altar. First go and be reconciled; then come offer your gift.'"

Father put in, "Yes, to be reconciled should come first. If our attitude is wrong, how can God accept our gifts? And how can we cover sin that is ongoing?"

Jahzeel interrupted, "Wait—if my brother has something against me, how is that my fault?"

Assenting to his logic, I replied, "It may not be your fault, but fellowship has still been broken. The attitude is bad. Jesus said, 'Settle matters quickly with your adversary who is taking you to court. Do it while you are still on the way, or your adversary may hand you over to the judge, and he to the officer, and you may be thrown into prison. I tell you that you will not get out until you have paid the last penny.'"

Father mused, "He is wise, this Jesus."

"Yes. But our sinful attitudes run deeper than I had realized. Listen to Jesus's words: 'You have also heard that it was said, "You shall not commit adultery." But I tell you that anyone who looks at a woman lustfully has already committed adultery with her in his heart. If your right eye causes you to stumble, gouge it out and throw it away. It is better for you to lose one part of your body than for you to be thrown into hell. If your right hand causes you to stumble, cut it off and throw it away. It is better for you to lose one part of your body than for you to be thrown into hell.'"

Jahzeel replied, incredulous, "So great a punishment for lust? Lust is natural."

Father disagreed, "Natural . . . and wrong. Some of my friends lusted after my sister, your aunt. It disgusted me. You have no sister, but I taught you that all women are the daughter or sister or wife of someone. Lusting is wrong. Jesus is right: the thief does not become a thief when he steals the lamb; that just proves he is a thief. He became a thief when he thought about stealing the lamb."

I agreed, "You taught us well. But we all have to repent of some of our thoughts. Jesus went on, 'It has been said, "Anyone who divorces his wife must give her a certificate of divorce." I tell you that anyone who divorces his wife, except for sexual immorality, makes her the victim of adultery, and anyone who marries a divorced woman commits adultery.'"

Mother murmured, "So many Pharisees have divorced their wives. So sad for the children."

Father nodded, pointing out, "God plainly said through Malachi that he hates divorce."

I concurred, "It is sad. Jesus went on, 'Again, you have heard from long ago, "Do not break your oath, but fulfill to the Lord the vows you have made." I tell you, do not swear an oath at all, either by heaven, for it is God's throne, or by the earth, for it is his footstool, or by Jerusalem, for it is the city of the Great King. Do not swear by your own head, for you cannot make even one hair white or black. All you have need of saying is "Yes" or "No"; anything beyond this comes from the evil one.'"

Father nodded again. "Yes, whenever someone makes a 'deal' for me, they swear by an oath. As soon as they do, I doubt whether they are honest."

"Yes, Father; you warned Jahzeel and me of that. Jesus went on, 'You have heard "Eye for eye, and tooth for tooth." But I tell you, do not resist an evil person. If anyone slaps you on the right cheek, turn to them the other cheek also. And if anyone sues you to take your shirt, hand over your coat as well. If anyone forces you to go one mile, go with them two miles. Give to the one who asks you, and do not turn away from the one who wants to borrow from you. Do to others as you would have them do to you.'"

Jahzeel shook his head. "That's going too far. If someone slaps me, I leave; I'm trying to be a peaceful man, and I don't slap back. But to stay for more . . . !"

Mother nodded to Jahzeel but explained, "I know, son, but listen again to the end: 'Do to others as you would have them do to you.' If we all did that, who would be hurt?"

Jahzeel agreed, "Your point is good, Mother. It's what you taught us, and you say it so plainly."

Father put in, "I have heard some of the Greek philosophers say, 'Don't kill if you don't want to be killed.' I think Hillel said that, too. But this is much deeper: do good because you want good done to you. It's so plain. In Proverbs Solomon says, 'A word fitly spoken is like apples of gold in a setting of silver.' This rule to live by is of pure gold."

I nodded. "That's well put, Father—a rule of gold to live by. I'll have to remember it. Jesus said further, 'You have heard that it was said, "Love your neighbor, and hate your enemy." But I tell you, love your enemies and pray for those who persecute you, that you may be children of your Father in heaven. He causes his sun to rise on the evil and the good and sends rain on the righteous and the unrighteous. If you love those who love you, what reward will you get? Are not even tax collectors doing that? And if you greet only your own people, what are you doing more than others? Do not even pagans do that? If you lend to those from whom you expect repayment, what credit is that to you? Even sinners lend to sinners, expecting to be repaid in full. But love your enemies, do good to them, and lend to them without expecting to get anything back. Then your reward will be great, and you will be children of the Most High, because he is kind to the ungrateful and the wicked. Be merciful, just as your Father is merciful.'"

Mother stated simply, "People often forget that even sinners want to be loved, yet we treat them with bitterness."

I looked at her tenderly. "Mother, you have a big heart. Jesus went on, 'Be careful not to practice your righteousness in front of others to be seen by them. If you do, you will have no reward from your Father in heaven.'"

Jahzeel remarked, "That sounds so much like the Pharisees; everything they do is to be noticed."

"Being noticed is their only reward. Jesus continued, 'So when you give to the needy, do not announce it with trumpets, as the hypocrites do in the synagogues and on the streets, to be honored by others. Truly I tell you, they have received their reward in full. But when you give to the needy, do not let your left hand know what your right hand is doing, so that your giving may be in secret. Then your Father, who sees what is done in secret, will reward you.'"

Father agreed generally, commenting, "Quiet generosity is good. Yet I do want all of me to know that I'm doing it."

I nodded, asserting, "I believe, though, that you know what he means. Jesus also talked about prayer: 'When you pray, do not be like the hypocrites, for they love to pray standing in the synagogues and on the street corners to be seen by others. Truly I tell you, they have received their reward in full. But when you pray, go into your room, close the door, and pray to your Father, who is unseen. Then your Father, who sees what is done in secret, will reward you. And when you pray, do not keep on babbling like the pagans, for they think they will be heard because of their many words. Do not be like them, for your Father knows what you need before you ask him.'"

Mother mused, "I don't know if you boys will ever know how often I have prayed for you."

Father confirmed, "*I* know. True prayer is because you care."

"I'm glad you did, Mother. Jesus gave us an example of how we should pray:

'Our Father in heaven,
hallowed be your name,
your kingdom come,
your will be done,
    on earth, as it is in heaven.
Give us today our daily bread.
And forgive us our debts,
    as we also have forgiven our debtors.
And lead us not into temptation,
    but deliver us from the evil one.'"

Mother sighed, "That's beautiful. It seems as though he simply talks to God in a personal way."

"We do talk to God when we pray. God also enjoys our reciting or singing psalms of praise to him. These are acts of worship, and we can even do them together. When we read Torah, we learn of him, but when we pray and sing, we talk to him."

Father agreed, "Yes. But this is so much shorter than the Shiminoph! Is this one to be said only silently, like the Shiminoph, and standing? He asks that the kingdom may come, but not that our enemies be annihilated. I know that line was not in the original 18. If the kingdom is here, what would be the need for destruction? He also asks that we not be tempted; what wisdom! It is so personal. But what is this 'Abba, Father, Daddy'? I've never heard anyone pray to 'Father.'"

Mother stood and began the Shiminoph, aloud, quietly reciting the praise section:

"'God of our forefather who shields Abraham
      The almighty and powerful One, who causes all events,
including the resurrection of the dead,
      God is holy.'"
Father stood and continued with the requests section:
      "'We ask for enlightenment and wisdom
      We desire to repent and be close to God
      We ask forgiveness
      We ask to be redeemed from pain and strife
      We ask to be healed
      We for produce good and plentiful
      We ask that all Jews should be returned to Israel
      We ask that Jewish judges shall return to rule
      We ask that the enemies of the Jews should be defeated
and annihilated
      We ask that the pious be rewarded
      We ask for God's presence to return to Jerusalem
      We ask that The Messiah may arrive
      We ask that Our prayers be heard and accepted.'"

Jahzeel stood and finished with the gratitude section:
      "'We give thanks that the Holy Temple and system has
been restored
      We give thanks to God for keeping us alive and providing
for us at all times
      We would have peace and goodness in our lives.'"

After an appropriate moment of silence, Jahzeel stated, "Most
of this Jesus gave in these few words. He asks for God's will, not
our own. That's great wisdom; many prayers given aloud sound
as though the petitioner knows better than God . . . but, '*Abba,
Father*'? I understand that he thinks—and perhaps you think—that
God is *his* father. But, '*Our Father*'? Is he saying that anyone can
address the Almighty in such a flippant way? It seems blasphe-
mous. Thomas, this is wrong; it is not what the rabbis teach."

Didymus

I answered each in turn. "Yes, Mother, it is beautiful. And yes, Father, it's shorter than Shiminoph, . . . and yet says much of the same. We say it aloud, often, but not always standing. He teaches us to still ask for the kingdom, which is most of the Shiminoph—just without the emphasis on our people. But because it is personal, he can ask that we be not tempted. Isaiah speaks of God as our father, but not so intimately. Jesus teaches us to pray intimately. When you think of it, why would we not pray that way? God knows our thoughts before they are on our lips; that's from Psalms. Why should we not intentionally talk to God all the time, as long as we are reverent about it? After all, isn't he already listening? Jahzeel, this prayer was not as the rabbis teach; it was better! Very reverent."

Father answered, "I have never thought about it that way. The prayer was still reverent. One could pray to God almost ceaselessly."

I agreed, "I like what you just said, Father. This prayer was a model; we don't always pray it exactly the same, but we include the honor first, before the requests, like the Shiminoph."

Jahzeel interjected, "If it could be shortened, then the rabbis would already teach it that way."

Father remarked, "The rabbis pray loudly on the street corners; yet you know that the Shiminoph, for one, is a prayer meant to be said only silently! I think the rabbis want to be heard by everyone on the street. I do not believe that is what God desires."

"That's it exactly, Father. The loudness does nothing; it is for the benefit of men, not God. Do you remember Nehemiah's short prayer before the king of Persia? At first he prayed and fasted for days; then he prayed instantly and *silently* before the king. His first prayer was aloud—of that the rabbis would have approved, even if it were not public and even though he confessed on behalf of the nation and not just of himself. God heard both . . . and answered both."

Father began, "When you put it like that . . ."

To which Jahzeel interrupted, "Yes, but Jesus teaches you to pray so . . . so *intimately*."

"Nehemiah could pray intimately because he had already prayed so piously; God had heard his earnest plea, and Nehemiah was close to God at that time. We still need the reverence. When you are in trouble or afraid, would you not call out to God? Would you not want to be close to God?"

Father confirmed, "I would. I have passed though areas where there were bandits; I had many quiet prayers on my lips, and I didn't want any bandits to hear me! I also said many loud and pious prayers of thanks when I returned home."

Jahzeel was not satisfied. "I still see Jesus's teaching as irreverent. To *Father* . . ."

I clarified, "No, Jesus would always have us be reverent. Jesus then spoke about our debts: 'If you forgive other people when they sin against you, your heavenly Father will also forgive you. But if you do not forgive others their sins, your Father will not forgive your sins.'"

Father agreed, "How important it is, then, to forgive! Even Jews who have cheated me are still sons of Abraham."

"Yes, but God loves all humankind; he has created us all of one blood, first through Adam and continuing through Noah. But then Jesus went on to teach about false fasting: 'When you fast, do not look somber as the hypocrites do, for they disfigure their faces to show others they are fasting. Truly, they have received their reward in full. But when you fast, put oil on your head and wash your face, so that it will not be obvious to others that you are fasting, but only to your Father, who is unseen; and your Father, who sees what is done in secret, will reward you.'"

Father, smiling, "He calls them hypocrites, play actors wearing masks, as the Greeks do. How true!"

Jahzeel, asking for clarification, "*When* you fast, not *if*? This sounds as though he assumes that *all* will fast."

"That's how I understood it." I admitted, "He expects fasting, but only genuine fasting with contrition."

Jahzeel agreed with the last part. "Yes, I hate it when people show their piety as pain. It's acting, as much as is the praying on street corners; they want to be seen as pious. I suppose that is the only reward for both false fasts and false prayers. Jesus says the reward from God comes to him who does these things in secret. I think he is right."

"You are wise, my brother. Jesus also talked about where true rewards are kept: 'Do not store up for yourselves treasures on earth, where moths and vermin destroy, and where thieves break in and steal. Store up for yourselves treasures in heaven, where moths and vermin do not destroy, and where thieves do not break in and steal. For where your treasure is, there your heart will be also.'"

Father stated, "I like to think I will have a reward for doing well."

"I believe you will. I see it in your eyes. Jesus said, 'The eye is the lamp of the body. If your eyes are healthy, your whole body will be full of light. But if your eyes are unhealthy, your whole body will be full of darkness. If then the light within you is darkness, how great is that darkness!'"

Mother interjected, "I have seen joy in your father's eyes. I see it today—and in yours, too."

"Thank you, Mother; you put others first and notice their needs. Jesus went on again: 'No one can serve two masters. Either you will hate the one and love the other, or you will be devoted to the one and despise the other. You cannot serve both God and money.'"

Jahzeel pointed out, "You may not be able to serve money, but you can't live without it."

Father conceded, "Yes, but Jesus is just saying not to put money first."

I agreed, "You are both right. Jesus wanted us to see that money is not to be our greatest concern: 'Therefore I tell you, do not worry about your life, what you will eat or drink; or about your body, what you will wear. Is not life more than food, and the body more than clothes? Look at the birds of the air; they do not sow or reap or store away in barns, and yet your heavenly Father feeds them. Are you not much more valuable than they? Can any one of you by worrying add a single hour to your life?'"

Mother smiled wryly. "Worry? I'm a mother; it's what we do."

Father put in, "I have worried too much. I can't get back the time I have spent worrying. Most of my fears have never come true. My energy has been wasted."

I tried to cheer Father up. "Father, you do well now. Jesus went on, 'And why do you worry about clothes? See how the flowers of the field grow. They do not labor or spin. Yet I tell you that not even Solomon in all his splendor was dressed like one of these. If that is how God clothes the grass of the field, which is here today and tomorrow is thrown into the fire, will he not much more clothe you, you of little faith? So do not worry, saying, "What shall we eat?" or "What shall we drink?" or "What shall we wear?" For the pagans run after these things, and your heavenly Father knows that you need them. But seek first his kingdom and his righteousness, and these things will be given to you as well. Therefore, do not worry about tomorrow, for tomorrow will worry about itself. Each day has enough trouble of its own.'"

Mother admitted, "I, too, have worried about how to feed and clothe my family, yet we were never really in want."

"I have been thinking about my priorities, too. Jesus continued, 'Do not judge, and you will not be judged. Do not condemn, and you will not be condemned. Forgive, and you will be forgiven. Give, and it will be given to you. A good measure, pressed down, shaken together and running over, will be poured into your lap. For with the measure you use, it will be measured to you.'"

Jahzeel admitted, "I find it hard not to condemn the wicked, especially when they are wealthy or in power."

"I, too, brother, but I know that we need to forgive. The promise of good measure is a gift. Jesus continued, 'Can the blind lead the blind? Will they not both fall into a pit? The student is not above the teacher, but everyone who is fully trained will be like their teacher.'"

Jahzeel remarked, "We have many blind leaders, and we will have trouble. But I am not blind."

"Yes, we will have trouble—and no, brother, you are not blind. But Jesus is no blind teacher. Listen to what came next: 'Why do you look at the speck of sawdust in your brother's eye and pay no attention to the plank in your own eye? How can you say to your brother, "Brother, let me take the speck out of your eye," when you yourself fail to see the plank in your own eye? You hypocrite, first take the plank out of your eye, and then you will see clearly to remove the speck from your brother's eye.'"

Jahzeel asked, "Did you recite that one especially for me?"

"No. It's for me, too, brother; I cannot judge you. I need to remove anything blocking me from seeing truth clearly, or I cannot help."

Mother, beaming her pride, exclaimed, "What sons I have!"

Father reflected, "Remember how David unknowingly condemned himself when Nathan confronted him about Bathsheba? When I hypocritically judge someone, I do the same."

I nodded and continued, "Jesus went on, 'Don't give dogs the sacred; do not throw your pearls to pigs. If you do, they may trample them under their feet and turn and tear you to pieces.'"

Father mused, "How funny that sounds, and yet to a pig a pearl is nothing but pain to his teeth, something that would anger them. We are not to judge but are to see people for what they are; if they are pigs, we are not to give them holy things. We can tell the difference without judging. We cannot condemn; God will handle that. Jesus is tossing out these pearls of wisdom to Pharisees who want to tear him to pieces."

"They do want to do so, but Jesus's words are for all of us. Jesus promised more: 'Ask and it will be given to you; seek and you will find; knock and the door will be opened to you. For everyone who asks receives; he who seeks finds; and to the one who knocks, the door will be opened.'"

Father admitted, "I have always been afraid to ask . . ."

"No longer, I hope. Jesus's words mean for us to keep on asking, keep on seeking, and keep on knocking. Listen to these words; they are for you! 'Which of you, if your son asks for bread, will give him a stone? Or if he asks for a fish, will give him a snake? If you, then, being evil, know how to give good gifts to your children, how much more will your Father in heaven give good gifts to those who ask him! So, in everything, do to others what you would have them do to you, for this sums up the Law and the Prophets.'"

Father acknowledged, "These words are for me. I always wanted the best for you. I'm not greater than God. God wants the best for me, and I should not be afraid to ask."

"No, Father, you shouldn't. But so few know what God really wants. Jesus went on in his sermon, 'Enter through the narrow gate. For wide is the gate and broad is the road that leads to destruction, and many enter through it. Small is the gate and narrow is the road that leads to life, and few find it.'"

Mother, looking somber, "Few? That is so sad . . ."

"It is. We need to show people the straight path. Jesus wants us to tell people the truth. He cautioned, 'Watch out for false prophets. They come to you in sheep's clothing, but inwardly they are ferocious wolves. By their fruit you will identify them. Do people pick grapes from thorn bushes, or figs from thistles? Likewise, every good tree bears good fruit, but a bad tree bears bad fruit. A good tree cannot bear bad fruit, and a bad tree cannot bear good fruit. Every tree that does not bear good fruit is cut down and thrown into the fire. By their fruit you will recognize them. A good man brings out the good stored up in his heart; an evil man brings evil things out of the evil stored up in his heart. For the mouth speaks what the heart is full of. Not everyone who says to me, "Lord, Lord," will enter the kingdom of heaven, but only the one who does the will of my Father who is in heaven. Many will say to me on that day, "Lord, Lord, did we not prophesy in your name and in your name drive out demons and in your name perform many miracles?" Then I will tell them plainly, "I never knew you. Away from me, you evildoers!"'"

Father confirmed, "Not all teachers are true. You can tell by what they preach. This Jesus knows the true from the false."

"Yes, and if he is true, why do people not believe him? Jesus again went on: 'Why do you call me, "Lord, Lord," and do not do what I say? Therefore everyone who hears these words of mine and puts them into practice is like a wise man who built his house on the rock. The rain came down, the streams rose, and the winds blew and beat against that house; yet it did not fall, because it had its foundation on the rock. But everyone who hears these words of mine and does not put them into practice is like a foolish man who built his house on sand. The rain came down, the streams rose, and the winds blew and beat against that house, and it fell with a great crash.'"

Jahzeel reflected, "I understand these parables; calling someone 'lord' but not obeying is asking to be punished. But what is our house to be built on? What rock is this?"

Father stated, "I think it is the Word of God."

"Yes, Father, I'm sure it is. The Word is true, dependable. It can be trusted. It never changes, can never be tossed aside or moved. It's a sure foundation. That finished Jesus's sermon. When Jesus finished, the crowds were amazed at his teaching, because he taught with authority and not as the teachers of the Law. Jesus has authority, and everyone who hears him knows it."

Father stated, "I have not heard him, other than in the distance at Passover when he cleared the temple. Yet I perceive his authority from what you say. You are very convincing in the way you recount his words and deeds."

Glad to receive Father's affirmation, I replied, "Thank you, Father. Telling others is the job that Jesus has given me. I need to do it. After this, Jesus went to Capernaum. There, a centurion's favored servant was sick unto death. The centurion had heard of Jesus and sent some elders of the Jews to him, asking him to come and heal his servant. When they came to Jesus, they pleaded earnestly with him: 'This man deserves to have you do this, because he loves our nation and has built our synagogue.' So, Jesus began to go with them."

Jahzeel asked, again incredulous, "Jesus went to a centurion's house? Even one who built a synagogue is still a Roman."

I corrected, "Jesus *began* to go. We were not far from the house when the centurion sent friends to say to Jesus, 'Lord, don't trouble yourself, for I do not deserve to have you come under my roof. I did not even consider myself worthy to come to you. But say the word, and my servant will be healed. For I myself am a man under authority, with soldiers under me. I tell this one, "Go," and he does; and to that one, "Come," and he comes. I say to my servant, "Do this," and he does it.'"

Jahzeel surmised, "Even the centurion realized that no prophet should enter a Roman house. He is wise for a Roman."

I continued, "When Jesus heard the centurion's words, he turned to the crowd following him and said, 'I tell you, I have not found such great faith even in Israel. I say to you that many will come from the east and the west and will take their places at the feast with Abraham, Isaac, and Jacob in the kingdom of heaven. But the subjects of the kingdom will be thrown outside, into the darkness, where there will be weeping and gnashing of teeth.'"

Jahzeel stopped me. "The centurion had *faith*? In what? His servants?"

Father reflected, "I think I know. Faith that Jesus would heal."

I agreed, "Yes, Father, that's it. Then Jesus said to the centurion, 'Go! Let it be done just as you believed it would.' Then the men who had been sent returned to the house and found the servant well, healed at that moment."

Mother mused, "Jesus had pity on the servant of a centurion? Most in Israel would not have anything to do with a centurion; we fear them."

"Yes, I know. Just over a year ago I would not have believed it."

Father pointed out, "Romans know sorrow, too. They probably know death and injury more even than we do."

I paused before announcing, "That's all for now. Jahzeel, how is the room coming?"

"It is well planned and looking promising. I am told that Anna is getting her preparation done as well, but the marriage is still nearly a year away."

"Yes, but the betrothal contract is completed. That is something you can have confidence in."

Didymus

Father affirmed, "Yes, it gives me joy."

And Mother agreed, "Yes, and having you both here today gives me great joy. Here, eat! That, too, will give me joy."

It had been a very good day.

XI

When Testimony Goes Sour

It was again a long while before I had another opportunity to visit my family. So much had happened, and I had so much to tell! I was afraid I would leave something out. Through the whole journey I tried to remember Jesus's words.

When I arrived, I saw Father first; he ran out to greet me with an embrace before I had even entered. As happy as I was, I felt rather embarrassed; I did not remember his ever meeting me like that before. It was so humbling to realize I meant that much to him that I felt tears in my eyes. He immediately called to Mother and to Jahzeel. Mother, too, embraced me; I wondered whether she would let me go. At first, I worried that something had gone wrong, but it was just joy. Even Jahzeel gave me a manly hug and was genuinely glad to see me.

Mother stated, "Come in, you must eat; you look so thin."

"Thin? I eat as much as ever. I have muscles from traveling."

Father stated, "Eat anyway; we need to hear about your travels."

Jahzeel confirmed, "Yes, I have heard much about this Jesus recently, but I want to hear it firsthand."

I began, "Certainly. But what have you heard?"

Jahzeel filled me in with information from his side: "He heals everyone. He preaches repentance and preaches against the Pharisees, but not Rome. Even more amazing tales."

I admitted, "That's pretty close to the whole story. He doesn't single out the Pharisees all the time—but does emphasize their hypocrisy."

Father commented with a rueful smile, "Their hypocrisy *is* most of the time . . ."

Jahzeel, with a grin: "I could not have put it better, Father."

I asked, "Where to begin?"

Father responded with "Again you must ask? Everything since we last spoke. Please, recline here and wait for Mother; she has raisin cake coming.

As Mother arrived to serve, I thanked her and began, "After Sabbath when I was here, we followed Jesus to Nain. We were accompanied by a great many joyous followers of Jesus. As we approached the town, a large group was coming out of the city. They were mourners following a widow whose only son had died."

Mother murmured, "How sad; she would have been helpless and without hope."

"Yes, Jesus had pity on her as well. He said simply, 'Don't cry.' The procession stopped. Jesus went up to the bier the youth was lain on and said, 'Young man, I say to you, get up!' The dead boy sat up and began to talk, and Jesus gave him back to his mother. The crowds were filled with awe and praised God. Many said, 'A great prophet has appeared to us.' Others said, 'God has come to help his people.'"

Mother, gasping, "What a wonderful gift!"

Father, taking in the ramifications, queried, "Jesus raised the dead?"

Jahzeel confirmed, "I had heard this, too; I just didn't want to repeat it until I received confirmation from you. Are you sure he was dead?"

"Everyone in the procession knew he was dead. Jesus raised the dead."

Father asked, "God raised him when Jesus prayed, like the prophets?"

"He simply said, 'Young man, I say to you, get up!' He didn't call on God with his lips."

Jahzeel wanted to hear details. "That can't be right, or at least not all of the story. Only God can raise the dead."

"I know. What does that say about Jesus?"

Jahzeel spoke, not angrily, but with feeling. "Thomas, I accept that Jesus may be a prophet, but this is more than the works of any prophet. You said the people there called Jesus a great prophet. But again, only God can raise the dead."

Father stated the obvious: "It would seem that Jesus is claiming to be the Son of God . . ."

"Yes."

Mother offered her perspective: "All I know is that he saved a widow in grief—why the concern over why he has done such a great work?"

I acknowledged her empathy for another mother. "Yes mother, you have a tender heart, but Father and Jahzeel are right: Jesus is performing wonders. Don't judge before you hear more."

Father pressed, "Tell on."

"News of Jesus spread quickly through Judea and the area around it. It even reached back to John the Baptist in prison. John sent two of his disciples who cared for his needs in prison to call upon Jesus, asking about his mission. When the men reached Jesus, they said, 'John sent us to you to ask, "Are you the one who is to come, or should we expect another?"' While they were there, Jesus cured many who had diseases, sicknesses, and evil spirits, as well as giving sight to many who were blind. He then replied to John's disciples, 'Go back and report what you have seen and heard: The blind receive sight, the lame walk, those with leprosy are cleansed, the deaf hear, the dead are raised, and the good news is proclaimed to the poor. Blessed is anyone who does not stumble on account of me.'"

Father went on, "Jesus said the dead are raised. I remember; this is in fulfillment of Isaiah's prophecy."

"Yes, it is. It's about the Messiah, or the kingdom."

Jahzeel asked, "So, you are saying Jesus is the Messiah?"

"I believe he is. Let me go on. When John's messengers had left, Jesus began to speak to the crowd of John: 'What did you go out into the wilderness to see? A man dressed in fine clothes? No, those who wear such clothes and are in luxury are in palaces. But what did you go out to see? A prophet? Yes, I tell you, and more than a prophet. This is the one about whom it is written:

"I will send my messenger ahead of you who will prepare your way before you."

'I tell you, among those born of women there is none greater than John; yet the one who is least in the kingdom of God is greater than he.

'From the days of John the Baptist until now, the kingdom of heaven has been subjected to violence, and violent people have been raiding it. For all the Prophets and the Law prophesied until John. And if you are willing to accept it, he is Elijah who was to come. Whoever has ears, let him hear.'

"Jesus continued, 'To what, then, can I compare the people of this generation? What are they like? They are like children sitting in the marketplace and calling out to each other:

"We played the pipe for you, and you did not dance;
we sang a dirge, and you did not cry."

'For John the Baptist came neither eating bread nor drinking wine, and you say, "He has a demon." The Son of Man came eating and drinking, and you say, "Here is a glutton and a drunkard, a friend of tax collectors and sinners." But wisdom is proven right by all her children.'

"All the people, even the tax collectors, when they heard Jesus, acknowledged that God's way was right, because they had been baptized by John. But the Pharisees and the experts in the Law rejected God's purpose of them, because they had not been baptized by John."

Jahzeel asked, "He says the Prophets and the Law prophesied *until* John. Meaning that the Law *ends* with John?"

"No, just the predictions of the Law; Jesus is saying the prophecies of the Law are being fulfilled."

Father, seeking clarification, "He says *John is* Elijah? He speaks of the kingdom? Will he throw out Rome?"

"No, John has the spirit of Elijah; remember that Elisha was given a double portion of the spirit of Elijah, too. Some of the disciples are hoping that Jesus will throw out Rome, but his plans are for a different kind of a kingdom."

Jahzeel echoed, "A different kind of kingdom? What would that be?"

"Brother, I'm not sure. The people would follow him anywhere, but he has never advocated overthrowing Rome. It's as though that is not important to him."

Father stated the obvious: "It's important to all Jews!"

"Not more important than raising a widow's dead son. He helps individuals, not just the nation. I can't really explain, but I discern a difference. I must go on."

Father invited, "Please."

"One of the Pharisees invited Jesus to dinner at his house. As Jesus was reclining at the table, a woman of the town who was known to have lived a sinful life learned that Jesus would be there. She came into the house with an alabaster jar of perfume. As she stood behind him at his feet, weeping, she began to wet his feet with her tears. Then she wiped them with her hair, kissed them, and poured perfume on them."

Jahzeel, clearly miffed, asked, "How could he allow this?"

"Many asked that. Jesus told us later that the Pharisee who had invited him had said to himself, 'If this man were a prophet, he would know who is touching him and what kind of woman she is, a sinner.' Jesus, knowing the Pharisee's thought, answered him aloud: 'Simon, I have something to tell you.' Simon answered, 'Tell me, teacher.' Jesus asked him, 'Two people owed money to a certain moneylender. One owed him five hundred denarii, and the other fifty. Neither had money to pay him back, so he forgave the debts of both. Now which of them will love him more?' Simon replied, 'I suppose the one who had the bigger debt forgiven.' Jesus said, 'You have judged correctly.'"

Father asked, "So, since she has had more forgiven, she has more love for him who forgives? That makes sense."

Jahzeel contended, "Only if he has power to forgive."

I continued, "The discourse went on. Turning to the woman, Jesus said to Simon, 'Do you see her? I came into your house, but you gave me no water for my feet. She wet my feet with her tears and wiped them with her hair. You gave me no kiss, but she has not stopped kissing my feet from the time I arrived. You did not anoint my head, but she has poured perfume on my feet. I tell you, her many sins have been forgiven, as she demonstrates by her love. But to whom little has been forgiven, little love has been shown.' Jesus looked at the woman and said to her, 'Your sins are forgiven.' The others in the house began to say amongst each other, 'Who is this who even forgives sins?'"

Jahzeel stated, "My point exactly!"

"It's not over, Jahzeel. Jesus said to her, 'Your faith has saved you; go in peace.'"

Jahzeel countered, "Faith? God forgives. She had no part in the forgiveness, if indeed she was forgiven."

Father asked, "No, but she showed faith in her repentance. Does that make sense?"

I continued, "Exactly. If she did not believe, she would not have repented."

Mother reflected, "Imagine what relief she felt!"

"Yes, Mother, what joy. What good news, that *anyone* can have forgiveness. We went on through cities and villages, proclaiming and bringing the good news of the kingdom of God. All twelve of us were with him, and also some women who had been healed of evil spirits and infirmities: Mary, called Magdalene, from whom seven demons had gone out; Joanna, the wife of Chuza, Herod's household manager; Susanna; and many others, who provided for us out of their means. Everyone knew of Jesus, all the way to Herod."

Father noted with concern, "Herod would do to Jesus what he did to John."

Jahzeel verified, "Father is right."

And Mother once again asked anxiously, "Are you safe?"

"I'm safe. There is no safer place than to be in the center of God's will—unless it is in the presence of Jesus."

Jahzeel exclaimed in awe, "I have never seen such confidence from you, brother."

"I have never before followed anyone like Jesus. Once we entered a house in Capernaum, but such a crowd gathered that we were not even able to eat. They brought Jesus a demon-possessed man who was both blind and mute, and Jesus healed him so that he could both see and talk."

Mother commented, "How wonderful. From blind and mute to seeing and talking. How could anyone in such a situation not have joy?"

"Most of them do; the crowd was shocked and asked, 'Could this be the Son of David?' Yet the Pharisees, who are always watching Jesus, heard and accused, 'It is only by Beelzebul, the prince of demons, that this fellow drives out demons.'"

Jahzeel muttered, "That is strange logic."

And Father put in, "They don't really believe that! What a disgusting accusation."

"It is. Jesus knew both what they said and what they thought. He told them, 'Any kingdom divided against itself, whether a city or a house, cannot stand: If Satan casts out Satan, he is divided, how can his kingdom stand? If I am casting out devils by Beelzebub, by whom are your children casting them out? They will be your judges. But if I cast out devils by the finger or Spirit of God, then the kingdom of God has come to you.'"

Father concurred, "His logic is accurate."

And Jahzeel pointed out, "I recall that Pharaoh's magicians of old, Jannes and Jambres, said that the works of God through Moses were by the finger of God."

I confirmed, "They did. Jesus asked them, 'How can one enter into a mighty man's house and use his goods, unless he first binds the man? He who is not with me is against me; he who does not gather with me scatters. All types of sin and blasphemy will be forgiven, but blasphemy against the Holy Spirit will not be forgiven. He who speaks against the Son of Man will be forgiven, but he that speaks against the Holy Ghost will not be forgiven, either now or in the world to come. Either the tree and the fruit are good, or they are bad; the tree is known by its fruit.' Jesus said this because they were saying he had an impure spirit."

Jahzeel asked, "What is this 'blasphemy against the Holy Spirit'?"

Father interjected, "I think I know. We feel shame because of the Holy Spirit, so we sacrifice to remove our guilt. But if the Spirit never causes us shame, we will never sacrifice. One does not repent unless the Spirit moves him. If you continue to chase away the Spirit, you will never repent. Is that it?"

"That's pretty close, Father; we feel guilt and then sacrifice or repent."

Jahzeel interjected, "I am not against Jesus, but I do not scatter. And what is this? No forgiveness?"

Father went on, "I think Jesus means that if you had the ability to witness to the good but did not, you would rightly be faulted."

I agreed. "If we know truth, not telling it lets the falsehood go unchecked. That constitutes a sin of omission. Jesus went on, in some of the strongest language I have heard from him, 'Make a tree good and its fruit will be good, or make a tree bad and its fruit will be bad, for a tree is recognized by its fruit. You vipers, how can you who are evil speak good things? Out of the wealth of the heart the mouth speaks! A good man from the riches of his heart brings forth good things. An evil man out of the evil of his heart will speak evil things. Truly, every empty or idle word that men speak they will give account of on the judgment day. By your words you will be justified or condemned.'"

Father recalled, "I have heard so many idle words . . ."

And Jahzeel stated, "He must have made them furious!"

"Yes, he did. Some of the Pharisees and teachers of the Law said, 'Teacher, we want to see a sign from you.'"

Father commented, "*I* have heard of enough signs; what more do they want?"

I continued, "Jesus answered them, 'A wicked and adulterous generation asks for a sign, but none will be given it except the sign of the prophet Jonah. As Jonah was three days and three nights in the belly of a huge fish, so the Son of Man will be three days and three nights in the heart of the earth. The men of Nineveh will stand up at the judgment with this generation and condemn it; they repented at the preaching of Jonah, and now something greater than Jonah is here. The Queen of the South will rise at the judgment with this generation and condemn it; for she came from the ends of the earth to listen to Solomon's wisdom, and now something greater than Solomon is here.'"

Jahzeel asked, "What sign of Jonah? Three days in the heart of the earth? Is he going to perform a sign from inside a cave?"

"I don't think so; how could it be a sign if no one were able to see it?"

Father confirmed my thought. "For him to bring up the Queen of Sheba implies that it must be a public sign. Just tell us what else happened."

"Jesus continued speaking to those gathered, 'When an impure spirit comes out of a person, it goes through arid places seeking rest and cannot find it. Then it says, "I will return to the house I left." When it arrives, it finds the house unoccupied, swept clean and put in order. Then it goes and takes with it seven other spirits more wicked than itself, and they go in and live there. The final condition of that person is worse than the first. That is how it will be with this wicked generation.'"

Jahzeel, picking up the thread of thought, "Then something has to occupy the house first."

"Yes. God must occupy it."

Father asked, "But how?"

"I believe this is about a commitment to God. As Jesus spoke, a woman of the crowd called out, 'Blessed is the mother who gave you birth and nursed you.'"

Didymus

Mother replied emphatically, "I agree."

I went on, "Jesus replied, 'Blessed rather are those who hear the word of God and obey it.'" Mother, when you hear and obey the Word of God, *you* are blessed!"

Mother looked thrilled. "What a promise. It feels as though he gave it directly to me."

"Yes, but Jesus's own mother didn't feel blessed by his other brothers right then. His half-brothers heard these things and went to take charge of him, thinking he was out of his mind. I think they believed the Pharisees would stone him right there. Someone told him, and he replied, 'Who is my mother, and who are my brothers?' Pointing to his disciples, he said, 'Here are my mother and my brothers. For whoever does the will of my Father in heaven is my brother and sister and mother.'"

Mother exclaimed, "Oh, the blessing of having sons who don't argue." Looking at her own with a laugh, ". . . and now I do!"

I spoke again, with a smile: "I'm blessed, too! Jesus continued with 'No one lights a lamp and puts it in a place where it will be hidden, or under a bowl. Instead, they put it on its stand, so that those who come in may see the light. Your eye is the lamp of your body. When your eyes are generous, your whole body also is full of light. But when they are stingy, your body also is full of darkness. See to it, then, that the light within you is not darkness. Therefore, if your whole body is full of light, and no part of it dark, it will be just as full of light as when a lamp shines its light on you.'"

Father recalled, "Light—I remember you talking about light when you first talked to Jesus."

I confirmed with a smile, "I did. As the light grows brighter, I see better. After Jesus finished talking to the people, another Pharisee invited him to eat at his home."

Mother, looking pleased, "Wonderful! Even the Pharisees are beginning to see the light."

"Perhaps. But not many. Jesus went to the table, but the Pharisee seemed surprised that Jesus did not ceremonially wash before the meal. Jesus must have known his thoughts and said to him,

'You Pharisees clean the outside of the cup and dish, but inside you are full of greed and wickedness. You foolish Pharisees! Did not the one who made the outside make the inside as well? Now as for what is inside you, be generous to the poor, and everything will become clean for you.'"

Father stated, "You can see only what is shown to be clean in the light; if you do not light the inside of the bowl, how can you know?"

"Father, you are so right. They did not see. Jesus went on, 'Woe to you, Pharisees, because you give God a tenth of you mint, rue, and all other kinds of garden herbs, but you neglect justice and the love of God. You should have done the latter while continuing to do the former.'"

Jahzeel affirmed, "He knows them so well!"

"Yes. Jesus went on further, 'Woe to you, Pharisees, because you love the most important seats in the synagogues and respectful greetings in the marketplaces.'"

Mother, looking troubled, "I don't think they would have liked this talk . . ."

"You know them, too! Jesus went still further: 'Woe to you, because you are like unmarked graves, which people walk over without knowing it.'"

Father, with a chuckle, "They remained silent? Their silence is itself a miracle!"

I smiled at Father's joke. "Before the Pharisees could answer, one of the expert lawyers, to justify himself, told Jesus, 'Teacher, saying these things you insult us also.' Jesus replied, 'Woe to you experts in the Law, because you load people down with burdens they can hardly carry, and you yourselves will not lift one finger to help them.'"

Mother stated, "I have seen people with such burdens, but the lawyers rarely care; we, the lowly people, have to take care of them on our own."

"God has given you a tender heart. Jesus said further, 'Woe to you because you build tombs for the prophets, and it was your ancestors who killed them. So, you testify that you approve of what your ancestors did; they killed the prophets, and you build their tombs. Because of this, God in his wisdom said, "I will send them prophets and apostles, some of whom they will kill and others they will persecute." Therefore, this generation will be held responsible for the blood of all the prophets that has been shed since the beginning of the world, from the blood of Abel to the blood of Zechariah, who was killed between the altar and the sanctuary. Yes, I tell you, this generation will be held responsible for it all.'"

Father, pushing back, "Wait—*this* generation will be responsible? For everything? How is that?"

"I don't know for sure."

Jahzeel put in, "But you must have an idea . . ."

I admitted again, "It is because they continue to reject Jesus. If you were to reject a gift, how would the giver respond?"

Father replied, "He would be angry. He would hold you responsible. That must be it. They rejected the prophets, those sent. You, too, have been named an apostle: a sent one. Rejecting you is bad, but rejecting one who can raise the dead—that would be ever so bad. By saying that they reject, Jesus is stating that they have heard and know what they are doing; they are not ignorant."

"Yes, they do know, at least some of them; Jesus said so, later. He went on, 'Woe to you experts in the Law because you have taken away the key to knowledge. You yourselves have not entered, and you have hindered those who were entering.'"

Mother asked softly, "Did we hinder you?"

"Not at all! You were only concerned. That was your responsibility. When Jesus finally went outside, the Pharisees and teachers of the Law began to oppose him fiercely and then besiege him with questions, waiting to catch him in something he might say. By this time a crowd of thousands had gathered, so that they were trampling on one another. Jesus began first to speak to all his disciples, saying, 'Be on your guard against the yeast of the Pharisees, which is hypocrisy. There is nothing concealed that will not be disclosed or hidden that will not be made known. What you have said in the dark will be heard in the day, and what you whispered in the ear in the inner rooms will be proclaimed from the rooftops.'"

Father exclaimed, "The Pharisees must be mad to oppose someone whom people saw raise the dead in front of a crowd. Even the Romans take a person away and oppose him elsewhere, away from a crowd."

"When we are mad, we stop thinking rationally. We simply react. That is what most of them were doing. Jesus continued, talking both to the others and to us, 'I tell you, my friends, do not be afraid of those who kill the body and after that can do no more. Fear him who, after your body has been killed, has authority to throw you into hell. Yes, I tell you, fear him. Are not five sparrows sold for two pennies? Yet not one of them is forgotten by God. Indeed, the very hairs of your head are all numbered. Don't be afraid; you are worth more than many sparrows.'"

Father, chuckling, "I have no idea how many hairs are on my head; God knows me better than I know myself." Then, thoughtfully, "Yes, all men have value."

Mother asked, concerned as always, "Jesus is saying that people who oppose the Pharisees may be killed? Are you safe?"

"He may be saying that, but I have never felt safer since when you tucked me into bed at night. Jesus told us why: 'I tell you, whoever publicly acknowledges me before others, the Son of Man will also acknowledge before the angels of God. But whoever disowns me before others will be disowned before the angels of God. And everyone who speaks a word against the Son of Man will be forgiven, but anyone who blasphemes against the Holy Spirit will not be forgiven.'"

Jahzeel asked, "Why does he speak of this 'Son of Man'?"

Father explained, "Ezekiel was also called Son of Man by God himself. It shows that he, too, has a relationship through Adam."

I agreed, "It does."

Father went on, "But again the warning on speaking against the Spirit. The warning this time was to tell the people how dangerous the attitude of the Pharisees is?"

"Yes. A man can be drawn to God only through the Spirit; without the Spirit, you will never repent. If you never repent, you will never be forgiven. That is a good lesson, but more, Jesus explained what the Spirit can help us do and why we need not worry about what to say: 'When you are brought before synagogues, rulers, and authorities, do not worry about how you will defend yourselves or what you will say, for the Holy Spirit will teach you at that time what you should say.'"

Father queried, "Have you had the Spirit tell you what to say?"

I replied candidly, "I'm sure that I have. I have been questioned and found myself answering with scripture that I didn't even realize I knew. It was both humbling and exciting."

Jahzeel admitted, "You do seem to know scripture better than you ever did before."

"Yes, I'm learning, but it's more than that. I know it to be true. At this point someone in the crowd said to him, 'Teacher, tell my brother to divide the inheritance with me.' Jesus replied, 'Man, who appointed me a judge or an arbiter between you?' Then he said, 'Watch out! Be on guard against all kinds of greed; life does not consist in an abundance of possessions.' Then he told us a parable: 'The ground of a certain rich man yielded an abundant harvest. He thought to himself, "What shall I do? I have no place to store my crops." Then he decided, "This is what I'll do. I will tear down my barns and build bigger ones, and I will store my extra grain. I'll say to myself, 'You have plenty of grain laid up for many years. Take life easy; eat, drink, and be merry.'" But God said to him, "You fool! This very night your life will be demanded from you. Then who will get what you have prepared for yourself?" This is how it will be with whoever stores up things for themselves but is not rich toward God.'"

Jahzeel stated, "You know I would not do that to you!"

"I've always known that."

Father interjected, "You miss the point, Jahzeel: the man of the parable thought only of himself. It is about greed."

"I got the point. I also realize you don't have to be rich to be greedy."

Mother agreed, "Good. I remember both of you boys growing up and not wanting to share. Sometimes all you had was the dinner in front of you, but it was so hard for you to share."

I nodded. "I remember. You both taught us to share. I don't think we are unusually greedy. I'm not sure we are always very grateful, though. We all experience a lot of worry about tomorrow. Jesus looked straight at us, his disciples, and said, 'Therefore I tell you, do not worry about your life, what you will eat, or about your body, what you will wear. For life is more than food, and the body more than clothes. Reflect on the ravens: They do not plant or reap; they have no store places or barns; yet God feeds them. How much more valuable are you than birds! Who of you by worry can add even an hour to his life? If you cannot do this little thing, why do you worry about the rest?'"

Jahzeel thought aloud, "If I did not worry about next year's grapes, we would have no harvest."

Father countered, "That is not what he is saying. You can plan—just don't be consumed with the planning."

I went on, "You are wise, Father. Jesus continued the thought: 'Think about the wildflowers. They do not labor or spin, yet I tell you that not even Solomon in all his splendor was arrayed like one of them. If that is how God clothes the grass of the field, which is here today and tomorrow is thrown into the fire to be burned, how much more will he clothe you, you of little faith! Do not set your heart on what you will eat or drink; do not worry about it. The pagans run after all such things, and your Father knows that you need them. Instead, seek his kingdom, and these things will be given to you as well.'"

Mother regretted, "I think I have worried too much about such things. Perhaps that is part of being a parent—you feel responsibility."

"It is good to feel responsible, just not to worry. Jesus went on, 'Do not be afraid, little flock, for your Father has been pleased to give you the kingdom. Sell your possessions and give to the poor. Provide purses for yourselves that cannot wear out: a treasure in heaven that cannot fail, where no thief can come near, and no moth can destroy. For where your treasure is, there your heart will be also.'"

Mother reflected, "That is profound; you can see someone's life in their desires. He talked about the lawyers; they are concerned only with themselves."

Father agreed, "Profound, yes, but think about this 'treasure in heaven'! I never thought about good deeds being treasure, but it is true: they can never be taken away. A good deed lasts forever, no matter what anyone may say."

Jahzeel remarked, "That sounds well and good, but I still need to sacrifice for my sin; no deed of mine can make up for it."

"You are exactly right, Jahzeel," I confirmed. "No number of good deeds can make up for a murder. But if my sin is covered, God will account my deeds for my profit. Then my deeds will last. Jesus talked more about sin later on. Covering and remittance are not the same. How could anyone remit or pay the price for murder?"

Jahzeel admitted, "I don't think anyone could."

Father urged, "So, tell us how, already."

I went on, "My question was rhetorical. As Jahzeel said, we cannot pay the price. God must. All we can ask is mercy from God. Jesus said, 'Be dressed and ready for service, and keep your lamp burning, like a servant waiting for his master to return from a wedding banquet, so that when he comes and knocks, he can immediately open the door for him. It will be good for the servant whose master finds him watching when he comes. Truly, he will dress himself to serve, will have them recline at the table, and will come and wait on them. It is good for the servant whose master finds him ready, even if he comes in the middle of the night, or at daybreak. Understand this: If the owner of the house had known at what hour the thief was coming, he would not have let his house be broken into. You also must be ready, because the Son of Man will come at an hour when you do not expect him.'"

Jahzeel asked, "So, we must all be ready both day and night? For Jesus to show up? Why, then, would he compare himself to a *thief*?

"The comparison was for effect, a warning to be prepared. You are in good company, Jahzeel, for Peter, who sees himself as our leader, was curious about that too. Even though Jesus had directed most of this at the 'little flock,' Peter asked, 'Lord, are you telling this parable to us, or to everyone?' Jesus answered, 'Who, then, is the faithful and wise manager, whom the master puts in charge of his servants to give them their food allowance at the proper time? It will be good for that servant whom the master finds doing so when he returns. Truly I tell you, he will put him in charge of all his possessions. But suppose the servant says to himself, "My master is taking a long time in coming," and begins to beat the other servants, both men and women, and to eat and drink and get drunk. The master of that servant will come on a day when he does not expect him and at an hour he is not aware of. He will cut him to pieces and assign him a place with the unbelievers.'"

Father commented, "It sounds as though some of the servants are lazy. I know that's not you."

"No, Father, that's not like us; you raised us well. But the warnings are real, and I believe they must be taken to heart—for all of the servants, including me. Jesus explained it this way: 'The servant who knows the master's will and does not prepare or does not do it will be beaten with many blows. But the one who does not know and does things deserving punishment will be beaten with few blows. For everyone who has been given much, much will be demanded; and from the one entrusted with much, much more will be asked.'"

Father stated with satisfaction, "He will be fair. That's better than most masters are. But *beaten*?"

Mother asked, "Have *you* been given much, Thomas? Will you be expected to do much or give much?"

I replied to both, "Father, fairness is only what I feel. God is equitable and will be just; God is always just. Mother, in a way I have been given much. *You* have given me much. You have taught me much. Now Jesus has taught me much as well and given me much shalom. I don't yet know what will be expected of me. There is so much that Jesus tells us will happen: 'I have come to bring fire on the earth, and how I wish it were already kindled! But I have a baptism to undergo, and what constraint I am under until it is completed! Do you think I came to bring peace on earth? No, I tell you, division. From now on there will be five in one family divided against each other, three against two and two against three. They will be divided, father against son and son against father, mother against daughter and daughter against mother, mother-in-law against daughter-in-law and daughter-in-law against mother-in-law.'"

Mother said, "I don't think we are against one another—not any longer. You said he gave you peace, and now this?"

Jahzeel stated, "We have been at peace for a time. That must be what he meant . . . for a time?"

Father also spoke: "You have already been baptized. Was it not for the remission of sins?"

I replied carefully, taking my time, "Good questions, all. We have much peace. My sins were remitted at baptism. But when I first believed in Jesus, it caused division for a time, didn't it?"

Jahzeel agreed, "I'm still not convinced. Oh, I believe that *you* believe."

Feeling disappointed, I continued, "Jesus wasn't finished: As surprised as the crowd seemed, he went on: 'When you see a cloud rising in the west, you say, "It's going to rain," and it does. When the south wind blows, you say, "It's going to be hot," and it is. Hypocrites! You know how to interpret the appearance of the earth and the sky. How is it that you don't know how to interpret this present time?'"

Father asked, "What is there to interpret? The Romans rule, and God will send, or perhaps has sent, his Messiah."

"That's it, Father. Jesus said, 'Why don't you judge for yourselves what is right? As you are going with your adversary to the magistrate, try hard to be reconciled on the way, or your adversary may drag you off to the judge, and the judge turn you over to the officer, and the officer throw you into prison. I tell you, you will not get out until you have paid the last penny.'"

Jahzeel stated, "I know that I would never take someone to the magistrate, unless I was sure I was in the right."

Father admitted, "I'm not sure I would take someone to the magistrate unless the situation was critical, even if I were in the right. I never have. It's probably better to just know you have been cheated and be more careful next time."

"That's exactly how you taught us. Some people then told Jesus about the Galileans whose blood Pilate had mixed with their sacrifices. Jesus answered them, 'Do you think that these Galileans were worse sinners than all the other Galileans because they suffered this way? I tell you, no! But unless you repent, you too will all perish. Or those eighteen who died when the tower in Siloam fell on them, do you think them guiltier than all others living in Jerusalem? I tell you, no! But unless you repent, you too will all perish.'"

Jahzeel exclaimed, "Oh, how they despise anyone from Galilee."

Father interjected, "Yes, but the point is that bad things don't happen *because* the victim is the worst of sinners. Look at Herod, a murderer! He is surely among the worst of sinners, having killed John just for telling the truth. No tower has fallen on Herod."

Mother confirmed, "Whenever anything bad happens, people wonder what that person has done to deserve the misfortune, even if that person is no worse than the rest."

Jahzeel added, "And people from Galilee are not always worse than those from Jerusalem."

Mother contemplated, "But such occurrences are tragic. I've seen much sadness: mothers losing children, children losing parents. Horrible things. This may sound callous, but as time has gone on, I've come to realize that we *all* die; the tragedy is not death but untimely death, suffering, or someone dying without repentance. The sadness is for those left behind, for the loss of the promise of

Didymus

a life. For those who cannot do what they were meant to do. Life is always precious to all around it. It is a happy mother who does not have to bury any of her children."

Father affirmed his wife. "Mother, you could never be callous, and you are quite profound! You are pointing out what we glean about life as we get old. To the Almighty, death is an appointment, not a surprise."

"You are both right. I'm not even sure that we Jews are always in the right. Jesus told us another parable: 'A man had a fig tree growing in his vineyard, and he went to look for fruit on it but did not find any, so he said to the vinedresser, "For three years I've been coming to look for fruit on this fig tree and haven't found any. Cut it down! Why should it use up the soil?" The vinedresser replied, "Sir, leave it alone for one more year, and I'll dig around it and fertilize it. If it bears fruit next year, fine! If not, then cut it down."' We apostles realized that Jesus was asking why we, Israel, are not producing fruit. It was humbling."

Father asked, "Why was a lone fig tree in a vineyard, not an orchard?"

I answered as best I could, "Israel is unique yet surrounded with cultures that creep upon us like a vine?"

Jahzeel agreed but asked, "Why complain about Israel when Rome is right here!"

Father ruminated, "We as a nation have not been producing much good fruit. How often has God had to punish Israel at the hands of a yet more wicked nation? When we have sinned, we should not only call for a deliverer—we must also repent."

"Truer words have never been spoken."

Jahzeel stated, "I've done nothing to repent of. Thomas, you know that is true. I am good."

I replied carefully, "Daniel repented for the nation; Ezekiel and Nehemiah did as well. So far, I've only repented for myself, though that has been more and more frequently. I'm not judging you, Jahzeel, but our nation has done much to repent of. Repentance makes one feel so clean."

Mother affirmed my explanation, smiling on both of her young men. "Thomas, you are both good boys. You have always behaved properly. You don't need to repent."

Father, dubious, reflected, "I remember several hardly veiled arguments not so long ago. . ."

Mother countered, "You know what I mean. Besides, I have chosen to forget those."

I tried to clarify. "I'm not judging any of us—only myself . . . and the nation."

Jahzeel spoke sharply: "Then judge yourself for leaving the family, and not me for working! You are no better than me, 'apostle.'"

Father tried to tone this down. "We need to quiet this before something happens that we do need to repent of."

Mother urged, "Come, eat some raisin cakes. Give thanks— and let us think carefully before we lose our tempers. I'm just glad to be together again."

Jahzeel spoke slowly, obviously still miffed. "I suppose."

And I put in, "I love you all. Jahzeel, you know I would not hurt you."

Jahzeel, his voice harsh, "Brother, keep still; you have laid hands on me before."

Mother, in shock, "No!"

Father spoke clearly and calmly. "They were boys then. They are men now; they have put away these childish things. That is enough. Shalom. Eat."

I felt tears welling up in my eyes. I had thought I was doing a good job witnessing but now realized that it is not so easy. Perhaps my family was harder to reach than others. Then I thought about Jesus's brothers; even they did not believe. Just as I was feeling sorry for myself, I thought of Nehemiah's short prayer before the king. I had not thought of praying for help. I had become too self-confident. Nehemiah's prayer was a simple, short petition for help before he had even spoken to the king. Without closing my eyes, I breathed a brief prayer asking for help and for the right words to say. Then I blurted aloud the first thing that came to my mind: "Mother, these raisin cakes are delicious. They taste better than all others because of your secret ingredient: love."

Mother looked up, a faint smile playing on her lips. Father looked at me, not with anger but with a degree of sorrow. I hoped my tears wouldn't show, but I could see from Father's expression that they did. Father seemed at a loss for what to say or do, but then Jahzeel, not wanting to be upstaged by his twin, commented, "Yes, Mother, you must show Anna how to make them this way."

A thin smile crossed Father's face; the reality is that tu bi'shvat, raisin cake, is easy to make, and there is little difference one from another. Father probed calmly, "Thomas, I suppose there is more to tell?"

Fighting hard for composure, I admitted, "A little."

"Tell on."

I gave a grateful smile and continued, "The whole point of that last parable is that for each of us our time on earth is short. As Mother said, we have each been put here for a reason. God has a plan and a purpose for our nation, and for each of us. Many times, God gave Israel, the nation, judges and prophets and time to repent, but when we did not he sent judgment on the whole nation. Repentance is one fruit. Many families, like ours, were living a righteous life in those days, but when judgment came the righteous also had to feel much of the pain—or had to watch friends experiencing a life made so much harder because of their own judgment. Sometimes they suffered, too.

"If we live well," I continued, "we show others how to live well, and to repent, so that judgment on the nation need not take place. That is some of the fruit we need to reflect. To have such fruit we need to be always attached to the vine, for that is where the life comes from that allows us to be God's witnesses for righteousness. We must live a life related to God, and we cannot ever really live a life that is not related to those around us. Jahzeel, I know you spend much time with Anna and her family."

Jahzeel replied, sounding slightly defensive, "I should."

"Yes, you should. Theirs is a good family. Would you have spent that time had Anna not been there?"

"No. Of course not. What would have been the point?"

Father picked up the thread. "I think I see the point. Theirs is a good family, and you have told me that you now have influence on them, influence you would not have had if you had not been there. I know many people to whom we sell that I should be influencing. I sell fermented wine to people who I know drink strong wine far too much. Some, I think, thus harm their families. I say nothing. I try to stay a quiet man, but perhaps I need to witness more openly to them. They want my wine, so they can have my advice and warning as well, for free! Perhaps I should not be so quiet."

I exclaimed, "That's it exactly, Father. If good men remain silent, the nation has no fruit, and we will fall. It does not begin with the king; it begins with each of us."

Mother chimed in, "Thomas, I am proud of you. I hear many tales from other women. It's time I talk to some of them about how they might fix their lives—about how we should all fix our own lives."

Jahzeel continued to protest. "But I do my job . . ."

I assured him, "I know you do, brother. You still have influence."

Jahzeel, pausing for a moment, relented, "I will think about it."

I was grateful that this visit was ending well. "Thank you all. Shalom."

As I returned to rejoin the apostles, I thought about what had happened. I had carefully rehearsed what to say to my family. I had thought that my recounting the strong words of Jesus would convince them of who he is. For a time, it had seemed to work well; then, suddenly, something adverse had happened. They had become defensive—especially Jahzeel. Had I not thought of Nehemiah's prayer, I didn't know what might have become of my witnessing attempt.

Why had I thought of Nehemiah? I had been talking about the nation falling, as it had before Nehemiah; that had in fact precipitated the confrontation. Nehemiah had offered a long prayer, a prayer of confession for the people . . . and himself. That prayer had brought him into the position whereby the later short prayer before the king would suffice. I had not offered a long prayer in preparation for my own; my preparation had consisted more of anticipation of the glory the words of Jesus would reflect. In truth, I had not been thinking of the kingdom of God as much as of my own glory.

These thoughts sobered me to realization: I was a vessel of the message of God's love. The Holy Spirit had brought to my mind Nehemiah's short prayer before the king at the very point when I realized that I myself had no power over the situation. I could only imagine how the meeting would have gone had I recognized before I had spoken at all that the power was all God's. I knew right then that the best preparation was humble prayer before God, not self-confidence. Jesus talked about binding the mighty man; I should pray that Satan would be bound so that those whom he had bound would be able to hear. Next time I would do better. Even after following Jesus so long, I still had so much to learn—and not just doctrine. I had to learn practical witnessing; I could not always rely on Jesus's miracles to witness for me.

During the next weeks I spent more time listening to Jesus and praying than I had before. Oh, I had always followed, but my following had been passive. The other apostles saw the change in me, and Nathaniel asked me what had happened. I replied, "I spent time with my family. I had thought that all the words of Jesus would change their attitudes. At first all went well, but then we had a fight. We were just as Jesus said: 'a family divided against each other.' I prayed, and the Spirit gave me words to say that brought us back to cordial terms. I want to pay more attention now, and to pray more, so that my witness to them is more effective. I know now that I cannot do it on my own."

Nathaniel acknowledged, "It is hard to talk to those closest to you; they know the old Thomas. Would you like one of us to talk to them?"

"No. They would know that I had sent you. I love them. I appreciate the offer, but even though they knew the old me, I know them, and I will be the one who tells them of Jesus. I know now that I can never convince someone about Jesus on my own. The Spirit must move them. This is why I pray so much more now. I'm sure I'm learning more, too."

"I will pray for you, brother."

XII

Testimony Immersed in Humility and Prayer

Months later, on a Sabbath afternoon while we were near home, I managed to find time again to return home. It had been so long, and there was so much to tell. As I walked, I prayed silently, asking God to give me the right words to help my family understand all that God was doing. I prayed that this would be about Jesus and not about me. I realized that, with God's help, I could do so much better than I had the last time. We did not have to fight about this. I recalled words from Proverbs: "A soft answer turns away wrath, but a harsh word stirs up anger." That was the way I must proceed.

When I got home, I realized from the voices that Anna had joined my family for the Sabbath meal, which was nearly over. Father greeted me at the door with an embrace. Mother, too, called out a greeting and quickly began to prepare me a place. Jahzeel grinned as he brought Anna to me. It was a happy moment. It was good to see them. I believe my prayers had already helped.

Father said quickly, "Mother, prepare him a place," as though he were unaware that she was already doing so. I think he simply wanted me to hear that he was still in charge. As I reclined, he continued, "Let us know all that has happened; we have heard so much of Jesus's ministry . . . of your ministry."

I nodded, smiling at Jahzeel and Anna and asking, "Do we have a better idea of a date?"

Jahzeel shyly responded, "Sooner rather than later."

Mother gave me some bread and paste, for which I thanked her. Her smile was from ear to ear.

I said another quick and silent prayer and began, "After I left last time, things were even more impressive than before. One Sabbath Jesus was teaching in one of the synagogues, and a woman was there who had been crippled by a spirit for eighteen years. She was bent over and could not straighten up at all."

Mother sighed, "That poor woman! When I see people like that, I feel so bad."

"You have a tender spirit. So does Jesus. When Jesus saw her, he called her forward and said to her, 'Woman, you are set free from your infirmity.' Then he put his hands on her, and immediately she straightened up and praised God."

Father recalled, "I have heard of such things. Did he pray?"

"Not that I could tell. The ruler of the synagogue said to the people, 'There are six days for work. Come and be healed on those days, not on the Sabbath.'"

Jahzeel exclaimed with compassion, "That's terrible. It sounds like a miracle; why couldn't he just have praised God?"

Father spoke up. "Moses said in Exodus; 'Six days you shall labor . . .' The ruler had probably never worked six days in *any* one week; that also breaks Moses's Law. How could he judge a miracle performed on Sabbath?"

Anna, speaking for the first time, almost in tears, "Why can't people be happy when they see such a burden lifted?"

Jahzeel asked, "It was envy, wasn't it? I expect it from the Pharisees, but not from a synagogue ruler who is there to minister to people."

"I'm sure it was envy," Jesus told him, addressing all the frauds. "You hypocrites! Doesn't each of you on the Sabbath untie your ox or donkey from the stall and lead it out to give it water? Then should not this daughter of Abraham, whom Satan had kept bound for eighteen long years, be set free on the Sabbath day from what had bound her?" At this his opponents were humiliated, but the people were delighted with the wonderful things Jesus did.

Father interjected, "They should have been humiliated. The woman was far more important than their cattle. Did Jesus say she had been bound by Satan? Was he saying her condition was not her fault?"

I replied, "I believe Jesus. Many of our problems are caused by our adversary, Satan. I don't believe the illness had anything to do with something she had done."

Jahzeel remarked, "The Sadducees say that anyone with a problem is at fault for their own problem. Many Pharisees agree. I have seen too many good people suffering to believe that."

I complimented my brother. "You are a wise man, Jahzeel."

Jahzeel smiled, and I realized that God was indeed helping me with my words. I went on, "Later that day, Jesus went out and sat by the lake. Such large crowds gathered around him that he got into a boat and sat in it while the people stood on shore. He told them many things in parables, starting with this: 'A farmer went out to sow his seed. As he was scattering the seed, some fell along the path, and the birds came and ate it up. Some fell on rocky places, where there was not much soil. It sprang up quickly, because the soil was shallow, but when the sun was high the plants were scorched, and they withered because they had no root. Other seed fell among thorns, which grew up and choked the plants. Still other seed fell on good soil, where it produced a crop, thirty, sixty, or even a hundred times what was sown. Whoever has ears, let them hear.'"

Jahzeel asked, "Why the parables?"

"We asked him the same thing. Jesus told us, 'The knowledge of the secrets of the kingdom of heaven has been given to you, but not to them. Whoever has will be given more, and they will have abundance. Whoever does not have, even what they have will be taken from them. This is why I speak to them in parables:

"Though seeing, they do not see;
    Though hearing, they do not hear or understand.

In them is fulfilled the prophecy of Isaiah:
  "You will be ever hearing but never understanding;
you will be ever seeing but never perceiving.
  For this people's heart has become calloused;
they hardly hear with their ears,
  and they have closed their eyes.
Otherwise, they might see with their eyes,
  hear with their ears,
understand with their hearts,
  and turn, and I would heal them.""""

Father confirmed, "Yes, that's from Isaiah. That has never sounded fair to me. I think I understood the parable, but not the passage from Isaiah."

"It's a hard passage. He was saying that not everyone is given all the knowledge of God. Parables actually make it easier, not harder, for us to understand. When you think about that, it's not so much that these things are being hidden from them but simply that they are not being given to those that would abuse the knowledge, like that synagogue ruler."

Jahzeel complimented me, "That's the best explanation I've ever heard of it. Brother, you are becoming a rabbi, and a good one!"

I began to feel a swelling of pride in my heart. I realized, however, that if I did not give the glory to God, I would not be able to continue with such openness. I prayed quickly, then continued, "Thank you, Jahzeel, but it's Jesus with the knowledge. He told us, 'Your eyes are blessed because they see, and your ears because they hear. Truly I tell you, many prophets and righteous people longed to see what you see but did not see it, and to hear what you hear but did not hear it. Listen to what the parable of the sower means. When anyone hears the message about the kingdom and does not understand it, the evil one comes and snatches away what was sown in their heart. This is the seed sown along the path. The seed falling on rocky ground refers to someone who hears the word and at once receives it with joy. But since they have no root, they last only a short time. When trouble or persecution comes because of the word, they quickly fall away. The seed falling among the thorns refers to someone who hears the word, but the worries of this life and the deceitfulness of wealth choke the word, making it unfruitful. But the seed falling on good soil refers to someone who hears the word and understands it. This is the one who produces a crop, yielding a hundred, sixty, or thirty times what was sown.'"

Father responded, "I thought as much. We who work the land understand how important it is to sow our seed properly, to prepare the soil. To get the best crop you must do your best."

Jahzeel mused, "I wonder if many in Jesus's audience understood that as we do."

"Probably not. That synagogue ruler has probably never sown seed. Jesus succeeded in telling us the parable, all the while hiding the implications from him. Isaiah was right. Jesus went right on, talking to people while that ruler stood there, puzzled. Jesus then told another parable, the first of many about the kingdom of heaven: 'The kingdom of heaven is like a man who sowed good seed in his field. But while everyone was sleeping, his enemy came and sowed weeds among the wheat, and went away. When the wheat sprouted and formed heads, the weeds also appeared. The owner's servants came to him and said, "Sir, didn't you sow good seed in your field? Where then did the weeds come from?" He replied, "An enemy did this." The servants asked him, "Do you want us to go and pull them up?" He answered, "No, because while you are pulling the weeds you may uproot wheat with them. Let both grow together until the harvest. At that time I will tell the harvesters: 'First collect the weeds and tie them in bundles to be burned; then gather the wheat and bring it into my barn.'"'"

Father asked, "Do you think the ruler understood any of that?"

I admitted, "Probably not much. Many of the disciples did not, either. Jesus left the crowd and entered a house. Some of us came to him and requested, 'Explain to us the parable of the weeds in the field.' Jesus answered, 'The one who sowed the good seed is the Son of Man. The field is the world, and the good seed stands for the people of the kingdom. The weeds are the people of the evil one, and the enemy who sows them is the devil. The harvest is the end of the age, and the harvesters are angels. As the weeds are pulled up and burned in the fire, so it will be at the end of the age. The Son of Man will send out his angels, and they will weed out of the kingdom everything that causes sin and all who do evil. They will throw them into the blazing furnace, where there will be weeping and gnashing of teeth. Then the righteous will shine like the sun in the kingdom of their Father. Whoever has ears, let them hear.'"

Father replied, "Even I would not have truly understood all of that. Oh, I get the weeds in the wheat, but in his parable they are people, planted by the devil. I would not have realized that. Angel harvesters? And when is this 'end of the age'?"

"We were not told when. But it does explain how someone like that synagogue ruler has not been plucked up; that would have ripped apart the synagogue."

Jahzeel agreed, "That would explain a lot. There are so many corrupt rulers."

Father continued, "This Jesus seems to understand so well. I've never heard this explained so plainly."

Feeling relieved that the glory was going to Jesus, I went on, "This proves what Jesus said: 'The knowledge of the secrets of the kingdom of heaven has been given to you, but not to them. Whoever has will be given more, and they will have abundance.' You . . . no, we, have been given much knowledge."

Father asked, "There is more? I mean . . . for us?"

"Far more. Jesus went on, 'Do you bring a lamp to put it under a bowl or bed? Don't you put it on its stand? For whatever is hidden is meant to be disclosed, and whatever is concealed is meant to be brought out into the open. If anyone has ears to hear, let them hear.'"

Mother commented, "Imagine how silly? To waste a light? A lamp is meant for light. Jesus seems to have been saying that the healing of that woman had to be done in public, or the miracle would have been a waste in terms of sending a message to others."

Father replied, "That's good, but I suppose this logic also would apply to a story like that of David and Bathsheba; it could not be hidden from God or the people."

"You are both right. Many of these parables have more than one application. Jesus went on with another: 'Consider carefully what you hear, with the measure you use, it will be measured to you, and more. Whoever has will be given more; whoever does not have, even what they have will be taken from them.'"

Father said, "I knew that from the vineyard, but I didn't realize the principle applied elsewhere. If you don't put work into the vineyard, or if you are stingy, you won't get much out of it. If you work hard, you will get better results. Jesus says that God watches in other areas and blesses as we give. I like that."

"Yes. Jesus also said, 'This is what the kingdom of God is like. A man scatters seed on the ground. Night and day, whether he sleeps or gets up, the seed sprouts and grows, though he doesn't know how. All by itself the soil produces grain, first the stalk, then the head, then the full kernel in the head. As soon as the grain is ripe, he puts the sickle to it, because the harvest is come.'"

Jahzeel commented, "Yes, it grows, but it is so slow that you can see the results only over time. I suppose it could be seen as a slow miracle; either way, God does the actual work."

"That's it exactly. Another parable followed, again about planting and harvest: 'The kingdom of heaven is like a mustard seed, which a man took and planted in his field. Though it is the smallest of all seeds, yet it grows to become the largest of garden plants, and becomes a tree, so that birds come and perch in its branches.'"

Father added, "The seed is not much of a representation of what is being grown. If you didn't recognize the seed, you would never know what it was. It can be hard to sort weed seeds from good seed."

"Yes, Father. Imagine how hard that would be for those from the city."

Jahzeel mentioned, "I don't much care for birds perching on anything I plant."

I nodded. "They don't do the plants any good. But adding to what Father said, Jesus had parables for city people, too. Jesus said, 'The kingdom of heaven is like yeast that a woman took and mixed into about sixty pounds of flour until it worked all though the dough.'"

Mother smiled. "Finally, one for me. It takes only a little yeast or leaven to work into much flour. You can't see its effect when you start; you see it only after you work it through. Was Jesus talking about something happening slowly, without the world noticing?"

Anna commented, "That's what I thought at first. The men notice only the bread; they don't see all that goes into it. All Jews know that leaven represents corruption. At Passover we remove all leaven from the house. Leavened bread rises, or puffs up, because of the effect of a little corruption over time that you would never notice at first. Perhaps the kingdom is like that. We all know people who are puffed up with corruption. Not very flattering."

I agreed again. "You both are right. This is happening right before us: a new kingdom! But beware that some of the people in the kingdom do not become puffed up due to corruption. Yet another parable, also about the kingdom being hidden, followed: 'The kingdom of heaven is like treasure hidden in a field. When a man found it, he hid it again, and then in his joy went and sold all he had and bought that field.'"

Jahzeel echoed, "A treasure? But one no one notices. So *that* is Jesus's kingdom? I expected more. Thomas, you expected more, too, didn't you?"

"You know me, brother. I still expect more over time. But I now am beginning to realize that it's about both now and later. The kingdom is hidden now, to be seen later. This kingdom is not for everyone. All will eventually hear of it, but many will not really take notice. Jesus told yet still another about a treasure; this time a pearl: 'Again, the kingdom of heaven is like a merchant looking for fine pearls. When he found one of great value, he went away and sold everything he had and bought it.'"

Didymus

Jahzeel asked, "Did he mean that one who finds the kingdom must give up all that he has in order to buy it?"

Father reflected, "I'm not sure. The merchant was searching for treasure—for pearls; they must have been of great value to him. Are we to be the merchant, as Jahzeel says, or is Jesus the merchant who has found you, Thomas, and redeemed you—bought you? From what you say, Jesus has given up everything for us as a redeemer. It reminds me of this from Isaiah:

'I have swept away your offenses like a cloud,
    your sins like the morning mist.
Return to me,
    for I have redeemed you.'"

I replied thoughtfully, "I assumed it to be as Jahzeel said: when I find Jesus, I give up everything, and that fits. Yet, Jesus has given up much, and I believe Jesus is our redeemer. If that was Jesus's point, then the second explanation that Father gave would fit better. Early on in our history as a nation, Boaz redeemed the entire estate to get Ruth, whom he loved. Will Jesus pay *everything* to redeem us? Pearls are valued more by Gentiles than by Jews; perhaps Jesus was talking about 'buying' the Gentiles. In either case, the kingdom is important.

"Jesus gave one last parable about the kingdom: 'The kingdom of heaven is like a net that was let down into the lake and caught all kinds of fish. When it was full, the fishermen pulled it onto the shore. Then they sat down and collected the good fish in baskets but threw the bad away. This is how it will be at the end of the age. The angels will come and separate the wicked from the righteous and throw them into the blazing furnace, where there will be weeping and gnashing of teeth.'"

Jahzeel commented, "A net? Jesus is also the prophet to the fishermen? So, all will be gathered in at this day in the future, and the bad will then be disposed of. That comparison will be popular with the fishermen!"

I found myself getting angry at Jahzeel, but, thankfully, Father intervened: "Jahzeel, you had no problem with parables speaking to farmers and vinedressers, no problem talking about a time of separating crops from weeds, or even about merchants; how can you complain if Jesus speaks in a way fishermen can identify with?"

Anna, too, spoke up. "My family are not farmers; Father is a baker. Do you think Jesus should speak only to farmers?"

Jahzeel backed down. "Yes, Father, I suppose you are right. Anna, I'm sorry . . . that came out wrong. I'm sorry, Thomas."

Breathing a sigh of relief before I spoke, I continued, "No, it is fine. Jesus speaks to many people. We do not all understand, even though we may claim to. Jesus asked us, 'Have you understood all these things?' We replied, 'Yes,' even though I am not so sure of the significance of the pearl of great price even now. Jesus had given us so many examples, and we each understood some of them. He said, 'Therefore every teacher of the Law who has become a disciple in the kingdom of heaven is like the owner of a house who brings out of the storeroom new treasures as well as old.'"

Father agreed, noting, "The Torah is good; I suppose that is the old treasure. These sayings of Jesus seem to be treasures, too. From all I have heard, they are. So, a disciple must use both kinds of treasure. Thomas, I think that is what you are doing."

Again, I prayed to suppress my pride before I spoke. "Yes, but this is still all about Jesus. There were many parables Jesus spoke to us. In fact, he did not say *anything* to us in front of the crowds without using a parable. But when he was alone with us, he explained everything. This fulfilled what was spoken in the Psalms:

'I will open my mouth in parables,
  I will utter things hidden since the creation of the world.'"

Father, seeming satisfied, "So, it is indeed about old treasure and new. Everyone will want such treasure."

Didymus

"Yes. There were crowds. When Jesus saw the crowd around him, he gave us orders to cross to the other side of the lake. Then a teacher of the Law came to him and said, 'Teacher, I will follow you wherever you go.' Jesus replied, 'Foxes have dens and birds have nests, but the Son of Man has no place to lay his head.' Jesus said to another man, 'Follow me.' The man replied, 'Lord, first let me go and bury my father.' Jesus said to him, 'Let the dead bury their own dead, but you go and proclaim the kingdom of God.' Still another said, 'I will follow you, Lord; but first let me go back and say good-bye to my family.' Jesus replied, 'No one who puts a hand to the plow and looks back is fit for service in the kingdom of God.'"

Jahzeel asked, "Does he not want disciples? One was a teacher of the Law! These people did not sound unreasonable."

I elaborated, "They were half-hearted. He wants people to listen and learn. Many are there for the miracles—to be healed or to watch others being healed. He knows who will really follow him. He knows who is truly willing."

Father asked meditatively, "Do you look back?"

I spoke carefully. "Father, I follow, and that is my path, but I will never leave you—any of you."

Mother confirmed, "We know you have not left us."

Suffused with joy, I continued, "Later that same day, as evening came, he said to us, 'Let us go over to the other side.' Leaving the crowd behind, we took him alone, just as he was, in the boat. There were also other small boats with us. A furious squall came up, and the waves broke over the boat, so that it was nearly swamped. Jesus was in the stern, sleeping on a cushion. We woke him and said, 'Teacher, don't you care if we drown?'"

Jahzeel smiled. "So, he is a sound sleeper?"

I continued without smiling, "There is more, Jahzeel. Jesus got up and rebuked the wind and the waves, 'Quiet! Be still!' Then the wind died down and it was completely calm. Instantly. He asked us, 'Why are you so afraid? Do you still have no faith?' We were terrified and asked each other, 'Who is this? Even the wind and the waves obey him!'"

Father reflected, "I'm no sailor, but doesn't it take time for water to calm after a storm?"

"It ordinarily does, Father. This was a miracle."

Jahzeel asked, "Did he pray for this?"

"All I saw was him telling the storm to stop."

Father spoke, reverence in his tone. "What power! You said you were all terrified after the storm? Even the fishermen?"

"Yes. They were amazed and frightened by the power he had."

Jahzeel pointed out, "But you had already seen miracles."

"I had. But to see such power over nature. Anyone would be terrified. We had been afraid from the storm, but now we saw that the storm had been no match for him. How can I fear anything but God now? When we finally got across the lake, we arrived at the area of the Gerasenes. As soon as Jesus got out of the boat, a man possessed with a demon came from the tombs. The man lived in the tombs, and no one could bind him any longer, even with a chain. He had been previously bound both hand and foot, but he had torn the chains and broken the irons on his feet. No one could subdue him. Night and day among the tombs and in the hills, he would cry out and cut himself with stones. When he saw Jesus even at a distance, the man ran to us and fell on his knees in front of Jesus. Jesus said to him, 'Come out of this man, you impure spirit!' The man shouted at the top of his voice, 'What do you want with me, Jesus, Son of the Most High God? In God's name don't torture me!' Jesus asked, 'What is your name?' He answered, 'My name is Legion, for we are many.' He begged Jesus again and again not to send them out of the area. A large herd of pigs was feeding on the nearby hillside. The demons begged Jesus, 'Send us among the pigs; allow us to go into them.' Jesus gave them permission, and the impure spirits came out of the man and went into the pigs. The herd, about two thousand in number, rushed down the steep hill and into the lake and were drowned."

Mother commiserated, "What torture that man must have endured!"

"Yes, Mother, but some people didn't care about the man. Those tending the pigs ran off and reported this to the town and countryside, and people came to see for themselves. They saw the man who had been possessed by the demons, sitting, dressed and in his right mind, and they were afraid. Those who had seen all this told the people what had happened to the man and to the pigs. The people began to plead with Jesus to leave their region."

Anna, in surprise, "They wanted him to *leave*?"

Father explained, "They cared more for their pigs than for the man. The region is Gentile. Jews should not be keeping swine. Either they were Gentile, or they profited from selling pigs to the Gentiles."

Mother added, "They were afraid, too, as you were after Jesus calmed the storm. When they saw his power over the demons, they probably felt the same sort of fear."

"You are both right. As Jesus was getting into the boat, the man who had been possessed begged to go with us. Jesus told him, 'Go home to your own people and tell them how much the Lord has done for you and how he has had mercy on you.' So, the man went and began to tell in Decapolis how much Jesus had done for him. Everyone was amazed. As you said, Father, Decapolis is Gentile; the man who was possessed is now telling Gentiles about Jesus."

Anna commented, "Of course the man was grateful."

Jahzeel continued the thought: "Some people would be grateful, too; I'm sure he still had family."

Father agreed, "Yes. The ones witnessing about Jesus's healing were also those who saw the power of God not as a threat, but as a blessing."

I went on, "We crossed over the lake again to Capernaum, and a large crowd gathered around him while he was still by the lake. One of the synagogue leaders named Jairus came, and when he saw Jesus he fell at his feet. He pleaded earnestly with him, 'My little daughter is dying. Please come and put your hands on her so that she will be healed and live.' Jesus went with him."

Anna expressed sympathy: "The poor girl."

Father put in, "Yes, but think about it. This Jairus must have believed that Jesus can heal, so much so that he risked the wrath of the Pharisees and Sadducees in order to see his daughter healed. He must at least see Jesus as a prophet."

"Exactly. A large crowd followed and pressed around him. A woman was there who had suffered bleeding for twelve years. She had spent all she had on doctors but continued to get worse. When she heard about Jesus, she came behind him in the crowd and touched his cloak, thinking, 'If I just touch his clothes, I will be healed.' Immediately, her bleeding stopped and she felt in her body that she was free of suffering."

Mother exclaimed, "Oh, what pain she must have endured . . . and to think she was unclean the whole time, apart from everyone! Twelve years! She told you this?"

"She told us afterward, but the story is not over. At once Jesus realized that power had gone out from him. He turned in the crowd and asked, 'Who touched me?' We answered him, 'You see the people crowding against you; how can you ask, 'Who touched me?' But Jesus kept looking to see who it had been. The woman, knowing what had been done for her, came and fell at his feet and, trembling with fear, told him the whole truth. He said, 'Daughter, your faith has healed you. Go in peace and be freed from your suffering.'"

Mother, a tear in her eye, empathized, "She must have been so embarrassed . . . and yet so glad."

Jahzeel expressed a different perspective: "A prophet would know who had touched him."

I replied, "I'm sure Jesus knew who touched him; he wanted it made public."

Jahzeel asked, "Wait, Jesus said *her faith* had healed her. Not Jesus?"

"That is what Jesus said. But who, or what, had she put her faith *in*?"

Father replied, "It is the same faith this Jairus had: faith in Jesus's ability to heal. When Jesus saw her faith, he healed her."

"Yes, Father. While Jesus was still speaking, some of the people from the house of Jairus came. They told him, 'Your daughter is dead; why bother the teacher anymore?'"

Didymus

Anna, nearly in tears herself, empathized, "That poor man . . . so close!"

"But there is still more. Ignoring those who had told him she was dead, Jesus told Jairus, 'Don't be afraid; just believe.' Jesus allowed only Peter, James, and John to follow him into the home."

Mother asked, "You could not go? Was the house too small?"

Jahzeel interrupted, "It's a synagogue ruler's house. It's large."

I did not disagree. "No, Mother, the house was large, but I did not go in. I stayed outside. Peter, James, and John are the leaders. I should have mentioned that by now."

Mother looked surprised. "I was sure you were a leader. I know Peter—he is loud. He *would* make himself a leader."

Father commented, "The sons of Zebedee are just as loud."

"No, it's not that. I'm sorry if I elevated myself. Those three have the most faith. I need to finish the story. John told me what happened next. Jesus saw a commotion, with people crying and wailing. He went in and said to them, 'Why all this commotion and wailing? The child is not dead but asleep.' They laughed at him. Jesus put them all out and took the child's father and mother and the three disciples with him and went in to where the child was. He took her by the hand and said to her, 'Talitha koum!' (which means 'Little girl, I say to you, get up!'). Immediately, the girl stood up and began to walk around, for she was twelve years old. At this they were completely astonished. He gave strict orders not to let anyone know about his and told them to give her something to eat."

Anna replied, her voice breaking, "So tender. He spoke to her in Aramaic, as though she were his lamb."

Mother spoke thoughtfully: "Twelve years? The same period of time the woman had been bleeding."

Jahzeel replied in his turn, "*Not to tell?* What would have been the use? Even if she were not dead, this would still have been a miracle witnessed, or told of, by many!"

I answered clearly, "No, she was dead. The people knew it. They laughed at Jesus before he raised her."

Anna mused, "What a marvelous work. I would see this Jesus."

Everyone looked at her, and Jahzeel spoke: "Yes, it was a work. What is it you would want to see?"

Anna, realizing that she had spoken before her betrothed, and without his consent, said quietly, "I was just speaking in the moment."

Mother, defending Anna and locking her eyes with Father's, spoke next: "We all wish to see him, dear, when the time is right."

Father added reassuringly, "Yes, all in good time. We wish to see these works, these miracles Jesus is doing. Thomas, is there more?"

"So much more. As soon as Jesus left, two blind men followed him, calling out, 'Have mercy on us, Son of David!' When he had gone indoors, the blind men came to him, and he asked them, 'Do you believe that I am able to do this?' They replied, 'Yes, Lord.' Then he touched their eyes and said, 'According to your faith let it be done to you'—and their sight was restored. Jesus warned them sternly, 'See that no one knows about this.' But they later went out and spread the news about him all over that region."

Jahzeel commented, "Son of David? They see him, then, as Messiah?"

"As do I, Jahzeel."

Father pointed out, "This time he heals by touch. Some he touches, and some he heals by other means. I do not see why. And telling them not to spread the news seems pointless; of course, they will tell. Everyone will know."

Jahzeel suggested, "Perhaps his saying not to spread it will incite them to do it all the more!"

I replied, "Perhaps, but I don't think so; we are surrounded all the time with people wanting healing. As far as why some are touched and some not, I'm not sure there is any one reason—perhaps to show he is not limited. While we were still going out, a man who was demon-possessed and could not talk was brought to Jesus. When the demon was driven out, the man could speak. The crowd was amazed and said, 'Nothing like this has ever been seen in Israel.' But the Pharisees again said, 'It is by the prince of demons that he drives out demons.'"

Didymus

Jahzeel spoke up. "That is too harsh. They only worry about losing their own disciples."

"You are right, Jahzeel. We left there and came to Jesus's hometown, Nazareth, which you know is a long walk from Capernaum. When Sabbath had come, he began to teach in the synagogue, and many who heard him were amazed. 'Where did this man get these things?' they asked. 'What's this wisdom that has been given him? What are these remarkable miracles he is performing? Isn't he the carpenter? Isn't this Mary's son, and the brother of James, Joseph, Judas, and Simon? Aren't his sisters here with us?' And they took offense at him. Jesus said to them, 'A prophet is not without honor except in his own town, among his relatives, and in his own home.' He could not do any miracles there, except to lay his hands on a few sick people to heal them. He was amazed at their *lack* of faith."

Father, seeking clarification, "He *could* not do miracles because of their lack of faith?"

"He did heal a few. But I don't think their lack of faith limited Jesus's abilities at all; Jesus can do anything. I have found that miracles must have a purpose; if the onlookers would not have believed even with the miracles, he would have had no reason to do them. He "cannot" do them in such a situation because it would not serve the purposes of God. When we don't demonstrate that we could believe, why should God offer demonstrations for us? Jesus went through all the towns and villages, teaching in their synagogues, proclaiming the good news of the kingdom, and healing every disease and sickness. When Jesus saw crowds, he had compassion on them, because they were harassed and helpless, like sheep without a shepherd. Then he said to his disciples, 'The harvest is plentiful, but the workers are few. Ask the Lord of the harvest, therefore, to send out workers into his harvest field.' It's tempting to try to convince God to see things my way. Prayer helps God get hold of my own heart and mold me. When I prayed, 'Oh Lord, send forth workers into the harvest,' I heard the call of God: 'Whom will I send?' And I answered, like Isaiah, 'Here am I—send me.'"

I took a bite of bread, praying that what I was about to say would not sound overly prideful, and then continued, "Calling us apostles to him, he began to send us out two by two and gave us authority to drive out impure spirits and to heal every disease and sickness! I went with Matthew, the tax collector. We were told, 'Do not go among the Gentiles or enter any town of the Samaritans but rather to the lost sheep of Israel. As you go, proclaim: "The kingdom of heaven is at hand." Heal the sick, raise the dead, cleanse those who have leprosy, drive out demons. Freely you have been given; freely give. Do not get any gold or silver or copper to take with you in your belts, no bag for the journey or extra clothes or sandals or staff, for the worker is worthy of his keep.'"

Jahzeel queried, "*You* were told to do miracles?"

I clarified, "Jesus allowed me the privilege of God doing miracles though me."

Mother, glowing, breathed, "I knew you would be used."

"Really, Mother, it's not about me; it's about Jesus. He told us, 'Whatever town or village you enter, search there for some worthy person and stay at their house until you leave. As you enter the home, give it your greeting. If the home is deserving, let your peace rest on it; if not, let your peace return to you. If anyone will not welcome you or listen to your words, leave that home or town and shake the dust off your feet. Truly I tell you, it will be more bearable for Sodom and Gomorrah on the Day of Judgment than for that town.'"

Father stated, "He still gives shalom."

"Only to those who are willing to accept it. Some people want nothing to do with peace. Did you hear the warning? Jesus continued to warn us as well: 'I am sending you out like sheep among wolves. Therefore, be as shrewd as snakes and as innocent as doves.'"

Father reflected, "Doves are harmless, and snakes are careful, hiding in corners and being patient. That doesn't sound flattering, but I think I get the meaning."

Jahzeel also commented, "If you are the sheep, then the wolves are the Pharisees."

Didymus

"I'm afraid so. Jesus went on, 'Be on your guard; you will be handed over to the local councils and be flogged in the synagogues. On my account you will be brought before governors and kings as witnesses to them and to the Gentiles. But when they arrest you, do not worry about what to say or how to say it. At that time, you will be given what to say, for it will not be you speaking, but the Spirit of your Father speaking through you.'"

Mother, in concern, echoed, "Flogged? Are you safe? You felt safe before because you were *with* Jesus."

"That's right, and I still do. I know I'm safe when I am doing the will of God. Jesus went on, 'Brother will betray brother to death, and a father his child; children will rebel against their parents and have them put to death. You will be hated by everyone because of me, but the one who stands firm to the end will be saved. When you are persecuted in one place, flee to another. Truly I tell you, you will not finish going through the towns of Israel before the Son of Man comes.'"

Father asked, "What is this 'You will not finish going through the towns of Israel before the Son of Man comes?'"

I answered as best I could. "He was talking about the future, as though he were preparing us for something yet to come. I need to finish telling you what we did, but first I need to finish reporting what he warned us of. Jesus said, 'The student is not above the teacher, or a servant above his master. It is enough for students to be like their teachers, and servants like their masters. If the head of the house has been called Beelzebul, how much more the members of his household!'"

Anna asked in consternation, "Have they called you those things?"

"Some have called us names, but Jesus said, 'Do not be afraid of them; there is nothing concealed that will not be disclosed or hidden that will not be made known. What I tell you in the dark, speak in the daylight; what is whispered in your ear, proclaim from the roofs. Do not be afraid of those who kill the body but cannot kill the soul. Be afraid of the one who can destroy both soul and body in hell. Are not two sparrows sold for a penny? Yet not one of them will fall to the ground outside your Father's care. Even all the hairs of your head are numbered. Don't be afraid; you are worth more than many sparrows.'"

Mother exhaled in relief, "God is watching over you, then."

"Yes. Jesus went on, 'Whoever acknowledges me before others, I will also acknowledge before my Father in heaven. But whoever disowns me before others, I will disown before my Father in heaven.'"

Father stated, "You have acknowledged him."

And Jahzeel interjected, "We have not disowned him."

I looked with surprise at Jahzeel and replied, "No, you have not, and I am glad. Jesus went on with a hard saying: 'Do not think that I have come to bring peace to the world. I did not come to bring peace, but a sword. For I have come to turn

"A man against his father,
   a daughter against her mother,
a daughter-in-law against her mother-in-law,
   a man's enemies will be the members of his own household."'"

Mother pointed out, "We are not against you!"

Father agreed, "No, certainly not. I think he was quoting Micah."

I nodded. "He was quoting Micah. No, you are not against me. But Jesus went on, 'Anyone who loves their father of mother more than me is not worthy of me; anyone who loves son or daughter more than me is not worthy of me. Whoever does not take up their cross and follow me is not worthy of me. Whoever finds their life will lose it, and whoever loses their life for my sake will find it.'"

Mother, in a barely audible voice, asked the hardest question so far: "Do you love Jesus more than us?"

I prayed as I answered. "I don't love you any less, but I cannot love anyone more than Jesus."

Mother, tears in her eyes, reflected, "That is enough. But what is this 'taking up your cross'? Are the Romans going to do something like that to you?"

Didymus

"Jesus was simply telling us to be willing, even if things get difficult."

Father mused, "Losing your life to find it. You are right: this is a hard saying."

"It means that, if I were to shy away from my calling, God would not protect me. But if I embrace my calling, God will give me purpose, power, and direction. Jesus went on, 'Anyone welcoming you welcomes me, and anyone who welcomes me welcomes the one who sent me. Whoever welcomes a prophet as a prophet will receive a prophet's reward, and whoever welcomes a righteous person as a righteous person will receive a righteous person's reward. And if anyone gives even a cup of cold water to one of these little ones who is my disciple, truly I tell you, that person will certainly not lose their reward.'"

Father stated, "You are always welcome here. Does this mean that *we* by extension welcome Jesus? I suppose it does."

Mother agreed, "I would give him more than a cup of cold water—and I would do the same for any of your friends."

I spoke with a slight smile. "Thank you—that means a lot, I knew you would. After giving us instructions, Jesus went on to teach and preach in the towns of Galilee. We set out and went from village to village, proclaiming the good news and healing people everywhere. As we went, Matthew, who is wealthy, left his bag with others. I was impressed. He is a humble man for a Levite— and one so well to do. I supposed this came from his having been ostracized by the Jews because he collected taxes for the Romans, but being alone with him I realized that his humility simply came from Jesus. Indeed, as I have stated, God did miracles though us. People came to see and be healed, and they willingly heard the good news of Jesus and the kingdom from us. It was never about us; it was always about Jesus."

Jahzeel asked, intrigued, "What sorts of miracles can you do?"

I nudged my brother away from this train of thought, replying softly, "God does the miracles; he just used me. When you prune a vine with a pruning hook, the hook is not in charge of the pruning—you are. I'm like the pruning hook; the work is commanded and done by God."

Jahzeel, not to be dissuaded, asked again, "I understand. Still, what sorts of things?"

"Many things. We healed. We proclaimed the good news of the kingdom; that Jesus had come. People listened because of the miracles. Had the miracles not been done, fewer would have listened. It is an amazing feeling to be used of God. Many times, I could not believe what God was doing through me. I have never before had such power channeled through me, but it was always about God."

Jahzeel, persisting, asked, "Can you do one now?"

I was grateful that Father answered quickly, "I don't think that would be right. To what purpose—that we should believe your brother?"

I explained again, "I only did what I felt led of God to do. I do not feel such power now. Even with such power, we cannot be everywhere. We later found out that, while this was happening, Herod had killed John in prison."

Father admitted, "We, too, heard about that."

Mother, looking uncharacteristically angry, blurted, "That woman Herodias and her daughter! What a terrible thing."

I proceeded, "When we returned, we reported to Jesus what we had done. Because so many people were coming and going that we did not even have a chance to eat, Jesus told us, 'Come with me by yourselves to a quiet place and get some rest.' We were exhausted, having done more than we could have imagined. We went by boat to the far shore of the Sea of Galilee to a solitary place. But many who saw us leaving ran on foot and got there ahead of us. We never got that rest, other than on the boat. When we landed, Jesus saw the crowd and had compassion on them, because they were like sheep without a shepherd. He began teaching them many things. He welcomed them and spoke about the kingdom of God, and he healed those who were sick. The Passover was near."

Mother asked anxiously, "Do you need to rest here?"

Didymus

"That was at Passover. I'm rested now. As it was late in the day, we came to Jesus, saying, 'This is a remote place, and it's already very late. Send the people away so they can go to the surrounding countryside and villages and buy themselves something to eat.' When Jesus saw the great crowd coming to him, he said to Philip, 'Where shall we buy bread for these people to eat?'"

Jahzeel pointed out, "Jesus was in charge, so why would he ask that question of you?"

I replied, "Jesus knew what he would do; he wanted to see if *we* knew what God would do. Philip answered him, 'It would take more than a half year's wages to buy enough bread for each to have a single bite!'"

Mother stated, "It takes hours to make bread. Unless someone had hundreds of loaves, it would take much work to feed a multitude."

Anna agreed, "Yes, if you did not have flour, you would have to use a mortar to grind the grain, then work it into dough with water or a mix with vinegar so it would not be bland. You would need the seor, the live yeast in the dough from the last batch to get the yeast, and then you would have to work it for hours before you baked it. This Philip understood the problem."

I agreed, "Jesus understood, too. Andrew, Simon's brother, spoke up, 'Here is a boy with five small barley loaves and two musht, but how far will they go among this multitude?'"

Father commented, "A fisherman with a big heart."

I went on, "Jesus directed them to have all the people sit down in groups on the green grass. They sat down in groups of hundreds and fifties. Taking the five loaves and the two fish and looking up into heaven, he gave thanks and broke the loaves. Then he gave them to us, the twelve, to distribute to the people. He also divided the two fish among them all. They all ate and were satisfied. Well, . . . all but a few Pharisees, who watched and sniffed and poked at the food without eating it. They were trying to figure out whether it was a trick. We picked up twelve basketsful of broken pieces of bread and fish. The number of men who had eaten was five thousand!"

Jahzeel put in, "I have heard much about this, and Anna has as well. I wanted to hear about it from your own lips. So many witnesses. Are you sure?"

I replied simply, "Yes."

Jahzeel asked, "Could Jesus just have done something to everyone to make them think their stomachs were filled?"

"No. It was real. We took up twelve basketsful of what was left over.

Jahzeel asked again, "Could he have put a spell on people so they could not tell?"

"This miracle was experienced by all—by five thousand men, plus women and children, in a desert place."

Jahzeel, still dubious: "There was no trick?"

"It was a miracle. In a trick, someone tries to deceive you. Jesus did this clearly. Jahzeel, this was awesome. Everyone realized it."

"You yourself were reaching into the baskets?"

"Yes, and every time the baskets were just as full as they had been."

Father commented, "It's like the miracle of the widow's oil that Elisha did."

"Yes, but everyone saw this miracle. I *felt* it! Do you know how long it took the twelve of us to feed thousands? I reached into baskets so many times my arms were worn out. Jahzeel, it was like picking grapes for hours. It was real!"

Anna stated, "It takes time to make bread, and to prepare the ingredients."

"I know."

Father stated further, "And fish take time to grow."

Jahzeel asked, "Did all the fish look alike?"

"Brother, you and I think alike: I thought about that as I passed them out. The boy had two small musht; I was passing out musht and biny—but the boy had carried no biny! These were mature fish that had never seen water. They had never been minnows. They had never been hatched as eggs. Jesus *made* them, just as they were, out of *nothing*—with his blessing."

Didymus

Jahzeel asked, "You know this is not possible, right? I am still sure most of these 'miracles' were illusions. Oh, I believe Jesus is a prophet. Perhaps if I were to see a miracle taking place, I could tell how he did it. This is too hard."

I pressed, "Harder than raising the dead? Harder than healing? In my own strength I can do neither. God can do both. He has not told me which is the harder."

Jahzeel, unmoved, replied, "Not just hard—impossible."

"But *both* are impossible. Yet with God all things are possible."

Father commented, "First the wine, starting from water, but no time and no work. Then bread, without flour or dough—again no time and no work. Now fish that have never been eggs, never grown but suddenly there—complete, perfect, and mature. Who can do such a miracle?"

I replied firmly, "God can. This miracle caused me think about how God has worked in the past. When God created the heavens and the earth, what did he use for material?"

Father replied, "He must have created it all out of nothing . . ."

"The Pentateuch tells us that God said, 'Let there be light.' He simply *spoke* it into existence. Jesus simply blessed, and either something multiplied or came into existence out of nothing. I could not tell the difference in this miracle, and I was right there, pulling fish out of baskets. The bread smelled wonderfully fresh, and, as I said, the fish were mature, complete, and lacking nothing—but who had caught them?"

Father pointed out, "God created animals, too . . . including fish."

"Yes, he did. I have had time to think about this, and I don't believe he created the fish as eggs in the account of Genesis; like those I handled, they also were mature when he created them. Imagine if he had created a sheep as an infant, a helpless lamb? It would have died the first night. No, God's creations were mature and complete, probably even with their bellies full."

Father agreed, "Some rabbis teach it that way. It has to be that way. Adam was never a baby or a child, with angels taking care of his needs. That would have been ridiculous. He was created as a man."

Jahzeel pointed out, "Adam had to have the ability to walk the day he was born . . . er . . . the day he was . . . created."

Father went on, "We know he could talk; he talked to God. God did not have to teach him language; he made him able to talk when he first awoke. He had a vocabulary. He knew how to pronounce. He understood words. This is all too hard for me to imagine. Creating Adam with thoughts and memories already in his mind . . ."

"Yes, it's too hard for me to imagine, too. Yet I ate the bread!"

Jahzeel asked, "Did it taste . . . fresh . . . er . . . new?"

"It was perfect. It smelled wonderful. It felt warm, as though right from the oven."

"The fish?"

"Perfect. You could not tell any difference at all. Jesus blessed, and that's what became."

"Did the fish look . . . old?"

"They looked a year old or more. But the reality is that they were not more than moments old. God controls age . . . and time. The fish appeared to have a history, but that was only apparent. Other than the two first little musht, these fish could never have lived."

Anna asked, "The boy had barley loaves?"

I smiled. "You pay attention well. What you really want to know is whether all the loaves we passed out were made of barley? I am sure there were wheat loaves also among the hundreds I passed out. Where did they come from? The blessings of God."

Father spoke clearly, "I, too, want to see Jesus. I believe you, Thomas, but I still want to see."

Mother confirmed, "We all do."

"I am glad. The people experienced the miracle, experienced Jesus's power! They knew what they saw, and what they tasted! It would be hard to deceive 5,000 men at once, not to mention the women and children. When there is a trickster, he will keep children away; they may look where the adults do not. After the people had seen the thing Jesus had performed, they began to say,

Didymus

'Surely this is the Prophet who is to come into the world.' Immediately, Jesus made us get into the boat and go on ahead of him to Bethsaida, while he dismissed the crowd. Jesus, knowing that they intended to come and make him king by force, withdrew again to a mountain by himself."

Jahzeel stated, "They wanted to be fed forever."

I agreed, "That's it exactly. Jesus knew it."

Father reflected, "If Jesus simply did everything for everyone, we would have no purpose."

"You are wise, Father. I thought of that after the miracle of turning the water into wine. Our vineyard would have become irrelevant. Our vineyard and its use are gifts from God to us."

I continued, "As we rowed across the Sea of Galilee, it became dark, and Jesus had not yet joined us. A strong wind was blowing, and the water got rough. Jesus saw us straining with the oars because the wind was against us. Just before dawn Jesus came to us, walking on the sea! When we had rowed about three or four miles, we saw Jesus approaching the boat, walking on the water. He appeared to be passing us by, and we thought he was a ghost. We cried out, all of us terrified. But Jesus spoke to us: 'Take courage! It is I. Don't be afraid.'"

Jahzeel echoed, "Walking *on water*? Why?"

"Jesus had sent us away, and the crowd saw us go. He wanted us to be apart for a while. Since the people didn't see him get into the boat, they thought he would still be there. That was what he was doing, but he also wanted us to see that he could walk on water. Peter shocked us. He sometimes acts before he thinks. He said, 'Lord, if it's you, tell me to come to you on the water.' Jesus said, 'Come.'"

Father, like Jahzeel before him, asked, "Why?"

"I don't really know. Peter got down out of the boat and walked on the water toward Jesus. When he saw the wind, though, he became afraid and began to sink. He cried simply, 'Lord, save me!' Jesus reached out his hand and caught him. Peter is a stronger swimmer than any of the rest of us, but he panicked in the wind and the waves. Then Jesus asked him, 'You of little faith, why did you doubt?'"

Jahzeel asked, "What was he thinking?"

"He had more faith than I did; I wasn't getting out of that boat. I suppose Peter wanted to impress us all—or to impress Jesus. It was pretty amazing. When they climbed into the boat, the wind died down. We were completely amazed. We in the boat worshipped Jesus, saying, 'Truly you are The Son of God.' We all knew then for sure. The first time when Jesus calmed the sea, he had wanted us to feel safe, no matter the storm, because he was with us; we were in his presence. This time Jesus wanted us to learn the lesson that we were safe despite the storm because his presence was with us, even though he was not even near the boat."

Jahzeel stated, "I know that's what you believe. I'll have to withhold judgment."

I replied, trying to be kind, "I would expect nothing less from you, brother. When we arrived at Gennesaret, people recognized Jesus. They ran throughout that whole region and carried the sick on mats to wherever they thought Jesus would be. Wherever we went, villages or towns, they brought him to the marketplaces. The same in the country; they placed the sick where he might pass. They begged him to let them touch even the edge of his cloak, and all who touched it were healed. He didn't have to do anything, just pass by. It was nothing like the prayers we had prayed for healing."

Father asked, "How can he avoid the press of the crowd?"

"He challenged the people, and many decided not to follow. The next day the crowd that had stayed on the opposite shore realized that only one boat had been there and that Jesus had not entered it with us, although he had also gone away. Some boats from Tiberius landed near the place where the people had eaten the bread after the Lord had given thanks. Once they reached there, seeing neither Jesus nor us, they got into the boats and went to Capernaum in search of Jesus."

Jahzeel stated with satisfaction, "He lost them."

Didymus

I agreed, "For a time. When they found him, they asked him, 'Rabbi, when did you get here?' Jesus answered, 'Very truly I tell you, you are looking for me, not because you saw the signs which I performed but because you ate the loaves and had your fill. Do not work for food that spoils, but for food that endures to eternal life, which the Son of Man will give you. For on him God the Father has placed his seal of approval.'"

Father stated, "He told them the truth."

"He did. Then they asked him, 'How must we do the works God requires?' Jesus answered, 'The work of God is this: Believe in the one he has sent.'"

So, they asked him, "What sign, then, will you give that we may see it and believe you? What will you do? Our ancestors ate the manna in the wilderness; as it is written: 'He gave them bread from heaven to eat.'"

Father, looking amazed, asked, "They think they can challenge him into doing more miracles? I have not met this man, but I know he will not fall for such a trick."

"You are right. Jesus said to them, 'Very truly I tell you, it was not Moses who has given you the bread from heaven, but it is my Father who gives you the true bread from heaven. For the bread of God is the bread that comes down from heaven and gives life to the world.' They said, 'Sir, always give us this bread.'"

Jahzeel stated, "There it is: they wanted something for nothing."

"Yes. Then Jesus declared, 'I am the bread of life. Whoever comes to me will never go hungry, and whoever believes in me will never be thirsty. But as I told you, you have seen me and still you do not believe. All those the Father gives me will come to me, and whoever comes to me I will never drive away. For I have come down from heaven not to do my will but to do the will of him who sent me. This is the will of him who sent me, that I shall lose none of all those he has given me but raise them up at the last day. For my Father's will is that everyone who looks to the Son and believes in him shall have eternal life, and I will raise them up at the last day.'"

Jahzeel probed, "Jesus says he is the bread of life? That he is the sustenance of life? And that he came down from heaven?"

"He has already produced life in the miracles, and he talks about the Father in heaven. I believe him."

Father, seeming a little surprised, "That is some promise—eternal life."

"It is. At this point some Jews there began to grumble about him because he said, 'I am the bread that comes down from heaven.' They said, 'Is this not Jesus, the son of Joseph, whose father and mother we know? How can he now say, 'I came down from heaven'?"

Jahzeel added, "I can see why they doubt; they have known him, and his father and mother."

I challenged Jahzeel, "They knew his earthly Father. His true Father is God. Jesus answered them, 'Stop grumbling among yourselves. No one can come to me unless the Father who sent me draws them, and I will raise them up at the last day. It is written in the Prophets: "They will all be taught by God." Everyone who has heard the Father and learned from him comes to me. No one has seen the Father except the one who is from God; only he has seen the Father. Very truly I tell you, the one who believes has eternal life. I am the bread of life. Your ancestors ate manna in the wilderness, yet they died. But here is the bread that comes down from heaven, which anyone may eat and not die. I am the living bread that came down from heaven. Whoever eats this bread will live forever. This bread is my flesh, which I will give for the life of the world.'"

Jahzeel, shuddering, "Even the pagans don't eat human flesh. That's disgusting."

"I'm not saying I understand all of this. The Jews began to argue sharply among themselves: 'How can this man give us his flesh to eat?' Jesus said to them, 'Very truly I tell you, unless you eat the flesh of the Son of Man and drink his blood, you have no life in you. Whoever eats my flesh and drinks my blood remains in me, and I in them. Just as the living Father sent me and

Didymus

I live because of the Father, so the one who feeds on me will live because of me. This is the bread that came down from heaven. Your ancestors ate manna and died, but whoever feeds on this bread will live forever.' He said this while teaching in the synagogue in Capernaum."

Jahzeel questioned, "Drink his blood? That's disgusting, too."

Father asked his own question: "That synagogue is near Simon's house, isn't it? How did Simon's friends take this?"

"Not well. When they heard it, many of Jesus's disciples said, 'This is a hard teaching. Who can accept it?' Jesus was aware of their grumbling and said to them, 'Does this offend you? Then what if you see the Son of Man ascend to where he was before! The Spirit gives life; the flesh counts for nothing. The words I have spoken to you, they are full of the Spirit and life. Yet there are some of you who do not believe. This is why I told you that no one can come to me unless the Father has enabled them.' From that time on, many of his disciples turned back and no longer followed him."

Jahzeel realized, "He not only scared away the crowds, but many of his disciples as well."

Father asked, "How are these words full of life?"

I replied, "Listen carefully; Jesus had just said that no one can come to him unless the Father has enabled them. The other 'disciples' could not truly come to him."

Father asked, "Does that mean we cannot choose to follow him?"

"You can, but if you do, that will mean that the Father had already enabled you; it would not be a surprise to the Father."

Jahzeel observed, "It sounds as though I can't decide for myself."

"You can, but your decision would have already been known by the Father. If he already knows, then he determined that you would choose to follow. As far as you are concerned, the decision is yours. To the Father, it was already determined. I chose to follow Jesus, but he had already chosen me to follow him. Does that make sense?"

Jahzeel replied reluctantly, "Not really."

I said a short prayer, then tried to graciously reply, "You are my brother, a wise man. No matter what you think, God has already thought that. He is abundantly wiser than any of us. I don't think any of us really understands, nor are we expected to. Jesus asked us, 'You do not want to leave too, do you?' Peter answered, 'Lord, to whom shall we go? You have the words of eternal life. We have come to believe and to know that you are the Holy One of God.'"

Father commented, "I know Simon. He's a brusque, unrefined sort. That sounds deeper than I would have expected from him."

"He has been with Jesus for two years. Jesus replied to us, 'Have I not chosen you, the Twelve? Yet one of you is a devil.' I was shocked. One of us? I wondered who it might be."

Mother replied emphatically, "You are *not* a devil. It's someone else."

Jahzeel ruminated, "The tax collector, perhaps?"

"No, I went with Matthew, and we did miracles from God. It is not him."

Jahzeel reflected, "All of you twelve went out."

"We went out two by two. Only one is needed to do miracles. I don't want to think about who it might be; we are all close. Shortly after this some of the Pharisees and some of the teachers of the Law who had come from Jerusalem gathered around Jesus and saw some of us eating food with unwashed hands. So, they asked Jesus, 'Why don't your disciples live according to the tradition of the elders instead of eating their food with defiled hands?'"

Mother chastened me, "Thomas, you know better . . ."

"I was very clean. The Pharisees were talking about ritual washing and prayer. We don't do that, even at home. Jesus replied, 'Isaiah was right when he prophesied about you hypocrites; as it is written:

Didymus

"These people honor me with their lips,
  but their hearts are far from me.
They worship me in vain;
  their teachings are merely human rules."

'You have let go of the commands of God and are holding on to human traditions. You set aside the commands of God in order to observe your own traditions! For Moses said, "Honor your father and mother," and "Anyone who curses their father of mother is to be put to death." But you say that if anyone declares that what might have been used to help their father or mother is Corban [a gift devoted to God] then they no longer need to do anything for their father or mother. Thus you nullify the word of God by your tradition that you have handed down. And you do many things like that.'"

Jahzeel commented, "I have heard such excuses for disobedience. Such people are nitpickers of the Law, and yet they disrespect it."

"Yes, they are. Jesus called the remaining crowd to him and said, 'Listen to me, everyone, and understand this. Nothing outside a person can defile them by going into them. Rather, it is what comes out of a person that defiles them.'"

Father agreed, "That is the truth. The things some people say reflect such defilement in their heart. It wasn't what went in; it's what came out."

"Yes. But we realized how he had offended them. They are proud of their traditions. He told everyone to listen to him! The Pharisees want people to listen to them, instead. We came to him, and some asked, 'Do you know that the Pharisees were offended when they heard this?' Jesus replied, 'Every plant that my heavenly Father has not planted will be pulled up by the roots. Leave them; they are blind guides. If the blind lead the blind, both will fall into a pit.'"

Father reflected, "Blind guides. That's funny, but only too true. I would like to listen to this Jesus."

I went on, "Peter said, 'Explain this parable to us.' Jesus said, 'Are you still so dull? Don't you see that nothing that enters a person from the outside can defile them? It doesn't go into their heart, but into their stomach, and then out of the body. What comes out of a person is what defiles them. For it is from within, out of a person's heart, that evil thoughts come, sexual immorality, theft, murder, adultery, greed, malice, deceit, lewdness, envy, slander, arrogance, and folly. All these evils come from inside and defile a person.'"

Mother interjected, "I thought you said Peter was a leader. He doesn't seem so bright."

"He leads, but that is in faith. Peter understood but wanted elaboration. I was glad to hear the details, too. After this Jesus went around Galilee. We did not go into Judea because the Jewish leaders there were looking for a way to kill him."

Mother asked again, "Are you sure you are safe?"

"The safest place in the world is at the center of his will, or in his presence. I am in both."

Father asked, "You said he will be around Galilee for a time?"
"Yes."

Speaking slowly, he ventured a further question: "Do you think we could see him? Not individually, but just to listen?"

"I'm sure of it."

Anna spoke up: "My parents heard of the feeding of the 5,000. They want to see him, too."

Jahzeel was more cautious. "I will think about it . . . perhaps if I have time."

I spoke gladly, "This is great news. I love you all so much. You must make up your own minds about Jesus."

"Jahzeel assured me, "Don't worry, I make up my own mind."

"I expect nothing less from you, my brother. Mother, this meal is great."

Didymus

As I returned to Peter's house in Capernaum, I thought about how well this visit had gone. I was grateful that God had answered my prayers and kept my family open to the claims of Jesus. After I prayed, I realized that God had done even more: he had changed my attitude. God had humbled me. My witness had improved. God had done more than I had asked; more even than I had imagined. I had asked God only to change my family, but God had changed me. I prayed again, this time with even greater thanks and a much humbler spirit. As I thought about it, I realized that I must also thank Nathaniel for praying for me.

XIII

Ikhthũs (The Fish)

Not long after this Jesus led us to the region of Tyre and Sidon, where we spent some time. During those days, even in this mostly Gentile area, another large crowd gathered. People must have come from as far away as Galilee. Since they had nothing to eat, Jesus called his disciples to him and said, "I have compassion for these people; they have already been with me three days and have nothing to eat. If I send them home hungry, they will collapse on the way, because some of them have come a long distance."

We asked, "But where in this remote place can anyone get enough bread to feed them?"

Jesus asked, "How many loaves do you have?"

We replied, "Seven."

Jesus told the crowd to sit down on the ground. When he had taken the seven loaves and given thanks, he broke them and gave them to the twelve, to distribute to the people. They had a few musht, as well; he gave thanks for them also and told the disciples to pass them out. The people ate and were satisfied. Afterward, we picked up seven basketsful of broken pieces that were left over. About four thousand were present. After he had sent them away, Jesus prepared to get into the boat with us to go on to the region of Dalmanutha.

Before we left, as the crowd was dispersing, Jesus seemed to be looking at one small group, smiling. I looked closely in that direction. It was my father, mother, Jahzeel, Anna, and her parents! I ran to them and embraced them.

I exclaimed to Father, "You are so far from home—halfway around the sea, a half-day's journey. How long have you been here?"

Father replied, "We heard of the crowds two days ago. We arrived only this noon, but it was enough."

Knowing what Father meant, I began to weep tears of joy. My father had come to believe! Mother assured me, "Don't weep—we listened, we saw miracles, we ate, and we believe." I was so happy. But my exhilaration was not to last. After a moment I noticed that, although Anna and her parents appeared to be happy, Jahzeel did not. Mother urged me, "Speak to your brother; he has no peace. He truly respects you. Quickly. Shalom." I took Jahzeel aside.

I spoke slowly: "Jahzeel, what is wrong?"

My twin replied, "I listened, yet I cannot follow just because others do. You have fished; you know that a dead fish simply follows the current, while a live fish can decide for itself. I decide for myself. I see why Jesus has followers. He has a dignity about him. Your Jesus is a great speaker; he has sway over the crowd. Much of what he says I know to be true. I saw 'miracles.' I watched the blessing of the bread. I did not eat of the bread or fish. I could not. At first, I was so angry as to be nearly apoplectic over it. My emotions had gotten the better of me. As I continued, I looked them over, carefully. I studied them. Fresh smelling, warm bread. Fresh fish. The fish appeared to be fully grown. Differing varieties. No apparent source. They seemed to have come out of thin air. Very convincing. But it is to me a show. I'm not sure whether he is a magician or a prophet. I'm sorry, Thomas; I know that all of you believe, but I cannot. I still see this as a trick."

Now I had new tears in my eyes, and not of joy. I tried to speak. "Jahzeel . . ."

He interrupted me with tact. "Your friends in the boat are motioning for you to come. You had better not keep them waiting."

I started again. "But, Jahzeel . . ."

My brother again cut in: "I will consider what I have heard. Even Anna believes. Her parents loved the bread; they believed when they saw Jesus make the bread. Perhaps after I sleep on this . . . No, I doubt I will believe; I do not need him. I have what peace I need. Go now."

Taking leave of my family, I went to the boat. Now fully in tears, I hid my face. The boat left shore. Nathanial came and put his arm around me.

"Brother Thomas . . ."

"My family . . ."

"They were the people you were talking to? The last one must be your twin."

"Yes . . ."

"They came so far. They did not believe?"

"My father did, and my mother . . . but not my brother."

"I'm sorry. Perhaps later he will believe. Jesus said, 'No one can come to me unless the Father who sent me draws them.' Perhaps he will yet be drawn."

"I remember, but it hurts so badly."

I began to remember more of Jesus words: "You will have shalom. Just as it takes time to make the wine in the grape skin, it will take time to make shalom in Jahzeel's heart. It will even take time in your heart. Do not lose heart. Just as the grapes appear, shalom, too, will appear in due season. Do not give up."

In due season. Jesus had said it would take time to produce shalom in my brother's heart. Jesus knew. Jesus had smiled to me, looking tenderly upon my family. Jesus knew! Of course—it was not God's will that any should perish! Jesus wanted my family to believe. I had been praying to say to them the right words, to do the right thing. That was exactly what I should pray, . . . but it was not all. I had not been praying that my family would believe.

Father and Mother had believed, of course, but I had not been praying specifically that Jahzeel would believe. Now I realized that I must pray that, as well. That, and wait for "due season," the time appointed in the Father's plan for this to happen. I had been so

Didymus

busy doing God's work that I had forgotten that *each and every one* of the people ministered to was important to God, and to their families. Oh, the marvelous love of God for each one individually! What was it that John had told me that Jesus had said to Nicodemus? "For God so loved the world that he gave his only Son, that whoever believes in him should not perish but have eternal life." God gave us Jesus so that the world could have eternal life. What incredible love!

Suddenly, I remembered that Nathaniel was still by my side. "Nathaniel, thank you for praying for me. My parents have believed; I praise God for that. Continue to pray for me, and also that my brother, Jahzeel, will trust Jesus. And that others will, as well."

Nathaniel replied reassuringly, resting his hand on my shoulder, "I will, my brother. Take some rest; we are all tired. I'm sure there is still much work to be done."

I thought back over the last two plus years. I had my mother and father and my brother, Jahzeel, as well as my friends Andrew and Philip. They were still close, but now Nathaniel and Matthew were at least as close. All the apostles were close. And I had Jesus, the one closer than any brother. Why had I so quickly doubted? I had received an answer to prayer, but it had not been enough to satisfy me. Jesus loved Jahzeel even more than I could myself. The best thing to do was to desist from weeping and instead to pray and continue to work. To follow Jesus's example. That's what I should do, too. But now I could barely keep my eyes open. As I settled in to take my needed rest, Jesus continued to give me shalom.

XIV

Be Ready to Give an Answer

For months we continued to follow Jesus as he taught and performed miracles. I had time near home just before the Festival of Dedication, and I was able again to return home on a cold Sabbath afternoon. On several Sabbaths I had been close by but not within a designated Sabbath day's journey. I wanted badly to see my family now that they believed, but I especially wanted to see Jahzeel, who still refused to believe. I wanted them all to have Jesus as Lord of their lives. I knew that Jesus loved Jahzeel even more than I could myself. I had been praying, but the work of ministry had kept me so busy.

When I arrived, Father literally ran out to meet and embrace me. He exclaimed, "Thomas, my son, it is so wonderful to have you home!" He was loud, and mother heard and came out as well.

I simply smiled and embraced them both for a moment. I first saw tears of joy in Mother's eyes, then realized that there were tears in Father's, as well. Suddenly, I felt tears welling up in my own. Jesus's promises to me were being fulfilled. We were all quiet for a moment, each in our own way taking in this realization. Then I asked, "Where is Jahzeel?" to which Father replied, "He is well. He will be coming shortly. Come in."

We entered the home I had grown up in. It was obvious that Jahzeel had added a room for himself and Anna, but other than that nothing had changed. Father motioned me to sit, and Mother looked as though she wanted to serve me, but I knew she would wait for Jahzeel. Mother explained, "Jahzeel and Anna are returning from synagogue, but they are not coming directly; they wanted to walk through the vineyard together."

I nodded and asked, "How are the preparations coming for the wedding?" Father replied, "You recall that Anna's parents were with us for the miracle of the fish and the bread?" I nodded. Father went on, "Anna's parents were impressed with Jesus, and, like Anna, they believe he is Messiah." I realized where this was going but let Father continue. "Anna's father is a just man, and all the preparations for the wedding are complete, but he will not make the call of the wedding because he knows that Jahzeel does not believe."

I remained quiet for a time. Mother said softly, "Anna is broken over this. She believed they were b'shert—soulmates. They are still betrothed, and we hope Jahzeel will yet believe, but for now there is nothing."

I had to ask, "And Jahzeel?"

Father spoke reflectively: "You know he is a proud man. He believes Jesus is a prophet, though he still refuses to acknowledge the miracles we experienced. He respects Anna's father so does not argue but remains quiet."

"Does he ask questions? Perhaps I can answer . . ." Father shook his head emphatically.

I realized that my parents knew Jesus but did not know how to guide Jahzeel at this time. They did not understand that seeing miracles and accepting Jesus are not synonymous. For Anna's parents it had been easy; they saw and believed. For Anna herself, the transition in belief had come after nearly a year of questions. For Mother and Father there had been three years of questions and answers, and much prayer, until finally the miracles had convinced them. Yet for Jahzeel, even that had not been enough.

I looked compassionately at my sad parents and invited, "Let us pray together for Jahzeel. Unless he is moved by the Spirit of

God, as you were, he cannot accept Jesus." I bowed my head and proceeded, "Father, we are grateful to you for your holiness, and for hearing our prayer. We also know that you love us and that you love Jahzeel just as much. We ask that you help us to say words to Jahzeel that will honor you and that you will guide and direct us as we witness to your love of him. We know that your timing is without flaw and that you may not answer us at the time of our choosing, but we know that it is not your will that he would live a life apart from you. We want your will to be done. Amen."

My parents were quiet for a moment, after which Father said, "Thomas, I have never heard such a prayer except when Jesus blessed the loaves and fishes. You do not pray as the rabbis or the priests; you *talk* to God. You address him as Father, yet it does not seem inappropriate. What a beautiful prayer."

Mother echoed, "Yes, beautiful . . ." and began to weep.

Father asked, "Do you think you could teach us to pray like that?"

"Of course. Jesus taught us. Andrew and John said that the Baptist had taught them to pray in a similar manner, except that the Baptist did not address God as Father. You are right; it is not as the rabbis pray."

Mother dried her eyes. Within moments Jahzeel and Anna entered. Now I said another quiet prayer, dried my eyes quickly, and greeted them with a smile.

Jahzeel looked surprised to see me, but he reached out and took my hand. Anna smiled. Jahzeel exclaimed confidently, "I would welcome you home, but I see Father and Mother already have."

Mother went to get bread for us, and Father sat us all down. I knew not to ask about the wedding preparations so instead asked about the vineyard: "Jahzeel, how are the grapes?"

Jahzeel knew what I was doing and curtly replied, "The grapes are good. All is ready. The room is done. Anna's father wants us to wait for a while."

I said another short prayer, this one silent. Then I blurted out a verse that I hadn't even realized I knew:

Didymus

"The LORD is good to those who wait for him,
   to the person who seeks him."

I finished by commenting, "I don't know how I remembered it. It's from Lamentations. Sometimes verses come to me that I must have read long ago."

Jahzeel looked at me strangely for a moment and then began to smile. The smile started small but ended in a huge grin. Suddenly, Jahzeel was laughing out loud. Anna looked embarrassed, and my parents looked surprised. Jahzeel gave me a huge hug. By then Anna was laughing too, and Father and Mother were smiling a little uncertainly. When Jahzeel had caught his breath, he remarked, "Thomas, you really are becoming a rabbi. You think scripture." I began to laugh, too. This was my brother. He would always be my brother, and I would always be his brother. Nothing would change that.

As we quieted, I realized that his manner had given me permission to talk to him bluntly. I breathed yet another quick and silent prayer before addressing him: "Jahzeel, I know you as well as anyone does." Then, looking at Anna, I corrected myself with a smile, "Well, almost anyone." I went on, "Jahzeel, I know how stubborn you are, because I am just as stubborn as you are." I watched his face and could see that he was taking this well. "Jahzeel, you are in every way just as good as I am." His expression did not change. "What would it take for you to believe? You have witnessed miracles firsthand with the loaves and the fish, you have heard the words of Jesus in person, and you have experienced a miracle with the wine. Many times we have discussed Jesus's teaching and how it fits with scripture. I've answered all of the questions you have asked. There are many people who have believed much more quickly after hearing much less. What is it you still are looking for?"

The smile had not completely left Jahzeel's face. He was silent for a moment before reflecting, "I think you said that well, Thomas. I trust you. Do you think I am not good enough for God?"

I realized that his question was honest and deserved an honest answer. I offered up yet another brief prayer, this one the simplest of all: "Lord, help me." Then I addressed my brother: "Jahzeel, you know that I know you. I am not without flaw, and neither are you. We have all sinned. God is without flaw, and when we sin we separate ourselves from God. We are no better than Adam. When we sin, we ignore the tree of life but choose the other tree for ourselves. The sacrifices of the Law are covering for our sin because God cannot look upon us in our sin. None of us is 'good enough' for his just and holy eyes. The sacrifices are temporary coverings. Samuel asked, 'Does the Lord take pleasure in burnt offerings and sacrifices as much as in obeying the Lord? Look: to obey is better than sacrifice; to pay attention is better than the fat of rams.'

"You know all of that. Our sin is disobedience to God; no, it's worse—it's rebellion against God. But I have repented and been baptized, and my sins have been washed away. Jesus has forgiven me. In some way I still don't understand, I belong to him. He is my Lord. It isn't a matter of me being 'good enough.' I'm not, but he is good, and now I am his. When God looks at me, he sees me as belonging to Jesus. It's just as when we used to go to market. Everyone knew we belonged to Father, and if we delivered grapes, it was as though he had delivered the grapes."

Jahzeel was silent for a time. Then he answered, pleasantly, but without the smile, "You said that very well, Thomas. You are obviously learning a lot of facts . . . no, as you would say, truth. You have always been honest about this. I can see a real change in you. I see a change in Father and Mother, too, as well as in Anna and her parents. Being with Jesus has a good effect. Yet I still have questions. I have been studying Torah a bit lately, too. I thought I could successfully refute the arguments you have made. I could not. I talked to a rabbi, and he gave me questions that I have not heard the answers to."

"Say on, please."

"The Messiah must be a Son of David. How does this apply to Jesus?"

Didymus

"I assumed you had heard. Jesus's earthly father, Joseph ben Heli, is a descendent of David under the Law, through Nathan, the son of David. Remember, Solomon's line was cut off from being king when God cursed Jeconia. His mother, Mary, is a descendent of David by the flesh, through Solomon. I say 'earthly' father, as I believe Jesus was conceived by the Holy Spirit before the marriage of Joseph and Mary had been consummated. I know the Pharisees are claiming he is the bastard child of a Roman soldier, but there are many who will corroborate the truth I just gave you."

"I have heard that, too. I just wanted to confirm what you believe. I'm not agreeing, but your explanation would be within the realm of possibility. The next problem is that Jesus is from Nazareth; he is a Nazarene, not a Bethlehemite. The Messiah must come from Bethlehem, the city of David."

"No, his birth was in Bethlehem. Joseph went there with his wife to pay the Roman tax—for the census, as required over thirty years ago. There is ample proof. Herod believed it well enough to kill all the male babies in Bethlehem in order to be assured of destroying the newborn Messiah. That was after a group of the Magi came to Herod. They had seen the Messiah's star arise and had come looking for him. Herod, in fear, ordered the slaughter of these innocents. Joseph took his family to Egypt to escape. Even that fulfills scripture. Hosea tells us that God would call his son out of Egypt, and so he did. When Herod died, the family returned from Egypt to Joseph's place of work, Nazareth. Father and Mother, do you remember hearing of Herod killing all the babies in Bethlehem?"

Father confirmed sadly, "Yes. Herod was brutal. The rumor was even then that he was trying to kill the Messiah. He was terrified when the entourage of the Magi came. The whole of Jerusalem was in an uproar about it. He sought information from the chief priests and scribes as to the where and when of the birth. Herod believed the reports, even if the priest did not. I cannot imagine how they could live with themselves. The same with the soldiers who committed the deed."

Mother added, shuddering involuntarily, "Yes, it was horrible. All the suckling children—the little boys—were killed."

Jahzeel continued, "The rabbi said you would offer some justification for claiming Jesus was born in Bethlehem. Perhaps the rabbi had already heard all of this. I don't know how the scribes or the Magi would have expected the Messiah to be born at that time, but I won't argue this. I have a much harder question for you. I found something from Isaiah with the help of a rabbi whom I trust, and he says there is no answer. The rabbi himself gave the passage to me. The rabbis, of course, all know about Jesus, and most doubt him. It is well known among the learned that this passage is speaking about the Messiah, and it constitutes their strongest argument against Jesus as Messiah. I paid a scribe to write it out for me; you know how thrifty I am, so you know I am serious about this. Perhaps you are familiar with it. If you could find an answer for this, I think I would be compelled to believe. Here, let me begin it aloud:

'Who has believed what we have heard?
And to whom has the arm of the LORD been revealed?'"

Jahzeel paused and then interjected, "There is much more. Does this sound like your master—is this Jesus?"

Again, I said a silent prayer because I really didn't know all the answers. "I believe it is about Jesus. I will do my best. Let's look at it, part by part, if that's alright?"

"I hoped you would."

I took the scroll and began with the first two verses, explaining what I thought I understood:

"Who has believed what we have heard?
And to whom has the arm of the LORD been revealed?"

"Many do not believe, it is revealed to the common people, not just the learned."

Didymus

"He grew up before him like a young plant
　　and like a root out of dry ground."

"Jesus appeared in a land that is dry. We have not had a prophet,
except for John the Baptizer, in hundreds of years."

"He didn't have an impressive form
　　or majesty that we should look at him,
no appearance that we should desire him."

"You have seen him; he is not dressed like a majestic king. He
is no taller than an average man."

"He was despised and rejected by men,
　　a man of suffering who knew what sickness was."

"The Pharisees, Sadducees, and Herodians have rejected him."
Jahzeel interrupted, "That may be considered suffering,
but where is this sickness? He heals the sick. I don't see ful-
fillment."
Again, I prayed silently, and then admitted, "I'm not sure.
Perhaps it has not happened yet. Should we go on?"
Jahzeel nodded.

"He was like someone people turned away from;
　　he was despised, and we didn't value him."

"Some people do not value him; they want to kill him. They
do despise him."

"Yet he himself bore our sicknesses,
　　and he carried our pains;
but we in turn regarded him stricken,
　　struck down by God, and afflicted."

"I believe he does carry our pains and sicknesses, but I have no idea why God would strike him down."

I stopped and prayed yet again; what could I say? I did say, "Jahzeel, I do believe Jesus is Messiah, though I am no longer sure this passage speaks of Messiah."

My brother pressed, "Most rabbis are. I know that most Pharisees and Sadducees reject Jesus out of envy—but not all do. Unless he fulfills this entire passage, I cannot believe."

My heart was pounding in my chest. My confidence was shaken, and I prayed again. Then Father spoke slowly. "Jahzeel, I do not understand how Jesus will fulfill this passage, or even if this passage is clearly speaking of Messiah. I do know in my heart that Jesus is Messiah. I hope you can come to that point, too."

"I wish I could. If Jesus were to fulfill this passage, he would have to die. Then how could his kingdom stand?"

"Jahzeel, you realize that anyone, any messiah, would have to die to fulfill this passage?"

Jahzeel looked shocked, as though he had not considered that.

My head hung in shame. I was an Apostle; I should be ready. I spoke softly, "Jahzeel my brother, I do not know all that Jesus will do. I will have to ask to find out."

I was silent for some time. I knew I must go on, but did not know how.

XV

Carry On

Mother, in an attempt to counteract the awkwardness, spoke. "Here, dates and raisin cakes. Let us not argue this; instead, tell us what has happened since we last spoke."

As humbled as I was, unable to satisfactorily answer the questions of my brother, I realized that I could still testify to what Jesus was doing in my life and in the lives of those around me.

I did not have all the answers, but I did have testimony, so I began, "Before you came, Jesus led us to the region of Tyre and Sidon. He entered a house and did not want others to know it; yet it was impossible to keep his presence secret. A Canaanite woman from the vicinity came to him, crying out, 'Lord, Son of David, have mercy on me! My daughter is demon-possessed and suffering terribly.' Jesus did not answer a word. So, we came to him and urged him, 'Send her away, for she keeps crying out after us.' Jesus answered her then, 'I was sent only to the lost sheep of Israel.' The woman came and knelt before him. She entreated, 'Lord, help me!' He replied, 'It is not right to take the children's bread and toss it to the dogs.'"

Mother spoke up in concern: "That does not seem like the compassionate man I have been hearing about."

"The story is not over. The woman answered, 'Yes, Lord, but even the dogs eat the crumbs that fall from their master's table.' Jesus said to her, 'Woman, you have great faith! Your request is granted.' And her daughter was healed at that moment."

Mother mused, "I know the term he used for dog is that of a pet, but still, you know we have never considered Gentile people to be dogs. He has healed other Gentiles, and he did heal her daughter."

I went on, "Yes, there is still more to the story. Jesus was drawing out her faith; it had to become stronger than her pride, and it did. We left Tyre and went through Sidon, down again to the Sea of Galilee and into the region of Decapolis. There some people brought to him a man who was deaf and could hardly talk, and they begged Jesus to place his hand on him. Jesus took him aside from the crowd and put his fingers into the man's ears. Then he spit and touched the man's tongue. He looked up to heaven and with a deep sigh said to him, 'Be opened!' At that moment the man's ears were opened, his tongue was loosened, and he began to speak plainly. Jesus commanded them not to tell anyone, but the more he did so, the more people kept talking about it. People were overwhelmed and amazed. Some said, 'He has done all things well,' or 'He makes the deaf hear and the mute speak.' Great crowds came to him, bringing the lame, the blind, the crippled, the mute, and many others, and laid them at his feet, and he healed them. The people were amazed when they saw the mute speaking, the crippled made well, the lame walking, and the blind seeing. They praised the God of Israel."

Father noted, "He seems to prefer the praise going to God. This is good."

"His intent is to glorify the Father. During these days, just before you came, even in this mostly Gentile area another large crowd gathered. People came from as far away as Galilee. Since they had nothing to eat, Jesus called us to him and said, 'I have compassion for these people; they have already been with me three days and have nothing to eat. If I send them home hungry, they will collapse on the way, because some of them have come a long distance.' We asked, 'But where in this remote place can anyone get enough bread to feed them?' Jesus replied with a question of his own: 'How many loaves do you have?' We replied, 'Seven.' Jesus told the crowd to sit down on the ground. You saw the rest.

Didymus

"When he had taken the seven loaves and given thanks, he broke them and gave them to us to distribute to the people, which we did. They had a few small musht, as well; he gave thanks for them also and told us to pass them out. The people ate and were satisfied. Afterward, we picked up seven basketsful of broken pieces that were left over. About four thousand were present. After he sent them away, he got into the boat with us to go on to the region of Dalmanutha. You may not have seen this, but the Pharisees and Sadducees had also followed all the way there. They came to Jesus and tested him by asking him to show them a sign from heaven."

Father asked, incredulous, "The feeding was not sign enough?"

I shrugged. "Jesus replied, 'When evening comes, you say, "It will be fair weather, for the sky is red," and in the morning, "Today it will be stormy, for the sky is overcast." You know how to interpret the appearance of the sky, but you cannot interpret signs of the times. A wicked and adulterous generation looks for a sign, but none will be given tit except the sign of Jonah.' Then he left them and got back into the boat to cross to the other side. As the crowd was dispersing, but before we left, Jesus seemed to be looking at one small group, smiling. I looked closely in that direction. It was *you!*"

Father, smilingly, "Yes, we saw and realized. You looked very happy."

"I was ecstatic! Jesus knew it was you; that's why he was looking your way, smiling. I thought that perhaps you might see him in a local synagogue, but I did not expect you there. When I left you, we took a boat across the sea. I fell asleep briefly but was awakened by commotion. Despite all that bread we had gathered up, we had left the baskets there, all but one loaf! We were a dozen hungry and tired men in a boat far from shore."

Father chuckled, followed by all of us. It was clear that we apostles were not without flaw, and that detail broke the tension in the room. I went on, "Jesus said to us, 'Be careful. Be on your guard against the yeast of the Pharisees and Sadducees.' We discussed this with one another and decided he had said this because we had no bread. Jesus asked us, 'Why are you talking about having no bread? Do you still not see or understand? Are your hearts hardened? Do you have eyes but fail to see, and ears but fail to hear? And don't you remember? When I broke the five loaves for the five thousand, how many basketsful of pieces did you pick up?' We replied, 'Twelve.' Jesus asked, 'And when I broke the seven loves for the four thousand, how many basketsful of pieces did you pick up?' We answered, 'Seven.' Jesus asked us, 'Do you still not understand? How is it you don't understand that I was not talking to you about bread? Be on your guard against the yeast of the Pharisees and Sadducees.' Then we understood that he was not telling us to guard against the yeast used to make bread but against the teaching of the Pharisees and Sadducees."

Father interjected, "All of you must have been tired. The yeast of the Pharisees and Sadducees must be their corrupt teaching or life. Even I get that."

"Yes, I do get it now. We came near Bethsaida, and some people brought a blind man and begged Jesus to touch him. He took the blind man by the hand and led him outside the village. When he had spit on the man's eyes, and put his hands on him, Jesus asked, 'Do you see anything?' He looked up and said, 'I see people; they look like trees walking around.' Once again Jesus put his hands on the man's eyes. Then his eyes were opened, his sight was restored, and he saw everything clearly. Jesus sent him home, saying, 'Don't even go into the village.'"

Jahzeel acknowledged, "The miracles I believe. He is a good man. A good prophet."

"He makes great claims. When we neared the area of Caesarea Philippi, Jesus asked us, 'Who do people say the Son of Man is?' We replied, 'Some say John the Baptist, others Elijah, still others, Jeremiah or one of the prophets.'"

Jahzeel pointed out, "See, his disciples know his limits."

"Wait, Jahzeel. Jesus asked us, 'And you; who do you say that I am?' Simon Peter answered first, 'You are the Messiah, the Son of the living God.' Jesus replied, 'Blessed are you, Simon bar

Didymus

Jonah, for this was not revealed to you by flesh and blood, but by my Father in heaven. I tell you that you are Peter. On this rock I will build my church, and the gates of Hades will not overcome it. I will give you the keys of the kingdom of heaven; whatever you bind on earth will be bound in heaven, and whatever you loose on earth will be loosed in heaven.' Then he ordered us not to tell anyone that he was the Messiah."

Jahzeel, with a twinkle in his eye, asked, "He ordered you not to tell anyone—and yet you tell us?"

I smiled back. "Yes, I know. But I had *already* told you some time ago that he was the Messiah."

"Yes, you had. What is this 'church' he speaks of? That sounds like a group of leaders of a community of some sort. Are these new plans?"

"I don't know. The word seems to signify a group, or community leaders. Perhaps we are becoming that group."

Father smiled, too. "Jesus plays with words; the name Peter, as we know, means a little stone. The rock on which this church, this group, is to be built is a cornerstone he calls a large rock. Didn't Isaiah say, 'I lay in Zion a stone for a foundation, a tried stone, a precious cornerstone, a sure foundation'? Jesus would be that cornerstone that Peter had just confessed.

"Yes. Everything is built on Jesus, or on those who know Jesus as Lord. He is clearly the cornerstone, but the church is to be built upon this faith, this knowledge, and this confession, as proof of this faith. Abraham believed the Lord, and God credited it to him as righteousness. The key to Abraham's righteousness was not what he did; it was his faith, his willingness to believe God. Peter confessed his belief in God and has that same relationship. Abraham failed God at times, as does Peter. But our relationship with God is not based on what we do; it is on our faith in God—a God who will never fail. We can all have that same faith. If we pass on to others this faith, we allow people to see heaven. If we do not . . . No, we simply must. But this must become *their own faith*, not simply a parroting of our statement of faith."

Father asked, "Gates are used to protect; is he saying that his church will defeat Hades?"

"I don't know exactly how it works. The meaning would be that those who confess him will defeat death."

Jahzeel asked, "How can he make such a claim, given what we just read in Isaiah? He would have to be ignorant of the passage."

Father took this to its logical conclusion: "If he were ignorant of the passage, neither could he be a prophet."

I explained, "He knew the passage. Peter was not the first to make such a confession; Nathaniel made a similar confession when he first met Jesus. Even before that, John the Baptizer confessed him, and from time to time all of us apostles have confessed him. The difference in this case was, according to Jesus, that *the Father in heaven* had revealed this to Peter. It was this communion with the Father that made the difference. That belief, and its confession, must come this way, though the Spirit. From this time Jesus began to tell us that he would go to Jerusalem and suffer many things at the hands of the elders, the chief priests, and the teachers of the Law, and that he must be killed and on the third day be raised to life."

Father, sighing, "Amazing, perhaps he will yet fulfill the Isaiah scripture . . ."

To which Jahzeel countered, "With all due respect, Father, I can't believe that."

I continued, "Peter didn't like it, either; he took Jesus aside and began to rebuke him: 'Never, Lord! This shall never happen to you!' We all felt that way, but Peter was the one who spoke out. Jesus turned and said to Peter, 'Get behind me, Satan! You are a stumbling block to me; you do not have in mind the concerns of God, but merely human concerns.'"

Mother pointed out, "Simon has a big mouth. He should not have rebuked the one he calls his Lord."

"No, Mother, he should not have. Jesus had just credited Peter's confession moments earlier, and now Peter tried to lecture him. Jesus called the nearby crowd to him, along with us disciples, he said, 'Whoever wants to be my disciple must deny themselves and take up their cross and follow me. For whoever wants to save their life will lose it, but whoever loses their life for me and for the gospel will save it. What good is it for someone to gain the whole world and yet forfeit their soul? Or what can anyone give in exchange for their soul? If anyone is ashamed of me and my words in this adulterous and sinful generation, the Son of Man will be ashamed of them when he comes in his Father's glory with the holy angels.'"

Jahzeel commented, "Gospel? Good News? Losing one's life for Good News?"

Anna finally spoke: "I am not ashamed."

I agreed, "He would be proud of you, Anna. Jesus said to us, 'Truly I tell you, some who are standing here will not taste death before they see that the kingdom of God has come with power.'"

Jahzeel asked, "And when will this kingdom come? Will he overthrow the Romans?"

I replied carefully, "I don't think that's what he meant. I'm still not sure. After six days Jesus took with him Peter, James, and John and led them up a high mountain by themselves. We were not told what they did."

Mother inquired, "Why were you not chosen?"

"I don't know. Perhaps I was too tired; the mountain was high. Perhaps they were the only ones with enough faith. When they rejoined the nine of us, there was a large crowd around us, and the teachers of the Law were arguing with us. As soon as all the people saw Jesus, they were overwhelmed with wonder and ran to greet him. Jesus asked us, 'What are you arguing with them about?' A man from the crowd answered, 'Teacher, I brought you my son, who is possessed by a spirit that has robbed him of speech. Whenever it seizes him, it throws him to the ground. He foams at the mouth, gnashes his teeth, and becomes rigid. I asked your disciples to drive out the spirit, but they could not.'"

Jahzeel, with a hint of sarcasm, "Your powers are waning?"

Father corrected him: "Jahzeel, you know Thomas has never claimed powers, but only that God has worked though him."

Jahzeel conceded, "You are right, Father. Thomas, I apologize. I should not make light of this."

"It is alright, brother, we were indeed failing. It was embarrassing to say that we could do something by the power of Jesus but yet failed. His power had not failed—we had. Jesus said, 'You unbelieving generation, how long shall I stay with you? How long shall I put up with you? Bring the boy to me.' They brought him. When the spirit saw Jesus, it immediately threw the boy into a convulsion. He fell to the ground and rolled around, foaming at the mouth. Jesus asked the boy's father, 'How long has he been like this?' He answered, 'From childhood, it has often thrown him into fire or water to kill him. But if you can do anything, take pity on us and help us.' Jesus repeated, '*If* you can?' Everything is possible for one who believes.' Immediately the boy's father exclaimed, 'I do believe; help me overcome my unbelief!'"

Jahzeel spoke seriously. "This is a man like me. He wants to believe but has doubts so great that he realizes they come from a spirit of unbelief."

I nodded. "When Jesus saw that a crowd was running to the scene, he rebuked the impure spirit. 'You deaf and mute spirit,' he said. 'I command you, come out of him and never enter him again.' The spirit shrieked, convulsed him violently, and came out. The boy looked so much like a corpse that many said, 'He's dead.' But Jesus took him by the hand and lifted him to his feet, and he stood up."

Father commented, "I feel the pain of this father—and the joy."

I continued, "After Jesus had gone indoors, we asked him privately, 'Why couldn't we drive it out?' Jesus replied, 'Because you have so little faith. Truly I tell you, if you have faith as small as a mustard seed, you can say to this mountain, "Move from here to there," and it will move. Nothing will be impossible for you. This kind can come out only by prayer.'"

Jahzeel asked, "Did Jesus pray?"

"Not that I could tell. When we had gone from there, we passed through Galilee. Jesus did not want anyone to know where we were, because he was teaching only us. He told us, 'The Son of Man is going to be delivered into the hands of men. They will kill him, and after three days he will rise.' We did not understand what he meant and were too afraid to ask him about what he was telling us."

Father observed, "So, perhaps you did not know the answers to the Isaiah passage because you were afraid to ask?"

I replied sheepishly, "Perhaps. After we arrived in Capernaum, the collectors of the two-drachma temple tax came to Peter and asked, 'Doesn't your teacher pay the temple tax?' Peter replied, 'He does.' When Peter came into his house, Jesus asked him, 'What do you think, Simon? From whom do kings of the earth collect duty and taxes, from their own children of from others?' Peter answered, 'From others.' Jesus answered him, 'Then the children are exempt. But so that we may not cause offense, go to the lake and throw out your line. Take the first fish you catch; open its mouth, and you will find a four-drachma coin. Take it and give it to them for my tax and yours.'"

Jahzeel asked, his inflection rising, "He claims to be higher than the temple?"

"He does, and I believe him. While we were in the house, Jesus asked us, 'What were you arguing about on the road?' We kept quiet because on the way we had argued about who among us was the greatest."

Mother stated, to no one's surprise, "You know whom I think is greatest."

I smiled. "Mother, I love you too, but it's all about Jesus. Jesus sat down and called us, saying, 'Anyone who wants to be first must be the very last, and the servant of all. Suppose one of you has a servant plowing or looking after the sheep. Will he say to the servant when he comes in from the field, "Come along now and sit down to eat"? Rather he will say, "Prepare my supper, get yourself ready and wait on me while I eat and drink; after that you may eat and drink." Will he thank the servant because he did what he was told to do? So, you also, when you have done everything you were told to do, should say, "We are unworthy servants; we have only done our duty."' Jesus then called a little child to him and placed the child among us. He said, 'Truly I tell you, unless you change and become like little children, you will never enter the kingdom of heaven. Therefore, whoever takes the lowly position of this child is the greatest in the kingdom of heaven.'"

Jahzeel protested, "That can't work. Someone has to be in charge—and not a child."

"Being in charge is not the point. Being in charge is not the same as being the greatest. Jesus continued, 'Whoever welcomes one of these little children in my name welcomes me; and whoever welcomes me does not welcome me but the one who sent me. If anyone causes one of these little ones who believe in me to stumble, it would be better for them to have a large millstone hung around their neck and to be drowned in the depths of the sea. See that you do not despise one of these little ones. For I tell you that their angels in heaven always see the face of my Father in heaven.'"

Anna stated, "Jesus loves children. I am glad, for I do, too."

I continued, "Yes, he does. Jesus went on, 'What do you think? If a man owns a hundred sheep, and one of them wanders away, will he not leave the ninety-nine on the hills and go to look for the one that wandered off? And if he finds it, truly I tell you, he is happier about that one sheep than about the ninety-nine that did not wander off. In the same way your Father in heaven is not willing that any of these little ones should perish.'"

Jahzeel observed, "The ninety-nine are of greater value; looking for one, he runs the risk of losing several."

Father corrected, "This shepherd cares for each one; that is the point. All have great value to him."

"Yes, Father. Jesus gave another warning: 'Woe to the world because of the things that cause people to stumble! Such things must come, but woe to the person through whom they come! If your hand or your foot causes you to stumble, cut it off and throw it away. It is better for you to enter life maimed or crippled than to have two hands or two feet and be thrown into eternal fire. And if your eye causes you to stumble, pluck it out. It is better for you to enter the kingdom of God with one eye than to have two eyes and be thrown into hell, where:

> "The worms that eat them do not die,
>   and the fire is not quenched.""""

Father shuddered. "What a terrible place!"

"Going there is a choice. No one has to go there."

Jahzeel asked, "But the choice! An eye?"

Father pointed out, "Temptation begins with the eye . . ."

I agreed. "Father, that is so true. If you are not tempted, you will not sin."

Jahzeel commented, "Still, he simply means it's very serious."

I continued, "I agree. Jesus went on, 'Everyone will be salted with fire. Salt is good, but if it loses its saltiness, how can you make it salty again? Have salt among yourselves, and be at peace with each other.' Jesus had talked about salt before, on the mount."

Father added, "He also wants peace for us with each other. A few years ago we had no peace between you two."

Mother seconded, "That is for sure."

"It's true. But we all still have tempers that get out of control. John told Jesus, 'Teacher, we saw someone driving out demons in your name and we told him to stop, because he was not one of us.' Jesus said, 'Do not stop him. No one who does a miracle in my name can in the next moment say anything bad about me, for whoever is not against us is for us. Truly I tell you, anyone who gives you a cup of water in my name because you belong to the Messiah will certainly not lose their reward.'"

Mother reflected, "That sounds too small to expect any reward."

I continued the thought, "Yes, but God gives a reward because the act was done in Jesus's name, or according to his will."

Father, seeking clarification, "It implies not just action, but intent?"

"Yes, it does. Jesus went on, 'If your brother or sister sins, go and point out their fault, just between the two of you. If they listen to you, you have won them over. But if they will not listen, take one or two others along, so that "every matter may be established by the testimony of two or three witnesses." If they still refuse to listen, tell it to the church, and if they refuse to listen even to the church, treat them as you would a pagan or a tax collector.'"

Jahzeel asked, "*Church?* You used that term before. What is this? Jesus will have a called-out organization? Called out from what? The world? That does not sound like any part of Judaism."

I tried to explain as best I could. "He seems to be describing how the organization will work. We know the rules of the synagogue, but those rules are not really part of the Law."

Father commented, "It sounds as though this church is in the future, like the kingdom he says is coming. Will this be part of the kingdom?"

"I really don't know. Jesus spoke more on power: 'Truly I tell you, whatever you bind on earth will be bound in heaven, and whatever you loose on earth will be loosed in heaven. Again, truly I tell you that if two of you on earth agree about anything they ask for, it will be done for them by my Father in heaven. For where two or three gather in my name, there am I with them.'"

Father exclaimed, "What power he gives, but only to groups of at least two or three! The testimony of two or three is required in the Law, and this is power based on the same sort of thing. But power to do what?"

Again, I admitted, "I don't really know yet. Before I could ask, Peter asked Jesus about forgiveness: 'Lord, how many times shall I forgive my brother or sister who sins against me? Up to seven times?' Jesus answered, 'I tell you, not seven times, but seventy times seven times. If your brother or sister sins against you, rebuke them, and if they repent, forgive them. Even if they sin against you seven times in a day and seven times come back to you saying, "I repent," you must forgive them.'"

Jahzeel commented, "It sounds as though he is *constantly* requiring forgiveness."

Didymus

Father corrected his logic: "Not quite—the offender must repent, and then the forgiveness must be given."

I agreed. "Yes, Father. He gave an example in a parable. He said, 'Therefore, the kingdom of heaven is like a king who wanted to settle accounts with his servants. As he began the settlement, a man who owed him ten thousand bags of gold was brought to him. Since he was not able to pay, the master ordered that he and his wife and his children and all that he had be sold to repay the debt. At this, the servant fell on his knees before him saying: "Be patient with me, and I will pay back everything." The servant's master took pity on him, canceled the debt, and let him go. But when the servant went out, he found one of his fellow servants who owed him a hundred silver coins, grabbed him and began to choke him, demanding, "Pay back what you own me!" His fellow servant fell to his knees, begging, "Be patient and I will pay it back." He refused, and had the man thrown into prison until he could pay the debt. When the other servants saw what had happened, they were outraged and told their master everything. The master called the servant in. "You wicked servant; I canceled all that debt of yours because you begged me to. Shouldn't you have had mercy on your fellow servant as I had on you?" The master handed him to the jailer to be tortured until he paid back all he owed. This is how my heavenly Father will treat each of you unless you forgive your brother or sister from your heart.'"

Jahzeel quipped, "Sounds like a Pharisee. They don't forgive *or* forget."

With a smile, I went on, "That brought us up to the feast of Tabernacles. We continued to follow Jesus as he taught and performed miracles, staying away from Jerusalem until the Feast was near. His half-brothers taunted him about staying away; they said, 'Leave Galilee and go to Judea, so that your disciples there may see the works you do. No one who wants to become a public figure acts in secret. Since you are doing these things, show yourself to the world.' His brothers have not believed in him. He told them, 'My time is not yet here; for you any time will do. The world cannot hate you, but it hates me because I testify that its works are evil. You go to the festival. I cannot now go to the festival because my time has not yet fully come.' At that time, he stayed in Galilee."

Mother commented, "It sounds as though Jesus's brothers don't trust him."

"They don't. I know that bothers him. After his brothers had left for the festival, he went also, not publicly but in secret. At the festival, the Jewish leaders were watching for Jesus and asking, 'Where is he?' Among the crowds there was widespread whispering about him. Some said, 'He is a good man.' Others said, 'No, he deceives the people.' But none said anything publicly about him for fear of the leaders."

Father stated, "There is much talk everywhere about him, some telling the truth and others telling opposing stories out of envy."

I nodded and went on, "The leaders are getting angrier. Jesus did not go to the temple courts to teach until halfway through the festival. The Jews there were amazed and asked, 'How did this man get such learning without having been taught?' Jesus answered, 'My teaching is not my own. It comes from the one who sent me. Anyone who chooses to do the will of God will find out whether I speak on my own. Whoever speaks on their own does so to gain personal glory, but he who seeks the glory of the one who sent him is a man of truth; there is nothing false about him. Has not Moses given you the Law? Yet not one of you keeps the Law. Why are you trying to kill me?'"

Mother asked, anxious as always about this issue, "Are you safe? Is he safe?"

I replied, "Yes. He knows the crowd better than they know themselves."

Father commented, "Yet it is hard to reason with a crowd."

Mother went on, "And yet he cares for each of the people in the crowd. Look how he fed us."

I continued, "The Jews responded, 'You are demon-possessed. Who is trying to kill you?' Jesus answered, 'I did one miracle, and you are all amazed. Yet because Moses gave you circumcision

Didymus

[though actually it did not come from Moses but from the patriarchs], you circumcise a boy on the Sabbath. Now if a boy can be circumcised on the Sabbath so that the Law may not be broken, why are you angry with me for healing a man's whole body on the Sabbath? Stop judging by mere appearances, but instead judge correctly.'"

Father remarked, "Yes, they do circumcision even on a Sabbath, if it is the eighth day after the birth, in order to keep the Law, even though it is work that breaks the Law. Jesus's logic is without flaw, but they will not listen."

Jahzeel pointed out, "Some are just looking for a problem."

I agreed. "You are right, Jahzeel. Some of the people from Jerusalem began to ask, 'Isn't this the man they are trying to kill? Here he is, speaking publicly, and they are not saying a word to him. Have the authorities really concluded that he is the Messiah? But we know where this man is from; when the Messiah comes, no one will know where he is from.' Jesus, still in the temple courts, teaching, cried out, 'Yes, you know me, and you know where I am from. I am not here on my own authority, but he who sent me is true. You do not know him, but I know him because I am from him, and he sent me.' At this they tried to seize him, but no one could lay a hand on him because his hour had not yet come. Still, many in the crowd believed in him. They asked, 'When the Messiah comes, will he perform more signs than this man?'"

Jahzeel mused, "There are always a few honest people."

"Yes. Yet when the Pharisees heard the crowd whispering such things about him, they and the chief priests sent temple guards to arrest him. Jesus said, 'I am with you for only a short time, and then I am going to the one who sent me. You will look for me, but you will not find me; and where I am, you cannot come.' The Jews said to one another, 'Where does this man intend to go that we cannot find him? Will he go where our people live scattered among the Greeks, and teach the Greeks? What did he mean when he said, "You will look for me, but you will not find me" and "where I am, you cannot come"?'"

Father noted, "He drives them crazy with what they don't understand."

I acknowledged, "Yes, but even I don't understand some things. On the last and greatest day of the festival, Jesus stood and said in a loud voice, 'Let anyone who is thirsty come to me and drink. Whoever believes in me, as Scripture has said, rivers of living water will flow from within them.'"

Jahzeel remarked, "This must be figurative speech. Water cannot flow from him in that way."

"It is figurative. When some heard his words, they said, 'Surely this man is the Prophet' and others, 'He is the Messiah.' Still others asked, 'How can the Messiah come from Galilee? Does not scripture say that the Messiah will come from David's descendants from Bethlehem, the town where David lived?' The people were divided because of Jesus. Some wanted to seize him, but no one could lay a hand on him."

Father stated, "He is protected from them by God."

"Yes. Finally, the temple guards went back to the chief priests and the Pharisees without Jesus."

Jahzeel commented, "That must have made them even more upset."

"It did. As people went home, we went to the Mount of Olives."

Mother sighed, remembering, "A beautiful place. A good place to rest."

"It is. And we did for a time. At dawn we returned to the temple courts. People gathered, and he sat down to teach. The teachers of the Law and the Pharisees brought in a woman caught in adultery. They made her stand before the group and said to Jesus, 'Teacher, this woman was caught in the act of adultery. In the Law, Moses commands us to stone such a woman. What do you say?'"

Jahzeel stated, "That was a trap."

Father agreed, "Yes, but if they know the Law and caught the woman, they should have caught the man, too. He, too, should be stoned, according to the Law."

"Yes, it was a trap," I agreed. "They let the man go free. Perhaps he was even one of them. They didn't care about the Law, just about getting Jesus. When they tried to trap him, Jesus simply bent down and started to write on the ground with his finger. They kept questioning him, so he straightened up and told them, 'Let any one of you who is without sin be the first to throw a stone at her.' Again, he stooped and wrote on the ground. When the accusers heard, they began to go away, one at a time, the oldest to the youngest, until only Jesus was left, with the woman. Jesus straightened up and asked her, 'Woman, where are they? Has no one condemned you?' She answered, 'No one, sir.' Jesus replied, 'Then neither do I condemn you. Go now and leave your life of sin.' We were all amazed at the ease with which Jesus had handled the accusers."

Father stated with satisfaction, "Jesus handled them perfectly."

And Jahzeel asked, "What did Jesus write?"

I answered as best I could. "I was too far away to see. Perhaps names? Or sins? Whatever it was, they felt guilty."

Father agreed, "By doing it quietly, he got the right result without anger or confrontation."

"Yes. When Jesus was again in front of the people, he said, 'I am the light of the world. Whoever follows me will never walk in darkness but will have the light of life.' The Pharisees immediately attacked him, saying, 'You appear as your own witness; your testimony is not valid.' Jesus answered, 'Even if I testify on my own behalf, my testimony is true, for I know where I came from and where I am going. You have no idea where I come from or where I am going. You judge by human standards; I pass judgment on no one. Yet if I do judge, my decisions are true, because I am not alone. I stand with the Father, who sent me. In your own Law it is written that the testimony of two witnesses is true. I am one who testifies for myself; my other witness is the Father, who sent me.' They sneered at him, 'Where is your father?' Jesus replied, 'You do not know me or my Father. If you knew me, you would know my Father also.' He spoke all this while teaching in the temple courts near the places of the offerings, yet no one seized him, because his hour had not yet come."

Jahzeel spoke thoughtfully. "Their logic was flawed; you can appear as your own witness as long as you have other witnesses in agreement with you. In fact, you would be expected to witness for yourself."

Father observed, "Jesus knows the Law better than they do. He uses it against them. They would have seized him if God had not forbidden them."

I continued, "Again Jesus said to them, 'I am going away, and you will look for me, and you will die in your sin. Where I go, you cannot come.' The Jews asked, 'Will he kill himself? Is that why he says, "Where I go, you cannot come"?' Jesus simply continued, 'You are from below; I am from above. You are of this world; I am not of this world. I told you that you would die in your sins; if you do not believe that I am he, you will indeed die in your sins.' They asked, 'Who are you?' Jesus replied, 'I have been telling you from the beginning, I have much to say in judgment of you. But he who sent me is trustworthy, and what I have heard from him I tell the world.' They did not understand that he was telling them about his Father. So, Jesus said, 'When you have lifted up the Son of Man, then you will know that I am he and that I do nothing on my own but speak just what the Father has taught me. The one who sent me is with me; he has not left me alone, for I always do what pleases him.' Even then, as he was speaking, many believed on him."

Father remarked, "He is careful in his use of words. They cannot use them against him, even though they know he is speaking against them."

I agreed, "Yes, but he is speaking to many Jews who will believe. Jesus said, 'If you hold to my teaching, you are really my disciples. Then you will know the truth, and the truth will set you free.'"

Jahzeel surmised, "So, there is a test of discipleship. It is obeying his teaching, which he says will set you free. Free from what? Death?"

I answered, "Eventually, yes. But for now, it's simply free from sin. Before Jesus could elaborate, the other Jews answered him, 'We are Abraham's descendants and have never been slaves of anyone. How can you say we shall be set free?'"

Father shook his head. "That is simply not true. Our people were slaves for hundreds of years in Egypt, as well as in the times of the judges and of the dispersions. They know better. To say this, they must be panicking."

"That's all true, Father. We are Abraham's descendants in the flesh, but all Jews know that not all of Abraham's descendants were children of promise. Jesus explained to them what freedom is: 'Very truly I tell you, everyone who sins is a slave to sin. Now a slave has no permanent place in the family, but a son belongs to it forever. So, if the Son sets you free, you will be free indeed. I know that you are Abraham's descendants. Yet you are looking for a way to kill me, because you have no room for my word. I am telling you what I have seen in the Father's presence, and you are doing what you have heard from your father.' In anger the other Jews answered him, 'Abraham is our father!'"

Father clarified, "They may be physical descendants, but they don't act like children of promise."

"They don't. Jesus replied to them, 'If you were Abraham's children, then you would do what Abraham did. As it is, you are looking for a way to kill me, a man who has told you the truth that I heard from God. Abraham did not do such things. You are doing the works of your own father.'"

Father commented, "Abraham may not have been without flaw, but he did not plot murder."

"They were so angry! They answered him again, 'We are not illegitimate children; the only father we have is God himself.'"

Father shook his head, "They also mention illegitimacy; they have researched Jesus's background and know that he was born before his parents were married. They see his conception as from an illegitimate relationship, not as a miracle. If they know this detail, then they also know that he was born in Bethlehem, not Nazareth. They know that, and yet they will not admit it because they know Messiah was prophesied to be born in Bethlehem."

Jahzeel commented, "They had just said God was their father!"

"They had. Isn't that amazing? They would stone Jesus for say-ing what they themselves had just said! How hypocritical! Jesus told them, 'If God were your father, you would love me, for I have come here from God. I have not come on my own. God sent me. Why is my language not clear to you? Because you are unable to hear what I say. You belong to your father, the devil, and you want to carry out your father's desires. He was a murderer from the beginning, not holding to the truth, for there is no truth in him. When he lies, he speaks his native language, for he is a liar and the father of lies. Yet because I tell the truth, you do not believe me! Can any of you prove me guilty of sin? If I am telling the truth, why don't you believe me? Whoever belongs to God hears what God says. The reason you do not hear is that you do not belong to God.'"

Jahzeel echoed, "He called them children *of the devil*? They will kill him!"

Mother reiterated her ever-present theme, "Are you sure you are safe?"

I looked calmly at her and replied, "I'm safe enough. The Jews were unable to answer him, so they continued to ridicule him, asking, 'Aren't we right in saying that you are a Samaritan and demon-possessed?' Jesus answered again, 'I am not possessed by a demon, but I honor my Father and you dishonor me. I am not seeking glory for myself; but there is one who seeks it, and he is the judge. Very truly I tell you, whoever obeys my word will never see death.'"

Father, incredulous, exclaimed, "Even now he offers them life!"

"He does. They don't even hear it. At that they answered, 'Now we know that you are demon-possessed! Abraham died and so did the prophets, yet you say that whoever obeys your word will never taste death. Are you greater than our father Abraham? He died, and so did the prophets. Who do you think you are?'"

Father stated, "They understand something of the claims, but they will not accept."

Didymus

"No, they will not accept. Jesus answered again, 'If I glorify myself, my glory means nothing. My Father, whom you claim as your God, is the one who glorifies me. Though you do not know him, I know him. If I said I did not, I would be a liar like you, but I do know him and obey his word. Your father Abraham rejoiced at the thought of seeing my day; he saw it and was glad.' Shocked, they answered, 'You are not yet fifty years old, and you have seen Abraham?' Jesus answered, 'Very truly I tell you, before Abraham was born, I AM!'"

Jahzeel exclaimed, "He is claiming to be God."

I acknowledged, "I believe he claims to be God—and that he claims rightly. They quickly took up stones to stone him, but Jesus slipped away from the temple grounds. They were left holding their stones!"

Father visualized, "He escapes. Here they are with stones, and he goes out among them."

I went on, "That was the last confrontation that day. On the Sabbath, Jesus came to a man blind from birth. We asked him, 'Rabbi, who sinned, this man or his parents, that he was born blind?'"

Mother commiserated, "The poor family! All those years being thought of as sinners. Or worse—that their son sinned before he was born."

Father remarked, "I have heard that Greeks believe that a man exists and could sin before he is born, but Jews should reject such rubbish."

I continued, "Jesus replied, 'Neither this man nor his parents sinned, but this happened so that the works of God might be displayed in him. As long as it is day, we must do the works of him who sent me. Night is coming when no one can work. While I am in the world, I am the light of the world.' After explaining this, Jesus spit on the ground, made some mud with the saliva, and put it on the man's eyes. He told the man, 'Go, wash in the Pool of Siloam.'"

Jahzeel interjected, "I have heard of such healings from Jesus. You did some . . . or God did some through you—is that right?"

"Yes, God did some though me, but this was right in the city. The man went and washed and returned home seeing. The neighbors of the man asked, 'Isn't this the man who used to sit and beg?' Other said, 'No, he only looks like him.' The man insisted, 'I am the man.' They all asked, 'How were your eyes opened?' He replied, 'The man Jesus made mud and put it on my eyes and told me to go the Siloam and wash. I did, and now I can see.' They asked him, 'Where is this man?' and he replied, 'I don't know.' People brought the man to the Pharisees. They asked him how he had received his sight. He said, 'He put mud on my eyes, and I washed, and now I see.' Some of the Pharisees said, 'This man is not from God, for he does not keep the Sabbath.' Others asked, 'How can a sinner perform such signs?' They were divided, so they turned to the man, asking, 'What have you to say about him? It was your eyes he opened.' The man replied, 'He is a prophet.'"

Father observed, "See, there are some people open to truth."

"Yes, there are. Most Pharisees still did not believe that the man had been blind and had received his sight, so they sent for the man's parents. They asked, 'Is this your son that you say was born blind? How is it that now he can see?' They answered, 'We know he is our son, and we know he was born blind. How he can see, or who opened his eyes, we don't know. He is of age, ask him. He can speak for himself.' His parents were afraid because of the Jewish leaders, who had already declared that anyone who acknowledged that Jesus was the Messiah would be put out of the synagogue."

Father added, "They had just talked about the testimony of two or three witnesses; here they had them and still didn't believe!"

Mother empathized, "That poor family. The dishonor of a son born blind was removed, but the leaders were now threatening them with removal. How cruel!"

I confirmed softly, "Yes, Mother, you have a tender heart. They have no heart. Again, the Pharisees summoned the man and declared, 'Give glory to God by telling the truth; we know this man is a sinner.'"

Didymus

Father asked, "How could he give glory to God without giving it to the one used by God to do the miracle?"

I smiled, acknowledging, "He couldn't. He replied, 'Whether he is a sinner or not, I don't know. One thing I do know; I was blind but now I see!' Then they asked him, 'What did he do to you? How did he open your eyes?' He answered, 'I have told you already and you did not listen. Why do you want to hear it again? Do you want to become his disciples, too?'"

Father remarked, "I think he was ridiculing them!"

"If so, he most certainly paid a price for it. They yelled insults at him. accusing, 'You are this fellow's disciple! We are disciples of Moses! We know that God spoke to Moses, but as for this fellow, we don't even know where he comes from.'"

Jahzeel confirmed, "They have spread rumors that Jesus is the illegitimate child of a Roman soldier. That's ridiculous; Jesus looks Jewish, and they know it."

I went on, "The man answered, 'Now this is remarkable! You don't know where he comes from, yet he opened my eyes. We know that God does not listen to sinners. He listens to the godly person. Nobody has ever heard of opening the eyes of a man born blind. If this man were not from God, he could do nothing.'"

Father stated with evident satisfaction, "There could be no answer to that. Only a prophet working through God could do that."

I agreed, "No, there is no reasonable answer, but they still tried. To this they replied, 'You were steeped in sin at birth; how dare you lecture us!' They had him thrown out."

Mother observed ruefully, "They won't let him escape the stigma of having been born blind."

"They won't. Jesus found the man they had thrown out and asked him, 'Do you believe in the Son of Man?' He answered, 'Who is he, sir? Tell me so that I may believe in him.' Jesus replied, 'You have now seen him; in fact, he is the one speaking with you.' The man said, 'Lord, I believe,' and worshipped him. Jesus said, 'For judgment I have come into this world, so that the blind will see and those who see will become blind.'"

Father, seeking verification, "He said the Pharisees are blind? They must not have liked that."

"They didn't. Some Pharisees who were there heard this and asked, 'What? Are we blind, too?' Jesus answered them, 'If you were blind, you would not be guilty of sin; but now that you claim you can see, your guilt remains.'"

Anna pointed out, "They cannot claim innocence if they say they can see."

"No, Anna, they cannot. Jesus went on, 'Very truly I tell you Pharisees, anyone who does not enter the sheep pen by the gate, but climbs in by some other way, is a thief and a robber. The one who enters by the gate is the shepherd of the sheep. The gatekeeper opens the gate for him, and the sheep listen to his voice. He calls his own sheep by name and leads them out. When he has brought out all his own, he goes on ahead of them, and his sheep follow him because they know his voice. They will never follow a stranger; in fact, they will run away from him because they do not recognize a stranger's voice.' Jesus said this knowing the Pharisees did not understand what he was saying about them."

Father replied, "I think I understand. Those who believe follow. They are the ones he calls and leads. They will not follow a stranger. The Pharisees are trying to come in some other way than through him."

"Yes, Father, you understood it well, but they simply failed to grasp that he was speaking about them. Jesus went on, knowing the Pharisees could not understand, 'Very truly I tell you, I am the gate of the sheep. All who have come before me are thieves and robbers, but the sheep have not listened to them. I am the gate; whoever enters through me will be saved. They will come in and go out and find pasture. The thief comes only to steal and kill and destroy; I have come that they may have life and live it to the full.'"

Father summarized, "He not only keeps the gate, he *is* the gate—the way in! All others were thieves and robbers, coming to kill and steal, while he gives life."

Didymus

"Exactly. Jesus went on, 'I am the good shepherd. The good shepherd lays down his life for the sheep. The hireling is not the shepherd and does not own the sheep. So, when he sees the wolf coming, he abandons the sheep and runs away. Then the wolf attacks and scatters the flock. The man runs away because he is a hireling and doesn't care about the sheep. I am the good shepherd; I know my sheep and my sheep know me, just as the Father knows me and I know the Father, and I lay down my life for the sheep. I have other sheep that are not of this sheep pen. I must bring them also. They too will listen to my voice, and there shall be one flock and one shepherd. The reason my Father loves me is that I lay down my life, only to take it up again. No one takes it from me, but I lay it down of my own accord. I have authority to lay it down and authority to take it up again. This command I received from my Father.'"

Father said, "He is right about the hireling. He again talks of laying down his life. This is sad."

Jahzeel asked, "Who are these 'other sheep?' People who are not Jews?"

I answered as well as I could. "Probably. We know that God has reached out to non-Jews in the past; remember Jonah preaching to Nineveh? There may have been others. Samaritans? Greeks? Romans? I don't know. The Jews who heard these words were again divided. Many said, 'He is demon-possessed and raving mad. Why listen to him?' Other countered, 'These are not the sayings of a man possessed by a demon. Can a demon open the eyes of the blind?'"

Father stated, "So, there are still some who are willing to be open. At least he has them thinking."

I agreed, "This brings us to this very day. We had been in Galilee now for a long time, but you know we never spend too long in one place. Mother, by the way, these cakes are delicious. It is so good to be home."

Father remarked, "It is good to see you, and to talk about these things. I wish for fellowship with other believers in Jesus. The synagogue does not seem like the best place for us any longer. Oh, we still learn the Law, but you have shown us so much more."

Jahzeel said, "Brother, do not be offended by my questions. If there is an answer, I would love to hear it."

I answered clearly, "I'm sure there is an answer. I still have so much to learn."

Mother warned, "Be careful!"

"I will. Shalom."

As I left to return to Jesus, I realized that, although the discussion itself had gone well, I still do not know all the answers. Even Jahzeel, who continued to question faith, had seen evidence that could not be denied. He didn't really deny the evidence but was looking for something else. His questions seemed valid; he was not simply trying to stump me. I also realized that miracles, though useful, do not convince everyone. Jahzeel had said that at one point he was angered by the miracles.

There were Pharisees who had seen the miracles, too, but also refused to believe. Perhaps some Pharisees had been blinded by pride in their vast knowledge. They'd had their guard up before they had even heard Jesus's words. They had seen miracles—and, more importantly, truth—but refused to acknowledge what they had seen. They were distracted so quickly that the Word couldn't have the right effect. Even if they believed a little, they would still refuse to follow Jesus as Lord. They were determined. Stubborn, like Jahzeel . . . and me.

What was it Jesus said had: "The soil is hard"? The seed does not even enter. For a few moments my fatalistic bent re-emerged, and I felt totally hopeless that Jahzeel would ever believe. I felt as though I should give up. But the feeling subsided. At least Jahzeel was somewhat open and willing to discuss. I remembered what Jesus had told me nearly three years ago: "Just as it takes time to make the wine in the grape skin, it will take time to make shalom in Jahzeel's heart. It will even take time in your heart. Do not lose heart. Just as the grapes appear, shalom, too, will happen in due season. Do not give up.'

I had a promise, but it was conditional, dependent on my not giving up. I couldn't give up. I realized the need to pray more and

Didymus

learn more. I realized the need to be more patient. I must wait upon the timing and work of the Spirit. Happily, I had learned to pray while walking—which I did right then, eyes wide open.

XVI

Telikós Martyras
(The Last Witness)

We spent winter and spring traveling and working. A week before Passover approached, we arrived at Jerusalem. On the fourth day of the week, I realized that this might be my only chance to talk to my family before the actual feast day. I knew where they usually stayed, so I sought them out, praying on the way.

As I arrived, Mother was already getting ready for the Passover meal, which would take place in just one day. As I entered, I was warmly greeted with an embrace from Father. There were smiles all around. Father asked how long I would stay, and I explained that I would be eating with Jesus that evening, a day before the actual paschal meal.

I stated, "I saw all of you in the crowd shouting hosanna as we entered Jerusalem on the first day of the week."

Father replied, "Yes, it was an inspiring scene. Jesus has so many followers now."

Jahzeel seconded, "Yes, many. Have you found an answer to my questions?"

Father chided, "Jahzeel, is that a greeting?"

I interjected, "No, Father, it is fine; Jahzeel knows I have little time. Not completely, my brother. I believe that Jesus will die, but I don't understand when or how."

Didymus

Mother looked shocked, as did Anna, but Father simply asked, "Why?"

I acknowledged, "I really don't understand all of what is to come. But let me fill you in on what has gone on. This has been a thrilling time."

Father, agreeing, "Yes, if you have time."

"As you know, we had spent two months in Galilee, but then Jesus set out for Jerusalem for the Festival of Dedication, after which we departed again. Now we have returned for this Passover. Do you realize that this will be the fourth Passover I have seen him in Jerusalem? I began following shortly after the first."

I continued, "As we came this way, Jesus sent a few of us on ahead, but when we entered a Samaritan village, the people would not welcome us because they understood that Jesus was not staying but heading for Jerusalem. James and John asked Jesus, 'Lord, do you want us to call fire down from heaven to destroy them?' Jesus rebuked them, and we went to another village."

Jahzeel observed, "First the Samaritans welcome him—when they expect miracles, but when he is passing through they don't want him. Just like them. Can you blame James and John?"

Mother and Anna looked shocked, and Anna echoed, "Jahzeel, *calling down fire from heaven?*"

Jahzeel looked embarrassed, so I spoke quickly. "Jesus rebuked them. And nothing happened. The path we took then was between Samaria and Galilee. As we were going into a village, ten men with leprosy met us. They stood at a distance and called out in loud voices, 'Jesus, Master, have pity on us!' When Jesus saw them, he said, 'Go show yourselves to the priests.' As they went, they were cleansed. One of them, when he realized he had been healed, came back praising God in a loud voice. He threw himself at Jesus's feet and thanked him. The man was a Samaritan. Jesus asked, 'Were not all ten cleansed? Where are the other nine? Has no one returned to give praise to God except this foreigner?' Then he said to the man, 'Rise and go; your faith has made you well.'"

Father pointed out, "You see, Jahzeel, there are good men among the Samaritans, too."

Mother added, "And some bad among our own people. Nine Jews healed without giving thanks! I suppose they were too excited to think properly."

"Yes, Mother, sometimes our emotions get the best of us. Perhaps their mothers hadn't taught them good manners. After that Jesus appointed seventy disciples and sent them out ahead of him into every town and place where we were about to go, much as he had sent the apostles before."

Father recalled, "Yes, I have heard of the larger group. Are they to be called apostles, too?"

"I don't think so. *Apostle* does mean sent out one, so in a way they are being sent out as we were. But Jesus specifically sent the seventy ahead of him into towns he intended to visit. They prepared the way for him. He told them, 'The harvest is plentiful, but the workers are few. Ask the Lord of the harvest, therefore, to send out workers into his harvest field. Go! I am sending you out like lambs among wolves. Do not take a purse or bag or sandals; do not greet anyone on the road. When you enter a house, first say, "Peace to this house." If someone who promotes peace is there, your peace will rest on them; if not, it will return to you. Stay there, eating and drinking whatever they give you, for the worker deserves his wages. Do not move around from house to house. When you enter a town and are welcomed, eat what is offered to you. Heal the sick who are there and tell them, "The kingdom of God has come near to you." But when you enter a town and are not welcomed, go into its streets and say, "Even the dust of your town we wipe from our feet as a warning to you." Yet be sure of this: The kingdom of God has come near. I tell you, it will be more bearable on that day for Sodom than for that town. Woe to you, Chorazin! Woe to you, Bethsaida! For if the miracles that were performed in you had been performed in Tyre and Sidon, they would have repented long ago, sitting in sackcloth and ashes. But it will be more bearable for Tyre and Sidon at the judgment than for you. And you, Capernaum, will you be lifted to the heavens? No, you will go down to Hades. Whoever listens to you, listens to me; whoever rejects you, rejects me; but whoever rejects me rejects him who sent me.'"

Jahzeel broke in, aloofly, "As though Chorazin or Bethsaida were to disappear! Besides, it sounds as though these seventy did a lot of the same things you did. Are you sure you are still 'special'?"

Father spoke firmly: "Jahzeel!"

I replied, "Father, it's alright. What they did was a lot like what we did. They have just seen less of Jesus. We twelve still have a distinct purpose. The seventy returned with joy and said, 'Lord, even the demons submit to us in your name.' Jesus replied, 'I saw Satan fall like lightning from heaven. I have given you authority to trample on snakes and scorpions and to overcome all the power of the enemy; nothing will harm you. However, do not rejoice that the spirits submit to you, but rejoice that your names are written in heaven.'"

Mother commented, "Imagine, having your name written in heaven!"

"Mother, I believe that when you trusted Jesus, your name was written there. At this point Jesus, full of joy through the Holy Spirit, said, 'I praise you, Father, Lord of heaven and earth, because you have hidden these things from the wise and learned and revealed them to little children. Yes, Father, for this is what you were pleased to do. All things have been committed to me by my Father. No one knows who the Son is except the Father, and no one knows who the Father is except the Son and those to whom the Son chooses to reveal him.' Turning to us, he said privately, 'Blessed are the eyes that see what you see. For I tell you that many prophets and kings wanted to see what you see but did not see it, and to hear what you hear but did not hear it.'"

Father exclaimed, "That's an amazing perspective—the idea of seeing things the prophets wanted to see!"

"Yes, it is. Jesus went on, 'Come to me, all you who are weary and burdened, and I will give you rest. Take my yoke upon you and learn from me, for I am gentle and humble in heart, and you will find rest for you souls. For my yoke is easy and my burden is light.'"

Jahzeel smirked, "Easier than handling the grapes, I'm sure . . ."

Father, looking disturbed, "Jahzeel, really, we don't have time for this."

I clarified, "Jahzeel, if your burden is too heavy, then perhaps it isn't the burden God intended for you. Perhaps the burden is one given by yourself and not a portion given by God. We have no need to take on more of God's affairs on top of the ones God has specifically given us. But going on, an expert in the Law stood up to test Jesus. He said, 'Teacher, what must I do to inherit eternal life?' Jesus answered him with a question, 'What is written in the Law? How do you read it?' The man answered, 'Love the Lord your God with all your heart and with all your soul and with all your strength and with all your mind, and love your neighbor as yourself.' Jesus answered simply, 'You have answered correctly, do this and you will live.' The man, wishing to justify himself, asked Jesus, 'And who is my neighbor?'"

Father pointed out, "Wait, this lawyer did not quote the Shema correctly; he added a fourth word, *dianoia*, or 'mind.' Jesus did not correct him. Should I take notice?"

I answered as best I could. "I'm not sure whether you should. We were promised by Ezekiel that God will create a new heart in us, and we need this because our original heart is wicked. The Hebrew for heart, *lebab*, refers to our inner self. The Greek word *kardias* is much weaker. The inner self, I believe, is what the Shema is talking about. Since God has *created* that new *heart*, it should belong to him. Yet our *soul* is *renewed*—transformed, not recreated.

"You know the rabbis teach that we are made up of three parts, like the three parts of the tabernacle. The outer court is like our body—profane. The Shema does not address the body directly. The holy place is like our soul, and our spirit is like the most holy place: the heart, the place enlightened directly by God. If we are not yielded, then the battle between the body and the heart takes place in the soul.

Didymus

"There is, of course, more detail in the Shema about the tabernacle, but this gives us something to think about. Jesus has not taught us this directly, but he responded to the lawyer's limited understanding by quoting the prophet Jeremiah: 'Behold, the days are coming, says the Lord, when I will make a new covenant with the house of Israel and with the house of Judah,' and then, 'I will put my Law in their minds, and write it on their hearts; and I will be their God, and they shall be my people.' The Law will be put in our *minds*.

"Perhaps Jesus was allowing this lawyer more detail, adding the aspect of mind to the message of the Shema. Perhaps this lawyer's temptation centered on his mind. I know that my temptation starts with my will—my pride, and I recognize that the temptation of some others begins with their emotions. Each of us may have different strengths or powers, not to mention different weaknesses. Jesus said, 'Do this and you will live.' If the lawyer added a word to the Shema, he was signifying that he would do more, not less."

Jahzeel reasoned, "Isaiah tells us that Lucifer's fall also began with pride, so our own sin certainly may as well. Still, the lawyer's question, 'Who is my neighbor?' seems applicable."

"Yes, when you get down to it, sin always begins with pride. As to being reasonable or applicable, perhaps it is. Jesus replied to him with yet another of his stories: 'A man was going down from Jerusalem to Jericho when he was attacked by robbers. They stripped him of his clothes, beat him, and went away, leaving him half dead. A priest happened to be going down the road, and when he saw the man he passed by on the other side. So too, a Levite, when he came to the place and saw him, passed by on the other side. But a Samaritan, as he traveled, came where the man was, and when he saw him he took pity on him. He went to him and bandaged his wounds, pouring on oil and wine. Then he put the man on his own donkey, brought him to an inn, and took care of him. The next day he took out two denarii and gave them to the innkeeper. "Look after him," he said, "and when I return, I will reimburse you for any extra expense you may have." Which of these three do you think was neighbor to the man who fell into the hands of the robbers?' The lawyer replied, 'The one who had mercy on him.' Jesus told him, 'Go and do likewise.'"

Jahzeel said, "Again a reference to a Samaritan. I understand mercy. That detail just seems like a strange choice."

Father interjected softly, "No, it's a good choice. Obedience to God's will is better than sacrifice. That message is all through the prophets. The priest and the Levite did not understand that, but the one who did what he should have was the one doing God's will. This Samaritan cared for the man and even opened his purse for him."

I replied, "Yes, that is it, Father. It's not *who you are* as much as *who you can become*. On our way we came to the village of Bethany, where a woman named Martha opened her home to Jesus. She had a sister, Mary, who sat at the Lord's feet listening to what he said. But Martha was distracted by all the preparations that had to be made. She came to Jesus and asked, 'Lord, don't you care that my sister has left me to do all the work by myself? Tell her to help me!'"

Anna added, "It is good to be of help."

"Yes, it is. But Jesus replied, 'Martha, Martha, you are worried and upset about many things, but few things are needed, indeed only one. Mary has chosen what is better, and it will not be taken away from her.'"

Mother replied slowly, "I think I understand, but this is a new teaching."

"Yes, it is new to me, too. After Jesus was praying one day, one of his disciples said to him, 'Lord, teach us to pray, just as John taught his disciples.'"

Father put in, "Had he not already taught this?"

"To us apostles, yes. This was directed to the seventy. Jesus offered a model prayer to these disciples, much as he had to us when we were on the mount."

Father asked, "Are all our prayers to be the same?"

"I don't think so. But always the idea is first to honor God and acknowledge that his will is best and then to ask for our petitions, to request forgiveness, to promise forgiveness to others, and to ask for protection. Any part of that prayer may be much longer or more detailed. Jesus himself can pray for hours. Jesus said to us, 'Suppose you have a friend, and you go to him at midnight and say, "Friend, lend me three loaves of bread; a friend of mine on a journey has come to me, and I have no food to offer him." The one inside will answer, "Don't bother me. The door is already locked, and my children and I are in bed. I can't get up and give you anything." I tell you, even though he will not get up and give you the bread because of friendship, yet because of your shameless audacity he will surely get up and give you as much as you need.'"

Father reflected, "At first that sounded shameless, but God wants us to realize that we can be serious about our requests."

I replied, "That's it, Father. Jesus went on, 'So I say to you: Ask and it will be given to you; seek and you will find; knock and the door will be opened to you. For everyone who asks receives; the one who seeks finds; and to the one who knocks, the door will be opened.'"

Jahzeel quipped, "So, it's as easy as asking? I should then ask for a bountiful harvest."

I replied again, "Only if that is good for you to have. God will not give you what you should not have. Jesus continued, 'Which of you fathers, if your son asks for a fish, will give him a snake instead? Or if he asks for an egg, will give him a scorpion? If you then, though you are evil, know how to give good gifts to your children, how much more will your Father in heaven give the Holy Spirit to those who ask him!'"

Father recalled, "I, too, remember wanting you boys to ask me for what I already desired to give you. It pleased me to hear your requests."

Mother reminisced, "I remember when you were small, making you wait to give you a raisin cake until you would say 'please.' That is what God wants."

I went on, "This was the Festival of Dedication, and we were back in Jerusalem. Jesus was in the temple courts walking in Solomon's Colonnade. The Jews who were there gathered around him, asking, 'How long will you keep us in suspense? If you are the Messiah, tell us plainly.' Jesus answered, 'I did tell you, but you do not believe. The works I do in my Father's name testify about me, but you do not believe because you are not my sheep. My sheep listen to my voice; I know them, and they follow me. I give them eternal life, and they shall never perish; no one will snatch them out of my hand. My Father, who has given them to me, is greater than all; no one can snatch them out of my Father's hand. I and the Father are one.'"

Jahzeel exclaimed, "Again, the audacious claims. They will kill him. Perhaps Isaiah was right."

"Perhaps, but his time has not yet come. Again, the Jews picked up stones to stone him, but Jesus said to them, 'I have shown you many good works from the Father. For which of these do you stone me?' They replied, 'We are not stoning you for any good work, but for blasphemy, because you, a mere man, claim to be God.' Jesus answered them again, 'Is it not written in your Law, 'I have said you are "gods"? If he called them "gods," to whom the word of God came, and scripture cannot be set aside, what about the one whom the Father set apart as his very own and sent into the world? Why then do you accuse me of blasphemy because I said, "I am God's son"? Do not believe me unless I do the works of my Father. But if I do them, even though you do not believe me, believe the works that you may know and understand that the Father is in me, and I in the Father.' Again, they tried to seize him, but he escaped their grasp—while they stood still holding their stones."

Father shook his head. "He escapes so easily. This must be of God."

"Yes, it was. We again went back across the Jordan to Perea, the place where John had baptized in the early days. There we stayed, and many people came to him. They said, 'Though John

never performed a sign, all that John said about this man is true.'
And in that place many believed in Jesus."

Father added, "He always goes where the people need him."

"Yes. Jesus went through the towns and villages, teaching as
we made our way back to Jerusalem. Someone asked him, 'Lord,
are only a few people going to be saved?' Jesus answered, 'Make
every effort to enter through the narrow door, because many will
try to enter and will not be able to. Once the owner of the house
gets up and closes the door, you will stand outside knocking and
pleading, "Sir, open the door for us." Yet he will answer, "I don't
know you or where you come from." You will answer, "We ate and
drank with you, and you taught in our streets." But he will reply, "I
don't know you or where you come from. Away from me, all you
evildoers!" There will be weeping, and gnashing of teeth, when
you see Abraham, Isaac, and Jacob and all the prophets in the kingdom of God, but you yourselves thrown out. People will come from
the east and west and north and south and will take their places at
the feast in the kingdom of God. Indeed, there are those who are
last who will be first, and first who will be last.'"

Father observed, "He turns Judaism on its head."

"He does. But some in Jewry know exactly who he is. Some
Pharisees came to Jesus and said to him, 'Leave this place and go
somewhere else. Herod wants to kill you.' Jesus replied, 'Go tell
that fox, "I will keep on driving out demons and healing people
today and tomorrow, and on the third day I will reach my goal."
In any case, I must press on today and tomorrow and the next day,
for surely no prophet can die outside Jerusalem!' His statements
on dying are now frequent. We are all getting uneasy. We had been
expecting a kingdom. Still, we all trust every word, and we feel
safe."

Jahzeel pressed, "So, is Isaiah right?"

"I don't understand yet. But Jesus lamented, 'Jerusalem,
Jerusalem, you who kill the prophets and stone those sent to you,
how often I have longed to gather your children together, as a hen
gathers her chicks under her wings, and you were not willing.

Look, your house is left to you desolate. I tell you; you will not see me again until you say, "Blessed is he who comes in the name of the Lord."'"

Father asked, "Then *this* is the time he comes to Jerusalem as Lord?"

"I don't think so. But there is more. On a Sabbath, as Jesus went to eat in the house of a prominent Pharisee, he was carefully watched. There in front of him was a man suffering from abnormal swelling of this body. Jesus asked the Pharisees and experts in the Law, 'Is it lawful to heal on the Sabbath or not?' They remained silent. Jesus, taking hold of the man, healed him and sent him on his way. Then he asked them, 'If one of you has a child or an ox that falls into a well on the Sabbath day, will you not immediately pull it out?' They had nothing to say."

Mother observed ruefully, "They don't give up."

And Jahzeel added, "It was a trap."

"It was. When he noticed how the guests picked the places of honor at the table, he told them this parable: 'When someone invites you to a wedding feast, do not take the place of honor, for a person more distinguished than you may have been invited. If so, the host who invited both of you will come and say to you, "Give this person your seat." Then, humiliated, you will have to take the least important place. But when you are invited, take the lowest place, so that when your host comes, he will say to you, "Friend, move up to a better place." Then you will be honored in the presence of all the other guests. For all those who exalt themselves will be humbled, and those who humble themselves will be exalted.'"

Father, chuckling, "They can't imagine themselves in a position of humility. They are the ruling class. We are the working class. Even if we had money, we would never be allowed to rule like them."

"Never. Jesus said to his host, 'When you give a luncheon or dinner, do not invite your friends, your brothers or sisters, your relatives, or your rich neighbors; if you do, they may invite you back and so you will be repaid. But when you give a banquet, invite the poor, the crippled, the lame, the blind, and you will be blessed. Although they cannot repay you, you will be repaid at the resurrection of the righteous.'"

Jahzeel noted, "He has compassion for the common people, I'll give him that."

"He does. When one of those at the table with him heard this, he said to Jesus, 'Blessed is the one who will eat at the feast in the kingdom of God.' Jesus replied yet another of his parables: 'A certain man was preparing a great banquet and invited many guests. At the time of the banquet, he sent his servant to tell those who had been invited, "Come, for everything is now ready." But they all alike began to make excuses. The first said, "I have just bought a field, and I must go and see it. Please excuse me." Another said, "I have just bought five yoke of oxen, and I'm on my way to try them out. Please excuse me." Still another said, "I just got married, so I can't come." The servant came back and reported this to his master. Then the owner of the house became angry and ordered his servant, "Go out quickly into the streets and alleys of the town and bring in the poor, the crippled, the blind, and the lame." The servant replied, "Sir, what you ordered has been done, but there is still room." Then the master told his servant, "Go out to the roads and country lanes and compel them to come in, so that my house will be full. I tell you, not one of those who were invited will get a taste of my banquet."'"

Father, laughingly, "Can you imagine buying a field without seeing it first?"

Jahzeel added, "Or buying oxen without knowing what they were capable of? These men are liars!"

Anna, picking up a different thread, "Can you imagine a man asked to a banquet and not bringing his bride? Or a bride not willing to come?"

Mother observed softly, "That's the point, isn't it? The high and mighty, the ruling class—those who are not willing are really not worthy, but the poor and lame may be. Why should they not be invited?"

I enthused, "Yes, that's it exactly. God loves *all* his children, but some expect special treatment. Large crowds were by that point traveling with us, and Jesus turned to them and said, 'If anyone comes to me and does not hate father and mother, wife and children, brothers and sisters, yes, even their own life, such a person cannot be my disciple.'"

Mother pointed out, "That seems harsh."

To which Father added, "Yes, it does, but I think he was really saying the same as we all say in the Shema, 'Hear, O Israel: The LORD our God, the LORD is one. Love the LORD your God with all your heart and with all your soul and with all your strength.' If he is not first before all others, then we don't really love him enough."

Father asked, "Who will the guests be if the invited do not come?"

"I don't know—perhaps the poor? But Jesus went on, 'When the king came in to see the guests, he noticed a man there who was not wearing wedding clothes. He asked, "How did you get in here without wedding clothes, friend?" The man was speechless. Then the king told the attendants, "Tie him hand and foot and throw him outside, into the darkness, where there will be weeping and gnashing of teeth." For many are invited, but few are chosen.'"

Father replied, "So, one must be ready for the occasion? Clean and prepared?"

I replied, "Yes, I'm sure that's it. But it gets even harder for believers. Listen to these words of Jesus: 'Whoever does not carry their cross and follow me cannot be my disciple. Suppose one of you wants to build a tower. Won't you first sit down and estimate the cost to see if you have enough money to complete it? For if you lay the foundation and are not able to finish it, everyone who sees it will ridicule you, saying, "This person began to build and wasn't able to finish." Or suppose a king is about to go to war against another king. Won't he first sit down and consider whether he is able with ten thousand men to oppose the one coming against him with twenty thousand? If he is not able, he will send a delegation while the other is still a long way off and will ask for terms of peace. In the same way, those of you who do not give up everything you have cannot be my disciples.'"

Mother echoed quietly, "Carry their cross? A Roman cross? Jesus has mentioned a cross before."

"That is what he said."

Jahzeel protested, "It's not reasonable to give up *everything*."

I replied, "No, but the *willingness* to do so must be present, and the love of God has to be there too. Jesus went on, as earlier, about salt: 'Salt is good, but if it loses its saltiness, how can it be made salty again? It is fit neither for the soil nor for the manure pile; it is thrown out. Whoever has ears to hear, let them hear.'"

Jahzeel mused, "Salt again. Are *you* salt?"

Mother explained, "I understand better than before. The purpose of salt is to add flavor and to preserve. If salt can do neither, it has no purpose. If we can't do what God purposed for us to do, we are fit for nothing."

I replied, "Yes, Mother, that is it. There were so many types of people there. Tax collectors and sinners were all gathering around to hear Jesus. But the Pharisees and teachers of the Law muttered, 'This man welcomes sinners and eats with them.' Jesus told them the same parable about the one lost sheep he had told us before. He finished, 'In the same way there will be more rejoicing in heaven over one sinner who repents than over ninety-nine righteous persons who do not need to repent.'"

Father replied, "Yes, it is amazing how much the one missing seems to matter to him. I have even seen this in people; a man can have five good sons, and the one who is not behaving properly has all his attention." He quickly added, smiling, "Of course, I have two good sons."

I smiled, too, and continued, "Jesus went on to enforce the point for others: 'Or suppose a woman has ten silver coins and loses one. Doesn't she light a lamp, sweep the house, and search carefully until she finds it? When she finds it, she calls her friends and neighbors together and says, "Rejoice with me; I have found my lost coin." In the same way, I tell you, there is rejoicing in the presence of the angels of God over one sinner who repents.'"

Mother noted, "Losing something you need shows the importance of that something to you. Yet it would be careless to misplace even one coin."

I went on, "Jesus continued again, showing how important the lost are: 'There was a man who had two sons. The younger one said to his father, "Father, give me my share of the estate." So, the father divided his property between them. Not long after, the younger son got together all he had, set off for a distant country and there squandered his wealth in wild living. After he had spent everything, there was a severe famine in that whole country, and he began to be in need. So, he went and hired himself out to a citizen of that country, who sent him to his fields to feed pigs. He longed to fill his stomach with the pods that the pigs were eating, but no one gave him anything.

'When he came to his senses, he said, "How many of my father's hired servants have food to spare, and here I am starving to death! I will set out and go back to my father and say to him, "Father, I have sinned against heaven and against you. I am no longer worthy to be called your son; make me like one of your hired servants." So, he got up and went to his father. But while he was still a long way off, his father saw him and was filled with compassion for him; he ran to his son, threw his arms around him, and kissed him. The son said to him, "Father, I have sinned against heaven and against you. I am no longer worthy to be called your son."

'But the father said to his servants, "Quick! Bring the best robe and put it on him. Put a ring on his finger and sandals on his feet. Bring the fattened calf and kill it. Let's have a feast and celebrate. For this son of mine was dead and is alive again; he was lost and is found." So, they began to celebrate.

'Meanwhile, the older son was in the field. When he came near the house, he heard music and dancing. So, he called one of the servants and asked him what was going on. "Your brother has come," he replied, "and your father has killed the fattened calf because he has him back safe and sound." The older brother became angry and refused to go in. So, his father went out and pleaded with him. But he answered his father, "Look! All these years I've been slaving for you and never disobeyed your orders. Yet you never gave me even a young goat so I could celebrate with my friends. But when this son of yours who has squandered your property with prostitutes comes home, you kill the fattened calf for him!" The father said, "My son, you are always with me, and everything I have is yours. But we had to celebrate and be glad, because this brother of yours was dead and is alive again; he was lost and is found.""'

Father stated, "I can't imagine how painful it would have been for this father to lose his son."

Jahzeel, getting in a jab, pointed out, "You lost Thomas . . ."

Father, shocked, "No, not at all. We still have him. He has not taken any inheritance. I gave him only a few coins three years ago, and he has never asked for more. It hurt a little, but imagine this father . . ."

Jahzeel backed down. "Yes, I'm sorry; it is not the same."

I continued, "Jesus changed the subject from the lost, and spoke directly to us: 'There was a rich man whose manager was accused of wasting his possessions. So, he called him in and asked him, "What is this I hear about you? Give me an account of your management, because you cannot be manager any longer." The manager said to himself, "What shall I do now? My master is taking away my job. I'm not strong enough to dig, and I'm ashamed to beg. I know what I'll do so that, when I lose my job here, people will welcome me into their houses." He called in each one of his master's debtors. He asked the first, "How much do you owe my master?" He replied, "Nine hundred gallons of olive oil." The manager told him, "Take you bill, sit down quickly, and make it four hundred and fifty." He asked the second, "How much do you owe?" The reply was, "A thousand bushels of wheat." The manager told him, "Take your bill, and make it eight hundred."

'The master commended this dishonest manager because he had acted shrewdly. For the people of this world are more shrewd in dealing with their own kind than are the people of the light. I tell you, use worldly wealth to gain friends for yourselves, so that when it is gone, you will be welcomed into eternal dwellings. Whoever can be trusted with very little can also be trusted with much, and whoever is dishonest with very little will also be dishonest with much. So, if you have not been trustworthy in handling worldly wealth, who will trust you with true riches? If you have not been trustworthy with someone else's property, who will give you property of your own?'"

Jahzeel stopped me. "Wait brother, this man was being dishonest! How could he be commended?"

Father interrupted, "Jahzeel, you know that sometimes we have people for whom we forgive part of their debt. It is better to get a little than none."

Jahzeel went on, "But being shrewd to gain friends? How can this be good?"

I explained, "No, the manager was *not* commended for dishonesty, but only for using something over which he had some control to set up a future situation. I don't think I would have thought to do that. Perhaps it's like giving a present to a governor in anticipation of gaining future consideration. He was not hurting the prospects of the man for whom he was steward at this point.

"Matthew, being a former tax collector, shared some perspective: tax collectors get a small portion of the revenue. Suppose a man cannot pay the full tax. If the tax collector throws the man in jail, the tax collector will get nothing. A wise tax collector realizes that it's more expeditious to reduce the charge a bit and get at least something. Jahzeel, you are a businessman, and you understand. But you are right: he was not trustworthy, so God would not trust him. Jesus addressed this issue of trust next, saying, 'No one can serve two masters. Either he will hate the one and love the other, or he will be devoted to the one and despise the other. You cannot serve both God and money.'"

Father agreed. "Now, that is true. If the priests are worried about money, they care little about God. If they care about God, money is not their main concern."

Didymus

I carried this still further. "Even more so the Pharisees. We saw that the Pharisees, who had listened in, and who love money, had heard all of this and had sneered at Jesus. He said to them, 'You are the ones who justify yourselves in the eyes of others, but God knows your hearts. What people value highly is detestable in God's sight.'"

Jahzeel confirmed, "Jesus knows them. They do not really love God."

"Yes, Jahzeel, he knows them. But he understands, too, that the Law the Pharisees love is necessary. Jesus went on explaining the danger of ignoring the Law: 'The Law and the Prophets were proclaimed until John. Since that time, the good news of the kingdom of God is being preached, and everyone is forcing themselves into it. It is easier for heaven and earth to disappear than for the last stroke of a pen to drop out of the Law.'"

"Perhaps, but what is this about John the Baptist?"

"John taught that the Law is good, but being close to God is more important than the Law. The focus of his preaching was on repentance, as demonstrated by baptism, for the remission of sins. The Pharisees seem to think that, if you sacrifice correctly, you need not repent or even say you are sorry—that the sin simply goes away. Sacrifice was never intended to be more than a covering. Then Jesus gave an example: 'Anyone who divorces his wife and marries another woman commits adultery, and the man who marries a divorced woman commits adultery.'"

Mother commented, "It is terrible how quickly some Pharisees and others put away their wives, for no cause. If I had a daughter, I would be careful before I let her marry a Pharisee."

"Yes, but riches are part of the issue, too. Jesus went on, again talking about riches, 'There was a rich man who was dressed in purple and fine linen and lived in luxury every day. At his gate was laid a beggar named Lazarus, covered with sores and longing to eat what fell from the rich man's table. Even the dogs came and licked his sores. The time came when the beggar died, and the angels carried him to Abraham's side.

'The rich man also died and was buried. In Hades, when he was in torment, he looked up and saw Abraham far away, with Lazarus by his side. So, he called to him, "Father Abraham, have pity on me and send Lazarus to dip the tip of his finger in water and cool my tongue, because I am in agony in this fire." Abraham replied, "Son, remember that in your lifetime you received your good things, while Lazarus received bad things, but now he is comforted here, and you are in agony. Besides all this, between us and you a great chasm has been set in place, so that those who want to go from here to you cannot, nor can anyone cross over from there to us."

'The man begged, "I beg you, father, send Lazarus to my family, for I have five brothers. Let him warn them, so that they will not also come to this place of torment." Abraham replied, "They have Moses and the Prophets; let them listen to them." He answered, "No, father Abraham, but if someone from the dead goes to them, they will repent." Abraham answered, "If they do not listen to Moses and the Prophets, they will not be convinced even if someone rises from the dead."''

Father commented, "I have never heard it explained so plainly what happens after death. Think about it: the rich man was in torment!"

Jahzeel blurted, "It can't be simply from his having had wealth."

Father agreed, "No, I'm sure it was about how he lived his life."

Jahzeel pointed out, "Well, he said the other man, Lazarus, ate crumbs from his table. . . "

Mother interjected, "That is barely pity from a rich man."

Father added, "No, it isn't. Jesus gave a name to a character. I have heard of no other parable with a name in it. Do you suppose this is someone the Pharisees knew of? And if they knew the poor man, then they must also have known the rich man."

I admitted, "I really don't know. Perhaps. They were furious at the story."

Didymus

Father noted, "He talks of torment for the rich man, and good for the poor man. It's as though he has seen the place. No scribe would say that."

"I believe he knows. Based on his expression, I can only conclude that he has seen the pain. Did you hear what the rich man wanted? Not just the water, but to be sure that no one else would follow him there. Jesus knows about this. It's real."

Mother, with a quiet shudder, "Can we move on?"

"Of course, Mother. I'm sorry to disturb you so."

I took a sip of wine. It was time to begin.

XVII

When the Kingdom?

The Pharisees asked when the kingdom of God would come. Jesus replied, 'The coming of the kingdom of God is not something that can be observed, nor will people say, "Here it is" or "There it is," because the kingdom of God is in your midst.'"

Jahzeel surmised, "It sounds as though it won't even be noticed."

Anna expressed softly, "Jesus *is* in their midst."

I continued, "After he answered the Pharisees, he spoke to us, announcing, 'The time is coming when you will long to see one of the days of the Son of Man, but you will not see it. People will tell you, "There he is!" or "Here he is!" Do not go running off after them. For the Son of Man in his day will be like the lightning, which flashes and lights up the sky from the one end to the other. But first he must suffer many things and be rejected by this generation. Just as it was in the days of Noah, so also will it be in the days of the Son of Man. People were eating, drinking, marrying, and being given in marriage up to the day Noah entered the ark.

'Then the flood came and destroyed them all. It was the same in the day of Lot. People were eating and drinking, buying and selling, planting and building. But the day Lot left Sodom, fire and sulfur rained down from heaven and destroyed them all. It will be just like this on the day the Son of Man is revealed. On that day no one who is on the housetop, with possessions inside, should go down to get them. Likewise, no one in the field should go back for anything. Remember Lot's wife! Whoever tries to keep their life will lose it, and whoever loses their life will preserve it. I tell you, on that night two people will be in one bed; one will be taken and the other left. Two women will be grinding grain together; one will be taken and the other left.' We asked, 'Where, Lord?' He replied, 'Where there is a dead body, there the eagles will gather.'"

Mother noticed, "First 'on that night,' and having two in bed—clearly in the nighttime. But then two women are grinding, which happens in the morning, and two are in the field, a reference to the middle of the day. That sounds like all parts of the day."

I answered, "I see your point. I don't know. It sounds like this extends to different times of the day, yet Jesus said to hurry."

Jahzeel reflected, "Jesus calls himself the Son of Man, yet he says they will long to see the days of the Son of Man. Is he saying that there will be a time when he will go away, and people will be searching for him, and some will claim they have found him, even though he cannot be found? Then, without warning, he will return? When will this be?"

"I'm not sure. Nor do I know how long he will be gone. But Jesus told yet another parable to us about praying without giving up. He said: 'In a certain town there was a judge who neither feared God nor cared what the people thought. There was a widow in that town who kept coming to him with a plea: "Grant me justice against my adversary." For a time, the judge refused. Finally, he said to himself, "Even though I don't fear God or care what people think, this widow keeps bothering me, so I will see that she gets justice so that she won't eventually come and attack me!" Listen to what the unjust judge says. Will not God bring about justice for his chosen, who cry out to him day and night? Will he keep putting them off? I tell you that he will see that they get justice, and quickly. Howbeit, when the Son of Man comes, will he find faith on the earth?'"

Jahzeel commented, "The judge was expedient, not just."

Father, changing the subject, asked, "So, he will go and then come again?"

I replied, "So it seems. I do not know. Most of his words are warnings for the wicked to repent and for those who think they are righteous not to have confidence in themselves. It's not about us, the followers; we will be fine. It's the others he wants to reach. Then to those who looked down on others and were confident of their own righteousness, Jesus told this parable: 'Two men went up to the temple to pray, one a Pharisee and the other a tax collector. The Pharisee stood by himself and prayed: "God, I thank you that I am not like other people, robbers, evildoers, adulterers, or even like this tax collector. I fast twice a week and give a tenth of all I get." Yet the tax collector stood at a distance. He would not even look up to heaven, but beat his breast and said, "God, have mercy on me, a sinner." I tell you that this man, rather than the Pharisee, went home justified before God. For all those who exalt themselves will be humbled, and those who humble themselves will be exalted.'"

Jahzeel stated, "Yes, I've seen Pharisees like this. I do not know who they are trying to impress. The normal people are not impressed."

Father agreed, "I think they try to impress each other and really don't care what the others think."

I continued, "Then Jesus spoke to us again about the kingdom of heaven, saying, 'For the kingdom of heaven is like a landowner who went out early in the morning to hire workers for his vineyard. He agreed to pay them a denarius for a day and sent them into his vineyard. About nine in the morning, he went out and saw others standing in the marketplace doing nothing. He told them, "You also go and work in my vineyard, and I will pay you whatever is right." They went. He went out again about noon and again about three in the afternoon doing likewise.'"

Jahzeel interjected, "I've seen this happen. This is why we don't pick people up this way. The hard workers are ready early."

"I know. Jesus went on with the story: 'At about five in the afternoon, he went out and found still others standing around. He asked them, "Why have you been standing here all day long doing nothing?" They answered, "No one has hired us." He said to them,

Didymus

"You also go and work in my vineyard." When evening came, the owner of the vineyard said to his foreman, "Call the workers and pay them their wages, beginning with the last ones hired and going on to the first." The workers hired about five in the afternoon came and each received a denarius. So, when those came who were hired first, they expected to receive more. But each one of them also received a denarius. When they received it, they grumbled against the landowner. "Those who were hired last worked only one hour, yet you have made them equal to us who have borne the burden of the work in the heat of the day."'"

Jahzeel exclaimed with irritation in his voice, "That does not seem fair! I would not pay this way."

"No, it doesn't seem fair on the surface. But there are payments that are not based on quantity. When I did my bar mitzvah, I became respected as a man. It did not matter if I had studied a longer or a shorter time—I had earned the respect. If I had done it twice, I would have earned no more respect than if I had done it just the once. Jesus went on with the story: 'The landowner answered one of them, "I am not being unfair to you, friend. Didn't you agree to work for a denarius? Take your pay and go. I want to give the one who was hired last the same as I gave you. Don't I have the right to do what I want with my own money? Or are you envious because I am generous?" So, the last will be first, and the first will be last.'"

Father reasoned, "It was true—the money was his to give. He could have given more to the men who worked less if he had chosen to; that still would have been his right as a generous man. He simply made sure everyone had enough."

Jahzeel asked, "But what does this mean *to us*?"

I replied, "It means that those who serve God for a long time and those who serve him a shorter time will both inherit eternal life. God cannot give *more* than eternal life."

Jahzeel pointed out, "But you have earlier told us parables about rewards."

"Yes, and I believe Jesus has taught about differing rewards, but there is only one eternal life. I must go on, as time is flying.

At about that time a man named Lazarus was sick. He was from Bethany, the village of Mary and her sister, Martha. So, the sisters sent word to Jesus: 'Lord, the one you love is sick.' When Jesus heard this, he said, 'This sickness will not end in death. No, it is for God's glory so that God's Son may be glorified through it.'"

I continued, "Now, we knew Jesus loved Martha and her sister, as well as Lazarus. Yet when he heard that Lazarus was sick, he stayed where he was for two more days and then said to us, 'Let us go back to Judea.' We replied, 'Rabbi, a short while ago the Jews there tried to stone you, yet you are going back?' Jesus answered us, 'Are there not twelve hours of daylight? Anyone who walks in the day will not stumble, for they see by sunlight. It is when a person walks at night that they stumble, for they have no light.' After saying this, he went on, 'Our friend Lazarus has fallen asleep; but I am going there to wake him.' We replied, 'Lord, if he sleeps, he will get better.' We assumed that Jesus was speaking of natural sleep, but Jesus had been speaking of death. So, he told us plainly, 'Lazarus is dead, and for your sake I am glad I was not there, so that you may believe. But let us go to him.' Then I said to the rest of the apostles, 'Let us also go, that we may die with him.' I thought I was being brave, but I was not showing faith. Some of the others asked me, 'Can't you believe that Jesus knows what is best?' I felt foolish. I don't know why I suddenly thought we might be killed by the leaders."

Mother queried, a tremor in her voice, "You thought he would lead you to your death?" Then she asked her habitual motherly question, "Are you safe now?"

Father was hiding a brief smile at my stumble, but Jahzeel displayed a grin, which he quickly wiped off his face, commenting, "You are still human, my brother."

I realized that my family, and probably everyone else, needed to see my human side; this showed the honesty of my testimony, which had to be of God's power despite my own weakness. And my foibles served to exemplify that God could literally use *anyone*. His story was not about me. I swallowed my pride and replied,

"Yes, I stumbled. And I'm safe now. In that moment I could not see any need to risk our lives for a dead man. I was scared and tried to sound brave. But Jesus allayed my doubts quickly. When Jesus arrived, we learned that Lazarus had already been in the tomb for four days. Bethany was less than two miles from Jerusalem, and many Jews had come to the home of Martha and Mary to comfort them over the loss of their brother.

"When Martha heard that Jesus was coming, she went out to meet him, but Mary stayed at home. Martha said to Jesus, 'Lord, had you been here, my brother would not have died. Yet I know that even now God will give you whatever you ask.' Jesus said to her, 'Your brother will rise again.' Martha answered, 'I know he will rise again in the resurrection at the last day.' Jesus said to her, 'I am the resurrection and the life. The one who believes in me will live, even if they die; and whoever lives believing in me will never die. Do you believe this?' She replied, 'Yes, Lord, I believe that you are the Messiah, the Son of God, who is come into the world.'"

Father noted, "She confessed him, too."

"Yes, she did. At that point Martha went back and called her sister, Mary, aside. She said, 'The Teacher is here, and is asking for you.' When Mary heard this, she got up quickly and went to him. Jesus had not yet entered the village but was still where Martha had met him. When the Jews who had been with Mary in the house comforting her saw how quickly she got up and went out, they followed her, supposing she was going to the tomb to mourn there.

"As Mary reached the place where Jesus was, she fell at his feet and said words identical to her sister's: 'Lord, had you been here, my brother would not have died.' When Jesus saw her weeping, and the Jews who had come along with her also weeping, he was deeply moved in spirit and troubled. Jesus asked, 'Where have you laid him?' They replied, 'Come and see, Lord.' Jesus wept. When the Jews saw this, they said, 'See how he loved him!' Some of them said, 'Could not he who opened the eyes of the blind man have kept this man from dying?'"

Jahzeel blurted, "A prophet should have known and been there . . ."

"Listen further! Jesus, deeply moved, came to the tomb. It was a cave with a stone laid across the entrance. He said, 'Take away the stone.' Martha replied, 'But Lord, by this time there is a bad odor, for he has been there four days.' Then Jesus said, 'Did I not tell you that if you believe, you will see the glory of God?' So, they took away the stone. Jesus looked up and said, 'Father, I thank you that you have heard me. I knew that you always hear me, but I said this for the benefit of the people standing here, that they may believe that you sent me.' After saying this prayer, Jesus called in a loud voice, 'Lazarus, come out!' The dead man did come out, his hands and feet wrapped with strips of linen and with a cloth around his face. Jesus said to them, 'Take off the grave clothes and let him go.'"

Jahzeel replied, "I have heard this story before. Many tell of it. Still, a prophet should have known and prevented the death."

Father reflected, "There is some glory in a healing, but there is great glory in someone being raised to life. Think of it, no one has ever heard of any prophet raising one to life after four days!"

"That was it, Father. Jesus did it so people would believe. Many of the Jew who had come to visit Mary and had seen what Jesus did believed in him. But some of them went to the Pharisees and told them what Jesus had done. We knew that in their unbelief they would continue to plot against Jesus."

Mother shook her head, murmuring, "Seeing one come from a tomb and still plotting against him!"

"Yes. They still see Jesus as a threat to their position."

Father noted grimly, "Envy."

"Yes, that is it. But because of them Jesus no longer moved about publicly among the people of Judea. Instead, he withdrew to a region near the wilderness, a village called Ephraim, where we stayed.

Father interjected, "I know the place."

"Even there some Pharisees came to Jesus to test him. They asked, 'Is it lawful for a man to divorce his wife for any and every reason?' Jesus replied, 'Haven't your read that at the beginning the

Didymus

Creator made them male and female and said, "For this reason a man will leave his father and mother and be united to his wife, and the two will become one flesh"? So, they are no longer two, but one flesh. Therefore, what God has joined together, let no one separate.' They asked, 'Why then did Moses command that a man give his wife a certificate of divorce and send her away?' Jesus replied, 'Moses permitted you to divorce your wives because your hearts were hard. But it was not this way from the beginning. I tell you that anyone who divorces his wife, except for sexual immorality, and marries another woman commits adultery.'"

Mother asked, "Why do they love divorce so?"

"When we were in the house alone, we asked Jesus about this. He answered, 'Anyone who divorces his wife and marries another woman commits adultery against her. And if she divorces her husband and marries another man, she commits adultery.' We replied, 'If this is the situation between a husband and wife, it is better not to marry.' Jesus went on, 'Not everyone can accept this word, but only those to whom it has been given. For there are eunuchs who were born that way, and there are eunuchs who have been made eunuchs by others, and there are those who choose to live like eunuchs for the sake of the kingdom of heaven. The one who can accept this should accept it.'"

Jahzeel exclaimed, "I want to marry."

I replied, "You should. Yet, we know there are some like John the Baptizer who did not; the same is true of some of the prophets. Their life would have been a burden to their wife. Remember what happened to Ezekiel's wife? He was not even permitted by God to mourn her death. Yet even here, in this remote town, people were bringing little children to Jesus for him to place his hands on them. We rebuked those bringing them, but when Jesus saw this, he was indignant with us. He said, 'Let the little children come to me, and do not hinder them, for the kingdom of God belongs to such as these. Truly I tell you, anyone who will not receive the kingdom of God like a little child will never enter it.' And he took the children in his arms, placed his hands on them, and blessed them."

Anna asked, "Why would you keep children from Jesus?"

"We were wrong in doing so. At the time it seemed as though they would be a burden to Jesus. At this point we started on our way back to Jerusalem. A man ran up to Jesus and fell on his knees before him. He asked, 'Good teacher, what must I do to inherit eternal life?' Jesus answered, 'Why do you call me good? No one is good except God alone. You know the commandments: You shall not murder, you shall not commit adultery, you shall not steal, you shall not give false testimony, you shall not defraud, honor your father and mother. The man declared, 'Teacher, all these I have kept since I was a boy.' Jesus looked at him and loved him. He told him, 'One thing you lack. Go, sell everything you have and give to the poor, and you will have treasure in heaven. Then come, follow me.' At this the man's face fell. He went away sad because he had great wealth."

Jahzeel pointed out, "The man was righteous; you said Jesus loved him!"

Before I could reply, father noted, "These are the commandments dealing with how we are to treat our fellow man, not how we are to respect God."

I answered him first, before my brother. "Yes, Father, you are right. Jesus asked for these specifically. And, yes, Jahzeel, Jesus did love him. I believe he loves every person on earth. Remember that all have sinned and fallen short of God's righteousness. This man was more worried about riches than about God. Jesus looked around and then said to us, 'How hard it is for the rich to enter the kingdom of God!' We were amazed at these words. But Jesus explained, 'Children, how hard it is to enter the kingdom of God! It is easier for a camel to go through the eye of a needle than for someone who is rich to enter the kingdom of God.' We were even more amazed and asked each other, 'Who then can be saved?' Jesus looked at us and said, 'With man this is impossible, but not with God; all things are possible with God.'"

Father exclaimed, "He chooses an impossibility, but then says that with God even the impossible is possible."

Didymus

Jahzeel remarked, "You realize that all the religious leaders except John prize wealth. The Sadducees say that if one is wealthy this proves his righteousness. A claim like this must make them furious."

"I know. But wealth is not a good measure of righteousness—any more than is a lack of wealth. Simon protested, 'We have left everything to follow you! What then will there be for us?' Jesus said to us, 'Truly I tell you, at the renewal of all things, when the Son of Man sits on his glorious throne, you who have followed me will also sit on twelve thrones, judging the twelve tribes of Israel. And everyone who has left houses or brother or sister of father or mother or wife or children or fields for my sake will receive a hundred times as much and will inherit eternal life. But many who are first will be last, and many who are last will be first.'"

Mother echoed, "Other mothers . . . and brothers? So, the other believers will mother you when you need it?"

I replied, gently touching her arm, "I prefer you."

Jahzeel spoke, clearly outraged, though he managed to speak in a normal tone. "So, you will have a throne, as *judge!* Now comes the promise and the real reason you follow . . . !"

Father chided Jahzeel, "You know that is not why he follows."

My elder twin apologized, "I'm sorry, brother. But what about the others? Simon?"

Mother interjected, "Jahzeel, if it is as he says, then you should be proud of your brother. I am."

"Thank you, Mother, but I can't speak for the others. I try not to seek glory for myself. As we were on our way up to Jerusalem, Jesus led and we were astonished, though many of us were afraid. Again, he took us aside and told us what was going to happen to him: 'We are going up to Jerusalem, and the Son of Man will be delivered over to the chief priest and teachers of the Law. They will condemn him to death and will hand him over to the Gentiles, who will mock him and spit on him, flog him, and kill him. Three days later he will rise.' We do not understand any of this. The meaning is hidden from us—we simply do not know what he is talking about.

That doesn't sound like glory to you, does it, Jahzeel?"

Jahzeel answered slowly, "So, he says he will be *killed* and *rise*? Who will raise him? You? Peter? John?"

"I have no idea what he meant. But I do know that some of us desire glory. The mother of Zebedee's sons came to Jesus with her sons and, kneeling down, asked a favor of him. He asked, 'What is it you want?' She said, 'Grant that one of these two sons of mine may sit at your right and the other at you left in your kingdom.' Then James and John, the sons of Zebedee, came and also asked him together, 'Teacher, we want you to do whatever we ask.' Jesus answered them, 'What do you want me to do for you?' They replied, 'Let one of us sit at your right and the other at your left in your glory.' Jesus replied, 'You don't know what you are asking. Can you drink the cup I drink or be baptized with the baptism I am baptized with?' They answered, 'We can.' Jesus said to them, 'You will drink the cup I drink and be baptized with the baptism I am baptized with, but to sit at my right or left is not for me to grant; these places belong to those for whom they have been prepared.'"

Jahzeel spoke then with the hint of a sneer: "See, not all of you apostles are so good."

"No, they are good, but none of us is as good as Jesus. When the rest of us heard about this, we were indignant with James and John. Jesus called us together and said, 'You know that those who are regarded as rulers of the Gentiles lord it over them, and their high officials exercise authority over them. Not so with you. Instead, whoever wants to become great among you must be your servant, and whoever wants to be first must be slave of all. For even the Son of Man did not come to be served, but to serve, and to give his life as a ransom for many.'"

Father commented, "Jesus needed to put them in their place."

"Yes, Father, we all needed it. Now we entered Jericho and were passing through. A man was there by the name of Zacchaeus; he was a chief tax collector and was wealthy. He wanted to see who Jesus was, but because he was short in stature he could not see over the crowd. So, he ran ahead and climbed a sycamore-fig tree to see him, since Jesus was coming that way. When Jesus reached that spot, he looked up and said to him, 'Zacchaeus, come down immediately. I must stay at your house today.' So, he came down at once and welcomed Jesus gladly. All the people saw this and began to mutter, 'He has gone to be the guest of a sinner.' But Zacchaeus stood up and said to the Lord, 'Look, Lord! Here and now, I give half of my possessions to the poor, and if I have cheated anybody out of anything, I will pay back four times the amount.' Jesus said to him, 'Today salvation has come to this house, because this man, too, is a son of Abraham. For the Son of Man came to seek and to save the lost.'"

Father remarked, "Even to a chief tax collector he shows mercy. And it works—he repays!"

I chuckled and replied, "He seemed to be a decent man. Matthew was a tax collector, and you must meet him; he is a wonderful friend. As we were leaving Jericho with a large crowd, a blind man, Bartimaeus, was sitting by the roadside, begging. When he heard that it was Jesus of Nazareth, he began to shout, 'Jesus, Son of David, have mercy on me!' Many rebuked him and told him to be quiet, but he shouted all the more, 'Son of David, have mercy on me!' Jesus stopped and said, 'Call him.' So, we called to the blind man, 'Cheer up! On your feet! He's calling you.' Throwing his cloak aside, he jumped to his feet and came to Jesus. Jesus asked him, 'What do you want me to do for you?' He answered, 'Rabbi, I want to see.' Jesus said, Go, your faith has healed you. Immediately he received his sight and followed Jesus, praising God. When all the people saw it, they also praised God."

Mother enthused, "Another act of mercy."

I went on, "As we continued to get nearer to Jerusalem, Jesus told us a parable because many with us believed that the kingdom of God would appear at once. He said, 'A man of noble birth went to a distant country to have himself appointed king and then to return. So, he called ten of his servants and gave them ten minas of money. He told them, "Put this money to work until I return." However, his subject hated him and sent a delegation after him to say, "We don't want this man to be our king." He was made king, however, and returned home.

'Then he sent for the servants to whom he had given the money, in order to find out what they had gained with it. The first came back and said, "Sir, your mina has earned ten more." The master replied, "Well done, my good servant! Because you have been trustworthy in a very small matter, take charge of ten cities." The second came and said, "Sir, your mina has earned five more." His master replied, "You take charge of five cities."

'Then another servant came and said, "Sir, here is your mina; I have kept it laid away in a piece of cloth. I was afraid of you because you are a hard man. You take out what you did not put in and reap what you did not sow." His master replied, "I will judge you by your own words, you wicked servant! You knew, did you, that I am a hard man, taking out what I did not put in, and reaping what I did not sow? Why then didn't you put my money on deposit, so that when I came back, I could have collected it with interest?"

'Then the master said to those standing by, "Take his mina away from him and give it to the one who has ten minas." They said, "Sir, he already has ten!" The master replied, "I tell you that to everyone who has, more will be given, but as for the one who has nothing, even what they have will be taken away. But those enemies of mine who did not want me to be king over them, bring them here and kill them in front of me.'"

Father commented, "He speaks of rewards—with tests to determine the outcomes."

Jahzeel asked, "Why did he even give the wicked servant one mina if he did not trust him?"

I replied, "Yes, Father, they are tests. And yes, Jahzeel, the nobleman is Jesus. He is just and gives everyone an opportunity. But some are simply not honest. We must work—must remain occupied until his comes. There is no excuse for being idle. After the parable Jesus went on ahead, going up to Jerusalem."

I paused before going on. We were nearly up to date. Then I continued, "Six days before the Passover Jesus came to Bethany, where Lazarus lived, whom Jesus had raised from the dead. Here a dinner was being given in Jesus's honor. Martha served, while Lazarus was among those reclining at the table with him. Then Mary took about a pint of pure nard, an expensive perfume, she poured it on Jesus's feet and wiped his feet with her hair, and the house was filled with the fragrance of the perfume. It was much the same as at Simon the Pharisee's house. But one of Jesus's disciples, Judas Iscariot, objected, asking, 'Why wasn't this perfume sold and the money given to the poor? It was worth a year's wages.' Judas always pays attention to money, as he is keeper of the money bag. Jesus said, 'Leave her alone. It was intended that she should save this perfume for the day of my burial. You will always have the poor among you, but you will not always have me. Truly I tell you, wherever the gospel is preached throughout the world, what she has done will also be told, in memory of her.'"

Mother commented, "The woman who washed his feet some time ago was grateful because she had been forgiven. This Mary is grateful because Jesus brought her brother back from the grave."

Jahzeel probed, "Then he will die?"

"It would appear so, but I don't know when. That part I don't understand. Meanwhile, a large crowd of Jews found out that Jesus was there and came, not only because of him but also to see Lazarus, whom he had raised from the dead. We heard that the chief priest had made plans to kill Lazarus as well, for on account of him many of the Jews were going over to Jesus and believing in him."

Mother, aghast, sought clarity. "They would *kill* him because people believed in Jesus after he was raised? How cruel!"

"They are cruel. Then, as Passover approached, on the first day of the week, as we approached Bethpage and Bethany at the hill called the Mount of Olives, he sent two of us, instructing us, 'Go to the village ahead of you, and as you enter it, you will find a colt tied there, which no one has ever ridden. Untie it and bring it here. If anyone asks you: "Why are you untying it?" say, "The Lord needs it."' We found the colt outside in the street, tied at a doorway.

As we untied it, some people standing there asked, 'What are you doing, untying the colt?' We answered as Jesus had told us to, and the people let us go. When they brought the colt to Jesus and we threw our cloaks over it, he sat on it."

Father commented, "*Sat on* a new, unbroken colt? That is a miracle in itself."

I agreed with a smile. "When he came near the place where the road goes down the Mount of Olives, the whole crowd of disciples began to joyfully praise God in a loud voice for all the miracles we had seen. Many people spread their cloaks on the road, while other spread branches they had cut in the fields. As we passed, I recognized *you* in the crowd. Some of the Pharisees gathered there said to Jesus, 'Teacher, rebuke your disciples!' Jesus replied, 'I tell you, if they keep quiet, the stones will cry out.'"

Father, excitedly, "Yes, we saw and heard."

"But there was more. As he approached Jerusalem and saw the city, he again wept over it and said, evidently to the city itself, 'If you, even you, had only known on this day what would bring you peace. But now it is hidden from your eyes. The days will come upon you when your enemies will build an embankment against you and encircle you and hem you in on every side. They will dash you to the ground, you and the children within your walls. They will not leave one stone on another, because you did not recognize the time of God's coming to you.'"

Anna spoke up, horrorstruck: "What is this? They will *kill children*? When will this be?"

Father remarked, "This doesn't sound like a kingdom."

"I don't know when yet. And I agree that it sounds terrible. When Jesus entered Jerusalem, the whole city was stirred and asked, 'Who is this?' The crowd answered, 'This is Jesus, the prophet from Nazareth in Galilee.' Now the crowd, many of whom had been with him when he called Lazarus from the tomb and raised him from the dead, continued to spread the word. Many people, because they had heard that he had performed this sign, went out to meet him. We heard the Pharisees say to one another,

Didymus

'See, this is getting us nowhere. Look how the whole world has gone after him!'"

Father reflected mournfully, "Why do they hate him? And when will children be dashed to pieces?"

I explained, "They hate him out of envy. They don't know that the children will someday suffer. Jesus entered Jerusalem and went into the temple courts. He looked around at everything, but since it was already late, he led us out to Bethany.

Father commented, "That was only a few days ago."

"Yes. On the following day, as we were leaving Bethany, Jesus was hungry. Seeing in the distance a fig tree in leaf, he went to find out whether it had any fruit. When he reached it, he found nothing but leaves, because it is not the season for figs. Then he said to the tree, 'May no one ever eat fruit from you again.' We heard him say it."

Jahzeel asked, "Why would he say this? He must have known it is not the season for figs."

Father explained, "Jahzeel, the first figs form before the leaves. It may not be the season for the main crop of figs or leaves, but if the tree is in leaf there should be a few figs."

I replied, "He was teaching us a lesson—and I will return to it. On reaching Jerusalem, Jesus entered the temple courts and began driving out those who were buying and selling there, just as he had on that first of the four Passovers at which we saw Jesus three years ago. He overturned the tables of the money changers and the benches of those selling doves, and he would not allow anyone to carry merchandise through the temple courts. As he taught them, he asked, 'Is it not written:

"My house will be called
a house of prayer for all nations?"
But you have made it a den of robbers.""'

Father recalled, "I remember him doing this three years ago. What a stir!"

"Yes, but this time the chief priests and the teachers of the Law heard this and began looking for a way to kill him; they feared him because the whole crowd was amazed at his teaching. Yet they could not find any way to do it, because all the people hung onto his words."

Mother asked yet again, "Are you safe?"

"Yes, I feel assured that I am safe. The blind and lame came to Jesus at the temple, and he healed them. But when the chief priests and teachers of the Law saw the wonderful things he did and the children shouting in the temple courts, 'Hosanna to the Son of David' they were indignant. They asked him, 'Do you hear what these children are saying?' Jesus replied, 'Yes, have you never read,

"From the lips of children and infants
   you, Lord, have called forth your praise'?"

Father enthused, "How well he knows scripture!"

"Yes. Now there were some Greeks among those who went up to worship at the festival. They came to Philip, who was from Bethsaida in Galilee, with a request. They said, 'Sir, we would like to see Jesus.' Philip went to tell Andrew, and Andrew and Philip in turn told Jesus. Jesus replied, 'The hour has come for the Son of Man to be glorified. Very truly I tell you, unless a kernel of wheat falls to the ground and dies, it remains only a single seed. But if it dies, it produces many seeds. Anyone who loves his life will lose it, while anyone who hates his life in this world for my sake will keep it for eternal life. Whoever serves me must follow me; and where I am, my servant also will be. My Father will honor the one who serves me.'"

Father pointed out tenderly, "See, Mother, he is safe. The Father will honor him."

Jahzeel said, still with a hint of scorn, "Yes, but Jesus expects to die as a kernel of wheat to make a harvest?"

I replied, "Thank you, Father. Jahzeel, I don't have an answer. Somewhere in the new grain there must be some remnant of the old grain, but you can't tell where it is. We know grapes. When the vine grows, it comes from a seed. Yet a new vine has no seeds in it—only the fruit has seed. Jesus spoke again, saying, 'Now my soul is troubled, and what shall I say? "Father, save me from this hour"? No, it was for this very reason I came to this hour. Father, glorify your name!' A voice came then from heaven: 'I have glorified it and will glorify it again.' The crowd that was there and heard it said it had thundered; others said an angel had spoken to him. Jesus said, 'This voice was for your benefit, not mine. Now is the time for judgment on this world; now the prince of this world will be driven out. And I, when I am lifted up from the earth, will draw all people to myself.'"

Father replied, "I heard the thunder—in a clear sky. I heard no words, but I was not nearby."

Jahzeel added, "I heard a noise, too. But what is this 'I am lifted up from the earth?' Does he expect to be taken away like Elijah?"

"No. I'm sure it won't be like that. People in the crowd spoke up: 'We have heard from the Law that the Messiah will remain forever, so how can you say, 'The Son of Man must be lifted up'? And who is this 'Son of Man'?" Jesus told them, 'You are going to have the light just a little while longer. Walk while you have the light, before darkness overtakes you. Whoever walks in the dark does not know where they are going. Believe in the light while you have the light, so that you may become children of light.' When he had finished speaking, Jesus left and hid himself from them."

Jahzeel asked, "With all this power, why does he hide? To avoid the crowd?"

"The time is not yet right. When evening came, we went out of the city and returned to Bethany. Yesterday, in the morning, as we went along, we saw the fig tree withered from the roots. Peter said to Jesus, 'Rabbi, look! The fig tree you cursed has withered!' When we saw this, we were amazed. We asked, 'How did the fig tree wither so quickly?' Jesus replied, 'Truly I tell you, if you have faith and do not doubt, not only can you do what was done to the fig tree, but also you can say to this mountain, "Go, throw yourself into the sea," and it will be done. If you believe, you will receive whatever you ask for in prayer. And when you stand praying, if you hold anything against anyone, forgive them, so that your Father in heaven may forgive you your sins.'"

Jahzeel queried, "So, the lesson was about the power to do miracles? Why pick on a fig tree?"

Father explained, "Jahzeel, Israel is the fig tree. We have had little fruit. It was about miracles, yes, but Jesus was saying that we are out of time and that God expects more of us. We are proud of our beautiful leaves but have no fruit to be proud of."

I continued, "In Jerusalem, as Jesus was walking in the temple courts, the chief priests, the teachers of the Law, and the elders came to him. They asked, 'By what authority are you doing these things? And who gave you authority to do this?' Jesus replied, 'I will ask you one question. Answer me, and I will tell you by what authority I am doing these things. Was John's baptism from heaven, or of men? Tell me!' They discussed it among themselves and said, 'If we say, "From heaven," he will ask, "Then why didn't you believe him?" But if we say, "Of men," we will have to fear the people, for everyone held that John really was a prophet.' So, they answered Jesus, 'We don't know.' Jesus said, 'Neither will I tell you by what authority I am doing these things.'"

Father, chuckling again, "They think themselves so wise, but he puts them to shame. He will not be trapped!"

I began to speak but then realized that what I was about to say might give Jahzeel a wrong idea. I breathed a quick and silent prayer but felt I should repeat what Jesus had said, even if it were to cause a misunderstanding. Jesus said that the truth would set us free. It was time to tell truth that would hurt. To stall, I took a long drink of the wine . . .

XVIII

Jahzeel's Conviction

I began, "Jesus went on, asking the leaders, 'What do you think? There was a man who had two sons. He went to the first and said, "Son, go and work today in the vineyard." He answered, "I will not." But later he changed his mind and went. Then the father went to the other son and said the same thing. He answered, "I will, sir." Yet he did not go. Which of the two did what the father wanted?' They answered, 'The first.'"

Jahzeel, with a red face, "Have you talked to Jesus about us? Did the others hear this too? What do you think—that he will curse me as he did this tree?"

I replied softly, "Jahzeel, I only spoke to him about you once, three years ago, and I know he loves you. I did not tell him anything about our working together."

Father answered too, "Jahzeel, you know there were times when you were younger when this kind of thing happened. More than once. It happened to me when I was a boy, too. We are much alike. Thomas had issues, too—we all do. Thomas was quick to resist work, and that angered me, but he invariably relented and did the job. You would have wonderful intentions but often did not complete all the work. It doesn't matter; you both grew out of it. Whether Jesus was speaking about you or not, I do not know. I do know you are both good sons and are both loved,"

After a moment of silence, in which I offered another silent prayer, I spoke: "Jahzeel, I love you, and deep down you know it.

The purpose of the story was not to embarrass you. None of the others know you, save Andrew and John, and they don't know how we worked together. The focus of the story was the religious leaders. Jesus said to all of them, 'Truly I tell you; the tax collectors and the prostitutes are entering the kingdom of God ahead of you. For John came to you to show you the way of righteousness, and you did not believe him, but the tax collectors and the prostitutes did. And even after you saw this, you did not repent and believe him.'"

Jahzeel was looking down, and we all saw it. I prayed and then spoke again: "Jesus went on, lecturing the leaders in parables about what they wanted to do to him: 'A man planted a vineyard. He put a wall around it, dug a pit for the winepress, and built a watchtower. Then he rented the vineyard to some farmers and moved to another place. At harvest time he sent a servant to the tenants to collect from them some of the fruit of the vineyard. But they seized him, beat him, and sent him away empty handed. Then he sent another servant to them; they struck the man on the head and treated him shamefully. He sent still another, and that one they killed. He sent many others; some of them they beat, and others they killed.

'He had one left to send: a son, whom he loved. He sent him last of all, saying, "They will respect my son." But the tenants said to one another, "This is the heir, Come, let's kill him, and the inheritance will be ours." So, they took him and killed him and threw him out of the vineyard. What then will the owner of the vineyard do? He will come and kill those tenants and give the vineyard to others. When the people heard this, they said, "God forbid!"'" Jahzeel, that is about the leaders, not us."

Father pointed out, "We never left our vineyard."

Jahzeel spoke up. "No, it is not about us. Can you imagine?"

Father noted, "This also means that some of them know who he is and want to take what is his from him."

I replied, "Yes, it's about the leaders knowingly trying to kill Jesus. Jesus said to them, 'Have you never read in the Scriptures:

Didymus

"The stone the builders rejected
　　has become the cornerstone;
the LORD has done this,
　　and it is marvelous in our eyes"?

'Therefore, I tell you that the kingdom of God will be taken away from you and given to a people who will produce its fruit. Anyone who falls on this stone will be broken to pieces; anyone on whom it falls will be crushed.'

"When the chief priest and the Pharisees heard Jesus's parables, they knew he was talking about them. I thought they would arrest him, but they were afraid of the crowd because the people held that he was a prophet."

Jahzeel stated, "Everyone knows he is talking about the leaders. They fear him. I think they will try to get Rome to kill him."

"Yes. The Pharisees went out and tried to trap Jesus in his words. They sent their disciples to him, along with the Herodians, spies who pretended to be sincere. They hoped to catch Jesus in something he said, so that they might hand him over to the power and authority of the governor. So, the spies questioned him: 'Teacher, we know that you speak and teach what is right, and that you do not show partiality but teach the way of God in accordance with the truth. Is it right for us to pay taxes to Caesar of not?' Jesus saw through the trap and said to them, 'Show me a denarius. Whose image and inscription are on it?' They replied, 'Caesar's.' Jesus said to them, 'Then give back to Caesar what is Caesar's and to God what is God's.' They could not trap him. They were astonished by his answer and became silent."

Father remarked, "Do they never give up? They cannot trap him."

Jahzeel added, "Their trap was used against them. The Romans will not be upset."

I continued, "The leaders don't give up. Then the Sadducees who claim there is no resurrection came to him with their own trick question: 'Teacher, Moses told us that if a man dies without having children, his brother must marry the widow and raise up offspring for him. Now there were seven brothers among us. The first one married and died, and since he had no children, he left his wife to his brother. The same thing happened to the second and the third brother, right on to the seventh. Finally, the woman died. Now then, at the resurrection, whose wife will she be for the seven since all of them were married to her?' Jesus replied, 'You are in error because you do not know the scriptures or the power of God. At the resurrection people neither marry nor are given in marriage; they will be like the angels in heaven. But about the resurrection of the dead, have you not read what God said to you: "I am the God of Abraham, the God of Isaac, and the God of Jacob"? He is not the God of the dead, but of the living.' When the crowds heard this, they were astonished at this teaching."

Father exclaimed, "Amazing. I know the Sadducees have claimed that no scripture of the Law talks of eternal life, and they have little respect for the prophets, only accepting the Pentateuch. The Pharisees and scribes have for years looked for a passage that proves eternal life in the Pentateuch, and in moments Jesus has put them to shame by proving it from there!"

Jahzeel remarked, "Jesus is good with the Law—I'll give him that. Did you catch what he said their problem was? They don't know the Law as they should, and they don't know the power of God. Jesus knows the Law, and he has power we don't understand. Even if they hate him, they should respect him."

I pointed out, "Some do. At this point one of the teachers of the Law who had heard the discussion realized that Jesus had given an excellent answer, so he asked him, 'Of all the commandments, which is the most important?' Jesus answered, 'The most important is this: "Hear, Oh Israel: The Lord our God, the Lord is one. Love the Lord your God with all your heart and with all your soul and with all your mind and with all your strength." The second is this: "Love your neighbor as yourself." There is no command greater than these.' The teacher replied, 'Well said, teacher. You are right in saying that God is one and there is no other but him. To love him with all your heart, with all your understanding, and with all your strength, and to love your neighbor as yourself are more important than all burnt offerings and sacrifices.' When Jesus saw that he had answered wisely, he said to him, 'You are not far from the kingdom of God.' From then on no one dared ask him any more questions."

Father observed, "This teacher was honest; he heard the truth, and he knew it. He understands loving his neighbor. I also see that Jesus showed him some respect; he said he was near the kingdom of God. He didn't say that about the others. This particular teacher made no attempt to justify himself. It appears that Jesus works with each person in exactly the way each one needs. You told us before that a lawyer asked a similar question, and that lawyer added to the Shema and then attempted to justify himself.

"That time Jesus followed up with a parable about who is a neighbor. To this teacher Jesus quoted the Shema succinctly, without asking how the teacher read the passage. I have thought about what you said before about Jesus allowing the use of the word *mind*. I agree with what you said then: the Greek word for 'heart' doesn't do the Shema justice. But I also see that Jesus used the Greek word *ex*, which makes the passage read 'Love the Lord *from* all your heart, *from* all your soul, *from* all you mind, and *from* all your strength'—going beyond the word *with*, which could have come from the Greek *apo*. Jesus expects depth of commitment to the Lord *from* our inner being."

I nodded and continued, "I believe you see the difference correctly. Certainly, Jesus made them all think. In their pride they knew better than to ask anything further. While the Pharisees were still gathered together, Jesus asked them, 'What do you think about the Messiah? Whose son is he?' They replied, 'The Son of David.' Jesus said to them, 'How is it then that David, speaking by the Spirit, calls him Lord? For he says,

> "The LORD said to my LORD:
>   'Sit at my right hand
> until I put your enemies
>   under your feet.'"

'If then David calls him "Lord," how can he be his son?' The large crowd listened to him with delight. No one could say a word in reply, and from that day on no one dared to ask him any more questions."

Father, thoughtfully, "No more questions? They are afraid."

"They are. They thought that if they could present their view it would persuade the crowds. Now they know that they can never win the people with their words. Jesus knows the scriptures much better than they do, and he engages the crowd far better than they can. Now Jesus addressed both the disciples and the crowds: 'The teachers of the law and the Pharisees sit in Moses's seat. So, you must be careful to do everything they tell you. But do not do what they do, for they do not practice what they preach. They tie up cumbersome loads and put them on other people's shoulders, but they themselves are not willing to lift a finger to move them. Everything they do is done for people to see: They make their phylacteries wide and the tassels on their garments long; they love the place of honor at banquets and the most important seats in the synagogues; they love to be greeted with respect in the marketplaces and to be called "Rabbi" by others.

'But you are not to be called "Rabbi," for you have one Teacher, and you are all brothers. And do not call anyone on earth "father," for you have one Father, and he is in heaven. Nor are you to be called instructors, for you have one Instructor, the Messiah. The greatest among you will be your servant. For those who exalt themselves will be humbled, and those who humble themselves will be exalted.'"

Father summarized, "So, we trust what they say but don't do what they do? I knew that. But he says not to show them the respect they desire—that it belongs to God alone. While I am certain of that, I can't imagine a time when the leaders will not require respect for themselves."

"I agree. Jesus went on, railing against the leaders, 'Woe to you, teachers of the Law and Pharisees, you hypocrites! You shut the door of the kingdom of heaven in people's faces. You yourselves do not enter, nor will you let those enter who are trying to. Woe to you, teachers of the Law and Pharisees, you hypocrites! You travel over land and sea to win a single convert, and when you have succeeded, you make them twice as much a child of hell as you are.'"

Jahzeel exclaimed, "He calls them children of hell! They will want him dead!"

I continued without commenting on my brother's remark; Mother was still in the room, and she worries so about me. "Jesus went on, again attacking the religious leaders: 'Woe to you, blind guides! You say, "If anyone swears by the temple, it means nothing; but anyone who swears by the gold of the temple is bound by that oath." You blind fools! Which is greater: the gold, or the temple that make the gold sacred? You also say, "If anyone swears by the altar, it means nothing; but anyone who swears by the gift on the altar is bound by that oath." You blind men! Which is greater: the gift, or the altar that make the gift sacred? Therefore, anyone who swears by the altar swears by it and by everything on it. And anyone who swears by the temple swears by it and by the one who dwells in it. And anyone who swears by heaven swears by God's throne and by the one who sits on it.'"

Father seconded, "He is right. When someone swears, I doubt him immediately. But you already knew that."

I smiled my acknowledgment and continued, "Jesus went on: 'Woe to you, teachers of the Law and Pharisees, you hypocrites! You give a tenth of your spices, mint, dill, and cumin. But you have neglected the more important matters of the Law: justice, mercy, and faithfulness. You should have practiced the latter without neglecting the former. You blind guides! You strain on a gnat but swallow a camel.'"

Jahzeel, now with a smile of his own, "Look how he makes pictures with words; swallow a camel! How unflattering . . . and yet how fitting!"

"And again Jesus pronounced over them woes: 'Woe to you teachers of the Law and Pharisees, you hypocrites! You clean the outside of the cup and dish, but inside they are full of greed and self-indulgence. Blind Pharisees! First clean the inside of the cup and dish, and then the outside will also be clean. Woe to you teachers of the Law and Pharisees, you hypocrites! You are like whitewashed tombs, which look beautiful on the outside but on the inside are full of bones of the dead and everything unclean. In the same way, on the outside you appear to people as righteous, but on the inside you are full of hypocrisy and wickedness.'"

Father noted, "Yet again he challenged them."

"He did. At this point Jesus pronounced one final woe—the most serious: 'Woe to you, teachers of the Law and Pharisees, you hypocrites! You build tombs for the prophets and decorate the graves of the righteous. And you say, "If we had lived in the days of our ancestors, we would not have taken part with them in shedding the blood of the prophets." So, you testify against yourselves that you are the descendants of those who murdered the prophets. Go ahead, then, and complete what your ancestors started! You snakes! You brood of vipers! How will you escape being condemned to hell?

'Therefore, I am sending you prophets and sages and teachers. Some of them you will kill and crucify; other you will flog in your synagogues and pursue from town to town. And so upon you will come all the righteous blood that has been shed on earth, from the blood of righteous Abel to the blood of Zechariah son of Berekiah, whom you murdered between the temple and the altar. Truly I tell you, all this will come on this generation.'"

Mother echoed in alarm, "*This* generation?"

"That is what he said. Some of us think this is the end, but I do not know yet. Jesus again lamented Jerusalem: 'Jerusalem, Jerusalem, you who kill the prophets and stone those sent to you, how often I have longed to gather your children together, as a hen gathers her chicks under her wings, and you were not willing. Look, your house is left to you desolate. For I tell you, you will not see me again until you say, "Blessed is he who comes in the name of the Lord."'"

Jahzeel commented, his face reddening, "Something is up. Something big. Something *now*. Will he die soon?"

"I don't know. In the temple Jesus sat down opposite the place where the offerings are placed and watched the crowd putting their money into the temple treasury. Many rich people threw in large amounts. But a poor widow came and put in two very small copper coins. Calling us to him, Jesus said, 'Truly I tell you; this poor widow has put more into the treasury than all the others. They all gave out of their wealth; but she out of her poverty put in everything, all she had to live on.'"

Mother murmured, "That poor woman. What faith in God!"

"Yes. I myself don't have that much faith. As Jesus was leaving the temple, one of us said to him, 'Look, Teacher! What massive stones! What magnificent buildings!' Jesus replied, 'Do you see all these great buildings? Not one stone here will be left on another; each and every one will be thrown down.'"

Father reflected, "I can't imagine. I've always admired the gates with the gold vines and grapes."

And Jahzeel interjected, breathing heavily, "Mark my words—he is saying this is the end."

"I don't know. He said much more. When we reached the Mount of Olives opposite the temple, Peter, James, John, and Andrew took him aside. Apparently, they had asked when these things would take place. When we joined them, Jesus was already answering the questions of the four: 'Watch out that no one deceives you. Many will come in my name, claiming, "I am the Messiah," and will deceive many. You will hear of wars and rumors of wars, but see to it that you are not alarmed. Such things must happen, but the end is still to come. Nation will rise against nation, and kingdom against kingdom. There will be famines and earthquakes in various places. All these are the beginnings of birth pains. Be on your guard. You will be handed over to local councils and flogged in the synagogues. On account of me you will stand before governors and kings as witness to them. And the gospel must first be preached to all nations. Whenever you are arrested and brought to trial, do not worry beforehand about what to say. Just say whatever is given you at the time, for it is not you speaking but the Holy Spirit.'"

Jahzeel put in, this time almost shaking, "Can't you see it? He is warning you. A trial. Before whom? The nations? Rome. I don't understand. What I do see it this new kingdom will not happen now!"

"Probably not. I just know Jesus will keep us safe. Jesus continued, 'Brother will betray brother to death, and a father his child. Children will rebel against their parents and have them put to death. Because of the increase of wickedness, the love of most will grow cold. Everyone will hate you because of me, but the one who stands firm to the end will be saved. And this gospel of the kingdom will be preached in the whole world as a testimony to all nations, and then the end will come.'"

Jahzeel, now standing, rigid, in front of me, cried in real alarm, "Thomas. He said that everyone will hate *you* because of him. That is not just the Pharisees—it's the nations. And the end will come . . ." Anna came up and put her hand on his.

I continued, "Jesus went on, 'So when you see standing in the holy place "the abomination that causes desolation," spoken of through the prophet Daniel, which will someday be understood, then let those who are in Judea flee to the mountains. Let no one on the housetop go down to take anything out of the house. Let no one in the field go back to get their cloak. When you see Jerusalem being surrounded by armies, you will know that its desolation is near. Then let those who are in Judea flee to the mountains, let those in the city get out, and let those in the country not enter the city. For this is the time of punishment in fulfillment of all that has been written.

'How dreadful it will be in those days for pregnant women and nursing mothers! Pray that your flight will not take place in winter or on the Sabbath. For then there will be great distress, unequaled from the beginning of the world until now, nor to be equaled again. There will be great distress in the land and wrath against this people. They will fall by the sword and will be taken as prisoners to all the nations. Jerusalem will be trampled on by the Gentiles until the times of the Gentiles are fulfilled. If those days had not been cut short, no one would survive, but for the sake of the elect those days will be shortened. At that time if anyone says to you, "Look, here is the Messiah!" or, "There he is!" do not believe it. For false messiahs and false prophets will appear and perform great signs and wonders to deceive, if possible, even the elect. See, I have told you ahead of time.'"

Jahzeel, deathly pale, breathed, "Thomas, this is the end of the world he is talking of!"

I didn't know what to say, but I uttered an urgent silent prayer for Jahzeel and continued, "Jesus went on, repeating warnings he had already given us: 'So, if anyone tells you, "There he is, out in the wilderness," do not go out; or, "Here he is, in the inner rooms," do not believe it. For as the lightning that comes from the east is visible even in the west, so will be the coming of the Son of Man. Wherever there is a carcass, there the eagles will gather. Immediately after the distress of those days

"the sun will be darkened,
    and the moon will not give its light;
the stars will fall from the sky,
    and the heavenly bodies will be shaken."

'Then will appear the sign of the Son of Man in heaven. And then all the people of the earth will mourn when they see the Son of Man coming on the clouds of heaven, with power and great glory. And he will send his angels with a loud trumpet call, and they will gather his elect from the four winds, from one end of the heavens to the other. There will be signs in the sun, moon, and stars. On the earth, nations will be in anguish and perplexity at the roaring and tossing of the sea. People will faint from terror, apprehensive of what is coming on the world, for the heavenly bodies will be shaken.

'At that time, they will see the Son of Man coming in a cloud with power and great glory. When these things begin to take place,

stand up and lift up your heads, because your redemption is drawing near. Now learn this lesson from the fig tree: As soon as its
twigs get tender and its leaves come out, you know that summer
is near. Even so, when you see all these things, you know that it is
near, right at the door. Truly I tell you, this generation will certainly
not pass away until all these things have happened. Heaven and
earth will pass away, but my words will never pass away.'"

Jahzeel, speaking hoarsely, "This generation will not pass
away! I won't even have time to marry or have children."

"Jahzeel, I don't know when this is for sure. Jesus went on,
'But about that day or hour no one knows, not even the angels in
heaven, nor the Son, but only the Father. As it was in the days of
Noah, so it will be at the coming of the Son of Man. For in the days
before the flood, people were eating and drinking, marrying and
being given in marriage, up to the day Noah entered the ark; and
they knew nothing about what would happen until the flood came
and took them all away.

'That is how it will be at the coming of the Son of Man. Two
men will be in the field; one will be taken and the other left. Two
men will be grinding with a hand mill; one will be taken and the
other left. Therefore, keep watch, because you do not know on
what day your Lord will come. But understand this: If the owner of
the house had known at what time of night the thief was coming, he
would have kept watch and would not have let his house be broken
into. So, you also must be ready, because the Son of Man will come
at an hour when you do not expect him.'"

Jahzeel was more ashen than anyone I had ever seen. He whispered, "Then he is warning that it will be soon."

I replied, "Jesus continued to warn us, 'Careful, or your hearts
will be weighed down with carousing, drunkenness, and the anxi-
eties of life, and that day will close on you suddenly like a trap. For
it will come on all those who live on the face of the whole earth.
Be always on the watch, and pray that you may be able to escape
all that is about to happen, and that you may be able to stand before
the Son of Man.

Didymus

'It's like a man going away: He leaves his house and puts his servants in charge, each with their assigned task, and tells the one at the door to keep watch. Who then is the faithful and wise servant, whom the master has put in charge of the servants in his household to give them their food at the proper time? It will be good for that servant whose master finds him doing so when he returns. Truly I tell you, he will put him in charge of all his possessions. But suppose that servant is wicked and says to himself, "My master is staying away for a long time," and he then begins to beat his fellow servants and to eat and drink with drunkards.

'The master of that servant will come on a day when he does not expect him and at an hour which he is not aware of. He will cut him to pieces and assign him a place with the hypocrites, where there will be weeping and gnashing of teeth. Therefore, keep watch because you do not know when the owner of the house will come back, whether in the evening, or at midnight or when the rooster crows, or at dawn. If he comes suddenly, do not let him find you sleeping. What I say to you, I say to everyone: "Watch!"'"

Father, who has been watching Jahzeel intently, said softly, "We all need to watch, Jahzeel."

I continued again, "Even though he was talking to his apostles, Jesus now gave us a parable—not because he did not trust us but to reinforce the need for us to be watchful: 'At that time the kingdom of heaven will be like ten virgins who took their lamps and went out to meet the bridegroom. Five of them were foolish and five were wise. The foolish ones took their lamps but did not take any oil with them. The wise ones, however, took oil in jars along with their lamps. The bridegroom was a long time in coming, and they all became drowsy and fell asleep.

'At midnight the cry rang out: "Here's the bridegroom! Come out to meet him!" Then all the virgins woke up and trimmed their lamps. The foolish ones said to the wise, "Give us some of your oil; our lamps are going out." They replied, "No, there may not be enough for both us and you. Instead, go to those who sell oil and buy some for yourselves." But while they were on their way to buy the oil, the bridegroom arrived. The virgins who were ready went in with him to the wedding banquet. And the door was shut. Later, the others also came. They said, "Lord, Lord, open the door for us!" He replied, "Truly I tell you; I don't know you." Therefore, keep watch, because you don't know the day or the hour.'"

Father, still watching Jahzeel, as we all were by now, spoke again: "Oil is a symbol of holiness. Some were not prepared, even though they were pure."

I answered, "That may be it, Father. Now Jesus told us how the judgment will be performed: 'When the Son of Man comes in his glory, and all the angels with him, he will sit on his glorious throne. All the nations will be gathered before him, and he will separate the people one from another as a shepherd separates the sheep from the goats. He will put the sheep on his right and the goats on his left. Then the King will say to those on his right, "Come, you who are blessed by my Father; take your inheritance, the kingdom prepared for you since the creation of the world. For I was hungry and you gave me something to eat; I was thirsty and you gave me something to drink; I was a stranger and you invited me in; I needed clothes and you clothed me; I was sick and you looked after me; I was in prison and you came to visit me."

'Then the righteous will answer him, "Lord, when did we see you hungry and feed you, or thirsty and give you something to drink? When did we see you a stranger and invite you in, or needing clothes and clothe you? When did we see you sick or in prison and go to visit you?" The king will reply, "Truly I tell you, whatever you did for the least of these brothers and sisters of mine, you did for me." Then he will say to those on his left, "Depart from me, you who are cursed, into the eternal fire prepared for the devil and his angels. For I was hungry and you gave me nothing to eat; I was thirsty and you gave me nothing to drink; I was a stranger and you did not invite me in; I needed clothes and you did not clothe me; I was sick and in prison and you did not look after me." They also will answer, "Lord, when did we see you hungry or thirsty or a stranger or needing clothes or sick or in prison and did not help you?" He will reply, "Truly I tell you, whatever you did not do for one of the least of these, you did not do for me." Then they will go away to eternal punishment, but the righteous to eternal life.'"

Father noted, "God will judge the nations based on how people have or have not treated others. Jesus sees how we treat others personally."

"Yes, Father, he does. At this point Jesus spoke clearly of his death—though we could not believe it. He said to us, 'As you know, the Passover is two days away, and the Son of Man will be handed over to be crucified.'"

Jahzeel spoke in horror. "Crucifixion? The Isaiah passage?"

"I really don't know. He has otherwise been acting as though this is a normal Passover. Perhaps his words are symbolic. Each evening we go out to spend the night on the Mount of Olives. Today Jesus was teaching at the temple, and all the people came early in the morning to hear him."

Father mused, "As though nothing were going to happen?"

"Yes. Even after Jesus had performed so many signs in their presence, the scribes and Pharisees still would not believe in him. Jesus preached openly: 'This is to fulfill the word of Isaiah:

"Lord, who has believed our message,
    and to whom has the arm of the Lord been revealed?"

And as Isaiah also says:
"He has blinded their eyes
    and hardened their hearts,
so, they can neither see with their eyes,
    nor understand with their hearts,
    nor turn, and I would heal them.'"

'Isaiah said this is because he foresaw Jesus's glory and spoke about him."

Father asked, "He knows they will not believe?"

"He knows who will believe and who will not. Jahzeel, you

asked if I had ever talked to Jesus about you. We did speak once, three years ago, and he said that I should be patient because you *would* believe."

Jahzeel was trembling but remained silent.

I went on, "At that time many even among the leaders believed in him. But because of the Pharisees they would not openly acknowledge their faith for fear they would be put out of the synagogue—for they love human praise more even than the praise of God."

Father said, "Yes, though I believe there were good men there, too. But think of the ones who would rather have the praise of men than of God! How tragic!"

I went on, "Jesus was silent for a moment. Then he cried out, 'Whoever believes in me does not believe in me only, but in the one who sent me. The one who looks at me is seeing the one who sent me. I have come into the world as a light, so that no one who believes in me should stay in darkness. If anyone hears my words but does not keep them, I do not judge that person. For I did not come to judge the world but to save the world. There is a judge for the one who rejects me and does not accept my words; the very words I have spoken will condemn them at the last day. For I did not speak on my own, but the Father who sent me commanded me to say all that I have spoken. I know that his commands lead to eternal life. So, whatever I say is just what the Father has told me to say.'"

Father reflected, "So, this is all from God."

"Jesus sent Peter and John, saying, 'Go and make preparations for us to eat the Passover.' They asked, 'Where do you want us to prepare for it?' Jesus replied, 'As you enter the city, a man carrying a jar of water will meet you. Follow him to the house that he enters, and say to the owner of the house, "The Teacher asks: Where is the guest room where I may eat the Passover with my disciples?" He will show you a large room upstairs, all furnished. Make preparation there.' They left and found everything just as Jesus had told them. So, they prepared the Passover. I had time, so I went there, too. As of now, I must return for this meal, and tomorrow the lamb of the Passover."

Jahzeel spoke quietly then. He had stopped trembling, but his eyes were staring into the distance. "I still do not believe. But if I see that it is so, I will believe. The lamb of Passover. That will be tomorrow. We will see."

I was puzzled by his words. Mother asked again whether I was safe, and I assured her that I was. Father embraced me and told me the family was learning to pray for me. Anna looked understandably worried about Jahzeel but said farewell to me. I told them I would like to see them again during or just after the feast and took my leave. When I left, I again prayed for Jahzeel. He looked more worried than I had ever seen him. He had stated that, if he saw, he would believe. He had already seen miracles. What more could he see? His concerns worried me. Still, I'd been with Jesus now for three earlier Passovers and eaten with him on two. I was now arriving at the room. I was not late.

XIX

Passover Eve
Early Morning

14TH DAY OF NISAN, JEWISH YEAR 3790 (THURSDAY, APRIL 3, EARLY MORNING, AD 30 GREGORIAN CALENDAR) ON CRUCIFIXION DAY, YOM KHAMSHI, (GOOD THURSDAY)

I knocked repeatedly in the dark. I could hear more than one man grumbling over the sleep disturbance. Finally, the keeper of the house opened the door with a lamp. He recognized me and let me in to see my father, who was shocked to see me at this late hour. The keeper left the lamp but told us to keep very quiet.

By now, Mother was also there, looking equally taken aback, and so, too, was Jahzeel. The look on Father's face was one of grave concern. He asked me quickly, "What has happened?"

Speaking softly, I replied, "They arrested Jesus." Mother started to weep, and Father asked, "Who did?" I replied, "Guards from the temple, along with some priests and Pharisees—a mob with swords and clubs."

Mother asked anxiously, "Are you hurt?" to which I replied, "No, just some scrapes and bruises from fleeing down the mountain in the dark."

Now Jahzeel whispered wonderingly, "This is what Isaiah prophesied."

Didymus

Father requested, "If you can speak softly, tell us all that happened. I'm sure you can't sleep now."

I knew he was right and proceeded in a hushed voice, "When I left, it was time for our meal. Jesus had arranged for us to be at a large upper room, and it was prepared. When the hour came, we reclined at the table. Jesus said to us, 'I have eagerly desired to eat this Passover with you before I suffer. For I tell you, I will not eat it again until it finds fulfillment in the kingdom of God.'"

Jahzeel acknowledged softly, "*Not eat it*. He knows Isaiah."

It was easier for me to simply recite what had happened than to speculate on the meaning, so I went on, "After taking the cup, he gave thanks and said, 'Take this and divide it among you. For I tell you that I will not drink again from the fruit of the vine until the kingdom of God comes.' He took bread, gave thanks and broke it, and gave it to us, saying, 'This is my body given for you; do this in remembrance of me.' In the same way, after supper he took the cup, saying, 'This cup is the new covenant in my blood, which is poured out for you.'"

Jahzeel reflected again, wonderingly, "New covenant *in blood*. Not the Passover lamb—*his own* blood. *He is the lamb*."

I was startled that I myself had not realized the implications of the words when Jesus had spoken them. The lamb would be sacrificed tomorrow . . . no, today! I could not think clearly, so I continued to recite what Jesus had said: 'The hand of him who is going to betray me is with mine on the table.' We began to question among ourselves which of us would do this."

Father queried softly, "An *apostle* would betray him?"

"*Has* betrayed him. A dispute arose among us yet again as to which of us was considered to be the greatest. Jesus corrected us, 'The kings of the Gentiles lord it over them; and those who exercise authority over them call themselves benefactors. But you are not to be like that. Instead, the greatest among you should be like the youngest, and the one who rules like the one who serves. For who is greater, the one who is at the table or the one who serves? Is it not the one who is at the table? But I am among you as one who serves. You are those who have stood by me in my trials. And I confer on you a kingdom, just as my Father conferred one on me, so that you may eat and drink at my table in my kingdom and sit on thrones, judging the twelve tribes of Israel.'"

Mother observed poignantly, "He still worries about you as though you are his own children."

She was right. I nodded and continued, "Jesus got up from the meal, took off his outer clothing, and wrapped a towel around his waist. After that, he poured water into a basin and began to wash our feet, drying them with the towel that was wrapped around him."

Mother began to weep again, and I felt hot tears coming, too, which I swiped at. "He came to Simon Peter, who said to him, 'Lord, are you going to wash my feet?' Jesus replied, 'You do not realize now what I am doing, but later you will understand.' Peter said, 'No, you shall never wash my feet.' Jesus answered, 'Unless I wash you, you have no part with me.' Simon Peter replied, 'Then, Lord, not just my feet but my hands and my head as well!' Jesus answered, 'Those who have had a bath need only to wash their feet; their whole body is clean. And you are clean, though not every one of you.'"

Father marveled, "What humility . . . !" His voice broke, then, and he did not finish.

"When he had finished washing our feet, he put on his clothes and returned to his place, asking, 'Do you understand what I have done for you? You call me "Teacher" and "Lord," and rightly so, for that is what I am. Now that I, your Lord and Teacher, have washed your feet, you also should wash one another's feet. I have set you an example that you should do as I have done for you. Very truly I tell you, no servant is greater than his master, nor is a messenger greater than the one who sent him. Now that you know these things, you will be blessed if you do them.'"

I caught my breath before forging ahead with Jesus's words. "'I am not referring to all of you; I know those I have chosen. But this is fulfilling scripture: "He who shared my bread has turned against me." I am telling you now before it happens, so that when it does happen, you will believe that I am who I am. Very truly I tell you, whoever accepts anyone I send accepts me, and whosever accepts me accepts the one who sent me.' After he had said this, Jesus was troubled in spirit and testified, 'Very truly I tell you, one of you is going to betray me.'"

I began to feel the tears welling up again. My voice broke, but I continued, "We were very sad and began to say to him, one after the other, 'Surely you don't mean me, Lord?' Jesus replied, 'The one who has dipped his hand into the bowl with me will betray me. The Son of Man will go just as it is written about him, but woe to that man who betrays the Son of Man! It would be better for him if he had not been born.'

"We stared at one another, at a loss to know which of us he meant. John, the disciple whom Jesus loved, was reclining next to him. Simon Peter motioned to John and said, 'Ask him which one he means.' Leaning back against Jesus, John asked him, 'Lord, who is it?' Jesus answered, 'It is the one to whom I will give this piece of bread which I have dipped into the dish.' Then, dipping the piece of bread, he gave it to Judas, the son of Simon Iscariot. I believe that, as soon as Judas took the bread, Satan entered into him. How else could he do such a thing? Then Judas, the one who would betray him, said, 'Surely you don't mean me, Rabbi?' Jesus answered, 'You have said so.'"

Father, again seeking clarification, "Jesus gave him the bread? He shows an act of loving fellowship and respect to the one who will betray him?"

"Yes."

Mother asked, "How can he show such love to one who should be his enemy?"

"I believe he wants us to show such love, as well."

Jahzeel reflected in a whisper, "Judas? I don't know him, do I?"

"No. We have two Judases among us. Jesus told him, 'What you are about to do, do quickly. None of us at the meal understood why Jesus said this to him. Since Judas had charge of the money, I thought Jesus was telling him to buy what was needed for the festival or to give something to the poor. As soon as Judas had taken the bread, he went out, and it was night. I wasn't sure what it all meant then, though I know now.

"When he was gone, Jesus said, 'Now the Son of Man is glorified and God is glorified in him. If God is glorified in him, God will glorify the Son in himself, and will glorify him at once. My children, I will be with you only a little longer. You will look for me, and, just as I told the Jews, so I tell you now: Where I am going, you cannot come. A new command I give you: Love one another. As I have loved you, so you must love one another. By this everyone will know that you are my disciples, if you love one another.'"

Mother, weeping softly, marveled, "What love he shows you. He must have known he was to be arrested."

"He must have. Simon Peter asked him, 'Lord, where are you going?' Jesus replied, 'Where I am going, you cannot follow now, but you will follow later.' Peter asked, 'Lord, why can't I follow you now? I will lay down my life for you.' Jesus said, 'Simon, Simon, Satan has asked to sift you as wheat. But I have prayed for you, Simon, that your faith may not fail. And when you have turned back, strengthen your brothers.' But he replied, 'Lord, I am ready to go with you to prison and to death.' Jesus answered, 'I tell you, Peter, before the rooster crows twice, you will deny three times that you know me.'"

Jahzeel, wonderingly, "He knows what *Satan desires*? And he knows that Simon will turn away? What is this?"

"I really don't know. Then Jesus said, 'Do not let your hearts be troubled. You believe in God; believe also in me. My Father's house has many rooms; if that were not so, would I have told you that I am going there to prepare a place for you? And if I go and prepare a place for you, I will come back and take you to be with me, that you also may be where I am. You know the way to the place where I am going.'"

Father interjected, "I don't really understand. He says a moment earlier that you cannot come, and now he speaks of preparing a place for you there? It is a hard saying."

Didymus

"It is hard, and I don't know. I can't even think about it now. I said to Jesus, 'Lord, we don't know where you are going, so how can we know the way?' Jesus answered, 'I am the way and the truth and the life. No one comes to the Father except through me. If you really know me, you will know my Father, as well. From now on, you do know him and have seen him.'"

Father, clearly baffled, "Wait! You just said, 'We don't know where you are going . . .'"

"I did say that, but then Jesus explained that *he* is the way to life."

Jahzeel stated, "Again, he basically says that he is somehow one with the Father."

Noticing that this time my brother was not protesting, I went on, "Philip said, 'Lord, show us the Father and that will be enough for us.' Jesus answered, 'Don't you know me, Philip, even after I have been among you such a long time? Anyone who has seen me has seen the Father. How can you say, "Show us the Father"? Don't you believe that I am in the Father and the Father is in me? The words I say to you I do not speak on my own authority. Rather, it is the Father, living in me, who is doing his work. Believe me when I say that I am in the Father and the Father is in me; or at least believe on the evidence of the works themselves. Very truly I tell you, whoever believes in me will do the works I have been doing, and they will do even greater things than these, because I am going to the Father. And I will do whatever you ask in my name, so that the Father may be glorified in the Son. You may ask me for anything in my name, and I will do it. If you love me, keep my commands.'"

Jahzeel nodded as if fully in agreement. Now I was perplexed with my brother, but I went on, "Jesus continued, 'And I will ask the Father, and he will give you another advocate to help you and be with you forever, the Spirit of Truth. The world cannot accept him because it neither sees him nor knows him. But you know him, for he lives with you and will be in you. I will not leave you as orphans; I will come to you. Before long, the world will not see me anymore, but you will see me. Because I live, you also will live.

On that day you will realize that I am in my Father, and you are in me, and I am in you. Whoever has my commands and keeps them is the one who loves me. The one who loves me will be loved by my Father, and I, too, will love them and show myself to them.'"

Father whispered three questions in rapid sequence. "He will not leave you? He prepares a place for you? Spirit of truth?"

"It's hard to follow; perhaps I will understand more about the place later. Jesus talks often of the Holy Spirit—as he does the Spirit of Truth, and I believe the two to be one and the same. Then Judas (not Judas Iscariot, who had already left) asked, 'But, Lord, why do you intend to show yourself to us and not to the world?' Jesus replied, 'Anyone who loves me will obey my teaching. My Father will love them, and we will come to them and make our home with them. Anyone who does not love me will not obey my teaching. These words you hear are not my own; they belong to the Father, who sent me.'"

Jahzeel had turned away, staring, but I went on, "Jesus continued: 'All this I have spoken while still with you. But the Advocate, the Holy Spirit, whom the Father will send in my name, will teach you all things and will remind you of everything I have said to you. Peace I leave with you; my peace I give you. I do not give to you as the world gives. Do not let your hearts be troubled, and do not be afraid.

'You heard me say, "I am going away, and I am coming back to you." If you loved me, you would be glad that I am going to the Father, for the Father is greater than I. I have told you now before it happens, so that when it does happen you will believe. I will not say much more to you, for the prince of this world is coming. He has no hold over me, but he comes so that the world may learn that I love the Father and do exactly what my Father has commanded me.'"

Father asked, "Before *it* happens? Before what happens?"

"I suppose his capture."

Jahzeel stated softly, "No. He speaks of his death."

I drew a deep breath, then replied, "I really don't know. Then

Didymus

Jesus asked us, 'When I sent you without purse, bag, or sandals, did you lack anything?' We answered, 'Nothing.' He said to us, 'But now if you have a purse, take it, and also a bag; and if you don't have a sword, sell your cloak and buy one. It is written, "And he was numbered with the transgressors," and I tell you that this must be fulfilled in me. Yes, what is written about me is reaching its fulfillment.' We said, 'See, Lord, here are two swords.' He replied, 'That's enough!'"

Jahzeel observed in a reverent tone, "It's from Isaiah again."

I continued, again surprise at how much Jahzeel seemed to be agreeing, "Jesus said, 'Come now, let us leave.' When we had sung the traditional psalm—you know, the one with the refrain 'His mercy endures forever'—we went out to the Mount of Olives."

Jahzeel mouthed "His mercy . . ." without finishing the thought.

Father asked, "Were they there waiting for him?"

"No. There is much more. As we walked, Jesus told us, 'This very night you will all fall away on account of me, for it is written:

"I will strike the shepherd,
   and the sheep of the flock will be scattered."

'But after I have risen, I will go ahead of you into Galilee.'"

Father reflected, "Then he knew you would flee. But what is this 'I have risen'? He talked before about rising."

"Yes, he did—and I don't know. At this point, Peter replied, 'Even if all fall away on account of you, I never will.' Jesus answered, 'Truly I tell you, this very night, before the rooster crows, you will disown me three times.' But Peter declared, 'Even if I have to die with you, I will never disown you.' And all of us said the same."

Mother observed in an undertone, "I'm sure you didn't think you would run."

"No, I didn't. But Jesus went on, 'I am the true vine, and my Father is the gardener. He cuts off every branch in me that bears no fruit, while every branch that does bear fruit he prunes so that it will be even more fruitful. You are already clean because of the word I have spoken to you. Remain in me, as I also remain in you. A branch cannot bear fruit by itself; it must remain in the vine. Neither can you bear fruit unless you remain in me.

'I am the vine; you are the branches. If you remain in me and I in you, you will bear much fruit; apart from me you can do nothing. If you do not remain in me, you are like a branch that is thrown away and withers; such branches are picked up, thrown into the fire, and burned. If you remain in me, and my words remain in you, ask whatever you wish, and it will be done for you. This is to my Father's glory, that you bear much fruit, showing yourselves to be my disciples.'"

Jahzeel noted, "He knows the difference between a pruned branch and a cutting. A branch by itself, even if planted, will die. We take cuttings from dormant vines, using straight year-old growth half a finger thick. We use the flat base of the cutting, keeping a forearm length right-side up with a handful of nodes, and plant deeply so that only one node is not in the ground. The top is cut at an angle. Only then can it take begin to root. Only an established vine will bear."

Father pointed out, "He knows what a vinedresser does; we prune and wash the grapes so they will bear well. Our nation has always been the vine; many of the prophets say so. God has indeed washed us much—and pruned us upon occasion. The fruit does nothing but remain on the vine; the sun shines and gives light to the vine, the vine supplies the nutritional needs of the fruit through the root, and the vinedresser provides water. But a vine with no fruit must be removed, and it doesn't even burn for long. This Jesus is so good with words. He knew you would all flee, so he said you must remain in him. If you remained in him, you could not flee. He is clever with words."

"I had not thought about remaining and fleeing. I see the contrast now; I don't think I knew how much I need him. I never did the miracles; God did them though me. I could not have done them unless I remained on the vine. I'm of no value off the vine. Jesus continued, 'As the Father has loved me, so have I loved you. Now remain in my love. If you keep my commands, you will remain in my love, just as I have kept my Father's commands and remain in his love. I have told you this so that my joy may be in you and that your joy may be complete.

'My command is this: Love each other as I have loved you. Greater love has no one than this: to lay down one's life for one's friends. You are my friends if you do what I command. I no longer call you servants, because a servant does not know his master's business. Instead, I have called you friends, for everything that I learned from my Father I have made known to you. You did not choose me, but I chose you and appointed you so that you might go and bear fruit, fruit that will last, and so that whatever you ask in my name the Father will give you. This is my command: Love each other.'"

Father whispered, "Again, he says to remain. You said that all of you fled. But here, he tells you to remain in love. That's something you *have* done." Father paused then and reflected, "But he says he *lays down his life*. It is his to lay down; it is not being taken from him. He describes his death, and he *allows* this. It is as though accepting or allowing this is within his own power."

I could not help staring at Father. He was reflecting such wisdom. I had not even noticed this nuance, but Father had. I was the apostle who had been with Jesus, but it was Father who demonstrated such insight and saw what was happening. I went on, "Jesus then warned us, 'If the world hates you, keep in mind that it hated me first. If you belonged to the world, it would love you as its own. As it is, you do not belong to the world. I have chosen you out of the world. That is why the world hates you.

'Remember what I told you: "A servant is not greater than his master." If they persecuted me, they will persecute you also. If they obeyed my teaching, they will obey yours also. They will treat you this way because of my name, for they do not know the one who sent me. If I had not come and spoken to them, they would not be guilty of sin, but now they have no excuse for their sin. Whoever hates me hates my Father as well. If I had not done among them the works no one else did, they would not be guilty of sin. As it is, they have seen, and yet they have hated both me and my Father.

'But this is to fulfill what is written in their Law: "They hated me without reason." When the Advocate comes, whom I will send to you from the Father, the Spirit of Truth who goes out from the Father, he will testify about me. And you also must testify, for you have been with me from the beginning. All this I have told you, so that you will not fall away. They will put you out of the synagogue; in fact, the time is coming when anyone who kills you will think they are offering a service to God. They will do such things because they have not known the Father or me. I have told you this, so that when their time comes you will remember that I warned you about them. I did not tell you this from the beginning because I was with you.'"

Father again spoke, sorrow lining his face. "You will face persecution, too." Mother turned pale at the realization, and Father continued, "But he has given you a charge: to testify of him. So, you will go on doing that. You are doing that now. You do it well." I perceived understanding in Jahzeel's eyes—understanding I had not expected.

I half nodded, not knowing what to say, but then continued: "Jesus went on, 'But now I am going to him who sent me. None of you asks me, "Where are you going?" Rather, you are filled with grief because I have said these things. But very truly I tell you, it is for your good that I am going away. Unless I go away, the Advocate will not come to you; but if I go, I will send him to you. When he comes, he will prove the world to be in the wrong about sin and righteousness and judgment: about sin, because people do not believe in me; about righteousness, because I am going to the Father, where you can see me no longer; and about judgment, because the prince of this world now stands condemned.'"

Jahzeel, frightened but sober, "This Advocate will convict the world of sin because they don't believe in Jesus."

I realized that Jahzeel had keyed onto the statement about the sin of unbelief and the judgment for that sin because he was not a believer, and I was at a loss as to how to respond. Father, seeing the fear in Jahzeel's eyes, asserted, "I am anxious for this advocate. Will you all have the Holy Spirit like the Baptizer?"

Grateful for Father's assistance in an awkward moment, I shook my head to show that I did not know, then went on, "Jesus now explained future guidance: 'I have much more to say to you, more than you can now bear. But when he, the Spirit of Truth, comes, he will guide you into all the truth. He will not speak on his own; he will speak only what he hears, and he will tell you what is yet to come. He will glorify me because this is from me, and he will receive what he will make known to you. All that belongs to the Father is mine. That is why I said the Spirit will receive from me what he will make known to you.'"

Father concurred, "Yes, the Advocate is the Spirit of Truth: the Holy Spirit. That is how you healed people when you went out in pairs. He was with you then. Now it seems that you will have him all the time, as the Baptizer did."

I realized that what Father had just said was true; this had not occurred to me before. I continued, "Jesus went on to say, 'In a little while you will see me no more, and then after a little while you will see me.' At this, some of us said to one another, 'What does he mean by saying, "In a little while you will see me no more, and then after a little while you will see me," and "because I am going to the Father"? We don't understand what he is saying.'"

Jahzeel stated, "None of you understands at this point, either."

"I still don't. Jesus saw that we wanted to ask him about this, so he said to us, 'Are you asking one another what I meant when I said, "In a little while you will see me no more, and then after a little while you will see me"? Very truly I tell you, you will weep and mourn while the world rejoices. You will grieve, but your grief will turn to joy. A woman giving birth to a child has pain because her time has come, but when her baby is born, she forgets the anguish because of her joy that a child is born into the world.

'So with you: Now is your time of grief, but I will see you again, and you will rejoice, and no one will take away your joy. In that day you will no longer ask me anything. Very truly I tell you, my Father will give you whatever you ask in my name. Until now you have not asked for anything in my name. Ask and you will receive, and your joy will be complete.'"

Father reflected again, "Now you mourn. Especially now. He knew. He does not promise you happiness, because happiness is based on circumstances, on what is happening around and to you. What is happening is sad, but he promises you joy. He promises us joy. He tells you to ask. You must pray for this joy."

I realized that Father was tracking with all of this—and that his conclusions were right, but I didn't feel it then. I did not fully realize yet that I had to choose to be joyful, so I went on without pursuing that subject with Father. "Jesus spoke further to us: 'Though I have been speaking figuratively, a time is coming when I will no longer use this kind of language but will tell you plainly about my Father. In that day you will ask in my name. I am not saying that I will ask the Father on your behalf. No, the Father himself loves you because you have loved me and have believed that I came from God. I came from the Father and entered the world; now I am leaving the world and going back to the Father.'"

Jahzeel noted again, "He speaks of his death."

"I don't know. Then we said, 'Now you are speaking clearly and without figures of speech. Now we can see that you know all things and that you do not even need to have anyone ask you questions. This makes us believe that you came from God.' Jesus replied, 'Do you now believe? A time is coming and is in fact come when you will be scattered, each to your own home. You will leave me all alone. Yet I am not alone, for the Father is with me. I have told you these things so that in me you may have peace. In this world you will have trouble. But take heart! I have overcome the world.'"

Jahzeel realized, "He even knew that you would be coming here."

Mother said, "Thomas, he has again promised you. This is not over."

Didymus

I realized her concern for me. At that moment I couldn't even look up to meet her gaze, but I still continued, "At this point, Jesus looked toward heaven and prayed: 'Father, the hour has come. Glorify your Son, that your Son may glorify you. For you granted him authority over all the people that he might give eternal life to all those you have given him. Now this is eternal life: That they know you, the only true God, and Jesus Christ, whom you have sent. I have brought you glory on earth by finishing the work you gave me to do. And now, Father, glorify me in your presence with the glory I had with you before the world began.'"

Father, thinking ahead, "He is going to God."

I realized that this must be so but chose in the moment not to confirm Father's conclusion, instead pressing forward with "Then Jesus prayed for us: 'I have revealed you to those whom you gave me out of the world. They were yours; you gave them to me, and they have obeyed your word. Now they know that everything you have given me comes from you. For I gave them the words you gave me, and they accepted them. They knew with certainty that I came from you, and they believed that you sent me. I pray for them. I am not praying for all the world but for those you have given me, for they are yours. All I have is yours, and all you have is mine. And glory has come to me through them. I will remain in the world no longer, but they are still in the world, and I am coming to you. Holy Father, protect them by the power of your name, the name you gave me, so that they may be one as we are one.

'While I was with them, I protected them and kept them safe by that name you gave me. None has been lost except the one doomed to destruction, so that scripture would be fulfilled. I am coming to you now, but I say these things while I am still in the world, so that they may have the full measure of my joy within them. I have given them your word, and the world has hated them, for they are not of the world any more than I am of the world. My prayer is not that you take them out of the world but that you protect them from the evil one. They are not of this world, even as I am not of it. Sanctify them by the truth; your word is truth. As you sent me into the world, I have sent them into the world. For them I sanctify myself, that they, too, may be truly sanctified.'"

Mother again spoke. "Thomas, he prayed for your protection. I see that you were safe, even in this night, when he protected you, but now God will protect you."

I realized that she was right. She was now more confident than me. I nodded and continued, "Jesus now prayed for all his followers: 'My prayer is not for them alone. I pray also for those who will believe in me through their message, that all of them may be one, Father, just as you are in me and I am in you. May they also be in us so that the world may believe that you have sent me. I have given them the glory you gave me, that they may be one as we are one, I in them and you in me, so that they may be brought to complete unity. Then the world will know that you sent me and have loved them, even as you have loved me.

'Father, I want those you have given me to be with me where I am and to see my glory, the glory you have given me because you loved me before the creation of the world. Righteous Father, though the world does not know you, I know you, and they know that you have sent me. I have made you known to them and will continue to make you known in order that the love you have for me may be in them and that I myself may be in them.'"

Father recognized, his hand on my shoulder, "He wants restoration for us with the Father . . . for all of us."

How could Father know so much? I merely nodded, going on, "When Jesus had finished praying, we crossed the Kidron Valley. On the other side there is a garden called Gethsemane, and we went into it. Jesus said to us, 'Sit here while I pray.' He took Peter, James, and John along with him, looking distressed, but left us behind. The hour was late, and we were weary. I slept."

Father noted, "This is just a short time ago?"

"Perhaps two hours. We were awakened when Judas Iscariot came into the garden. He knew the place because Jesus had often met with us there. Judas came guiding a detachment of soldiers and some officials from the chief priests and the Pharisees. They were carrying torches, lanterns, and weapons. Judas approached Jesus to kiss him, but Jesus asked him, 'Judas, are you betraying the Son of Man with a kiss?' Going at once to Jesus, Judas said 'Rabbi!' and kissed him."

Jahzeel hissed, attempting to keep his voice low, "How could he?"

"I don't know. Jesus went out and asked them, 'Who is it you want?' They replied, 'Jesus of Nazareth.' Jesus answered, 'I am he.' At this, they drew back and fell to the ground! Again, he asked them, 'Who is it you want?' Again, they replied, 'Jesus of Nazareth.' Jesus answered, 'I told you that I am he. If you are looking for me, then let these men go.'"

Father exclaimed, "The soldiers fell to the ground at his word. He still has complete power—power over the soldiers, *complete* control. He could have stopped this. He didn't."

Jahzeel whispered yet again, "It's the Isaiah passage."

I went on, "The men seized Jesus and arrested him. When we saw what was going to happen, we cried out, 'Lord, should we strike with our swords?' Simon Peter, who had a sword, drew it and struck the high priest's servant, cutting off his right ear. Jesus said to him, 'Put your sword back in its place, for all who draw the sword will die by the sword. Do you think I cannot call on my Father, and he will at once put at my disposal more than twelve legions of angels? But how, then, would the Scriptures be fulfilled that say it must happen in this way? No more of this!' And he touched the man's ear and healed him."

Mother wondered, "He heals one of his captors. How can they still do this to him?"

Father commented, "It is not them on their own; this is of Satan."

I nodded my head again. "Then Jesus said to the chief priests, the officers of the temple guard, and the elders, who had come for him, 'Am I leading a rebellion, that you have come with swords and clubs? Every day I was with you in the temple courts, and you did not lay a hand on me. But this is your hour when darkness reigns.'"

Father spoke knowingly. "He knows them. The crooked are at their worst at night."

I continued, "Then the detachment of soldiers with its commander and the Jewish officials arrested Jesus and let us go, as Jesus had asked. Then we all deserted him and fled, terrified." I again confirmed that I had fled, just as Jesus had predicted.

Father nodded before pointing out, "Jesus commanded them to let you go. They had no choice. And you came here."

"I didn't realize how difficult it would be to flee out of the garden and down the Mount of Olives. I was grateful for the full moon. I could hear the others tripping and running into things as well. I did not want to yell out my position in case the guards decided to round us all up, too. It was clear that they were taking Jesus back for some sort of trial. I knew that it was near midnight and that the Sanhedrin never met at night, so I thought they would be taking him somewhere else until morning. I suddenly realized that I had no idea where to go. I determined that I must return to you; at least I knew where you were staying. I would be safe here.

"I didn't realize how difficult it would be even with the full moon to find my way through Jerusalem in the dead of night. In the daytime, that is not a problem, but the streets are winding, and now the shadows are long. I could tell the general direction at first from the Mount of Olives and the temple Mount in the distance, but once I was down in the streets, I rarely could see either. It was quiet, so I could not tell the area of any of the markets or businesses. The cattle were even still. I was glad this was not the actual Passover night; it will be even more quiet tonight. By the time I reached where you were staying, it was the middle of the night.

Jahzeel confirmed, "You had to come here. Jesus said you would."

Father spoke thoughtfully. "I am not sure if there will be a real trial; the Sanhedrin never meets at night, and this is the morning of the day of the feast. I can't see how they could do it. You have told us several times that he has escaped with ease those who meant him harm. It seems that he intended this arrest."

Didymus

Jahzeel spoke softly, his eyes wide in astonishment: "He will be a Passover sacrifice."

"No Jahzeel, that cannot be. Perhaps he will die, but he cannot be that. God has always forbidden human sacrifice. It cannot be. Stoning, perhaps . . ."

Father reasoned, "The Romans control death sentences. Oh, they may ignore a random stoning, but this is public. Perhaps they will send him to King Herod; Jesus is Galilean and under Herod's jurisdiction. We know what he did to John the Baptizer."

I remembered Jesus speaking of carrying a cross. No, it could not be that; there wouldn't be time before Passover. I asked, "But who would send him to Herod?"

Father spoke in an urgent whisper. "Thomas, you must find the other apostles. You have said that Simon Peter sees himself as a leader, as do the sons of Zebedee. Or one of the others? Do you think you can find them?"

It was already nearing dawn, and I was exhausted, but I knew he was right. I conceded, "I must try."

Jahzeel unexpectedly offered, "You have not slept—would you like help?"

I was surprised but realized that my brother spoke in love. I thought for a moment before responding and then said, "No, Jahzeel, you look like me. They may be looking for me as well. I do not want you arrested. You have Anna to worry about. Besides, you know only a few of them. I know many more disciples, as well as Jesus's family. Let me look."

Jahzeel pointed out, "Jesus ordered them to let you go. They had no choice."

Mother, who had been quiet for a time, spoke: "Yes, you must go. First, though, eat something. You look terrible. I know you cannot rest now, but you need energy, not a fast."

I thought and then consented. "You are right. First, may we pray?" There were nods. I prayed, "Father, I do not know what they are doing to Jesus. I do not know where the others are, but if there is anything I can do, please help me, and [as an afterthought, realizing how demanding the prayer must have sounded] let your name be glorified in what is done this day. Amen." I felt Father's arms encircling me first and then Mother's, which were trembling. Then I felt Jahzeel's strong embrace as well. I also felt my own tears coursing unabated down my cheeks, and this time I did not try to stop them.

Mother moved away, and I reclined for a moment. My eyes were so heavy. Suddenly I awoke, finding myself looking at Father. I asked, "Did I fall asleep?"

"Yes, but only for a short time. There is no shame in it. You are cut and bruised, not to mention exhausted. Mother has food. Eat—then you may go." I nodded. I saw that the bread was ready and still warm. The sun was up. Things looked safer in the light. I offered a hurried thanks and ate, asking "Where is Jahzeel?" Father, looking serious, responded, "He is asking about your friends. He took your advice seriously, and he will not go far; he promised. He will return very soon."

I continued to eat for a moment. Then I saw Jahzeel, looking worried, "Shalom," he said somberly.

I replied automatically, "Shalom." I was finished eating. Mother came in, too.

Jahzeel began to speak, "I didn't find out anything about your friends . . . well, almost nothing. The city is filled with the story. Jesus was brought before the Sanhedrin early in the morning, before light."

Father surmised, "They could not have had many members present. Besides, that's against tradition."

"They don't care about tradition now. They had enough there to have a trial. First before Annas, the chief priest."

Father commented, "They needed time to call the leaders."

"Yes. Then he was sent to Caiaphas."

"Neither of them wanted to go out, so they brought Jesus to them."

"Well, by then it was daybreak. The chief priests and most of the Sanhedrin met. They looked for evidence, but their statements did not agree. Of course, that didn't stop them. Finally, the high priest charged with the case adjured Jesus to testify whether he was the Messiah."

"He did not deny it, did he?"

"Jesus said, 'I am'—and that they would see so for themselves. The high priest called this blasphemy." Pausing a moment to glance at me, my brother went on, "They all condemned him to death."

I protested, "But they have no right to execute."

"They are sending him to Pilate."

"Pilate? The Roman Governor of Judea? A Roman doesn't care about blasphemy. That's a matter for the religious courts."

Father interjected, "But they will think of something. They would prefer that the Romans do the dirty work, so they can relieve their consciences a little."

Jahzeel added, again looking at me to gauge my reaction. "There is one more thing: Judas, the one who betrayed him, hung himself. Apparently, he turned over Jesus for thirty pieces of silver. When he found they were going to kill him, he tried to give the money back. Of course, they didn't care. He couldn't face what he had done, so he hung himself."

I was silent. It was so hard to believe. Then I said, "I can't imagine. For the price of a slave. He seemed no different from any of the rest of us."

Jahzeel proceeded, "Jesus is at Pilate's palace now. I suspect some of your friends must be nearby."

"Thank you, Jahzeel. Stay here; if anyone from this family is arrested, it must be me. Think of Anna."

"I will stay here for now, brother." He embraced me then. So did Mother, in tears, followed by Father, who offered, "I don't look like a disciple; would you like me to go with you?"

"No, I don't know what I can do, and Mother will need you here."

Father nodded, and with a final look back I started out. It was a long way to Pilate's palace.

XX

Tetelestai (It Is Paid For)

I t was finished. As we walked back to the family, Jahzeel put his arm around my shoulder; I was grateful for the support. The apostles were my brothers, but this was my twin. He understood. We walked in silence for a time, until Jahzeel asked, "When will you return to the apostles?" I didn't answer. I could not even think about it.

When we arrived, it was almost evening. Father and Mother both greeted us. They knew what had happened; everyone knew what had happened. They had felt the earthquake. The darkness. We sat together for a time, Mother weeping. I wept, too, and Father looked shaken. I realized that, although Jahzeel was somber, he did not share our grief. Now I was puzzled. He had shown me such love, but for him the emotion of the hour did not seem like sorrow. Why not? Finally, I blurted out, "Jahzeel, where is your grief?"

Father looked stunned, but Jahzeel answered back immediately, "I now believe."

This was even more shocking. I had on this day lost my own faith. How could Jahzeel say this? I was unaccountably angry.

Jahzeel could see my ire, and he raised a hand, signifying for me to wait, before beginning to speak softly. "Thomas, remember the Isaiah passage?" He walked over to his satchel and removed the scroll. He opened it and began to read, line by line:

Didymus

"Who has believed what we have heard?
   And to whom has the arm of the LORD been revealed?

"He grew up before him like a young plant
   and like a root out of dry ground.

"He didn't have an impressive form
   or majesty that we should look at him,
   no appearance that we should desire him."

Jahzeel stopped. "Did you see his frame? No one would particularly be drawn to him. This was *fulfilled, today, in our presence.*"

"He was despised and rejected by men,
   a man of suffering who knew what sickness was.

"He was like someone people turned away from;
   he was despised, and we didn't value him."

Jahzeel stopped again, "No one was ever despised or rejected like Jesus just was. He suffered as no other man has. Did you watch? Many, even I, had to turn away from him. The Jews despised him. Again, you watched it happen."

"Yet he himself bore our sicknesses,
   and he carried our pains;
but we in turn regarded him stricken,
   struck down by God, and afflicted."

Jahzeel paused yet again, "No one has ever been struck down by God or afflicted like him. All those healings? He bore the pain of each and all today. You saw it happen, Thomas!"

"But he was pierced because of our rebellion,
   crushed because of our iniquities;

the punishment for our peace was on him,
    and we are healed by his wounds."

"Thomas, we saw him pierced. It wasn't for his sin; it was for our rebellion. Our iniquities. He was punished and wounded for us. You saw it."

"We all like sheep have gone astray;
    we all have turned to our own way,
and the LORD has laid on him
    the iniquity of us all.
He was oppressed and afflicted,
    yet he did not open his mouth.

"Like a lamb led to the slaughter
    and like a sheep before her shearers is silent,
he did not open his mouth."

"Did you not all flee like sheep in the middle of the night? Each on his own. You heard him before Pilate—he did not defend himself."

"He was taken away because of oppression and judgment,
    and who considered his fate?"

"Has there ever been greater oppression? Worse judgment?"

"For he was cut off from the land of the living;
    he was struck because of my people's rebellion."

Jahzeel stopped again. "Today I am ashamed of my people— the Jews—for our rebellion. He was cut off for our open rebellion and sin."

"He was assigned a grave with the wicked,
    but he was with a rich man at his death,

Didymus

because he had done no violence
   and had not spoken deceitfully."

"He was buried in a rich man's tomb—Joseph is rich! Yet no one was ever able to accuse him of violence or deceit."

"Yet the LORD was pleased to crush him severely.
When you make him a guilt offering,
   he will see his seed, he will prolong his days,
and by his hand the LORD's pleasure will be accomplished."

"The guilt offering is to make reparations to God. Did he not tell you that this was the will of God?"

"After his anguish,
   he will see light and be satisfied."

Jahzeel turned and faced me, his eyes glowing. "He will see light. You told us he said he would rise in three days. This will happen!"

"By his knowledge,
   my righteous servant will justify many,
and he will carry their iniquities."

"He will justify us because he carried our iniquities. He has carried mine!"

"Therefore, I will give him the many as a portion,
   and he will receive the mighty as spoil."

"I don't understand this part yet; didn't he say that they who pierce him will see him? Perhaps that will happen later. I don't know, . . . but I know this is true!"

"Because he willingly submitted to death,
   and was counted among the rebels;
Yet he bore the sin of many
   and interceded for the rebels."

My brother finished, "Have you ever seen someone die so willingly? He was crucified between two rebels. He bore the sin of many, including mine. I even heard him intercede for one of the rebels who had earlier railed on him, as soon as the man had repented. Thomas, Jesus fulfilled the scripture concerning the Messiah! You believed after seeing the miracles. Now I saw scripture fulfilled. I didn't think I would ever trust anyone but myself, but I now trust Jesus—The Christ. I trust that he will accomplish all that needs to be done."

I was silent, at a loss for what to say. What he had just said sounded so true. It was all so rational, so right. But I knew that I no longer believed. It had been too much, too tragic. And I was too angry. Angry against God. I stated simply, "I can no longer believe. It was too much."

Father spoke gently. "Jahzeel, I am glad you now believe. And Thomas, you need time. Passover is a reflective time. Use it wisely. I know there is much more to tell and to discuss. Right now, we have no time. It is still Passover, time for the Passover Seder." He launched into the usual rhetoric, beginning with the age-old formulation, "How is this night unlike any other night?" Mother was weeping. I knew what must be said, of course, but right now wanted to scream: "It is unlike any other night; they killed the Messiah! Jesus is dead!"

The next morning, I arose quietly. It still seemed impossible. Mother was up, preparing food. Father was awake, too, looking thoughtfully though a window out at the city. Jahzeel was staring at the Isaiah scroll he had paid to have made. I said quietly to him,

Didymus

"You must have paid handsomely to get that scroll made."

"I did. You know me; I would never pay much for anything I didn't need. I think God led me to have it made. Several times I thought it was a mistake; I got it to convince you." Then, with a chuckle, he mused, ". . . And I was the one it convinced."

Father put in, "God works in mysterious ways . . ."

I thought about that for a moment. Jesus was dead. No mystery about that. It was wrong. It was a mistake.

Father continued, "Isaiah also said,

'As the heavens are higher than the earth,
    so are my ways higher than your ways
    and my thoughts than your thoughts.'"

I refused to think about this and remained silent.

Father reflected, "Thomas, you and Jahzeel both have strong wills. Like me; it is hard for you to accept anything from others."

I thought to myself: "This is true of Jahzeel," rationalizing that it could not be true of me. I, after all, had accepted Jesus first.

Father asked kindly, "Do you care to tell us all that happened yesterday?"

I remain silent, looking down. Finally, I stated, "Jahzeel was there. I cannot speak of it right now."

Jahzeel nodded to Father and then to Mother and began, "I followed Thomas at a distance. He was talking to another apostle, I think, when I found him near Pilate's palace."

I filled them in, "It was Nathaniel—a good man."

Jahzeel nodded. "He said that Jesus had already been taken before Annas, Caiaphas, and the Sanhedrin. Jesus was found guilty of blasphemy and sentenced to death. Since this was public, they could not stone him; as we know, the Jews are no longer allowed to execute, so they sent Jesus to Pilate on the basis of some other charges."

Father queried, "They met so early?"

"John had told Nathaniel that Pilate had already sent Jesus

to Herod: Jesus if from Nazareth and under Herod's jurisdiction. Pilate didn't want to deal with the priests, since he knew they had sentenced Jesus out of envy, and he knew Jesus was not leading an insurrection. Jesus taught peace, which Pilate well knew. Imagine a charge of insurrection without huge numbers of people dying. Pilate wanted no problems with the Jews over the Passover, with so many people in residence in Jerusalem, and so preferred to have Herod deal with this thorny issue. Peter and John had listened in on the trial after midnight—John knew the family of Caiaphas and had somehow managed to get them in."

Father noted, "Zebedee has a fish market in Jerusalem, bringing salted fish from Galilee; John probably has delivered to the palace and to all of the wealthy many times."

Jahzeel continued, "People recognized Simon as a disciple, but he denied three times that he even knew Jesus. Simon and John went to Herod's palace to see what would happen next. The two were able to get in because a disciple named Joanna is the wife of Chuza, Herod's household manager. She got them close enough to hear what Herod said. They were gone for only an hour or two. Herod didn't want to deal with the priests, either."

Mother observed, "I'm surprised that Herod didn't keep him, as he had John the Baptizer."

Jahzeel nodded his agreement and said, "We stayed in the shadows of an alley. Others came—I expect they were apostles— but all remained quiet."

I entered the conversation at last, admitting, "I was too troubled to even introduce them. I'm sorry that I didn't remember my manners, Father."

Father nodded to me with a wry half-smile, and Jahzeel continued, "After a time, we saw a procession of soldiers returning to the Praetorium, the Roman court, with Jesus bound in their midst. When they entered, we saw Simon Peter and John following at a distance. They came into the alley with us. John told us, 'It went poorly. Herod asked Jesus to perform some miracle, as though he were a court magician. When Jesus didn't answer, he asked many frivolous questions. All the while, the chief priest stood there accusing him. Finally, Herod mocked and ridiculed him, put him in a king's robe, and sent him back. He would do nothing.'"

Father reflected, "Herod thought he was a magician . . ."

"He was simply getting rid of Jesus. Pilate, sitting there on his judgment seat, looked upset. He called together the chief priests, the rulers, and the people and said to them, 'You brought me this man as one who was inciting the people to rebellion. I have examined him in your presence and have found no basis for your charges against him. Neither has Herod, for he sent him back to us; as you can see, he has done nothing to deserve death. Therefore, I will punish him and then release him.'"

Father remarked, "I'm surprised. Pilate usually has a taste for blood."

Jahzeel spoke again. "Pilate was afraid of Jesus. I could see it in his mannerisms; he did not look like a strong ruler when Jesus was nearby. Everyone has heard of the miracles, and the Romans are very superstitious. Pilate has a tradition each year at the festival of releasing one prisoner. Given Jesus's popularity, he had hoped it would be Jesus. The crowd came up and asked Pilate to do what he usually did. He asked, 'Do you want me to release to you the king of the Jews?' But the chief priests stirred up the crowd to have Pilate release a real insurrectionist and murderer, Barabbas. He was the only prisoner in Jerusalem at the time who posed a threat to Rome."

Mother lamented, "I don't even have words to say about how bad those men are! At Passover, yet!"

Jahzeel went on, "The crowd shouted, 'Away with the man! Release Barabbas!' I think Jesus's disciples who were present kept silent for fear of the leaders of the Jews. They would be put out of the synagogue at the very least if they were to petition on behalf of Jesus. Pilate asked again, 'What shall I do, then, with Jesus, who is called the Messiah?' They shouted as one, 'Crucify him!' Pilate asked yet a third time, 'Why? What crime has this man committed? I have found in him no grounds for the death penalty. Therefore, I will have him punished and then release him.'"

Father pointed out, "Herod does not need Barabbas starting a real insurrection; soldiers died in the last."

Jahzeel nodded, continuing, "Pilate had Jesus flogged. The soldiers mocked him and put a crown of thorns on his head and a robe on him, taunting, 'Hail, king of the Jews!' They spat upon him and struck him again and again. We could see it from the alley."

Mother began to weep again, and my brother went on, "Once again Pilate came out and said to the Jews gathered there, 'Look, I am bringing him out to you to let you know that I find no basis for a charge against him. Here is the man!' They shouted, 'Crucify!' but Pilate answered, 'You take him and crucify him. As for me, I find no basis for a charge against him.'"

Father reflected, "I'm not sure what the priests did to gain the crowd's approval; it does not make sense to me."

Jahzeel explained, "The priests brought their own disciples in. Perhaps Satan persuaded them. The Jewish leaders insisted, 'We have a Law, and according to that Law he must die, because he claims to be the Son of God.' When Pilate heard this, he was even more afraid; he asked Jesus in our hearing, 'Where do you come from?' but Jesus gave no answer. Pilate pressed him with, 'Do you refuse to speak to me? Don't you realize I have power either to free you or to crucify you?' Jesus answered, 'You would have no power over me if it were not given to you from above. Therefore, the one who handed me over to you is guilty of a greater sin.'"

Father marveled, "Even now, he does not condemn Pilate?"

Jahzeel answered, "Pilate tried to set Jesus free, but the Jewish leaders were shouting, 'If you let this man go, you are no friend of Caesar. Anyone who claims to be a king opposes Caesar.' When Pilate heard this, he brought Jesus out and sat down on the judge's seat on the stone pavement, called Gabbatha; it was now before the sixth hour on Preparation Day for the Passover. He said, 'Here is your king.' But they shouted, 'Crucify him!' Pilate asked again, 'Shall I crucify your king?' to which the chief priests answered, 'We have no king but Caesar.'"

Didymus

Father muttered, "These priests have Pilate in fear over what they will write to Rome."

Jahzeel agreed. "Pilate realized an uproar was starting—one led by the priests. Pilate took water and washed his hands in front of the crowd, declaring, 'I am innocent of this man's blood. It is your responsibility!' The people answered, 'His blood is on us and on our children.'"

Mother wept aloud. "They don't know what they are saying."

Jahzeel again agreed, "They don't. Children should not be responsible for the sins of their parents. Pilate did not know what he was saying, either; I think Pilate judged himself through his action, and he can never wash himself clean of his guilt over this. The Romans forced Jesus to carry his own cross, even after the beating. They led Jesus to the place called Golgotha. Jesus was so weak they had a man passing by carry his cross for him."

Father empathized, "After that sort of beating, the cross would have been too much for *Samson* to carry!"

Jahzeel was quiet for a moment, then continued, "A large number of people followed him, including us and the women who had been attending to his needs. All of the apostles were in the group following him, as well as his mother, Mary, and his half-brothers. The weeping was unforgettable. The apostles, except for John, who was with Mary, stayed far back. Jesus turned and addressed the women: 'Daughters of Jerusalem, do not weep for me; weep for yourselves and for your children. For the time will come when you will say, "Blessed are the childless women, the wombs that never bore and the breasts that never nursed!" Then

"they will say to the mountains, 'Fall on us!' and to the hills, 'Cover us!'"

'For if people do these things when the tree is green, what will happen when it is dry?'"

Mother breathed, "Do you see how much he cares for the people, even now? He is a true king."

Jahzeel continued his report. "Two other men, criminals, were led out with him to be executed. When they came to the place called the Skull, they crucified him there, along with the criminals, one on his right and the other on his left. Jesus prayed for those crucifying him: 'Father, forgive them, for they do not know what they are doing.' Then they offered him wine mixed with myrrh, but he did not take it. It was after the sixth hour when they crucified him."

Father shook his head. "So much happened in the morning."

Jahzeel continued, "Pilate had a notice prepared and fastened to the cross, which read 'JESUS OF NAZARETH, THE KING OF THE JEWS.' Many of the Jews read this sign, for the place where Jesus was crucified was near the city, and the sign was written in Aramaic, Latin, and Greek. The chief priests protested, but Pilate answered, 'What I have written, I have written.'"

Father noted, "They can't control everything."

Jahzeel went on, "The solders took his clothes, dividing the kingly robe into four shares with the undergarment remaining. The robe was seamless, woven in one piece. They said to each other, 'Let's not tear it but decide by lot who will get it.'"

Mother, weeping, "What shame they made him endure."

Jahzeel shed tears now, too. "Yes, and those passing by hurled insults at him, shaking their heads and saying, 'You who are going to destroy the temple and build it in three days, save yourself! Come down from the cross, if you are the Son of God!' In the same way the chief priests, the teachers of the Law, and the elders mocked him. They said, 'He saved others, but he can't save himself! If he's the king of Israel, let him come down now from the cross, and we will believe in him. He trusted in God. Let God rescue him now if he wants him, for he said, "I am The Son of God."' The soldiers also came up and mocked him. They offered him wine vinegar and taunted, 'If you are king of the Jews, save yourself.'"

Father asserted, "I'm glad I did not see this. Thomas, I think I understand a little of what your feel. I think Jesus believed that, if he had opted to save himself, he would not have been able to save us."

Didymus

Jahzeel responded, "I had not realized that. I could not think—only watch. At first, both criminals on the other crosses profaned Jesus. One of the criminals who hung there continued to hurl insults at him: 'Aren't you the Messiah? Save yourself and us!' But the other rebuked him, asking, 'Don't you fear God, since you are under the same sentence? We are punished justly, for we are getting what our deeds deserve. But this man has done nothing wrong.' Then he turned toward Jesus and said, 'Jesus, remember me when you come into your kingdom.' Jesus answered him, 'Truly I tell you, today you will be with me in paradise.'"

Mother marveled, "Even now he thinks of a criminal before himself!"

Jahzeel went on, "When Jesus saw his own mother there, and John by her, he said to her, 'Woman, here is your son,' and to John, 'Here is your mother.'"

Mother, crying unabashedly, "He cares for his mother at this time? He trusts her to John instead of to her own sons?"

Jahzeel acknowledged her but continued, "He agonized in pain from noon until three in the afternoon. Then darkness came over all the land. At about three in the afternoon Jesus cried out in a loud voice, 'Eli, Eli, lema sabachthani?' Or My God, My God, Why have you forsaken me? When some of those standing there heard this, they reported, "He's calling Elijah."

Father interjected, "We saw the darkness, too, of course. I heard this morning that everyone in the entire land experienced it, and that all were terrified. He was not calling Elijah; he was quoting from the psalms. In fact, all that you have spoken about Jesus's passion, his extreme emotion, harks back to one of David's Psalms: 'My God, my God, why have you forsaken me? Why are you so far from saving me, so far from the words of my groaning? O my God, I cry out by day, but you do not answer...

Jahzeel continued, "Jesus said, 'I am thirsty.' Immediately one of them ran and got a sponge. He filled it with wine vinegar, put it on a staff, and offered it to Jesus to drink. The rest said, 'Now leave him alone. Let's see if Elijah comes to save him.'"

Father interjected, "They thought that Elijah had more power than Jesus? Ridiculous."

Jahzeel replied, "It was near the end. After receiving the drink, Jesus said, 'It is finished.' He called out in a loud voice, 'Father, into your hands I commit my spirit.' With that, he bowed his head and give up his spirit. Think of it; Jesus says tetelestai at the end! It is finished!"

I quipped cynically, "Yes, it is finished indeed. We all are."

Jahzeel answered quickly, "No, brother. It's a business term. Jesus was stating that the contract is complete. Our sin account is paid in full. He finished his work. There is nothing more to do."

I knew what Jahzeel meant, but I could not think about that now. To my disillusioned mind, it was over.

Father declared, "He gave up his spirit. He was strong. He could have lasted for hours; he died of his own choice."

Jahzeel agreed, "Yes, Father, he did. The earth began to shake, and rocks split. People were terrified. The centurion and those with him who were guarding Jesus saw the earthquake and all that was happening and were terrified, exclaiming in wonder and alarm, 'Surely he was the Son of God!' Some women were watching from a distance. When all the people who had gathered to witness this exhibition saw what had taken place, they beat their breasts and went away.

Mother asked in wonder, "Did we not hear Jesus say that, if he were not praised, the rocks would cry out? The noise we heard as the rocks split was horrifying!"

Father confirmed, "We, too, felt the quake. Everyone did."

Jahzeel took up the story. "This morning I was told that the veil of the temple was split in two, from top to bottom, at that very moment. They say it was the earthquake. Yet how could an earthquake tear a veil from top to bottom without toppling the temple itself? I say it was the hand of God."

Father reflected, "That veil hid God from us. I believe God has removed that separation."

Didymus

Unable to take it any longer, I shouted out to my whole family, "Jesus is in a tomb!"

All were quiet for a moment. Then Jahzeel spoke. "I am only saying what I heard this morning. Yesterday, the Jewish leaders, not wanting the bodies left on the crosses during the Sabbath, asked Pilate to have the legs of the crucified broken and the bodies taken down. The soldiers came and broke the legs of the first man who had been crucified with Jesus and then those of the other. When they came to Jesus, they found that he was already dead and did not bother to break his legs. Instead, one of the soldiers pierced Jesus's side with a spear, bringing forth a sudden flow of blood and water."

Subdued now after my outburst, I recalled sorrowfully, "That was the hardest thing to see. . ."

Father pointed out, "They couldn't break his legs; you can't have a proper sacrifice of a lamb with a blemish like broken legs."

Jahzeel went on, "We stayed near the cross until the body was taken down. Jesus's blood was on the cross; so much like the blood we spread at Passover where the lintel and the door jamb come together. It had never occurred to me that the point at which they come together also forms a cross. Joseph of Arimathea, a member of the Council, asked Pilate's permission to take down the body, and he and Nicodemus did so, anointing it with myrrh and aloes—a very large amount. These two wrapped it in strips of linen and took it to Joseph's tomb, which was cut out of rock, laid it there before sunset, and rolled a stone in front of the entrance. Pilate set a Roman guard and sealed the tomb to prevent anyone from entering."

Father remarked, "There is much talk about Roman guards posted at the tomb. Whoever heard of such a thing? No one has ever escaped from a tomb, and all of Jesus's followers are afraid of being arrested for this 'insurrection.'"

Jahzeel again picked up the thread of the narrative. "We stayed together for a time, weeping, until Thomas decided it was time for us to return. John asked when Thomas would return. And he said he didn't know. John pointed out that Jesus had told them that all of this would happen. Then the two of us returned here."

Father asked, "When will you go to John and the others?"

Jahzeel looked at me for guidance, and I simply repeated, "I don't know."

I remained quiet during the day. Each time Father, Mother, or Jahzeel tried to bring me back to reality, I shut them down. I was glad for them, but I was also mourning deeply. I nursed my wounds, and although I knew that they were wounded, too, I found it impossible to emerge from my place of utter and unremitting pain. I had thought during all my time with Jesus that I had found the shalom I had been looking for, . . but I had been wrong. Jesus was dead!

XXI

Resurrection Sunday

17ᵀᴴ Day of Nisan, Jewish year 3790,
First Resurrection Sunday, April 6, AD 30

A t dawn on the morning of the first day of the week, we felt a brief earthquake, not nearly as long or as strong as the one at the time of Jesus's death. Under normal circumstances, this would have been the subject of conversation for days.

My agony still ran deep. It was to the point that I was hurting the ones I loved. I simply remained in my sulk. At one point Mother began talking about Anna and her family, who were staying nearby; I lashed out, "Jahzeel can now become her husband, since he, too, believes. Perhaps the reason he believes is so that he can have her as wife."

Mother began to cry, and Father responded quickly and harshly, "Thomas, we know you are hurting; we all are, though your wound is deeper than ours. But you disrespect your brother and Anna's parents by such talk, and you hurt your mother. You know your brother has genuine faith. I do not know what Anna's parents now plan; they are hurting as well. Jesus still has many followers. None of us knows what to do next. We thought you apostles would show us, but you appear unable."

I realized that he was right. I knew my father was still my authority, but more than that, I knew that I had hurt them all acutely, perhaps especially Jahzeel. I knew that I was not behaving as Jesus had commanded, in love; instead, I was acting in bitterness, as the devil would have me behave. How long since I had prayed? I couldn't even recall. I knew that I should repent, but instead I weakly apologized to my family.

"Father, you are right. Jahzeel, I'm sorry for the way I am treating you. I'm sorry for the way I am treating you all. I believe your faith is more genuine than mine. Mother, I should not have spoken that way. Forgive me. Jahzeel, you and Anna can enter the time of a joyful wedding soon. Passover is ended; it was a time of reflection, of gratitude. I have been ungrateful to all of you and to God. Our people have been delivered. I honor that."

I was silent for a moment before going on, "I must find the other apostles and discuss what we are to do now. It is a responsibility. I must do it before we all return home."

Father asked, "Will you stay in Jerusalem?"

I answered, "We have no income. The Pharisees here will now punish any known followers of Jesus. They will have Rome's support, to protect against any new 'insurrection.'"

Father replied, "Do what you need to do. If you need a place to stay, our home is always your home. The Pharisees will not bother us much in Galilee."

I spoke again, "I will likely be back in a few hours. Perhaps the apostles have already gone home. Or perhaps they have all been arrested. I'm not sure it matters which . . ."

After I left, I realized that again I was hurting the ones I loved. I didn't care. I had descended into a deep funk and I did not want out. I didn't know what I would do when I returned home, but I had no hope for any future. I was in a state of disillusioned apathy. Briefly, I thought about praying, but my anger suppressed that impulse. My emotions would not allow reason to creep into my spirit. My mind was made up, and my will, as Father had more than once pointed out, is very strong.

Didymus

When I returned, I simply came into the building and stopped. I knew my family would want to know what had happened, but I didn't care. Father spoke first, "Did you find your friends?"

"I saw the apostles."

Mother asked, "Did they say anything?"

"Yes."

Father again, "What did they say, Thomas?"

I replied, again churly, "They were all there. Peter had denied Jesus three times on Passover, just as Jesus had said. So much for being a model leader. John had fallen asleep when Jesus asked him to watch that night in Gethsemane."

Father replied, "You all scattered . . . "

"We are all cowards."

Mother said, "No, it was prophesied; you said so yourself."

"Prophesied or not, I still ran."

Father asked, "What all did you talk about for over an hour?"

"A few of the women went to the tomb to anoint the body again, . . . as though that would help."

Mother pointed out soothingly, "Son, that is a good work. Who went?"

"Mary Magdalene, Mary the mother of James, and Salome. The body had already been wrapped by Joseph of Arimathea and Nicodemus, and I'm sure they spent more on spices than the women could; after all, they have favor; they are rich."

Father spoke softly. "It is not the money; it is their love."

"It did no good! None at all! Someone took the body already."

Mother dropped her dish. Father looked shocked and gasped, "Who would do this? There was a Roman guard!"

"I don't know. Does it matter?"

"Of course, it matters! Do any of the followers have courage to take down Roman soldiers? The priests or Pharisees would not have done this! Romans would not attack Romans. This was God!"

"So, God takes him now when it is too late? Fine. There is no reason for it now. It is too late. God failed."

Father took me by the shoulders and looked me in the eye before saying, "No one will disrespect God in my house, Thomas—no matter how you feel!"

I realized how bad that had sounded, and although I didn't care, I respected him as my father and said, "Father, I repent. God has not failed. He does as he chooses, so he does not fail."

Mother was crying openly now. I continued, "Mary Magdalene came back from the tomb and said the stone had been rolled back and the guards were gone. Peter and John ran to the tomb to see. They came back and verified that this was true. John thinks Jesus arose."

Mother looked up, a new light in her eyes. "Why, that is wonderful! Why would you not have said that earlier?"

"John is always hopeful. Peter came back with him—not hopeful."

Father reminded me, "Thomas, you said he had denied Jesus. Perhaps Peter is ashamed?"

"Even if Jesus did arise, it could never be the same—we are all ashamed. And I don't believe he arose . . ."

Mother, through her tears, "Thomas, you must find out what has happened; there are many depending on you and on all the apostles. You, and others, must know the truth."

Just then Jahzeel came in and asked, "Thomas, is there any news?"

I stared at the floor, and Father reported succinctly, "The tomb is empty, and John believes Jesus arose!"

Jahzeel asked, "Then why, Thomas, are you still so upset?"

"John may believe. I do not."

"Why are you here?

"The others don't know what to do, either. What *can* we do?"

"You must find out."

"Oh, if you all insist. Still, it is over; Jesus is gone." With that I stomped out of the house.

As I walked back, I realized I was yet again hurting my family, but I didn't care whom I hurt.

Didymus

I returned an hour later, having decided to simply tell the family the news and be done with it. Father greeted me at the door, but I declined to say Shalom. I came in and simply recited what I had heard. "When Peter and John left the tomb, Mary Magdalene stayed. Mary claimed that, as she stood outside the tomb crying, she stooped and looked in to see two angels in white, sitting at the foot and head of where Jesus had lain. They asked her why she was crying, and she said, 'They have taken away my Lord, and I don't know where they have put him.'"

Father echoed, "Angels? What else did she say?"

"The women claim they were told that he had arisen and would go before us into Galilee. Mary claims that, as she turned, she saw a man, who also asked her, 'Woman, why are you crying? Who is it you are looking for?' Thinking him to be the gardener, she said, 'Sir, if you have carried him away, tell me where you have put him, and I will get him.' The man said to her, 'Mary,' and she turned to him and called out 'Rabboni!' She said it was Jesus, and that he said to her, 'Do not hold me here, for I have not yet ascended to the Father. Go instead to my brothers and tell them, "I am ascending to my Father and your Father, to my God and your God."'"

Jahzeel, thrilled, exclaimed, "He has arisen!"

I spat, "The women thought so. When Mary and the other women returned to tell the apostles the news, they reported that Jesus had met them, saying, 'Greetings' and that they had fallen down and worshipped him. He reportedly said to them, 'Do not be afraid. Go and tell my brothers to go to Galilee; there they will see me.' The women told the others all these things, but it seemed like nonsense to them, as it did to me—we simply did not believe them."

Mother stated sternly, "You do not believe simply because they are women!"

Father and Jahzeel both looked at her, and I realized with them that she was on the brink of true anger! So, I responded, more gently, "It's just so incredible. If Jesus were to arise, would he not speak to his apostles first?"

Mother chided, "To you who refuse to believe? If the other apostles are acting like you, then I am sure Jesus would *not* choose to come to you first."

Father interjected softly, "Thomas, she makes a good point. . ."

I realized that she did. It was nearly dark now, so I conceded, "I will inquire of the others in the morning. I will find out whether there are any *facts*."

It was a quiet night, though filled with anxiety.

XXII

My Despondency

18ᵀᴴ DAY OF NISAN, MONDAY, APRIL 7, AD 30

The next morning, I was again the last to rise. Jahzeel was filled with news, announcing almost as soon as my eyes were open, "An angel rolled away the stone at the time of the earthquake on the first day of the week, and his appearance was so bright that the guards had first quaked and then had frozen with fear. Later, they went to the chief priests instead of to their commanding officers, because they were afraid of execution for letting the Roman seal on the tomb be broken. The elders gave the solders money, telling them to say, 'His disciples came during the night and stole him while we were asleep. If the governor finds out, we will satisfy him.' So, the soldiers took the money and did as they had been instructed. Although the Jews had circulated the story, the truth was also circulating. I was told that other tombs opened also and that saints came out and were seen by many."

This report was amazing, but at this point I didn't care. My family had decided to stay in Jerusalem for a few days, until we knew what was happening. I thought briefly about the soldiers. They could be executed. It would take a lot of money to buy off the governor or the commanding officers. The Jews still saw Jesus as a real problem. It was curious; they had won, yet they were not acting that way. After listening to some small talk, I left for the house the other apostles were staying at.

I was gone less than an hour. As I returned to my family, I nursed my wounds. Jesus was dead. Others had seen a vision, or something, but not I. It was not the same for me as it had been. I saw myself now as less than the remaining apostles. Apostles and other disciples had seen visions of Jesus. Even the women had seen visions of Jesus. Why not me?

When I arrived, my family wanted to know of any news. Anna was there, too. They gathered, and I told them what had been told to me, dutifully reporting as "fact," though I couldn't bring myself to believe. I began, "When I arrived, there were several people trying to tell me of more visions of Jesus. Cleophas, one of the disciples, and a friend had left Jerusalem yesterday, but they were back already. They claimed that, as they talked about all these things on the way, Jesus himself came up and walked with them but hid his identity from them.

"He had asked, 'What are you discussing together as you walk along?' They stopped, amazed that anyone coming from Jerusalem would not know of the crucifixion. They asked, 'Are you the only one visiting Jerusalem who does not know the things that have happened in these days?' Jesus asked them, 'What things?' and they told him, 'About Jesus of Nazareth, a prophet, powerful in word and deed before God and all the people. The chief priests and our rulers handed him over to be sentenced to death, and they crucified him; but we had hoped he was the one who was going to redeem Israel. What is more, it is the third day since all this took place. Some of our women went to the tomb early this morning but didn't find his body. They came and told us that they had seen a vision of angels, who said he was alive. Some of our companions went to the tomb and found it just as the women had said, but they did not see Jesus.' Jesus, they further reported, had said to them, 'How foolish you are, and how slow to believe all that prophets have said! Did not the Messiah have to suffer these things and then enter his glory?' And beginning with Moses and all the Prophets, he explained to them what was said in all the Scriptures concerning himself."

I continued, "Cleopas told us that, when they approached their destination, Jesus seemed as though he were going farther. They urged him, 'Stay with us, for it is nearly evening; the day is almost over.' So, he went in with them. When he was at the table with them, he took bread, gave thanks, broke it, and began to give it to them. Then their eyes were opened, and they recognized him, and he disappeared from their sight. They asked each other, 'Were not our hearts burning within us while he talked with us on the road and opened the scriptures to us?'"

I sighed and almost stopped, but my family looked thoroughly engrossed in what I saw as an unlikely account—so I went on, "Cleopas said that they returned at once to Jerusalem. There, on the evening of the first day of the week, while they were in the house with locked doors for fear of the Jewish leaders, they came in and told them, 'It is true! The lord has risen and has appeared.' They told them what had happened. While they were still talking about this with Cleopas, the doors still locked, Jesus himself appeared and stood among them and said to them, 'Peace be with you.'"

Mother raised her hands, gasping, "He lives!"

I decided to continue. My family deserved to hear this. "So they said. They were startled and frightened, thinking they were seeing a ghost, or psuche, soul life only. Jesus said to them, 'Why are you troubled, and why do doubts rise in your minds? Look at my hands and feet. It is I myself! Touch me and see; a spirit does not have flesh and bones, as you see I have.' When he had said this, he showed them his hands and feet. And while they still did not believe it because of joy and amazement, he asked them, 'Do you have anything here to eat?' They gave him a piece of broiled fish, and some honeycomb and he took it and ate it in their presence. He said to them, 'This is what I told you while I was still with you: Everything must be fulfilled that is written about me in the Law of Moses, the Prophets, and the Psalms.'"

Father spoke, "Don't you see, son? He must fulfill all scripture."

Jahzeel also spoke. "He is showing everyone that he is indeed the Messiah. He entered a room without using the door. Thomas, you know the scriptures; he has risen with a body capable of so much more than his old one."

Father agreed, reflecting, "I have often wondered what we will be in the resurrection. We have God's promise that there will be one. You told us that Jesus talked about a grain falling to the ground to die, in order that new life may come forth. We know this happens with grapes, too. We also know the large white caterpillar. We usually destroy them when we find them, because we don't want them eating the grape leaves. When a large white caterpillar climbs on a leaf, it makes a chrysalis around itself. We usually ignore them at this point because they aren't eating anything. At this stage, if you break the chrysalis, you find only juice; there is no evidence of the caterpillar that went inside. But if you wait, a large white butterfly emerges. It bears no resemblance to the caterpillar, but you know it once was the very same caterpillar. God may have such a metamorphosed body that can even pass through closed doors, as Jesus did. What a wonderful thing to imagine."

I knew he was trying to encourage me, but I continued without comment, my tone flat, "The others also told me that Jesus said, 'Peace be with you! As the Father has sent me, I am sending you.' And with that he breathed on them and said, 'Receive the Holy Spirit. If you forgive anyone's sins, their sins are forgiven; if you do not forgive them, they are not forgiven.'"

Mother spoke in alarm. "You were not there. You received no commission?"

Father put in, "Your mother is right; you should also receive the Holy Spirit."

I waited a moment. Then I said, "If this were truly Jesus, then no, I did not. But if it were Jesus, he would have come while I was there. He would have sent me, too; am I not an apostle? And I was promised the Holy Spirit as well!"

Didymus

Jahzeel observed, "Thomas, you are like me! You are stubborn. You are envious. You are bitter. You are angry. The Holy Spirit *is* God. As you are now, how can God still alight on you, as you say the dove did on Jesus, when he was baptized? You must calm down. I had to accept God's will. You must do the same. No one has done you wrong. How can you expect to receive anything from God when you are like this?"

I replied curtly, "As I said to the others, 'Unless I see the nail marks in his hands and put my finger where the nails were, and put my hand into his side, *I will not believe!*' I left them then and came back here."

There was silence before Father replied, "When you were a child, I punished you when you would not forgive your brother. I punished you when you would not respect my will, or that of your mother. You are too old, now, to put over my knee. When you were older, I gave you a time out or sent you to the field. You are too old for that now, too. But you are not too old for God to correct. Do you really want that?"

I was still angry. I knew he was right, but this was my life, and I was acting more willfully than I ever had. I was actually proud of how I was standing up to the will of God. This was a terrible place to be, and I knew it. I replied, "He can do as he chooses," and walked back into the street. I could hear my mother beginning to weep and saw that Anna had her arm on Mother's, to comfort her, . . . but none of it mattered to me.

My family stayed in Jerusalem for another week. The vineyard would be fine, but I was sure they were doing this for me. What of it? Why should they not? I was a bit surprised that Anna's parents had stayed, too; her father's occupation, that of a baker, did not lend itself to a week off. Not my concern. On occasion, I went to the other disciples, who were mostly infused with joy, though Peter seemed more stoic than the others. I spoke with Peter briefly. He said that he was sure it was Jesus he had seen but that the relationship could never be the same after he had denied him. I almost felt sorry for him, but I felt sorrier for myself.

XXIII

Pistós (Faithful and Believing)

During one visit a week after Jesus had appeared to the others, I was locked in the house with the other apostles, still fearing the Jews. Jesus came and stood among us and said, "Peace be with you!" He looked at me and said, "Put your finger here; see my hands. Reach out your hand and put it into my side. Stop doubting and believe." I dropped to my knees and exclaimed, "My Lord and my God!" Then Jesus told me, "Because you have seen me, you have believed; blessed are those who have not seen and yet have believed."

I took his hand, wanting to never let go. His other hand was on my shoulder. I wept harder than I ever had in my entire life. Jesus still loved me. I had not denied him in the way Peter had. But worse yet, I had denied his lordship over me. I had stopped praying; stopped believing; stopped identifying as, or acting like, an apostle, or even a believer; I had lashed out at all who loved me—at Jesus's apostles . . . and even at God! But I knew that was over now. Jesus was alive, and because he lived, I also had a new and abundant life. My heart and will had been broken, but my self-imposed separation was over. I suddenly realized that, all during the last week, I had been doing the will of Satan, not that of God. But I also knew that I was forgiven and forever free. I *was* the rebellious prodigal son from the parable who had returned home—home to Jesus.

Didymus

Much was said over the hour, but all I knew was joy. What love! I saw the smiles of all the other apostles; they could see what I had gone through and were glad it was over. They cared for me. They loved me. I no longer feared the chief priests, the Pharisees, the Romans, or even Satan. I still had a strong will, but now it was channeled in the right direction; I was *for* Jesus, and if Jesus could give me victory over Satan, what chance would a mere man have against me?

This time, I did not want to leave the others. After Jesus was gone again, I confessed to all of them my willful pride and doubt, and they rejoiced with me upon my confession and repentance. I told them how I had mistreated my family—and this after they had all become believers. I realized that my family's belief was no testimony to my witnessing ability. No, Jahzeel had become a believer more despite me than because of me. God had called them, too, and now I knew it. Everyone embraced me. I was not the only one in tears. They all had loved ones, too. I knew I had to make an apology to my family, so I took my leave. John asked me before I left whether I could bring Jahzeel back the next time I came. I assured him that I would.

Walking back, I prayed every step of the way, asking forgiveness of God and giving him the praise that had always been due him. I had never felt this close to God before, even at my baptism. I was his, to do with as he chose. His plans were beyond mine: He is Lord. He did not need to tell me why he had done what he had. Yet, what had Jesus said—"I have called you friends, for everything that I learned from my Father I have made known to you"?

He had given us warnings about what would happen to us, but now it did not matter, for Jesus loved me. What else was it that Jesus had said—"But whoever has been forgiven little loves little"? I had now been forgiven more than any other. My form of denial, I knew, had been worse than Peter's. How could I have doubted? How could I ever again doubt? Only God's grace had brought me back. Then I thought of Jesus's words, "Blessed are those who have not seen and yet have believed." That was a picture of Jahzeel! Jesus had done something very special for me. Yet Jahzeel had been granted an even more special blessing, one that would be given to anyone who believed without a direct experience.

When I arrived at the house where we were still staying, I did not make a quiet entrance. I was loud and boisterous—as loud and exuberant as Simon Peter had ever been. I announced, "Father, Mother, Jahzeel, you must know: I believe! Jesus is alive! It is bios, physically alive!"

They all came to greet me, Mother gushing fresh tears. I took her in my arms and would not let her go. I exclaimed, "Jesus talked to me. Jesus forgives my unbelief. It is glorious!"

Father's eyes had a sparkle, too, and he wore a huge smile. Jahzeel slapped me on the back, hard, but I didn't mind. I knew that, as in the story Jesus had told, I had become a prodigal. Now I was home, and they were all happy.

After a time of weeping, I apologized sincerely for my behavior, beginning with Father: "Father, I don't deserve all the kindness you have shown me. You have tried to lift me out of the pit of despondency I had climbed down into. For all your help, I fought you off, like a cat scratching the one who tries to help it. I don't deserve your love. You have shown me so much wisdom. You understand God's purpose for me better than I do myself. I know that you only want what is best for me. When you questioned me, it was only to help me to probe my own motives. I see now what you had known all along: that my initial belief, although real, was only emotional.

"I had seen genuine miracles, and I believed. When I did not see the miracles I wanted, I ceased to believe. I had phileo (brotherly) love when I felt loved. But when I felt abandoned, I stopped loving and struck out at everyone around me. Phileo was a love of reaction—not love by a decision—agape. My belief was superficial. In my strong will I ignored any explanation of what was happening and continued in my wrong emotions until I was bitter, resentful, and unbelieving. I did not want to let love, or even any rational thought, enter my mind and heart. My stubborn will had won out. For this I am truly sorry."

Father smiled and embraced me again, saying, "What you said was beautiful. Jesus has made you a proclaimer of his will. I always knew it was in you. You were the one who forgot."

I smiled and then turned to Mother. "Mother, I have hurt you so deeply. I know that you have never wanted anything but the best for me. I don't deserve your love, either. I never realized how well you understood the feelings of others until you showed me. I also saw how much you love the people I was hurting. Your belief and love run deep—far deeper than mine. Even when I thought everyone had abandoned me, which I was pushing them to do, you would not. I am truly sorry. I love you, Mother. I can tell you right now that I have true shalom again.

Mother lifted a hand to God and said simply, "Thomas, I am so proud of what Jesus has made you become. He must receive any glory."

Now I spoke to my twin. "Jahzeel, I'm sorry. I know that I have always been envious of you. I know, too, that you've always had me in your heart. I was actually proud that Jesus had chosen me, and not you, to be an apostle. I know that was wrong. He has chosen you for some other purpose, no less significant than what he has chosen for me. I was bitter that you refused to believe based on my words. I was angry when you saw miracles but still did not believe. I realize now that, in your own way, you were actually nobler than I, receiving all I said but then seeking to discern whether these things were true.

"You trusted me, but you knew the scripture could never be broken, so you tested what I said against scripture. This is the correct way to receive God's word and his will. It's so much easier to just watch miracles and participate in the excitement of the moment. I see now how wrong that can be; some of the people who shouted 'Hosanna!' with the giddy crowd when Jesus entered Jerusalem also shouted, 'Crucify him!' only a few days later. Excitement is never an excuse for not taking God at his word. Before you were certain of your own faith, you risked your life going out into the city to try to help me, knowing that, because we look alike, you could have been arrested.

"At the darkest hour in history, when we apostles were filled with doubts, you began to truly believe. Like me, you have a strong will. God gave us all a will as part of the dominion Adam needed in the garden, but I abused it. Your strength of will, on the other hand, has never failed. I remember the story Jesus told about the soils; some shallow soil, like me, allows for quick growth. But my growth was nearly dead. It has taken me the experiences of this last week to truly find my roots. Your soil, in contrast, ran rich and deep. When the seed was established in you, it flourished. My brother, God has a plan for your life."

Jahzeel openly wept. I went on, "I have already confessed all of this to the apostles. I know that they, too, forgive me. They love me, and they sorrowed along with you about how I was behaving. I was a shame to Jesus, a shame to you, and a shame to them. Jahzeel, John has asked whether you would come back to meet with us. I still have not introduced you to all of the apostles. Perhaps Jesus will come again to us. I know that we are to go back to Galilee and that he will appear to us there. Father, Mother, I want you to meet him in person as well."

Jahzeel replied, "Of course, my brother, when you are ready."

Father announced, "It is time for us to return to Galilee. There are so many people I want to tell about Jesus."

Mother added, "Yes, I also have so many friends who need to know him. I believe I have already met Jesus, but to see him face-to-face would be wonderful."

Father enthused, "This is a time of celebration. And not just for you, son; we must celebrate the risen Jesus! We must celebrate this often. We honor God on the Sabbath; now we might celebrate the resurrection on the first day of each week. It would only be appropriate."

Didymus

I responded, "You are right. He deserves our worship. Jahzeel, whenever you are ready, return with me to meet my friends. Father, Mother, I want you to meet them, too."

"We want to meet them," asserted Father. "Take Jahzeel now. We can meet in Galilee."

I offered a short prayer: "Father, I thank you for your magnificent name, even when I would not respect it. I thank you for your glory, even when I refused to see it. I thank you for your perfect will, even when I did not understand it. I thank you for your provision, even when I did not appreciate it. I thank you for your forgiveness, even when I would not accept it. I thank you now for my family; you have given them to me, though I did not deserve them, either. In the name of Jesus, and according to his will, Amen."

After a moment, Father asked, "Do you mind if I try to pray aloud?"

I nodded, and he began, "Holy Father, to whom I owe all I have been given, all I have, and all I will ever have, I am grateful. I also give thanks for returning Thomas to us. May you be praised. Amen."

Jahzeel, looking up, interjected, "My turn. Thank you, blessed Father, for all you have bestowed on me, your unworthy servant. Make me into one you can be proud of. Amen."

Mother, looking slightly uncomfortable, as though out of her usual element, volunteered, "I, too, will pray. Father of all blessings, I thank you for putting up with me. For giving me so much joy. For giving me such a wonderful family. And for Jesus. Amen."

I realized then how close they all were to God, and I silently praised him.

XXIV

Fellowship of Believers

After we took leave of Father and Mother, Jahzeel and I began to walk and chatter loudly, as in old times. No more hiding under a cloak. I inquired, smiling, "So, has Anna's father now consented to your marrying a woman who is also a believer?"

Jahzeel replied, "He is enthusiastic. Anna is enthusiastic. You must stand up for me at the ceremony, which will be soon. We will need a rabbi. Do you think John would officiate? He may not have the tassels of a rabbi, but I consider him one."

I answered, "I never thought about that, but John is a something like a rabbi now. I'm sure he would do it. Think of the guests you will have!"

Jahzeel answered, "So many. We must wait for the wine!" We both laughed, remembering.

I went on, "Anna can help her father plan. I'm sure Mother will be preparing, and Anna's father can make the best bread and cakes. I'm sure Zebedee will get you the finest biny you have ever seen—or tasted. You must invite everyone!"

Jahzeel laughed again. "Thomas, my joy has never been so full." I agreed, and then Jahzeel asked, "John, then, is a rabbi of Jesus? Is that what his followers are to be called?"

I answered, "Some are calling us, as a group, 'the Way.' Think of faith in Jesus as the way to the Father. I'm sure you remember

Didymus

Jesus saying, 'I am the way and the truth and the life. No one comes to the Father except through me.'"

Jahzeel pondered. "The Way—that fits. Any Jew will want a way to the Father. I suppose even Samaritans would."

"Yes, there is so much we have not yet understood. We ministered to Samaritans, too. Jesus even ministered to Romans. First, though, we must reach our friends. . . and the other Jews."

Jahzeel asked with a twisted grin, "Even the Pharisees?"

I gave him a poke, as I had been in the habit of doing for most of our lives. "I suppose. You know that Nicodemus is a Pharisee. He is also a believer. They are not all bad. And the bad ones need him more than anyone else does!"

Jahzeel chuckled again. "Do you think Jesus will appear to them now?"

I thought before answering. "I don't know. He said we would be given instruction in Galilee, not in Jerusalem. That tells us where we will start.

Jahzeel nodded. We had arrived. The door was still locked, but there was unmistakable joy wafting outward from the inside. I knocked and announced myself, and the apostles opened to us.

When we returned to our parents, our joy must have been obvious to Father, Mother, and Anna, who had come to wait to see what had happened.

We told them that all of those present had tried to make Jahzeel comfortable. They had all practiced what Jesus had taught us: "In everything, do to others what you would have them do to you, for this sums up the Law and the Prophets."

I went on, "First, there was talk about how much the two of us resemble each other. Eventually, though, we became more serious. They wanted the details of how Jahzeel had come to believe; almost all of the believers we had known previously had come to Jesus after hearing him speak or witnessing miracles. We believe that Jahzeel may be the first convert after the crucifixion."

I went on, "I was thrilled when Jahzeel started to give a testimony of how he had listened to what I had said and then talked to a rabbi about it. He told about his having paid a lot of money to have a scroll made of the passage in Isaiah, after which he pulled it out from a fold in his robe. He had set about to investigate the most difficult proof the rabbi had challenged him with—and had fully expected God to deny the claims of Jesus. He read the passage to the group then, explaining step-by-step how the words verified Jesus's claim to be Messiah."

I continued, "Jahzeel went line by line, with many comments and tears. When he had finished the passage, he declared, 'Jesus fulfilled this scripture! Most of you believed from seeing the miracles—I from seeing scripture fulfilled!'"

Jahzeel went on to explain, "James said, 'It is clear that some will believe as they see the scriptures fulfilled, but how sad that we don't have access to all of the scriptures. So few people own even a single scroll; they are so expensive.'"

Father asked, "Do you need money?"

I replied, "Perhaps," and then went on, "Nicodemus is a Pharisee. I'm sure he has scrolls. After having wrapped Jesus's body, though, he has all he can do trying to keep his position in the Sanhedrin. He will be into trouble even if he doesn't meet with us. Besides, he is old; it would be hard for him to do more."

Father looked serious. "Yes, I'm sure he will end up fleeing Jerusalem. How sad!"

Jahzeel continued, "Peter said we need someone well trained, with scrolls and parchments, and someone young enough to go everywhere to teach. Thomas told the apostles, 'God will provide. We can pray for such a person. Perhaps the Holy Spirit will give us scripture when we need it. Remember that Jesus told us, "When they arrest you, do not worry about what to say or how to say it. At that time, you will be given what to say, for it will not be you speaking but the Spirit of your Father speaking through you."'"

Didymus

Mother asked, her habitual anxiety exerting itself, "Do you think you will all be arrested?"

I replied, "No. I have no worries; what can man do to me? I did express my concern about my having missed out on Jesus's breathing of the Holy Spirit upon the other apostles. Matthew assured me, 'That was a preliminary, a promise of a gift yet to be fully given. You will be given it with us.'"

I asked, "'When?' to which Peter replied, 'We were told he would meet us in Galilee.'"

Father looked joyful, and I continued, "Then James said, 'The women told us that Jesus had said, "Do not be afraid. Go and tell my brothers to go to Galilee; there they will see me." That is where we must go. He will find us, as he did here.' I asked again, 'When?' This time John simply answered, 'We should go soon.'"

Jahzeel exclaimed, "Yes, we will all go. There is more. Simon Peter said he had room at his house, and I volunteered ours as being nearby as well. James pointed out that all of our homes are nearby. Simon's is the largest, and he suggested that we could meet there daily."

I continued, "At that point John said, 'We need to seek God's will.' There were nods of agreement, and we all prayed. The prayers lasted for some time. When they had ended, we were all convinced. Jahzeel and I decided to return here and tell you of our plans. But before we left, I took John aside and asked a favor of him: 'My brother, Jahzeel, is soon to marry a fine believer, from a family of believers. John, I consider you a "rabbi," a teacher of The Way, would you consent to officiating the wedding ceremony?'"

Jahzeel remembered, "John smiled greatly and admitted, 'I suppose I am a rabbi. I have never performed a wedding, but I would indeed be honored, my brother.'"

I spoke again. "Then we came here. We will return tomorrow to make plans."

Anna looked delighted, and there was much joy all around. Jahzeel walked Anna to where her parents were staying. I don't think I have ever seen my parents more joyful. They were going to see Jesus!

Jahzeel and I returned in the morning. The other apostles, disciples, and the women there had decided to leave for Simon's house in Capernaum the following morning. Father, Jahzeel, and I had already discussed traveling together with the disciples. This would give us a chance to meet and get to know one another. We could break bread together. After much discussion and prayer, we returned to tell our parents where we would meet.

The journey to Judea was a joyous one. My family melded perfectly with the group. There was koinonia; the fellowship, as well as the sharing of goods; much singing; and much discussion of our families, our occupations—and, of course, about Jesus. We reminisced about how only four Passovers ago Jesus had first gotten attention by clearing the moneychangers from the temple. To many, this seemed like a short time, yet we, his followers, felt as though we had known him all our lives. It was hard to remember when he had not been an integral part of our lives. We did not know the details of what he had planned for us, but we knew we could trust him.

The apostles and many disciples met regularly at Peter's house in Capernaum for fellowship, prayer, and food. One night as we waited, Peter told us about the time when he, James, and John had gone alone up the mountain without us, and Jesus had been transfigured before them. Jesus's face had shone like the sun, and his clothes became as white as the light. Just then Moses and Elijah had appeared before the trembling apostles and had talked with Jesus.

Peter had said to Jesus, "Lord, it is good for us to be here. If you wish, I will put up three shelters, one for you, one for Moses, and one for Elijah." While Peter was still speaking, a bright cloud had covered them, and a voice from the cloud had said, "This is my Son, whom I love; with him I am well pleased. Listen to him!"

Didymus

When the three of them heard, they had fallen facedown to the ground, terrified. Jesus had come and touched them. "Get up," he had said. "Don't be afraid." When they looked up, they saw no one except Jesus.

As the three were coming down the mountain, Jesus had instructed them, "Don't tell anyone what you have seen, until the Son of Man has been raised from the dead." They asked him, "Why, then, do the teachers of the Law say that Elijah must come first?" Jesus replied, "To be sure, Elijah comes and will restore all things. But I tell you, Elijah has already come, and they did not recognize him, but have done to him everything they wished. In the same way the Son of Man is going to suffer at their hands." Then they understood that he was talking to them about John the Baptist.

The three had not told anyone at that time what they had seen. John and James verified the story. I wasn't sure why only the three had been chosen, but that had been Jesus's decision, and I knew now that his decisions are always without flaw. When I told my family the story later, my mother was not quite as accepting; I suspect all Jewish mothers think their child is the best at everything.

XXV

Fishers of Men

I returned home one morning with some excellent biny. Jahzeel greeted me and asked about the apostles. When the family had gathered, I began my update with "Last night, Simon Peter, Nathanael, James, John, and two other disciples were together, and Peter suggested going fishing. We went out, got into the boat, but caught nothing all night."

Jahzeel grimaced, "I would rather be in bed than getting seasick."

"Jahzeel, you would get used to the boats in time. I should have told you that years ago. I was seasick at first, too. Early in the morning, Jesus stood on the shore, but we didn't realize who it was. He called out to us, 'Friends, haven't you caught any fish?' We answered, 'No.' He said, 'Throw your net on the right side of the boat, and you will find some.' When we did, we were unable to haul in the net because of the large number of fish. They were huge biny! John said to Peter, 'It is the Lord!' As soon as Simon Peter heard him say that, he wrapped his outer garment around himself and jumped into the water."

Jahzeel pointed out, "You told me it is hard to swim in a garment. He covers himself like Adam after his sin . . ."

Father remarked, "Simon is impulsive and impatient. God must have created him that way for a reason."

I nodded and went on, "I think Peter wanted to be alone with Jesus. We followed in the boat, towing the net full of fish, for we were about a hundred yards out. When we landed, a fire of burning coals was there on the shore with fish on it, and there was bread. Jesus said to us, 'Bring some of the fish you have caught.' So, Simon Peter dragged the net ashore. It was full of biny—163 of them—but even with so many the net never tore. Jesus invited us, 'Come, have breakfast.' Jesus took the bread and gave it to us and did the same with the fish."

Jahzeel pointed out, "Peter and his clothes were wet. He would have needed to warm himself near the fire. Was Jesus reminding him that he had warmed himself at a fire when he betrayed Jesus?"

I realized how much insight Jahzeel had. "Yes, Peter did have to warm himself. Jesus does nothing by chance. When we finished eating, Jesus said to him, 'Simon, son of Jonah, do you love me more than these?' Peter said, 'Yes, Lord, you know that I love you.' Jesus said, 'Feed my lambs.' Again, Jesus asked,' "Simon, son of Jonah, do you love me?' Peter answered, 'Yes, Lord, you know that I love you.' Jesus said, 'Take care of my sheep.' The third time Jesus said to him, 'Simon, son of Jonah, do you love me?' Peter was hurt because Jesus asked him the third time, 'Do you love me?' and he said, 'Lord, you know all things; you know that I love you.' Jesus said, 'Feed my sheep.'"

Jahzeel exclaimed, "Three times he asked? Was it not three times Peter had denied him, after claiming that he would die for him?"

"Yes, it was. I'm sure that is part of the reason Jesus asked Peter this three times. But the first two times Jesus asked whether Peter's love was selfless—agape, unconditional, based on his own choice or will—and whether it was greater than the love the rest of us have for him. I could see Peter's embarrassment. His answer at first was that he had reciprocal, or brotherly (phileo) affection for Jesus. Peter was afraid that he had demonstrated at Jesus's trial that his love was incomplete.

"The second time Jesus left off the comparison to us but still asked whether Peter's love was selfless, like God's. Peter still felt inadequate to make that claim. When Jesus asked the third time, he questioned whether Peter's love was even brotherly affection. Peter was certainly hurt. Jesus had already shown us that he who has been forgiven much loves much. Peter, and all of us, realized that Jesus had indeed forgiven us much, and that we should willingly choose to love him much, regardless of the situation."

Jahzeel commented, "Peter, the fisherman, was asked to feed sheep. Didn't he really want a crown, not a shepherd's hook?"

"Yes, we all did. We should have seen from David's psalms that people without God are but sheep. Shepherding people is what David did as king. This is not something to be ashamed of—although we well know that the shepherding profession is looked down upon by many of our people. But then Jesus said, 'Very truly I tell you, when you were younger you dressed yourself and went where you wanted, but when you are old you will stretch out your hands, and someone else will dress you and lead you where you do not want to go.' Then he said to him, 'Follow me!'"

Mother pondered, admitting, "I don't really understand this."

"I think he was telling Peter that he would someday be executed because of what Jesus would say next."

Father pressed, "Don't keep us in suspense . . ."

"Peter turned and saw John following the two of them. When Peter saw him, he asked, 'Lord, what about *him*?' Jesus answered, 'If I want him to remain alive until I return, what is that to you? You must follow me.'"

Father reflected, "So, Peter suspects that this is how he will die, too. He does not want to go through anything that John doesn't go through. Misery loves company!"

"That was it. We knew that Peter, James, and John had all fallen asleep on the Mount of Olives the night of the arrest. We slept, too, and fled, but Jesus had specifically set aside the three of them to keep watch with him. Perhaps Peter was implying that he wasn't the only one who had done wrong."

Jahzeel queried, "Is Jesus saying that John will not die?"

"I don't think so—just that it isn't Peter's business what God determines for John. Peter had said that he would never deny Jesus, even if he would have to die for him. Jesus was reminding Peter of that. Besides, Jesus had earlier told both James and John that they would go through a baptism like his when their mother had requested that they be given a special place in the kingdom. Jesus's baptism was a cross."

Mother asked quietly, "And you . . . ?"

"I don't know. I do know that Jesus loves me and wants the best for me. You know that, too. Mother, *everyone* dies."

Mother answered softly, "I won't stop being your mother. After we had all met when we came back to Galilee, I saw pain in the eyes of Mary, Jesus's mother. She has joy now, especially now that all her other sons and daughters believe—but I can still see the scars of pain."

"We must always trust that Jesus knows best. Jesus asked for the apostles to meet with him on Olivet, a Sabbath day's journey from Jerusalem. I know that is far from here. We know where, and we know when—that will be nearly forty days after the resurrection. I'm sure the seventy disciples who were sent out will be there, too, and others as well. I want you all to see Jesus. Jahzeel, bring Anna and her parents."

Father thought aloud, "So many others; we will have to watch from afar, as we did when he broke the bread. But we will be there."

Jahzeel added, "I'm sure Anna and her family will want to be there."

"Do you know why the meeting will be back on Olivet?" Father asked. "And will there be significance to this being midway between Passover and Shavuot?"

I answered, "I'm not sure. We were freed from Egypt by Moses at Passover, but we did not have the law until Shavuot. It's also the festival of First Fruits. We commemorate both events. Olivet is a garden. Perhaps it signifies we are freed by the Cross and we will soon have fruit? We may be sent out again. The others who will be there may witness our being sent out—or perhaps they will be sent out, too.

Jahzeel put in, "If you are being sent out soon, then our wedding should be before you go."

I answered, smiling, "Oh, you are eager! And understandably so. I'm sure we will have the ceremony soon. We have some time before we are to meet at Olivet. I would not want to delay, since Jesus may send us all off on that very day. Tell Anna's father. Perhaps he will send out the call soon. Are you ready to breakfast?"

Anna's father agreed to initiate the call before we had gathered at the Mount of Olives; he had been ready for some time—and Jahzeel was beyond ready! It was to be the biggest wedding anyone in the area could remember. The day before, Peter baptized my parents, Jahzeel, Anna, and her parents. Philip joked that Peter should not baptize because he walks on top of water. Peter took the jibe good naturedly, and we all declared how impressed we were that he had actually gotten out of the boat.

John officiated the wedding, as he had promised, and Anna's father made bread and even cakes. It was the best bread I had ever tasted—with two earlier, miraculous exceptions. Father provided the best fresh wine we had, nearly as good as what Jesus had made. Miraculously, we did not have to wait for the wine; one small section of the grapes had come ten weeks early, two weeks before Pentecost! Zebedee brought huge biny for roasting.

All of the apostles were there, as were most of the seventy disciples Jesus had earlier sent out. The wedding celebration lasted for three days. It was the first wedding officiated by a rabbi of the Way that anyone knew of. I took the role of Friend of the Groom, a tradition going back at least to Samson. My brother and I had, after all, always been best friends—with that one notable exception for both of us. The form we used was almost exactly like that of a Jewish wedding, but our prayers were to the Father in Jesus's name.

Mother, Anna's mother, and Jesus's mother all cried. Jahzeel grinned, and Anna glowed. The ceremony was beautiful and meaningful. I helped out a bit in the vineyard. Even a few of the fishermen learned what it is like to work a vineyard! It seemed like

Didymus

a welcome for a short time. So many from the Way were here. We started meeting together at the synagogue, with permission from the ruler, on the first day of the week, when the building was not otherwise being used. Jahzeel had shown the rabbi, the synagogue ruler, how the prophecy on the scroll of Isaiah that he had suggested had been fulfilled; and we are praying that he would accept Jesus as Lord. We were experiencing a real community of the Way.

XXVI

Appearing to Five Hundred and Scriptures Opened; the Ascension

27TH DAY OF IYAR, THURSDAY, MAY 16, AD 30,

FORTY DAYS AFTER RESURRECTION DAY

The ensuing days passed quickly. We had a three-day distance to travel and knew that many people would be there to see Jesus.

We eleven apostles went to the Mount of Olives. I expected the seventy disciples and others, but more than five hundred were actually present, the vast majority of whom were believers. We both saw and worshipped Jesus. Sadly, a few of the people who had arrived unbelieving left in the same way. Jesus commissioned us with "All authority in heaven and on earth has been given to me. Therefore, go and make disciples of all nations, baptizing them in the name of the Father and of the Son and of the Holy Spirit and teaching them to obey everything I have commanded you. And surely, I am with you always, to the very end of the age."

He continued, "Go into all the world and preach the gospel to all creation. Whoever believes and is baptized will be saved, but whoever does not believe will be condemned. All these signs will accompany those who believe: In my name they will drive out demons; they will speak in new tongues; they will pick up snakes with their hands; and when they drink deadly poison, it will not hurt them at all; they will place their hands on sick people, and they will get well."

Jesus then opened the minds of his apostles so that we could truly understand the scriptures. His words were incredibly enlightening. He told us, "This is what is written: The Messiah will suffer and rise from the dead on the third day, and repentance for the forgiveness of sins will be preached in his name to all nations, beginning at Jerusalem. You are witness of these things. I am going to send you what my Father has promised, but stay in the city until you have been clothed with power from on high."

When Jesus had led us out to the vicinity of Bethany, he lifted up his hands and blessed us. Then we gathered around him and asked, "Lord, are you at this time going to restore the kingdom to Israel?" He answered, "It is not for you to know the times or dates which the Father has set by his own authority. But you will receive power when the Holy Spirit comes on you, and you will be my witnesses in Jerusalem, and in all Judea and Samaria, and to the ends of the earth."

After he had said this, he was taken up before our very eyes, and a cloud hid him from our sight. We were looking intently up into the sky as he was going, when suddenly two men clad all in white stood beside us. They said, "Men of Galilee, why do you stand here looking into the sky? This same Jesus who has been taken from you into heaven will come back in the same way you have seen him go into heaven."

We left Bethany and the area of the Mount of Olives to wait in eager expectation in Jerusalem, as we had been instructed. All of the apostles came, along with most of the seventy and many other disciples. Mary, the mother of Jesus, was there, as were Jesus's half brothers, James, Joseph, Judas, and Simon, all of whom had come to faith in Christ. We spent much time in prayer and fellowship. Even Jahzeel and Anna came for a few days until Pentecost.

XXVII

Paraclete (The Helper, or Holy Spirit)

8ᵀᴴ Day of Sivan, Sunday, May 26, AD 30,
fifty days after Resurrection Day, Pentecost

When the day of Pentecost came, we were all together in one place. Suddenly a sound like the blowing of a violent wind came from heaven and filled the whole house where we were sitting. What seemed to be tongues of fire separated and came to rest on each of us. We were filled with the Holy Spirit and began to speak in other tongues as the Pneuma, the breath of the Holy Spirit, enabled us. I had never before experienced such power and felt as though there was no limit to what I could do through Him.

The Spirit had used us in healing when Jesus had sent us out, but now he indwelt us! The power was according to his will—as we allowed it. We quickly realized that it had not been given for our own use but was intended to reach the multitudes. The proof was immediate. A few scoffers accused us of being drunk on new wine—as though anyone can get drunk on unfermented wine. Peter preached. When people heard his sermon, they were cut to the heart and asked Peter and all of us, "Brothers, what shall we do?"

Peter replied, "Repent and be baptized, every one of you, in the name of Jesus Christ for the forgiveness of your sins. And you

Didymus

will receive the gift of the Holy Spirit. The promise is for you and your children and for all who are far off, whom the Lord our God will call."

People gladly received his word and were baptized, and that day about three thousand souls were added to our number. We continued steadfastly in the doctrine and fellowship, in the breaking of bread, and in prayers.

It was an amazing day. I praised Jesus for all that was happening. Happily, Jahzeel and Anna were there as well. We talked, and I asked, "Can you imagine how many people just believed?" I knew that he and Anna would have to return to the vineyard, which was certainly too much at this point for Father to handle alone. I knew, too, that Jahzeel would tell Father and Mother, as well as Anna's family, what had happened. He would be a powerful witness to so many back in Galilee.

XXVIII

The Baby Church

On the first Passover after the church was formed, my family journeyed again to Jerusalem. It was a time of joy, of the celebration of both the Passover and the resurrection for the fledgling church. I found my family, and we also celebrated, as well as discussing what was happening among the believers.

I greeted my family at the inn early on the day of Passover with a hearty Shalom. After much embracing, Mother commented on the gray hairs in my beard. I responded that they had come from various responsibilities and concerns. Father asked how the church was doing. I responded, "We are blessed with a great number of converts. Most are genuine. We work hard to help them grow."

Jahzeel asked, concerned, "You appear to be stressed—are there problems?"

"Yes. We have authority as apostles, but we also have great responsibilities. Our days are no longer than they ever were, but our responsibilities exceed the number of hours. People come to Christ, for which we praise God, though often with great emotion but little direction. We all need to grow in Christ. We apostles spent three years with Jesus but still feel less than mature. These new converts are babes in faith. They learn mostly by watching others, often their own peers. When you wean children, you slice the meat thinly because they are not able to chew and digest solid food. We must present God's word in such a way that those not ready for hard food can digest it."

Father shook his head. "In some of these areas, I fear that I, too, remain a child."

"We all do. I'm sure that during the three years I followed Jesus I was no more than a babe. Our time devoted to teaching Christ is exciting, but teaching of the Gospel is not our only charge. We were not called to simply listen but to act. These children don't know what to do."

Father asked, "What would you have them do?"

"Our commission was to reach the world. Do you remember what happened after Jesus fed the five thousand?"

Jahzeel recalled, "They wanted to make Jesus king."

"Yes, but why?"

Father answered, "So that he would fill their bellies and they would not have to work."

"Exactly. That's human nature. Working is hard. The meetings of the church are all about fellowship, and there is often a festive atmosphere. Yes, we celebrate Christ, but one cannot live on festivity alone. Our people, as we recall so well, wandered aimlessly in the wilderness for forty years on their way from Egypt to the promised land. God had a plan and purpose for each and provided for them. Even then, with all the ongoing miracles, the food provided, even the presence of God, they never even gained faith. God expects more of us. Even Adam was expected to tend a garden."

Mother pointed out, "There are some who cannot work."

"Yes, Mother. We well know that you have a tender heart. We must take care of widows and orphans, yes, but a problem has arisen. Many wealthy people have given to the church to help the needy. This is a great and impressive act, and others see it and determine to give as well. They close their businesses and donate to the church all of their means. But this expectation of a Christ to return quickly is premature. When a farmer has given away his wheat and his land, who will then support *his* needs?"

Jahzeel answered, "They will expect the church to support them."

Father queried, "They feel somehow *entitled* to support?"

I nodded. "They do. Jesus gave us a charge to go out into the whole world and make disciples. We now have thousands who are comfortable listening to the words of Jesus but doing little else. They are, as I indicated, babes. Eventually, they will grow, but for now we feel as though we are simply running both a nursery and a charitable institution. We have appointed seven men to serve as deacons to relieve some of the distraction for us, so we can be freed to study and pray."

Father asked, "If no one were to fish or farm or be a vine-dresser or a baker, who would eat?"

I replied, "That is precisely the problem. The church is becoming impoverished. The apostles all knew a trade. Now, some young believers never learn one. Young men of working and marriage age are not feeling responsibility. If the Lord tarries in his return, we cannot keep doing this."

Anna, alarmed, commented, "That is terrible. What will happen if there are no new families?"

"That cannot be allowed to happen. Those who will not work cannot eat. Only with that harsh stipulation will they grow."

Jahzeel put in with a twinkle in his eye, "Our family has not grown yet, but hopefully soon."

XXIX

Paul

Nearly four years after the birth of Christ's church, I finally had an opportunity for a quick visit with my family. I felt guilty for not having reached out to them but knew that, when God used persecution to scatter the church into the broader world, believers had gone to Galilee and updated the believers there. When I arrived, I greeted Father with a joyful "Shalom!"

Father embraced me and then called the others. Mother was there, with Anna. Most of my earlier visits had been on Sabbath; this one was not, so Jahzeel was in the vineyard.

Mother, with tears in her eyes, reported, "Ever since the persecution has broken out, we have worried about you. I know you are in the center of God's will, but you are still my son."

"We apostles have stayed in Jerusalem, but most of the other believers are finally following Jesus's commission and leaving Jerusalem. It was after all a command, not a suggestion. When we did not go out as Jesus commanded, God used others to compel the Church to spread the Good News. I know that you have been told about Stephen and Philip. I will bring you up to date on the rest."

Mother mouthed her habitual refrain: "Are you safe?" to which I answered honestly, "I feel no fear—only agape love. Perfect love casts out fear."

Father responded, "That is true; when you were young, a tremor once caused the rocks on a terrace to begin to tumble. I had no fear for myself; I could think only of rescuing you!"

"I remember you scooping me up. I could not have been more than five years old. You held me tightly, and I felt safe. Your concern for me pushed all fear out of your heart. It's the same principle when relating to God."

Mother asked, "Should you be afraid?"

"No, the Spirit has revealed much work for all of us to do. We now have a new witness. Only God could do such a thing. I need to tell you about it."

Mother went and got raisin cakes; as she returned, Jahzeel came in from the vineyard. We embraced quickly and greeted each other. Father motioned for me to continue, so I took a cake and began, "Have you heard of a young Pharisee named Saul?"

Jahzeel answered, "Yes, he is a terror to those of the Way. He tries to force people to deny Christ. Is he coming?"

I concurred, "That is him—or it *was* him. The story is complex. He acquired letters from the high priest commissioning him to go to Damascus, as he knew some believers had fled there. His plan was to persecute them. But Jesus appeared to him en route."

Father asked, incredulous, "He simply *appeared* to Saul?"

"No, a brilliant light blinded Saul, and those with him fled. Saul himself fell to the ground. A voice from heaven spoke to him, asking, 'Saul, Saul, why do you persecute me?' Saul asked, 'Who are you, Lord?' Jesus answered, 'I am Jesus, whom you are persecuting. It is hard for you to kick against the goads. Now rise and go into the city, and you will be told what you must do.' The men traveling with Saul heard the sound but did not see anyone, nor could they discern what the voice had said. When Saul got up from the ground, he could see nothing. They led him by the hand into Damascus. For three days he was blind and did not eat or drink anything."

Father remarked, "Goads? Those are sharp objects placed behind animals who stubbornly kick. When they do, they hurt themselves, so they stop quickly. Jesus was saying that Paul was hurting himself in his stubbornness."

I nodded and continued, "The Lord called in a vision to a disciple named Ananias, saying, 'Go to the house of Judas on Straight

Street and ask for a man from Tarsus named Saul, who is praying. In a vision he has seen you, Ananias, coming to place your hand on him to restore his sight.' Ananias was confused and asked, 'Lord, I have heard that this man has harmed your holy people in Jerusalem and has come here with authority from the chief priests to arrest all who call on your name.' The Lord answered Ananias, 'Go! This man is my chosen instrument to proclaim my name to the Gentiles, and to their kings and to the people of Israel. I will show him how much he must suffer for my name.'

Father answered, "This Ananias must be a willing servant; this must have seemed like a trap."

I agreed, continuing, "Ananias did as he was bid; he went to the house and placed his hand on Saul, saying, 'Brother Saul, the Lord Jesus, who appeared to you on the road as you came here, has sent me so that you may see again and be filled with the Holy Spirit.' Immediately, Saul could see again. He was baptized and, after eating some food, regained his strength. Saul stayed for several days with the disciples in Damascus, preaching in the synagogues that Jesus is the Son of God. All who heard him were astonished and asked, 'Isn't this the man who raised havoc in Jerusalem among those who call on the name? Hasn't he come here to take them as prisoners to the chief priests?' Saul baffled the Jews living in Damascus by proving that Jesus is indeed the Messiah."

Father reflected, "If Jesus can reach out to such a man, then anyone may be won."

"Yes, isn't it wonderful? Soon there was a conspiracy among the Jews to kill Saul, but he learned of it. The Jews kept watch on the city gates day and night to kill him, but the believers took him by night and lowered him in a basket through an opening in the wall so that he escaped."

Mother asked, "The Pharisees would kill one of their own?"

"To stop the Way, they would. Paul came to Jerusalem and tried to join us, but we were afraid of him, thinking it was a trap. Then Barnabas brought him to us, telling us that Saul had seen the Lord, that the Lord had spoken to him, and that he had preached without fear in Damascus in the name of Jesus. Saul stayed with us, speaking boldly in the name of the Lord. He debated with the Hellenistic Jews, but they tried to kill him. When we learned this, we sent him down to Caesarea and then to Tarsus, his hometown."

Jahzeel asked, "Could not God use such a man elsewhere?"

"Yes, but he needs time. Much else has us occupied. There have been great miracles—too many to recount. How are things here?" I could see that Anna was great with child.

Jahzeel spoke with a smile, "You see that our family grows, but not as fast as the church."

Everyone chuckled. We enjoyed a fulfilling, although short, time of fellowship. After only a few hours, I had to return the Jerusalem.

XXX

Update on
the Gentiles

It had been nearly three years since I had last been home. I had wanted to tell the family about the Gentile believers when this new phenomenon had first occurred, but by now I realized that they must have already been told. I wanted to see Jahzeel's and Anna's child, whom I had been told was a son. So, I took the three-day journey back to the vineyard.

When I arrived, Mother greeted me with an embrace even before we could say "Shalom." She appeared to be very happy. Father also hugged me, and I immediately noticed a young boy following close behind him. Bringing up the rear was Anna, again with child. While we were still greeting each other, Jahzeel came in from the vineyard. Mother went for more raisin cakes, and Father motioned for us to sit on cushions on the roof for the breeze.

Jahzeel introduced me to his son, yet another Jahzeel the third. The lad was curious about me, especially since I looked so like his father! He was asked by Mother to pass the dish of cakes, which he did politely.

Jahzeel stated apologetically, "We have been somewhat nervous about going to Jerusalem for Passover after the persecution broke out, especially with the lad. We had him circumcised here. You had mentioned that there was a period of quietness, but we heard that James bar Zebedee was killed and Peter arrested."

"Yes, both are true. We have all been both arrested and flogged by this point. James was the first of the apostles to be killed."

Mother looked at me but said nothing, and Father asked, although I knew he didn't expect an answer, "Why did God not rescue James?"

"The Spirit has not revealed why James was taken and Peter remains."

Anna offered, "Could it be because Peter has a family?"

"It's possible, but God can care for any family better than the man of the house. We don't know any such thing unless it is revealed to us."

Mother asked anxiously, "Will you remain in Jerusalem?"

"That is what I have been shown. The Spirit seems to tell us that we will leave at some point, but there is as yet no detail. There is much news. You have heard of the Gentile believers?"

Father replied heartily, "Yes. It was confusing at first, but we now accept that this is God's will. We had not heard any details— only that Gentiles have believed."

"Many have. There is a new name for Christ's followers, too— disciples were first called Christians (Christ-like ones) at Antioch. Unbelievers had seen Christ-like behavior among believers and gave them this name. Perhaps they first did it to ridicule them, but that is immaterial now."

Father spoke, "We have heard the name Christian. It fits—if we truly follow. I had heard that Paul travels, preaching. He demonstrates the works of an apostle?"

"He is a true apostle."

Mother insisted on our eating before I left. We enjoyed wonderful fellowship.

XXXI

The Missions Calling

Three years later in Jerusalem, many apostles began to feel led by the Spirit to go on journeys to reach the lost in more distant lands. This experiential knowledge was called eido: knowing by perception through the Spirit. We all continued to grow in faith and in reliance on the Lord. We were given the impression that, eventually, few or none of us would remain in Jerusalem. Bathed in much prayer, the church sent each of us off to our respective destinations. Bartholomew wanted to travel to Armenia and to the southern Arabian regions but felt some desire to journey to Ethiopia as well. After prayer, he agreed to travel with me to Syria and Iraq and even to the far east—to India.

Peter, along with James, the half-brother of Jesus, felt compelled, at least for the time being, to stay in Jerusalem. In each case, after much prayer and discussion and by the leading of the Spirit, the church determined that no one would travel alone. Jesus had sent us out in pairs, and we determined that at least two of us would travel together. We assumed that we would return to Jerusalem after our journeys. Bartholomew and I were not the first to leave Jerusalem, nor the last. There was a commissioning by the church and much prayer, followed by a small celebration with each leave-taking, at least in part to cover the tears over parting.

I had enjoyed only a few brief visits to the vineyard since Jesus's ascension and felt in my spirit that I would not be returning to Jerusalem or Galilee again. I was uncertain whether word of our journeys would even be brought back to the church. We determined to visit with my family before embarking on this journey; they were now part of a strong congregation of converted Jews. Jahzeel had been ordained as an elder by the church, and Anna had by now given birth to three children. Jahzeel and Father were proud that the first two were boys, and Mother finally had the daughter she had dreamed of.

Jahzeel and Anna had also adopted a Greek girl with a disability. She had trouble walking, after having fallen into a fire. The girl's father had quickly rescued her, but her burns were substantial. A Greek doctor had suggested a poultice of ground grape seeds, and her parents had taken her to Jahzeel to get the poultice, as our vineyard was the only one in Galilee that made it. While they were with Jahzeel's family, both of the child's parents came down with a fever. Father prayed with both for recovery and then, when that seemed impossible, for salvation. The girl's father, already injured with burns, passed quickly, but the mother lingered for days. Jahzeel and Anna promised that they would take care of her daughter, Angelina. The mother died at peace with God. The poultice helped Angelina in the healing of her burns, and the little one became part of the family.

We were greeted with joyful tears when we reached the vineyard. The family knew I would be traveling—perhaps never to return. Father greeted me at the door with my younger nephew, my namesake Jezer, holding his hand, along with the other grandson, Jahzeel's namesake, who bore the same name as his father and grandfather. The children appeared shy; Anna said they were simply startled by how much I look like their father.

I reintroduced Bartholomew to my parents; they had not seen him since Jahzeel's wedding. Father sent the younger Jahzeel off to get my brother from the vineyard. It was amazing how much the boy looked like Jahzeel . . . and me. Had I been privileged to have a family, like Peter, I would likely have remained in the vicinity. As it was, I was free to serve at the discretion of the Spirit. We are not all called to be apostles, nor are we all called to be fathers. Yet,

Didymus

together we make up the body of Christ, the church. I am no more important, I realized, than Jahzeel; without people like him, where would the children come from, or the money to reach others? Nor would he ever suggest that I was unimportant; I was going on a journey to tell people about Jesus! There is no room for pride in the body of Christ.

Mother, always the hostess, already had us on the roof, reclining around a plate of raisin cakes. We had begun some small talk when Jahzeel entered. I rose, and we twins embraced. It felt so good. After their father's entrance, I found the children venturing closer to get a better look at me, which in the old days would have made Father angry over the breach in decorum. Now he simply smiled, with a look of pride clearly etched on his face. I also met for the first time my adoptive niece, Angelina. Shyly she approached me, limping. I took her hand.

Anna introduced us properly. "This is our daughter Angelina."

I spoke with a slight bow. "Shalom."

Her reply betrayed her Greek upbringing, as she mouthed the lovely Greek greeting, "Chari," or grace. I took her hands, knowing that the family had prayed much for healing and expected me to pray for a miraculous healing as well. Feeling tears in my eyes. I held one of the child's hands and offered Bartholomew the other. We both prayed. We could feel the Spirit—as well as the palpable tension of the family.

After a time, I spoke: "Anna, Jahzeel, I could feel the Spirit's touch, but also His message. Angelina, you have been given a miracle. God has taken away the lameness and the pain from the burns, but he has left on you the scars from the burns as a mark of ownership."

As Anna gathered up Angelina and inspected her arms, Bartholomew stated, "You can see for yourself, her lameness is gone. Rejoice—we are not always given a miracle."

As Anna and Mother wept, Angelina looked startled; then, with glee, she began to dance about the room with the other children, all of whom were laughing. Jesus was right: We must all become as little children. Jahzeel spoke, his voice cracking: "Thank you. . . We have prayed much. . . Angelina has lost so much. Perhaps we did not have enough faith. . ."

Bartholomew explained, "On occasion lack of faith is an issue when a miracle doesn't happen, either on the part of the person in need or of the intercessor. Faith is the substantiation of things we hope for and the conviction of things not seen. This time, though, it was not about a lack of faith. God can perform a miracle even with no faith involved. You will recall that, in the garden just before his arrest, Jesus reattached the ear of Malchus, the servant of the high priest, without anyone demonstrating faith.

There are many other possibilities: Perhaps God has a better plan—or different timing. Sometimes, we might become lifted up in pride based on an earlier answer to prayer, causing us to become overconfident or even arrogant. Or there may be a lesson to be learned—a lesson not necessarily for the person we are praying for or for us; others may for one reason or another need to see our afflictions. Of one thing we can be sure: God's will and timing are always impeccable. We pray to be in communion with God, to come alongside him in terms of our will, to show him our desires, and to recognize his. Sometimes, we understand the reason for a miracle, or its absence, though often God simply says that his grace is sufficient. See how much you have already learned from this healing."

Father, always desiring propriety, wanted Angelina to give thanks, too. I stopped him, saying, "Father, in time Angelina will show gratitude to God and to us. At the moment, her joy is gratitude enough." I spoke more loudly then to all. "Her scars are a reminder, nothing more. She may need them when she is older, to testify of the grace of God. We need reminders, especially of miracles that have happened in times past. The marks will become a beautiful reminder. We saw the scars Christ still bears. They are physically unpleasant, but they are the most beautiful marks in the world. Angelina was given a miracle—a proof that God loves her even after all she has been through, a testimony of his love."

Didymus

Jahzeel stated pensively, "What happened to her didn't seem fair."

I countered, "Fairness is a measure of our human judgment. We cannot see the end from the beginning. God is equitable and always perfectly just."

Jahzeel nodded, and the conversation turned to other matters.

I had expected Father to initiate the dialogue, but I realized that he had given Jahzeel that honor. My twin began with a smile. "Brother, you are looking well. I see that you, too, have kept much of your hair, though you are very gray. You look as though you spend too much time reading and not enough working; I see, too, that you have gained some weight."

I answered with a smile of my own, "My gray hair comes from worrying about what is happening in the churches. Yours comes, I have no doubt, from worrying about children, grapes, and your own church. I have put on a little weight, but we will be doing a lot of traveling, and where we are going there will be very little kosher, so I'll need that weight."

There was a little chuckling, after which Mother asked, "I know Gentile believers are not required to eat kosher, but you still do, don't you?"

"Yes, Mother, I have always eaten as a Jew. But I know that on these journeys to Gentile lands I will eat what is given me with thanks. I will eat kosher when I can."

Jahzeel asked, "You will be traveling to the east?"

"After much prayer, Bartholomew and I plan on going first to Syria and then to Iraq. We believe that the Spirit is directing us on from there to India. Bartholomew also feels led to return through Armenia and the southern Arabian regions, and perhaps through Northern Africa or Ethiopia. The church has agreed and is sending us to these places. Remember Jesus's commission: 'But you will receive power when the Holy Spirit overflows you; and you will be my witness in Jerusalem, and in all Judea and Samaria, and to the ends of the earth.' You were all there; I can hardly contain the gift given me!"

Jazeel smilingly quipped, "I will take Galilee, and you may have the ends of the earth."

Father commented, "I have never even met a Roman or a Greek who has been to India."

Bartholomew seconded, "Nor have I. The trade routes have been there since Alexander, so the way is known. They have so far been used only by merchants and soldiers. God will provide."

Jahzeel looked at me somberly and asked, "Thomas, do you feel that you will return?"

With tears in my eyes, I caught his gaze. "No, brother, I do not. If the venture is successful, I expect to start a series of churches and either travel between them or pastor a single fellowship and oversee others, much as John does at Ephesus. We apostles now understand far better what God has planned for both our nation and for his church. At times what we are told is theopneustos (simply given directly by the Spirit of God). Sometimes an event we did not expect, or an opportunity or turn of events, we also recognize as given by the Spirit to show us direction.

"We now realize that the kingdom is not yet, and perhaps not even imminent. Even Pilate was told that Jesus's kingdom is not of this world. These are, we believe, the final times before it is instituted in its fullness, and we now know that the Gentiles have been grafted into the root."

I proceeded, "Jesus spoke of wars and rumors of wars before his kingdom is complete. He also said that our people will fall by the sword and be taken as prisoners to all the nations. Jerusalem will be trampled on by the Gentiles until the time of the Gentiles is fulfilled. For now, Jesus said that we are to preach the Word to *every person*. He also said that the gospel, the good news, will be preached *in the whole world as a testimony to all nations*... and then the end will come. That will take a while. I doubt that it will even be in our generation. Jesus will return for a coronation as King. He will indeed sit on the throne of David. I used to think that would be soon, but I'm no longer sure. By the time I return from India, if God allows me to, I will no longer be a young man."

Didymus

Father replied with a twinkle in his eye, "You will still be young. . ."

Mother looked at Father with a smile playing on her lips, chuckling, "A second childhood does not count as young. . ."

Everyone laughed, but Jahzeel's oldest son asked, "Is India farther than Jerusalem?" In the old days (as in my own childhood), a child would not have spoken out in an adult conversation, but Father and Mother had begun a new tradition whereby children were always valued and included, as Jesus had taught.

Jahzeel replied, "Yes, much farther. Farther even than Rome. But God oversees us all."

Anna, gazing meaningfully at the children, said, "You will not be children when Thomas returns, if he is able to return at all."

The younger girl began to cry, and Mother scooped her up and assured her, "We will always pray for him. We will know that he is in God's care. Besides, Jesus may return for us all first."

I went on softly, "I may try to write, but I'm not much of a writer, and we have some fear of the Romans reading our letters. Some think the gematria, the cipher code replacing letters with numbers is a good and secret way to keep from alarming them. Regardless, happiness is based on what is happening, whereas joy is based on Jesus. You can't have an effect without a cause. Jesus is the cause for my joy. Right now, I have happiness as well. You are the cause of that happiness. I always have joy, for I always have Jesus. Mother, the little one takes after you; I remember your fears when I first went with Jesus. The prophet Joel once said to rend our hearts, not our garments, in contrition. I felt at that time as though your heart was about to be torn from you."

Mother answered, "It's true. Yet I remember what you said: 'The safest place in the world is the center of his will, or in his presence.' I didn't understand it then. My heart was too broken. I do now. I have turned it over to Jesus. The worst thing for you now would be to avoid or circumvent this will."

I nodded. "We don't know the future, what will be meta autos (after these things). I do fear. Yet my greatest fear is to let down my Lord. I was tempted with power and glory. All of us were." I watched Bartholomew nodding and continued, "When my dreams were not coming to fruition, I fell. Now I realize that, whenever we are tempted, it is not God who is tempting us, for God cannot be tempted by evil, nor does he tempt anyone. No, each of us is tempted when we are enticed by *our own* evil desires. After desire has conceived, it gives birth to sin—and sin, when full-grown, gives birth to death. My evil desire began in my mind, thinking that I was entitled to more. That gave birth to sin. God allowed me to be tested and humbled by failing. I had a childish tantrum. God had to tear worldly ambition out of me.

"The Spirit has taught us that we must put on the armor of God against Satan's schemes. Our struggle is not against flesh and blood, but against the rulers, against the authorities, against the powers of this dark world and against the spiritual forces of evil in the heavenly realms. We must put the belt of truth around our waist and the breastplate of righteousness in place. Our feet must be fitted with the readiness that comes from the gospel of peace. We must take up the shield of faith, daily, to extinguish all the flaming arrows of the evil one. Most importantly, we have the helmet of salvation and the sword of the Spirit, which is the Word of God. And we are to pray with alertness. Oh, the grace of Jesus that brought me back! I could not see at the time that he has *everyone's best interest* in mind, *all the time*. We have his favor. That was hard for me to believe. Even now, I tend to think I know what's best."

Father recalled, "Growing up, both you and your brother had that tendency to give in to that desire, but you came by it honestly; I've struggled with it, too. Your mother and I always wanted what was best for each of you, individually. Others saw you as 'the twins,' but we could discern the differences between you, and we did not train you in an identical way. We didn't have the complete or perfect knowledge of God, though we did our best. I think you both believed that you could parent better than we could." Looking at Jahzeel with a smile, he finished, "Now, with the help of the Holy Spirit, you can."

Didymus

I exclaimed, "God's hand was on us through you and Mother. I used to worry that I did not have the favor of God. I looked at my circumstances and compared them to the situations of others whom I believed had it better. The truth was that, though others had what *looked* like better circumstances, I had *always* had God's favor. Even in the lowest moments of my life, after the crucifixion, I still had God's favor. I thought things were against me, but the Spirit has apokalyptria (convinced me) that *all* things work *together* for the good of those who have been called according to his purpose.

"So many things were revealed to us after Jesus was glorified. I realized that God *allowed* those difficult things to happen to me to make me who I am. I now can empathize with doubters. I didn't know the early history of Jesus then, but Mary, his mother, has told us about Jesus's birth and childhood over these last years. His birth was announced by angels—to lowly shepherds, of all people! The people with the least favor according to the world were given the favor of the best message in the world. Here is what we are told: 'Suddenly a great company of the heavenly host appeared with the angel, praising God and saying, 'Glory to God in the highest heaven, and on earth peace to those on whom his favor rests.'

"God's favor was on poor shepherds, and on all who would receive his Shalom. My envy was wrong. Now I know that his favor had been on me from the beginning. I now love the *high* title: *shepherd*. I should have been grateful for all that God had given me, first though my family and then through Jesus. When you know something you should do and don't do it, you are sinning. We have the favor of having been chosen by Christ before the foundation of the world, that we should be holy and blameless before him. I know through the Spirit that I can do all things through Christ and his strength! How marvelous! Now, as with Jeremiah, his word burns within me."

Jahzeel admitted, "I have a willful bent. I was concerned about having charge over situations. I wanted the decisions to be mine, and I wanted to be recognized as always being in the right. It goes way back to our days together in the vineyard, brother; I wanted to rule over you. When you became an apostle, I feared that your position gave you authority over me. Now that I have learned of the humility of Christ and grown in his grace, I've repented of this sin, though I still fight it."

Father nodded, remembering, "It was a hard time, the crucifixion. Jahzeel handled it better than any of the rest of us."

Now Jahzeel looked uncomfortable. "For me, it was simply believing what God had said through Isaiah."

Anna commented, "You believed it because you first knew it."

Mother asked her, "How do you mean?"

"The Isaiah passage seemed impossible to fulfill, although those of us who did not really know it couldn't see how improbable it was. Jahzeel, along with many rabbis and Pharisees, knew that it could not be fulfilled because they had studied it so well. After it was, in fact, fulfilled, people who did not understand the passage were unimpressed, but the ones who understood it were absolutely amazed. Thomas, did you not tell us that many priests and Pharisees have since been converted? Saul, for example."

"Yes. Many did believe through fulfillment of scripture. Saul, or Paul, had a direct encounter with the risen Lord, but once he came to understand the detail of Jesus's life, he recognized the fulfillment. Until he paid attention to the truth, he had refused to believe."

Jahzeel observed, "Brother, believing is always a decision. Before I knew the Isaiah passage, my refusal to accept was an act of my will. I refused to believe even after seeing the truth of the fish and the loaves. When I found the Isaiah passage, *it* was what I trusted in. When Jesus fulfilled the passage, I had nothing to rely on but him. It was only then that I put my trust in Christ, not in myself. After the crucifixion, *you* had plenty of people offering you truth, yet you became willful in your decision *not* to believe."

"Yes, I willfully refused to trust. People who have been presented with the evidence and don't believe fail willfully. Men love darkness, or evil, rather than light. Agape love is a willful decision. God gives us the free will to choose to love; that's part of our being created in God's image. Yet we can use what God gives us for evil. When we do, Satan wants us to blame God, not ourselves. Judas Iscariot was among the Twelve. The Holy Spirit may have used him, but remember that the Holy Spirit had also come upon King Saul, *while he was trying to kill David!* Even though God knew what Judas would do, that did not excuse Judas for his choice. God chose Judas to do what he did, yet Judas also chose to do what was in his heart to do. God cannot be faulted for his choice; he is perfect in justice.

Judas chose his own sin, and God's choice was to not stop him. I should know: I also chose to rebel and reject the resurrection itself. *I deliberately rebelled against God's sovereign will,* and God did not stop me. Now I realize that my act of will is the strongest part of my personal testimony. God allowed me the free will to remain miserable, but the Spirit of God worked through my misery. Therefore, I can witness to those who are refusing to accept. Jahzeel and I are willful and stubborn like Abraham's son Ishmael, that wild donkey of a man. Unrepentant man is always like a wild donkey. I do not deserve even to be a doulos, or bond slave, of Jesus."

Father stated with a wry smile, "Perhaps God would like me to witness to the elderly?"

I smiled and said, "Father, I know you are a good martus, a good witness. Right now, you have at your side two young boys who will not let any word of yours fall to the ground; they are fertile ground in which to plant seed."

Father looked down, but I knew he had become content. He had become the tranquil man he had always desired to be, but not in the way he had expected. One can never enter rest through the works of the Law, but only by grace through faith. Moses was faithful, yet never led the people into the land of rest. What he had preached to them had not profited because it was not mixed with faith on their part. Joshua faithfully led the people into that land, yet not into that rest. Joshua spoke of another day, the day of Jesus. Jesus was far greater than Joshua or Moses.

Now Father had ceased from his works, trusting Christ and resting fully in the completed work of Jesus. Father had relinquished all he had, all of his plans and purposes, to Christ. Such trust in the wisdom and love of God had brought him complete shalom. I realized that, until after the crucifixion, none of us apostles had really relinquished our selfish desires. Being crucified with Christ required true Shalom. I realized that the Holy Spirit was allowing me, an apostle, to still learn from observing my own father; his serenity was eloquent and clear.

I broke the silence with, "Father, several years ago we had a deep conversation. I told you from my heart how much respect I had for you. If anything, that respect has grown. When Jahzeel and I were boys, we studied Torah, went to synagogue, and celebrated the holy days. You taught me to be careful, honest, and truthful. To believe God.

"You were afraid, though, that you had somehow let me down. You wanted me to have peace. I told you that the peace Jesus gave me reminded me of when I was little and we had to work at the vines until after dark. I was afraid. But I had peace when you held my hand. Jesus has given me that peace." I reached out and took Father's wrinkled hand. We both wept. Jahzeel's children at first looked surprised, but then they all came to touch his hand as well.

Mother reflected, "You boys both have shalom now. I thought your father and I had shalom before, but now we have it in abundance. We have no worry about ourselves, only a concern for others who do not have peace with God, the Shalom of Christ. You and Jahzeel have done so much for God—and I so little."

I answered quickly, "No, Mother! You have done so much. You have raised two sons to become honorable men. You now watch two grandsons and two granddaughters. You have helped so many in need. You both tell others of Jesus. You took exactly the path Jesus had chosen for you. You are in the center of God's will."

Anna shared as well, "I have been in love with Jahzeel since we were young. I chose him to spend my life with before he chose me; I suppose this is somewhat like the way God chooses us before we choose him. I was eager to marry, yet patient. When my father said we could, my heart leapt for joy. After our family came to faith, and Jahzeel had not, my father said we must wait, and my heart broke. I was still sure of Jahzeel. His hard work at discovering the truth made him in my eyes a much better man. I cannot imagine a life without him. Jahzeel told me that his father had often told him, 'The only true reason to marry is that you know that is the only path for your life.'"

Bartholomew, who had been observing with a smile, spoke again. "Without taking that path, you are incomplete, imperfect. This is much the way I feel about serving God—this is my only path, based on the clear direction of the Holy Spirit. In the prophets we are told many times that obedience is better than sacrifice. None of us is without flaw, but obedience, *doing what God asked*, is what made David a man after God's own heart."

I picked up the thread, also with a smile. "Satan is the one who binds people in sin. Jesus frees us. Usually, it's our mind that is held captive. Satan poisons our minds against the gospel, and we are captive until we acquire the mind of Christ. People worry about what they would have to 'give up' to follow Jesus, not recognizing that they are already bound by Satan! How can a drunkard still believe he is free? Satan tells him that he is, though in reality he is in darkness. Through the Spirit of God, we, the church, can pray and release others to be open to the gospel, to see the light of truth. If we do so, we have been instrumental in releasing them from Satan's chains, to become a part of the family of God!"

Bartholomew confirmed, "That's true. Under Satan's influence, the grace of God looks like bondage, while the truth is that it's exactly the opposite. The Spirit-led prayer of believers binds Satan from holding unbelievers, allowing them to hear and respond to the gospel. Too often, we offer up hopeful prayers like 'God save him' or 'God save her.' God already desires to save; our prayer should be, 'God, bind Satan from influencing this person so they can hear the gospel. Loose their ears.' Our prayers can set them free *so they can truly hear the gospel!*"

I continued, "You remember I told you that after Peter's confession Jesus promised, 'Whatsoever things you bind on earth will be bound in heaven, and whatsoever things you loose on earth shall be loosed in heaven?'"

Father replied, "Yes, I remember. I never believed that Simon alone would be determining what would happen in heaven."

"Jesus also said, 'I say to you that if two of you agree on earth concerning anything that they ask, it will be done for them by my Father in heaven. For where two or three are gathered together in my name, I am there in the midst of them.' He was talking to us, those who have been indwelt by the Holy Spirit. We set others free from bondage through prayer. If we don't ask for them to be released, we are leaving them in bondage. It isn't just about Peter or the apostles. If we do not pray for God to unbind people, who will? If we don't pray for God to bind the enemy, who will? The work is of the Spirit, not of any one man."

Father, speaking somberly, "I finally understand! You teach so well. God will give you a great reward."

Bartholomew explained, "We act because we have already been rewarded. God knows our motives, even when we don't realize them. My motive for serving before the resurrection was a reward in Christ's kingdom; I went so far as to compete for it. Working through the Spirit, God's Word has made all the difference; it is sharp enough to correctly divide my motives, good and bad. All the ways of a man are pure in his own eyes, but the Lord weighs the motives of his heart."

Father remarked, "Things you work for are more fulfilling than things requiring no effort. When we speak of Sabbath, we often forget that we need to labor for six days, not just to rest for one! The vineyard is not easy to maintain. The vines must be trained, or they are of little value. Raising a family is not easy, either. There must be training. Children without training are still of value, of course, but training them in Christ's ways magnificently increases their worth to him. These things are fulfilling, and they are good. We are made to work, to obey the will of God."

Didymus

Jahzeel observed, "It's natural to want an easy way out. I have seen some of the wealthy who believe there is nothing they need to do. What a horrible life. Following Jesus is exciting! Thomas, do you remember when you told us the difference between fact and truth? Sometimes I assume I know the truth, but often all I have is fact. If it were not for the Prophets or the Holy Spirit, I could never be sure of the truth."

Bartholomew agreed. "Scripture is the test. The truth is that the devil can easily deceive us; our only real solution is to keep putting our trust in the completed work of Christ when the devil lies to us. Only God knows the truth all the time. Even with scripture, we must devote much prayer and fasting in order to know how to use it. Knowledge puffs up, but agape love edifies. There is no easy way. Jahzeel, your testimony of what Christ has done in your life is also truth. You, also, will overcome Satan not only by the blood of Christ but by the word of your testimony."

I interjected, "I found it amazing to realize how much God wants to give both grace and peace to all people. We Jews grow up wishing Shalom—peace—to others. I never realized until after the Spirit spoke to me that the greeting of the Greeks is "Chari"—grace. All people realize their need of both peace and grace."

Father reflected, "I never even thought about the Greek greeting; I simply took it for granted. Of course, the Greeks desire grace. What a magnificent thought."

I continued, "Remember these words of Jesus: 'By this everyone will know that you are my disciples, if you love one another.' When we show his love, those around us will know we are his disciples."

Jahzeel remarked, "God is agape. Yet sometimes what I see in his working does not look like love—that is because I cannot see as God does. Words like this have already become a sad refrain in the church: How can a loving God allow this or that sad or evil thing? People want to judge God."

Bartholomew exclaimed, "We *can* trust God. His motive is pure. Do you recall that, in the Garden of Eden, that old serpent tempted Eve to question Elohim, The Almighty God himself? The serpent said to the woman, 'You will not surely die. For God knows that in the day you eat of this tree your eyes will be opened, and you will be like God, knowing good and evil.' That very first temptation was to judge God's motives! Unless the Holy Spirit reveals it, I have no right to judge the motives of another. I cannot even honestly judge my own motives without the help of the Spirit."

I agreed. "We have no right to judge God. In ancient days, Job found that out. God is love. He is also a jealous God—literally a consuming fire. Sometimes loving acts seem harsh. I wanted to touch fire as a young boy. Father, you seemed harsh in keeping me from hurting myself. Eventually, I did touch fire, and only then did I realize that your punishment had protected me.

"Jahzeel, if you did not have a jealous love for Anna, you would not truly love her. You are a loving man, and I know that you reserve vengeance for God, but if someone were to threaten or hurt your daughter, it would be the most loving thing you could do to protect her, even by force. We are commanded, in fact, to do so. Yet you know that Jesus died for that very person, and you would lovingly witness to him at any other time."

Father pointed out, "God has told us that we have a responsibility to take care of our family. Without genuine, selfless love—God's love—we are not his. Marriage, or even more, a family, is much like the church."

I replied, "Father, I like what you said; marriage and the family are indeed much like the church. I see clearly that the cornerstone of the family and the church is trust. Without trust in one's spouse, a marriage is a very unhappy place. Selfless love can occur in a marriage only through trust. Likewise, selfless love in the church can occur only through trust. When each one knows that he or she has been trusted with an important role, the family functions well. If a trusted person fails, we must lovingly restore them. If we cannot, then the family remains incomplete, imperfect. In a church setting, when each one knows that they have been entrusted with an important role, one appointed for them by the Holy Spirit himself, the fellowship works well. If someone in the church who has been trusted fails, we are to try to restore them. God makes no mistakes in either of these covenants. This is a beautiful way to see these relationships."

Bartholomew observed, "Jesus said, 'I have no greater joy than to hear that my children are walking in the truth.' We, even the adults, are his children. His family. The family of God."

I gave one final admonition: "Jahzeel, before you believed, my goal was to do all I could to bring about your belief. Your believing was God's will also. Yet if I concentrate all my energy or faith on a single goal, I will not appreciate the journey. Our lives are journeys. Each moment is important. Each is a gift from God. I need to be grateful for each moment, even when I cannot understand the why of whatever is going on. All things work together, or in combination, for good to those who have been called according to Christ's purpose. We can try to determine how they work together, or we can simply rest in his will and give him praise for the gift of today."

I noticed that the last of Jahzeel's children had fallen asleep. It was time for all of us to rest; there could be more talk tomorrow. Often while in Jerusalem we had stayed up late discussing such things; the difference was that this was home and family. Mother and Anna quietly put the children to bed. Bartholomew and I, along with Father and Jahzeel, had a time of prayer before retiring for the night.

XXXII

The Need for a
Written Testament

The next morning, everyone rose early. I sought to help in the vineyard, but Jahzeel insisted that he needed our fellowship. We made small talk at first. Jahzeel mentioned that there was talk of it becoming too hot for grapes. Father smiled and recalled, "When my father settled here, he was told it was too hot and dry here for grapes. To succeed, he would have to water them by hand. The people blamed the drought on Alexander the Greek having burned the land, or perhaps on the Persians having done so before him. Others lamented that conditions were simply becoming hotter and dryer every year. Yet, these things have a way or working out in the end. Didn't God promise seedtime and harvest, way back in the beginning?"

I concurred, quoting the passage from the Pentateuch, and Jahzeel quipped, "Do all apostles simply call any scripture to mind at will, as you two do?"

I laughed. "Only when the Spirit gives us these verses or the knowledge needed. I'm no Solomon. The Spirit won't let us use this knowledge to impress people."

Bartholomew explained, "We have all spent many days and nights studying the Word, and in prayer. We apostles may begin to speak and suddenly recall something we don't remember ever having heard. That's an amazing feeling—you know that you are being used by God. But this happens only when necessary, and exactly when the Spirit determines the need. The words may be profound or simply expedient. I may also begin to speak expecting to make a point when it seems as though what I intended to say is just not there. That must mean that the Holy Spirit doesn't want the words spoken at that time."

Father reflected, "At my age, I begin to speak, too, and many things I want to say are just not there. In my case, it's memory loss!"

We shared a chuckle, and Father went on to ask, "Thomas, when Jesus sent you out by twos, he told you not to carry money—that worthy believers would see to your needs. When you leave the lands inhabited by the Jews, who will meet your needs?"

"As brother Paul travels, he meets with people and looks for Jews, in their own synagogue or in a house or even by a riverside if there are few. Then he attempts to start a new fellowship of believers. He is a tentmaker by trade, so he can always earn money if the need arises. All apostles and most disciples know some sort of trade. I, for instance, know a lot about farming. If necessary, I can help someone in the fields until a church is established. We have also spent much time fishing, repairing nets, and otherwise helping in the fishing trade. If there are believers in Christ, we will look for the Ichthys, the symbol of the fish, which indicates that a Christian fellowship is nearby. That symbol reminds us of Jesus's feedings of the thousands. There is also a new symbol being used for Christians—a cross. The true sacrifice is, as we know so well, Christ's blood. We commemorate communion, as Jesus commissioned us to do, but we don't mark a doorpost with the blood, as at Passover. We have no lasting symbol for the blood within the church."

Jahzeel thought aloud, "There can be no lasting symbol, since blood is always fresh. I realize how favored we were, brother, to have been brought up in a vineyard. From our experience we know that wine spoils! Dried wine, in fact, is a stain of death. The life is in the blood, and it is the blood of life that makes atonement for each of our lives. Would you join us in a final communion supper before you leave?"

I answered, "The Lord's Supper we will certainly celebrate together as a congregation. How often do you partake?"

"Irregularly. Perhaps every month or so."

"Jesus told us to do so as a memorial, a remembering, though he did not tell us how often. Some do it weekly. Some far less often. Do you ever commemorate Jesus with a foot washing, as he did for the apostles in the upper room?"

"We have heard little about that idea and have not done so."

"Jesus told us that we should practice this in humility for others. Shall we do so here?"

"Certainly. We will need instruction."

"We can do it after communion. I will explain it first, and the men and women will do it separately. I will go over it with Mother and Anna, and they can explain the washing to the other women. We can watch the children as the women wash."

Jahzeel asked a complex, though unrelated, question: "When we were younger, we had the Law. We knew what sin was, and we knew what we could and could not do. Now, in the church, I have young people asking me whether a particular act is sin. They want a written code, like the Law. Yet we are no longer under the Law. What am I to tell them?"

"You are right, we are not under the Law but under grace. You and I were in grace, briefly, when we were very young, since we were alive before we understood Law. The Law, as we now understand, is insufficient; as an example, Jesus told us that, if we look at a woman with lust in our heart, it is as though we are committing adultery. That is a much harder test, because it deals with our spirit, not just with outward actions. Christians will sin, but sinning should not be our practice. When we do sin, we must confess to God and ask forgiveness.

"Isaiah says, 'Your iniquities have separated you from your God, and your sins have hidden his face from you, so that he will not hear.' We want God to hear us. And we know that, if we confess our sin, he will forgive our sin and cleanse us from all unrighteousness. The Spirit brings genuine conviction. Look at those who delivered up Christ to be crucified; they clearly sinned in shedding innocent blood, yet they had not in their own minds broken the letter of the Law!

"This should not be confusing, nor is God the author of confusion. When Gentiles who do not know the Law do by nature the requirements of the Law, they demonstrate God's Law unto themselves. The Law in itself is good—but it saves no one. It is only by grace that we have been saved, through faith. To us believers no longer living under the constraints of the Law, 'all things' are lawful, but we certainly know that not all things are helpful. Our bodies are members of Christ. We are his workmanship, created in Christ Jesus for good works, which God prepared in advance for us to walk in. We all know the story of the potter and the clay. We are clay, crafted for the potter's purposes—so we are to do as Christ the potter would have us do. The Law was only our schoolmaster; without it we would not have known how depraved we are without Christ."

Jahzeel appealed, "You are saying so many things so fast that I cannot keep up. All of this must be written down, allowing us to read the words again and again and to reflect on their meaning!"

"Yes, these discussions are excellent, but there is a critical need to have all of this encapsulated as written word, to be sent out to all the churches. I listened personally to the very words of Jesus, as did Bartholomew. There is a Dedike—an informal guideline on whom to trust—but that's simply practical; it's not to be considered scripture, or even a document the Spirit specifically asked us to write. We quote Jesus, as we should. But suppose neither of us were here; in most churches, there is neither an apostle nor a prophet immediately available. There would certainly be a need for a written record of the words and teachings of Jesus and his Spirit. Something that can be trusted, just as we Jews trust the Law and the Prophets. This must meet the criteria for real scripture, unlike the Targums, which were at best loose paraphrases.

"As a matter of fact, even as we speak, John Mark is writing what the Holy Spirit is calling to his mind, mostly by the mouth of

Peter. James has also written a letter of doctrine—and Paul several, including epistles that are circulating through the churches. We can verify that these are scripture. Such things can never be opinion; the words of Jesus, or the Spirit-led Word of God, must always be the final authority when it comes to acceptance of newer material."

Bartholomew pointed out, "You see how much the church has grown through the testimony of the apostles and the disciples. Imagine how much more the church could grow if we had these words written down for all to read and reflect upon!"

Jahzeel noted, "Thomas, when you apostles were first sent out by twos, you were paired up with Matthew, the tax collector. Did you not say he kept a journal of all that was happening? How is it that John Mark is writing based on the recollections of Peter instead of using Matthew's journal as his source material?"

"Matthew has an excellent journal. He was not one of the first apostles, but we have filled him in on what came before, and he has added that to his journal. He says with all seriousness that he will have it copied when he returns from the trip he has felt led by the Spirit to take: traveling the coasts of the Mediterranean and perhaps visiting Ethiopia. He says, however, that the Spirit has not led him to present it yet. Peter and John Mark are taking this very seriously, and the Spirit is leading them as well.

"The Greek physician who accompanies Paul, a man named Luke you have not met, has also taken notes from all the apostles and witnesses. Originally the servant of a Roman nobleman, he was sent to find out the truth about 'The Way,' as we called our movement then, and to report back to his master, Theophilus. What he shared with Theophilus was persuasive enough that he has been granted the freedom to continue following Paul to record what is still happening. He asked many questions of Mary, Jesus's mother, especially about the births of Jesus and of John the Baptizer.

"I've spoken with him only a few times, but he took many notes and asked good questions. All of this will be copied and circulated. It is conceivable that, if Matthew had already presented his notes, those of John Mark and Peter would not have been completed, and the records Luke is taking would never be copied. Besides, what Matthew learned or thought was important might not be what John Mark encountered or thought important. Whatever is significant to the Holy Spirit must be recorded."

Father mused, "Perhaps we will someday have three records. Thomas, would you write one, too?"

"No, I have recited some things to John Mark, and even a few to Luke. From what I have overheard of Peter's recollections, there is no need to duplicate. The Spirit leads me to the East, and the church has sent me. Besides, you remember what my teacher said about my writing abilities . . ."

Father chuckled, "Yes, your teacher said he thought that, because you are a twin to Jahzeel, you must not be trying, as Jahzeel could write twice as fast as you. You remembered everything and read well, but writing was tedious for you."

Jahzeel remembered, "You were always obsessed with detail. Every letter had to be without flaw. I was happy if my scribbles could be read at all. The Holy Spirit knows what he is doing."

I smiled and concurred, "We, the church, are also the body of Christ; I suppose I am a foot, not a writing hand." All chuckled.

Bartholomew interjected, "There is more. I'm sure you have heard that Jesus taught us by parable about not being able to sew new fabric onto an old garment; to make sure we got the message, he adding the example of sewing new fabric to old wine skins. You vinedressers of all people know that they would fail."

I pointed out, "The church is a new institution. It is not a new sect of Judaism. Faith in God to provide a solution to our sin is not new; that is all through scripture. Sometimes God showed his love to people beyond the Jews, as he did to the Ninevites generations ago through the prophet Jonah. Before Moses, God dealt with people in a different way—and before Abraham, differently still. God does not change, nor has his love for people changed. He has provided specific covenants for humanity at various times.

"In truth, all righteous men before the cross of Christ looked forward to redemption; now we look back on it. We are enjoying an

age of grace—a favor we do not deserve, and something the saints
of old looked forward to. What is new is an individual relationship
with God, with no human priest as mediator between God and people. The Spirit comes and indwells us to stay. Believers are God's
own special people, that we may proclaim the praises of him who
called us out of darkness into his marvelous light.

"Jesus was with all twelve of us apostles for a few years, but
the church did not actually come into being until Pentecost, when
the Holy Spirit came upon us all. This was a new thing, ushering
in a new age and a new way to see God's grace! The Holy Spirit
has been speaking to all the apostles and showing us the marvels
of God's love. These things will indeed be written down. But the
Spirit has also shown us that, when all is written, the testament
will be complete; sufficient. There will be nothing added . . . or
removed.

"There will be a time when people will cast doubt on our written testimony of what Jesus said and the instructions he has given
through the apostles, just as Satan did upon God's words in the
garden. Already people claim that Paul does not have the authority
of an apostle. In the future, they will ask, 'Did Jesus actually say
. . .?' They will say that what we are teaching is wrong and that
God changes. The written testament must be totally authoritative.
Doctrine must be based upon it, and only it."

Jahzeel recalled, "We turned away Judaizers because we see
the Spirit working with the Gentiles. We now know that Christ has
canceled the record of debt that stood against all people, that all
who believe in his name are redeemed. We also recognize that we
are not under the Law but under grace. We also turned away Gnos-
tics because we saw the risen Lord in the flesh. We need this written
testimony. Right now, anyone can claim that God himself has told
him something. We can dispute false claims by the Spirit, or by
logic or example or our memory of the words of Christ. But often,
I don't know the answer." Then, after a pause, "Then something
else always seems to come up that I can't answer, such as to what
degree are women allowed to minister in the church."

I smiled and asked a question of my own: "How much will men decline to do? Many women serve in the church. I think immediately of Mary, the mother of our Lord; Mary Magdalene; Martha and her sister, also Mary; the mother of James and Joses; Lydia; Phoebe; Chloe; Claudia; the mother of John Mark; and of course of note of all the apostles; Junia. There are many more. All of these willing servants are appropriately modest, and none is disruptive. They minister to the needs of others and do not usurp authority. They have been entrusted with the same Holy Spirit, indwelling and gifting them, as have the men. They, too, are members of the body of Christ. Their thoughts matter just as much as the men's whenever decisions need to be made. They help much, often taking responsibility only when men will not. When your right hand is hurt, would you not expect your left hand to take on more responsibility?"

Father began to nod in agreement, and Mother spoke up, smiling: "I am always happy to help."

"Mother, you are certainly a helper fit for a king—or, in this case, for the head of the family: Father. Even when you banter with him, he knows how you honor him. He responds by showing you the love you deserve. Many families do not have this blessed relationship. You have always walked in love."

Jahzeel observed, "You mentioned that women have received the gifts of the Spirit. I know that some of us have gifts, but I don't know much about this subject, other than a gift of teaching."

Bartholomew began, "There are different kinds of gifts, but all are given to believers to build up the body of Christ, the church. Some are given wisdom, for example, and others knowledge, faith, healing, miracles, prophecy, discernment, tongues, and interpretation. All are given by the same Spirit, to each believer individually as he wills, and to the degree he wills. The purpose of these giftings is never pride but to build up others within the body, as required. Need is determined by the Spirit. The fruits are the result of the work of the Spirit in the members of the church. Paul has listed them for us as love, joy, peace, patience, kindness, goodness, faithfulness, gentleness, and self-control—although many other characteristics would qualify as well. The Holy Spirit enables the gifts to work the fruit into our lives. Eventually, as we obey, we are being conformed more and more to the image of Jesus."

Jahzeel noted, "I need to write this down, too."

I nodded and went on, "Our gifts are simply that; we did not earn them, and they are never intended for our own glory. It's not about what God can do for us but about what we can do for God. Our job is simply to witness.

"The church in Jerusalem became too comfortable. We were meeting together in joy, but our commission from the Lord was to go into all the world to preach and baptize. Later, people began to follow individual apostles, saying, 'I am of Paul,' or "I am of Peter.' This was childish and carnal, and it brought discord—even competition. Remember, brother, how you and I competed? It gained us nothing. We must all be of the same Spirit!

"When we in the Jerusalem church did not do as we should have, God used shame from our lack of means, and even persecution, to get us to fulfill Christ's commission. My time as a Christian has in some sense been something like climbing a steep, sandy terrace. You can't stand still, and if you stop climbing, you start to slide backward. I tried that once, after the crucifixion; and, as you will recall, I slid back quickly. We have to keep pressing forward, or eventually we will reach rock bottom."

Father replied, "Thomas, you paint a wonderful and yet painful picture with words."

"Thank you, Father. You grasp the truth because you have the Spirit and can discern these things. You have a new heart and have been renewed in spirit and in mind. For by him all things were created; he is before all things, and in him all things hold together. And he is the head of the body, the church. The Spirit has shown us that we have to work at our growth, our sanctification; we are to make every effort to add to our faith goodness; and to goodness, knowledge; and to knowledge, self-control; and to self-control, perseverance; and to perseverance, godliness; and to godliness, mutual affection; and to mutual affection, love. As we possess these qualities in increasing measure, they will keep us from being ineffective and unproductive. It's not automatic; *it is work.*

"The Spirit of Christ will indeed help me grow. I am obedient to my Lord, doing what he commands—and I receive in return his friendship. He also tells me his business. Isaiah says, 'You, Israel, my servant, Jacob, whom I have chosen, you are descendants of Abraham my friend.' As sons of Jacob, we are God's chosen, and as descendants of Abraham, we are God's friends. In Jesus we are friends of God, as Abraham was! In Proverbs it is said, 'There is a friend who sticks closer than a brother.' Jesus is this friend!"

Jahzeel smiled and confirmed, "Brother, he is my friend as well. Jesus understands me even better than you do . . . better even than I understand myself!"

Turning toward Father and changing the subject, I mentioned, "Father, you brought up money. Others bring up the Romans, or other pagans—all sorts of reasons not to go out among the lost. They live in fear. Mother, there is no agape in fear. We love only because Jesus loved us. In fact, God loved us so much that he sent his own Son to die for us, *while we were* sinners!

"Whatever happens to us, we will not fear because we love those to whom we are trying to witness. We demonstrate patience with them, also out of agape; we cannot expect them to understand the truth immediately. Even though their background may be pagan, we will not dishonor them; in order to represent Christ well, we must show them agape love. Agape is greater than any other gift.

"If I have all gifts, all prophecy, all understanding, all faith, but no agape, then I am *nothing.* If I work hard to help the poor but have no agape, I am still nothing. Agape is patient and kind. It shows no envy, is not demanding or rude. It is not easily provoked. It has no suspicion. It always thinks the good. It wants no unfairness. It rejoices with truth. It can bear hardship. It trusts, hopes, and endures. Agape does not fail.

"Gifts fail. They pass away. The best of what we do now is incomplete, as is our understanding. I was once a child, and I acted childishly because I could not discern as a man. As I became a man, I gave up my childish ways. But someday, when I am perfected, what I now see only vaguely I will perceive as Christ does. Because of the changes taking place in me, the time will come when what I am now will appear as less than that which is expected of an adolescent."

Bartholomew explained, "At the ascension, we were told to preach to all the world. The message of the church is good news to the world—that Christ died for our sins, according to the scriptures, and that he was buried, and that he rose again the third day, again according to the scriptures. We were given the Holy Spirit on Pentecost to empower us to preach that gospel message. It's a simple, straightforward message of faith that we proclaim: If you declare with your mouth, Jesus is Lord, and believe in your heart that God raised him from the dead, you will be saved. For it is with your heart that you believe and are justified, and it is with your mouth that you profess your faith and are saved. Salvation cannot be the result of our effort, so God forbid that we should boast!

"There were Jews who tried to add to that gospel, perhaps so they could boast about their efforts. But the glory must be his. Isaiah told us this: 'I am the LORD: that is my name, and my glory I will not give to another.' Or perhaps they wanted to bring the kingdom of heaven to us *now*—which is not our charge. Jesus made it clear to us that these things are not yet. He said, 'See to it that you are not alarmed. Such things must happen, but the end is still to come.'

"So, we apostles declare that, if anyone preaches any other gospel, they are to be accursed. There will be a time for the gospel of the kingdom—the kingdom *will* come in its fullness. Yet the Spirit has given us no idea when that time will be. We asked, and Jesus simply said, 'Heaven and earth will pass away, but my words will never pass away. But about that day or hour no one knows, not even the angels in heaven, nor the Son, but only the Father.' So, for now, we must preach this simple gospel of faith to the world."

Didymus

I added, "In this present age Christ is already our high priest, the only mediator between the Father and us—not of the line of Aaron, who was designated a high priest only for the Jews, but like Melchizedek of Abraham's time, a high priest for all peoples."

Jahzeel asserted, "A high priest I can respect!"

I answered cautiously, "I was proud. Pride, like envy, is of Satan. Proverbs says, 'Pride goes before destruction, a haughty spirit before a fall.' I felt proud that Jesus had chosen me. In my mind, that made me better than others. I worked at saying I was not proud—but the truth is that, then, I became proud of my humility! What rubbish! I also thought I was better than you who were not apostles, and that I must take care of you—the ones not quite up to my standard as an apostle. It increased my feelings of superiority to see myself as doing good for those who could not help themselves. I really did want the best for you, but at the time that meant that *I wanted you to become just like me.* I was doing exactly what I hated in the Pharisees. Then I fell, and God lifted *you* up. That made me bitter. Now I know that there is no room for pride in a life devoted to following Jesus. We have to become as children. The Spirit is still working on me. Love cannot be proud."

Jahzeel replied, "That you wanted me to follow you was not a secret; it showed when you spoke. I knew you wanted what you thought was best for me, but I resented your attitude. Had I made a decision about Christ based on emotion, I would have rejected him *because* of you. As it was, God was even using your attitude to shape me. It forced me to make a rational decision."

I acknowledged, "With favor comes responsibility. I thought I had to flee responsibility in order to remain free. That's a lie. Sinners believe they are free when they are in reality slaves to sin. When you and I were little, we felt free because Father and Mother were watching over us. It's wonderfully freeing for me now to know that Christ is watching over me. I see his hand protecting me all the time. Freedom is being able to do what God created us to do. Doing God's will can never be a burden—it's a joy! The will of God is that by doing good we put to silence the ignorance of foolish people. We are to live as people who are free, not using our freedom as a cover-up for evil but living as servants of God."

Jahzeel replied, "I have felt the 'burden' of responsibility as well. Jesus said, 'To everyone to whom much is given, from him much will be required, and to whom much has been committed, of him they will ask the more.' These gifts are given to be used for others. People are counting on me—people in the church, people in the vineyard, and (looking at Anna) my family. Satan wants me to feel that I have lost my freedom; that is a lie. When I know I am doing God's will, I no longer feel it to be a burden. My perceived guilt over not doing what was never my responsibility to do is gone. You are right: Freedom is found only in Christ."

I nodded and continued, "Jahzeel, you have become a true prophet. Jesus said, 'Come to me, all you who are weary and burdened, and I will give you rest. Take my yoke upon you and learn from me, for I am gentle and humble in heart, and you will find rest for your souls. For my yoke is easy and my burden is light.' When I have become burdened, it is because I am trying to carry a burden that Christ never intended for me to bear. The Holy Spirit may have gifted someone else to bear that burden, or perhaps only Christ can bear it. The yoke he gave me is light; he carries the load. It is a privilege that he allows me to carry any of the load at all.

"Father asked why I am not writing a history of our time with Jesus. I was not gifted for that task—to me it would have been a burden, though to John Mark it is a joy! Perhaps if there were no one else who could do the task, the Holy Spirit would give me a gift to do so. You, Jahzeel, must avoid laying burdens on individuals in your church for which they have not been called.'"

Jahzeel mused, "Would I want to be told I must give money if I had none? Would I want to be directed to speak if I stuttered? Would I want to be instructed to repair a roof if I were afraid of heights? For any of these tasks, there is someone whom God has purposed for it. God has a plan and purpose for each of us."

Didymus

I nodded. "Let nothing be done through strife or vainglory, but in lowliness of mind let each esteem others better than themselves. We are right with the Father only because of Christ. His Spirit leads us. We are naos, the inner sanctuary of the temple of God, because the Spirit of God indwells and protects us. If anyone defiles the temple of God, God will destroy him. For the temple is holy, and that is *us*. It doesn't matter if the defiler is within or without."

I added, "We are simply stewards of the mysteries of God. We handle his valuables with care. They are revealed only though the Spirit."

Jahzeel asked a harder question: "Did not Jesus ask us to remain on the vine? Is one who has known Christ but falls into sin no longer on the vine?"

"No. Jesus loved us while we were still sinners. We came to Christ through faith—not when we stopped sinning. Jesus said clearly, 'Remain in me, as I also remain in you. No branch can bear fruit by itself; it must remain in the vine. Neither can you bear fruit unless you remain in me. I am the vine; you are the branches. If you remain in me and I in you, you will bear much fruit; apart from me you can do nothing. If you do not remain in me, you are like a branch that is thrown away and withers; such branches are picked up, thrown into the fire, and burned. If you remain in me and my words remain in you, ask whatever you wish, and it will be done for you. This is to my Father's glory, that you bear much fruit, showing yourselves to be my disciples.'"

Jahzeel further inquired, "How does a branch abide or stay on the vine of its own accord?"

Father remarked, "Perhaps we carry the analogy of the fruit and the vine too far. We say that the branch has fallen off the vine, as though it were responsible for holding on to it."

Jahzeel asked, "Did you not quote Jesus as saying, 'I give them eternal life, and they shall never perish; nothing can pluck them out of my hand'? Yet the command Jesus gave was to remain, or to abide, as though that's our choice. If the command is given to believers, then the two teachings don't seem to agree."

I answered slowly, knowing that this issue would be difficult to clarify. "Jesus is talking about branches, new vines that are growing off the main vine. We are told to abide or to remain. Yet since no one can pluck us from his hand, why are we given this directive? Jesus would not have requested our effort as believers if this were not something we should do. Perhaps in his sovereignty he allows us this choice. Or perhaps to us it is a choice, although from his perspective the choice has already been made. The Spirit has shown all the apostles that whoever would come may come—and yet that we have been chosen from before the foundation of the world. My mind cannot grasp those two ideas in combination, though I know they are both true.

"Jesus would not want us living either fearfully or carelessly. The Spirit has not made this as clear as I would like, but that too is *his* choice. *He* must want us to actively study and pray instead of simply revealing to us all of the detail. Such detail might be another Law like that of Moses—I am only conjecturing here.

"We of all people understand grapes and vines. It is true that a branch cannot of its own accord either stay attached to or separate itself from the vine—and branches don't ordinarily fall off. As Father stated, perhaps we carry the analogy too far. I am uncertain how to reconcile these two realities: Jesus commanded us to remain, but if we do not remain, we can do nothing. I do know that nothing that is of value comes without effort. Responsibility must be ours, yes, but it would seem as though all the exertion would still some from the vine and the vinedresser: God. We know that, despite all our work, *we don't make the wine—God does*."

Jahzeel mused, "Chosen, yet I can choose to come. It sounds as though two different parties—one on each side of the relationship—are making the same choice."

I nodded and asserted, "God is absolutely sovereign. Yet we are still absolutely responsible." What more could I say? Being an apostle did not give me all the answers—only the ones the Spirit wanted to reveal to me, either in the past or at any given moment.

Didymus

Father lamented, "This is too deep for me. All I know is that Jesus will not fail us."

With no clear resolution, we moved on. There was more talk about reaching the lost. We agreed that we must simply reach out to everyone. After all, the Father does the drawing, according to his will and on his schedule; we are simply instruments and witnesses.

XXXIII

Service at a Young Church and Koinonia

I t was clear that there were issues with meeting in the synagogue on the first day of the week. It was expedient, but there was contention. Jahzeel talked of building a major addition onto the house and meeting there, as Peter had done in Capernaum. My brother had been allowed to use the synagogue ruler's scrolls so far, but even that had become an issue of dispute. Most in the church had never before seen Jesus, or even an apostle. People simply accepted what Jahzeel said, and he was afraid of what might happen if he were gone.

The ruler of the synagogue greeted me on this morning. He was not the ruler from my youth; we had, in fact, first met at Jahzeel's wedding. He was still not a believer, but he respected those of us who were; this church has not suffered the persecution that has spread over the land. Jahzeel had gone over the Isaiah passage that this very rabbi had given him over and over again with him since his wedding. The rabbi still claimed that other parts of Isaiah had not been fulfilled and that Jesus was not a king—Rome still ruled.

The synagogue ruler no longer seemed offended by the gospel, at least not for us who are Jews—the people of the Covenant. He knew that good deeds, mitzvahs, do not earn us a place with Jehovah-Tsikenu, God our Righteousness; our best deeds are but filthy rags in God's sight. He had witnessed a few miracles with keen interest, but he was, in his own words to Jahzeel, "not ready." The ruler had told my brother than he believed God just as Abraham had; so, he reasoned, he, like Abraham, was considered righteous in God's eyes.

The ruler acknowledged that we are all sinners but believed that we Jews still had the temple and sacrifices to cover our sins; he saw no personal need for Jesus. I asked what he would do if the temple were to be destroyed again. He responded that we would again have to rely on the mercy of God, as our people did when there was no temple. I explained that we can rely only on the mercy of God—not receiving the punishment we deserve—even with the temple intact.

I did not try to explain to him that all of the temple and its symbolic furnishings, as well as the tabernacle before it, were representations of Jesus and his sacrifice. The ruler was not ready for that truth. I asked him whether obedience was not better than sacrifice. He did not see it that way, claiming that true obedience demands continuing sacrifices. The temple, I recognized, is a stumbling block to some, while a steppingstone to others. I realized the truth of Jesus's words, 'I am the way, the truth, and the life. No one comes to the Father except through me' and 'Most assuredly, I say to you, he who does not enter the sheepfold by the door, but climbs in some other way, is a thief and a robber.' I would pray for the ruler to receive saving faith. All of us apostles had been told by the Spirit that, without faith, it is impossible to please the Lord. The ruler left quietly as the church members entered.

There was much small talk as people arrived. The atmosphere was quite unlike that of a synagogue service, which entailed little more than a simple reading. We prayed, and a small offering was taken. In Jerusalem I had thought this was critical, probably because the Jerusalem church had become so needy after so many had given up their livelihoods that the church could no longer provide for itself. But the Spirit had since revealed to us that the true offering had been Christ's own. The physical and financial needs were ours, not God's. He would provide, likely though his people.

Bartholomew and I explained the decision of the Council of Jerusalem regarding removal of the Jewish requirements for Gentile believers and went over the few requirements for Gentile Christians. Several of us recited words of Jesus and expounded on the scriptures. Then we clarified application of the commands of Christ. I pointed out that it is the goodness of God that brings a man to repentance. I also explained that the Spirit usually gives us only enough knowledge of his will for our next steps, although as we obediently take them, more knowledge of his will is shown. I spoke of our forefathers, prophets of old who died in faith while embracing the future promise we now see clearly. We, I emphasized, must be the people of whom God would not be ashamed to be called our God: "I am not ashamed of the gospel of Christ, for it is the power of God to salvation for everyone who believes, for the Jew first and also for the Greek." I also explained that all men, not only the Jews, are aware of God from nature, so that none has an excuse for unbelief.

I felt led by the Spirit to talk about friction in the church, even though Jahzeel had not told me of any. I warned about misuse of the tongue and asked the gathered congregants, 'What is the source of fighting among you? Does it not come from your own lust that is warring in your members?' I challenged them with the self-test of agape—love by decision—and shared with them the ramifications of this kind of love: to be longsuffering, to be kind, not to envy or to be rude, not to be provoked, to think no evil, to bear all things, to hope all things, to believe all things, to be winsome.

How could we best show this love? By sharing the gospel of grace. How could we share? By first helping the needy. I explained that the worst of sinners know they need a savior but that many believe they are good enough or righteous enough for God based on their own merits. How wrong that belief! *All* have sinned and fallen short of the glory of God, and the just wage for sin is death. Confessing Jesus as Lord and believing that he has risen is the requirement—the only requirement—for salvation.

That led to my own testimony of how I had refused to believe in the resurrection until I had seen and even touched Jesus. I explained that *all* those outside of faith have been blinded by Satan. I explained how a personal testimony of God's grace is necessary if we are to be a witness. And I prayed that all the believers might be filled with the knowledge of his will in all wisdom and spiritual understanding and that Christ might dwell in their hearts through faith.

Bartholomew also spoke for a time, elaborating on the subject of the church no longer having expectations of Christ returning quickly, as we at first had thought; instead, we must be ready for him whenever he chooses to come. In the fullness of time, Christ will unite all things to himself.

Then he explained forgiveness in the church: If one is overtaken in a trespass, we who are Christians must restore that one in a spirit of gentleness, knowing that we also are subject to temptation. We must help bear one another's burdens in order to fulfill the royal law of love, yet without the hypocrisy of pride. Nothing should be done through selfish ambition or conceit, but in lowliness of mind each should esteem others better than themselves. Each one should look out not only for their own interests but also for the interests of others.

We sang a few psalms, with Anna's father leading with his booming voice; he had joyfully sung for years as he baked, to the edification of those around him. There was much testimony on the work of Christ in individual lives, and a few asked that we lay our hands on the sick.

There were questions about Bartholomew and my own calling and plans, as well as updates on the other apostles, missionaries, and local churches.

We ended with communion. There were only a few Gentiles, and most of the Jews allowed them to sit in the larger group. A few did not. I sat with Gentiles for a time to lead by example. I confessed to them that I do not always walk in the Spirit. The service—or celebration—as I think of it, was not a large affair, but we did break bread and share the cup with thanksgiving. Anna's father had made his best bread, as good as the loaves he had contributed at Jahzeel and Anna's wedding.

Afterward, we all took part in the humility service of foot washing, enjoying wonderful koinonia and celebration with God's children. Jahzeel wept when I washed his feet.

There was a final farewell, and it was finished. Many stayed and talked for a time, and there were tears. It was excellent fellowship. I came away reflecting that church—a congregation or fellowship—is a group of believers in various stages of their walk with Christ: some babes, some mature, and some simply present, with no true commitment at all, or at that time. Some have much spiritual insight and knowledge, others little. The Spirit has promised us that, although even the most insightful of us see only a wavy reflection as in a mirror, the time will come when we shall see our Lord face-to-face. Now we know in part; then we shall know fully, even as we are fully known. Perhaps that is why the service in the church can never be as intimate as the discussions in our homes, where we know each other intimately.

Before our family returned home, many went with us to the water, where I baptized Jahzeel's older son and namesake, based on his confession of faith and the belief in his heart after his conversion. Baptism is the public demonstration of the faith already held in the heart. This little boy had come to Christ while he was still too young for a bar mitzvah, but Father had led him in a prayer of faith at his own request.

That night was a time of celebration: of the resurrection, of young Jahzeel's baptism, and of family. Anna's parents joined us. Each one, from Father to the youngest daughter of Jahzeel and Anna, was celebrated individually. Jahzeel and I determined to show each of the four little ones that they were loved and that they had the favor of God, of Jesus, and of family. As twins, we knew from experience that each and every one of us has to be seen as an individual, and as special. There was much joy, and joyful tears.

I slept very well that night, bathed in true Shalom. I know my family had peace as well. I had wanted freedom and now had it in abundance. My family was free as well; the truth had set all of us free. We were one in the Spirit—and a stronger family unit

Didymus

than ever before. Jesus's promise to me had been fulfilled. Our visit had not been flawless, but it was perfect in that it was now complete. Tetelestai; it was finished.

The next morning, we broke bread, talked briefly, and said our farewells. There were tears. Our final farewell was a simple, yet profound one.

Shalom.

Epilogue

Tradition teaches that Thomas was martyred by envious Hindu priests at Kali on a hilltop (now known as Saint Thomas Mount) in n Chennai, Tamil Nadu, India, on December 21, AD 72, two years after the destruction of Jerusalem by Titus and nearly forty years after the ascension of Christ. The site is home to a church and a national shrine.

Thomas's doubt of the resurrection was in many ways an even deeper denial of Jesus than Peter's impulsive denying that he knew Christ. Both apostles were forgiven much—as is true for all of us. Jesus said that the person who has had much forgiven will love much. By that measure Thomas must have loved Jesus intensely.

Bibliography

The Daily Bible in Chronological Order by F. LaGard Smith.
(Eugene, Oregon: Harvest House Publishers).
Blue Letter Bible
BibleGateway.com
BibleHub.com

www.ingramcontent.com/pod-product-compliance
Lightning Source LLC
Chambersburg PA
CBHW072340020726
47506CB00004B/939